Chris let go of D.J.'s hands to clasp her upper arms tightly. He'd had enough of her "I don't believe in love" nonsense. They both could have been killed earlier. The time for prevaricating was past, the time for truth at hand. He gave her a little shake, hoping to jiggle some sense into her. "Don't call me McCall. I know you're trying to push me away when you do that, and it won't work. I'm here to stay. I know more about screwed-up minds than you think. Yours isn't so bad—when compared to my own."

He could see the hope flickering in her eyes, the desire hovering upon her lips. They could have so much, if she'd only believe.

She closed her eyes and turned her mouth toward his hand. Her lips touched the softer skin at the center; then her tongue flicked out and tasted him. The caress made him catch his breath against the desire surging through him.

She turned her head, rubbing her cheek along his palm once more, and her eyes met his. He read the same desire in those eyes that tingled throughout his body.

"Now, Christian. Make love to me now." She leaned toward him, her eyes shining bright green in the reflection from the lamplight. "Show me the difference between having sex and making love. Make me believe. I think you're the only one who can."

D.J.'s Angel

LORI HANDELAND

LOVE SPELL ◆ NEW YORK CITY

LOVE SPELL®

September 1995

Published by

Dorchester Publishing Co., Inc.
276 Fifth Avenue
New York, NY 10001

Printed in the United States of America.

For the only grandma I ever knew, Josephine Emma Rebecca Killian Gross, and the two I married into along the way, Lillian Buelow Bertolus and Viola Varner Handeland. When I grow up I want to be just like you.

D.J.'s Angel

Prologue

"Dear God, I'm going to die."

Though she'd been thinking the words for hours, hearing them said aloud in her own hoarse, desperate voice made Josie Belmont cringe. The movement sent another wave of agony cascading through her body. Thunder shook her bed, reminding Josie of the storm raging outside—the storm that prevented any hope of rescue, leaving Josie on her own.

Her husband hovered somewhere at the edges of her consciousness, but he could do nothing more than hold her hand and sponge her sweating brow. During childbirth, a woman learned the true meaning of solitude. The world became a struggle between one's self and one's body.

Despite her exhaustion, Josie gathered a last reserve of strength and pushed one final time. The child slipped from her body into the waiting hands of her husband. Joy flooded Josie, followed by profound relief. The ordeal had ended. She wanted nothing more than to open her eyes and view the life she'd worked so desperately to bring into the world, but she was just too tired. She became aware of the stillness around her. Why hadn't she heard the squall of her child, or the announcement of the baby's sex?

The question receded along with the pain and Josie's consciousness. Just before she slipped into what she thought would be a refreshing sleep, Josie heard her husband speak at last. Instead of the joy and wonder she'd expected, he sounded hoarse and desperate, just as she had been only moments before.

"There's so much blood. I don't know what to do. It won't stop. Josie, hang on, please. I have to—" *Smack.* The sharp crack of flesh against flesh. "Breathe, damn you. Breathe." Silence once more.

Panic filled Josie. Something was wrong with the baby. She needed to open her eyes—to see, to help. Why couldn't she seem to make her body obey her mind's command?

A harsh, guttural cry interrupted her musings. "No! Josie, don't leave me! Not my wife *and* my baby. Dear God, I've lost them both."

Thunder crashed once again, as though God had heard his desperate prayer and answered.

The panic dissipated as love filled her. Josie wanted to reach out and touch her husband, to tell him she'd never leave him. *Never.* But the peaceful darkness awaited, and she had no choice but to slip into it.

In that darkness Josie had no awareness of herself, of the world, or anything beyond.

Perfect solitude.

Gradually awareness returned, creeping from the void into her consciousness. The quiet was all-consuming.

What had happened to the storm?

Then a storm of a different type whirled through the darkness, damp air against her hot face, dank wind in her hair. Sadness and grief shrouded her.

Josie put a tentative hand on her stomach, and a soft sob escaped her at the emptiness there. For nine months she had carried a life, and now that life was gone.

Despair threatened, icy cold and terrifying. If possible, the darkness became darker, heavier, more oppressive. The wind was still and suddenly a light beckoned. Drifting forward, she became aware of a tunnel and voices all around her, though she couldn't distinguish any words. The voices soothed her fear. No longer would she be alone.

This place held no pain, no sadness, only joy. Josie stopped in front of the light, fascinated with the myriad of colors within the brightness. Colors she had never seen but merely imagined danced before her awestruck gaze. The voices she had heard emanated from the light, and Josie was drawn to their happiness. Still she hesitated. Should she go through?

A figure appeared on the other side, the silhouette of a man. He beckoned to her, then held out his hand.

Josie turned and took a hesitant step back toward the darkness.

"No." Though the word was soft, the sound whirled around her like an autumn wind. Josie froze at the underlying command. "That door is closed to you. You must come to me now. Enter the light."

Turning back, Josie raised her hand and inched forward, drawn to the promise she sensed beyond the light. But a part of her was missing, and just before her fingertips touched the shadowed fingers, she jerked away with a soft cry. "I can't. I want my baby. If we both have to be dead, can't I at least have my baby with me now?"

The man's shoulders lifted and lowered with a deep sigh. "You will see your child in due time. This I promise. But first, there is something you must understand." He flexed his fingers in invitation. "Come, Josie. Trust me. I'll help you make everything all right once more."

Funny, she did trust him, whoever he was. How could she not? With one last lingering look back the way she had come, Josie reached out and took the offered hand, stepping forward to join the man within the colored light.

As she stepped through the doorway, the light became so bright she closed her eyes, relying on the hand she held to guide her. The man squeezed Josie's fingers in reassurance. Peace and joy flooded through her, warming and filling Josie's soul with love.

"You can open your eyes now," he said, his voice making her think of golden honey sliding across warmed bread.

Josie followed his command. She couldn't describe

the place she now existed in as anything other than heavenly. She was nowhere, yet somewhere, in another realm from the one she'd known only a short time ago. Slowly she turned to meet the impossibly blue gaze of the man who had been her guide.

Tall, shoulder-length red hair—and three pairs of red wings the color of flames.

The peace that had invaded her within the tunnel continued to calm Josie—so much so that she barely blinked at the wings. Why he had wings wasn't important. How he could help her was. Since he'd been sent to greet her at the doorway, he must carry a degree of importance in this realm. He could tell her the things she needed to know—namely, how she could find her child.

"Who," she asked, "are you?"

He bestowed upon her an expression of tolerance for a lost lamb. "I am the Archangel Raphael."

Josie was silent. She hadn't been expecting that. Maybe St. Peter or some other saint, even a lesser angel. But the Archangel Raphael? If she remembered her theology at all, he had something to do with . . .

"Guardian angels," she blurted out before she could stop herself.

Raphael smiled. "Very good. I am chief of the guardian angels in this realm, and you are Josie."

"Yes. You told me I could see my baby. When?"

"Your baby is not here."

Josie gulped against the fear his statement caused. She had distinctly heard her husband cry that he'd lost both his wife and his baby. If she was here, then where would her child be? Surely God couldn't be so cruel as to separate them now?

"Calm yourself," Raphael admonished. "Your child is safe. You will see her soon enough."

"Her?"

Raphael nodded. "Yes."

Josie hugged that knowledge to herself—a little girl. She'd always dreamed of having a daughter. Too bad she wouldn't be able to enjoy the gift the way she'd imagined. Despair threatened once more.

Raphael brushed his hand back and forth, as if waving away her pain. "None of that, Josie. We have no time for despair now, and there is no need."

Hope chased away the despair. "I can see my little girl?"

"Soon," he repeated. "But before you can reside in heaven, God has decided you will return to earth and help someone there." He held up his hand, staving off her denial. "He was quite specific when He insisted you would be the best one for her. If you can complete your task, then you will enter heaven as one of my angels—a guardian angel."

Raphael said the last with such pride, Josie wondered if she had missed something. She was dead. Her baby was dead. And here sat this angel telling her she had to be a guardian and complete a mission to get into heaven. Right now she could care less about anything except her child.

She narrowed her eyes. "I don't recall anything in the Bible about completing missions to earn heaven."

"Nevertheless, you will do as you are asked. You are the one God has chosen for this particular mission. Only you can help her."

"I don't think so. Just give me my baby and I'll stay out of everyone's way. You won't have to worry about

us for a minute. You won't even know we're here."

"Heaven doesn't work in such a way, Josie. Everyone has his place, his purpose, just as they do on earth. Until you complete this mission, you can't enter heaven." He fixed her with a long look from his sapphire eyes. "And if you don't agree, you can't see your baby."

Anger flooded Josie at Raphael's manipulation. "Why are you doing this to me?" she shouted. Raphael flinched at the volume of her voice, which echoed in the silence surrounding them. She lowered the volume, but allowed the anger to remain as she hissed, "I don't know this girl. She's nothing to me."

"She's more than you think," he said in the same quiet tone of authority in which he'd told her to come into the light. His sigh fell heavily between them. Neither her words nor her tone had made him happy. "I can see you need a more earthly explanation. I forget sometimes that you are used to judging a situation with your mind and senses, not on faith alone, as we do here. There is a reason for everything—in heaven and on earth. Look, Josie Belmont. You now have the ability to see with your heart. Feel her pain. Then tell me you don't care."

Josie looked. She felt. She couldn't help but care.

Raphael had been right—the young woman in question was more than what Josie had thought. She was everything.

Her daughter.

Chapter One

The bullet whizzed past D.J. Halloran's cheek, so close a wisp of air touched her skin like an angel's kiss. She threw herself onto the ground, cursing as the cement met her hipbones with a bone-jarring crack.

"Damn, kids," she muttered. "Where do they get the guns?"

Tentatively she peeked around the end of the squad car. Another well-aimed shot rewarded her curiosity. She jerked back and sat up, careful to keep all body parts out of view. A quick glance around the area reinforced her isolation. Just her, the gun-toting kid, who must be on something to shoot at a cop, and a neighborhood full of people cowering inside their homes. Unless she could get to the radio in the squad car, or one of the citizens decided to be helpful, she would have to get out of this mess on her own.

Had it only been fifteen minutes ago when she'd stopped at the all-night gas station for a cup of coffee?

D.J. checked her watch. More like twenty minutes, but who was counting now?

Another shot shattered the window of the squad car above her, raining glass onto her head. D.J. sighed. This kid was getting on her nerves.

"How about you give me the gun, and we have a talk with juvenile?" she shouted. "If you quit using me for target practice and tell me where you got the gun, I'll even drive you there myself." The pop of her back tire as a bullet rendered it useless was her answer.

"Guess not," D.J. mumbled, and allowed her thoughts to return to the gas station.

She had filled her cup and, while taking a sip, her gaze had strayed to the front of the store where a kid, no more than fourteen or fifteen, stood speaking with the clerk. As she watched, the boy slammed his fist onto the counter. "Don't tell me I can't come in here, old man," he shouted. "I'll make you sorry you said that to me. Just wait and see."

The kid turned and ran out of the store.

As threats went, it wasn't much. But the clerk looked upset, so D.J. nodded to say she would take care of it and followed the boy outside.

Expecting to find no sign of him, she stopped short when she nearly bumped into the kid on the curb.

"I think we'd better have a talk."

Expecting the blubbering apology that usually followed such an outburst, D.J. was shocked when the kid turned and shoved her so hard she fell. She had time to register the frenzied look on the boy's face and the glazed cast to his eyes. Strung out, big time. By the time she was on her feet the boy had disappeared down an alley.

She would have let the matter drop if the incident had only involved a smart remark and a little shove, but the drugs were another matter. When the clerk came outside and told her where the boy lived D.J. drove to the boy's house to have a talk with him and his parents. But before she could get anywhere near the front door the kid appeared at the window, and she'd had to dive for cover behind her squad car.

"A hell of a way to end my day," D.J. grumbled as the memories faded and reality returned with the sound of another random shot over the roof of her squad car.

How was she going to get out of this? From the sound and the look of things, the kid had plenty of ammunition, and he knew what to do with it. As opposed to herself, who would have to make due with the three clips she had for her service weapon—a .9 mm semiautomatic. She carried two clips in her belt and one in the side arm, plus an extra round in the chamber, which gave her 46 bullets in all. She could hold out for quite a while on that, though she'd rather not have to. Her best bet would be to stay where she was until the gunfire attracted another squad car. She had nowhere to go but home, and nothing waiting for her there beyond a television and a solitary bed. She could sit here for the rest of the night, though the coolness of a mid-October evening in Wisconsin had started to seep through her uniform, especially in the area of her anatomy possessing intimate knowledge of the damp cement.

Shifting her rear end in discomfort, D.J. glanced to her right, her gaze coming to rest on the driver's side door of the squad car. It wouldn't hurt to try and call this in. If she kept her head low, the kid would have trouble blowing her brains out through the car door. Once she got her hands on the little creep she'd make him tell her where he'd gotten the gun—another semiautomatic from the sound of the thing—and the drugs. Only a kid who'd altered his reality would bother to start a shoot-out with a cop over nothing. Usually troublemakers kept a low profile.

For weeks she'd been trying to track down the sudden influx of guns and drugs into the hands of teenagers in Lakeview, Wisconsin. Someone was trying to start up a system of gangs in her happy little town, and D.J. planned to put a stop to it before things got any more out of hand than they already were. Perhaps tonight, with this kid, she'd found a break in the case.

Once she made a decision D.J. never hesitated. Crawling on her hands and knees, she reached the car door in seconds. She jerked on the handle and dove for the radio with her left hand, her gun still clasped in her right.

A shape shifted beyond the passenger window. D.J.'s neck gave a creak of protest as she jerked her head up. Her eyes met those of the kid through the glass. He smiled. Her gaze switched to the barrel of death staring her in the face. The finger on the trigger tightened. She had time to swear once before she fired.

The window exploded. The kid disappeared. D.J. bit her lip until she tasted blood. She should get up and walk around the car to check on the kid. She could hear him crying and the sound made her want to cry, too, but she couldn't make her legs obey the command. Instead, she dropped her head and rested her cheek against the cool vinyl of the seat. She opened her left hand. The radio fell to the floor of the car.

A siren wailed in the distance.

"My baby," Josie whispered. Tears filled her eyes as she met Raphael's gaze. "What have you done to her?"

The fallen child lay on the pavement, clutching his shoulder and shrieking. Violent tremors shook D.J. as she lay half in and half out of her squad car.

"I haven't done anything." Raphael gave an offended sniff. "You wanted to see your child. There she is."

"She's not a baby. She's a woman." Josie frowned. "How long was I in that tunnel?"

"Time moves differently for us than it does for them. When you have eternity to contemplate, a few moments here can be a lifetime down there."

Josie was stunned. Her daughter had grown into a woman. A very different woman than Josie had ever envisioned a daughter of hers becoming.

"I can't believe you made me watch as my daughter almost got killed. She must be terrified."

"She might be terrified, but she'll never let anyone know. By the time help arrives she'll be back in control. The other cops call D.J. Halloran 'Officer Ice.' She never allows anything to get to her."

"That doesn't sound like any child of mine."

"You haven't been there to teach her. D.J. is a product of her upbringing."

Jose frowned. "My husband, Ed, is the most loving man I know."

"The man you knew no longer exists. Something inside of him died with you. The man D.J. had for a father is a far cry from the one you married."

Josie took a deep breath. "I don't like the sound of this."

"I didn't think you would."

"Why doesn't D.J. allow anything to get to her?"

"According to D.J. emotions get in the way of doing her job."

Josie tilted her head, remembering the sound of the gunfire, the speed at which a disaster could happen. "I can see how they might. But what about her personal life?"

"She doesn't have one."

"She had one at some time if her name's Halloran and not Belmont. She must be married."

"She was. No longer. Her marriage, an unmitigated disaster, also contributed to the person she's become."

Josie watched as D.J. forced herself to stand and meet the arriving officers and the ambulance, cool and collected, just as Raphael had promised. Pulling

21

her attention away from the scene with difficulty, Josie returned to the conversation at hand. "I'm sorry to hear she's divorced. But that isn't the end of the world. A young, attractive girl like that should be out dating again. Why isn't she?"

"D.J. doesn't believe in love. That's where you come in."

"If I'd been around to raise her, we wouldn't be in this predicament. What do you expect me to do now?"

"Right now, all you have to do is watch."

Christian McCall pressed the button on his disposable camera.

Click. Click.

The roll was nearly finished. He'd taken almost all the shots he needed—the dispatcher, the captain's office, and the officers' desks. He could start sketching ideas for his new children's book on the police department as early as this evening. He'd finish this role with some shots of the evidence room and the holding cells at the back of the station. Colleen, the desk sergeant, had been too busy to let him into those locked areas when he'd taken her picture earlier. He would have to make a point to get back to them later.

Chris glanced around the room. The place was a madhouse, people running everywhere, and the phones ringing like an MD telethon. Something was going on at the Lakeview Police Department, something that had caused an extra amount of hustle and bustle in the station this morning.

There'd been a shooting during the night.

Not that a shooting would be unusual—crime existed in Lakeview, though not in as great an abundance as in a larger city. But this time a fifteen-year-old boy had been shot by a police officer, and the media was raising a hue and cry. Even though the kid had been involved in a shoot-out with the officer, in a small town like Lakeview his age made him the stuff of martyrdom.

A flurry of activity at the front of the station drew Chris's attention. He turned to see a young woman walk through the double doors, reporters buzzing at her heels.

Despite the anger in her stride, her face reflected no such emotion. Fascinated, Chris stared at her. Tall and lean, she carried herself with a confidence found only in women well able to defend themselves. Her russet hair had been cropped close to her head, short enough to remove the curls but not enough to erase a natural wave. Fine bones defined a regal face that matched her bearing. Ivory skin that would have looked pale on someone else did not dare on this woman.

She stopped short, just inside the door, and glared at her band of followers.

"No comment," she snapped, staring down those who would have questioned her further. Surprisingly, the reporters backed off.

When she turned, her eyes met Chris's, and they widened, revealing an evergreen hue. Then she caught sight of the camera in his hand and frowned, obviously deciding the enemy had invaded her sanctum.

Without so much as a hello, she walked over, snatched the camera from his hand, and strode toward the captain's office.

"Hey, who do you think you are?" he shouted to her retreating back, irritated with his lack of defense. He hadn't allowed himself to be surprised by anyone for a long time. "I want my film back." Chris started after the woman.

"Come and get it," she returned, opening the door to the captain's office and taking a step inside.

She stopped short and Chris, who had been following at full speed, bumped into her from behind. The woman tensed, and Chris took advantage of her momentary lack of attention to snatch his camera out of her hand. He waited for an attack, verbal or otherwise, but none came. Her gaze focused on the people in front of them. She had no interest in the man who stood close enough to smell the tang of her shampoo.

"Hell's bells," she said, her voice so soft only Chris heard her.

Inside the office, several men and one woman in gray suits huddled around the captain's desk. At their entrance, the crowd of suits parted, revealing one man in a uniform sitting behind the desk. Chris recognized the no-nonsense captain he'd met earlier. In his fifties, with the build of a wrestler and the face of a boxer, Captain Miller radiated a formidable presence. His dark gaze sought out the woman, then flicked toward Chris. The captain hesitated, then shrugged. Pointing a finger in their direction, he crooked it backward in command.

"Just the two I wanted to see. McCall, shut the

door behind you and take a seat."

Chris complied. The gray suits never looked at him. All their attention remained on the woman.

"What's this all about?" she asked, nodding at the circle of suits.

"Sit, Halloran; then I'll explain."

She shook her head and leaned back against the door. "I prefer to stand for my execution, thank you."

"D.J.," the captain said, the name ripe with warning.

A flash of recognition shot through Chris. *D.J. Halloran. Officer Halloran.* The officer who had shot a fifteen-year-old kid a few hours before.

He stared at her with renewed interest. How could she look so together after what had happened?

Officer Halloran ignored her captain's warning, and after a moment he sighed, obviously used to her. "You know who they are. You know why they're here."

The officer's gaze settled on Chris, reclined in a metal folding chair much too small for his tall frame. She dismissed him for the moment, turning her attention back to the captain. Never once did she acknowledge the suits.

"I explained everything on the phone. I had to shoot. I didn't want to. That kid was too young to be playing with guns. I want to get the guy who's turning my town into a pre-gang playground."

"Don't we all? But the gang problem's not the issue right now. The kid is the issue. He's in surgery right now. His parents are freaking out."

"As well they should be. Their kid shot at a police officer." She let out a sigh ripe with impatience. "I had no choice but to shoot—he was going to blow my head off. Would you have preferred a dead cop on the morning news?"

The captain rubbed the bridge of his nose. "Not now, Halloran. Let's just get this over with, and then you can give me attitude all you want."

She didn't answer, just continued to stare at Miller with an unreadable gaze.

Captain Miller turned to the suits. "I'll handle this from here."

One of the men stepped forward. "She's on suspension until the investigation of the shooting is complete. Rules are rules." The rest of the suits nodded in agreement before moving toward the door.

Officer Halloran straightened and opened the door for them. Each one gave her a frown of reproof as they left the room. When they were all in the hallway she slammed the door behind them.

" 'Rules are rules,' " she mimicked at their retreating backs. Turning, she stalked forward, placing her palms on the desk and leaning toward Miller. "What's going on here, Captain?" She jerked her head in Chris's direction. "Who's the stiff?"

Chris raised his eyebrows. He didn't much like her description. Despite a height that easily could be used to intimidate, he was a gentle, soft-spoken man. People liked him. Kids and dogs trusted him. What was the matter with her?

The captain ignored the officer's question, addressing his next words to Chris. Chris jerked his attention back to the small stuffy office and the near physical touch of Officer Halloran's glare from the corner where she'd retreated. "When the mayor first called me about you, McCall, I have to admit I figured you for a pain in the posterior." He silenced the snort of derision from Officer Halloran with a mere narrowing of his eyes toward the corner before he continued. "I was wrong. You've turned into a neat solution to today's problem."

"Oh, oh," Officer Halloran muttered under her breath.

"Captain?" Chris asked, uncertain how to respond to the undercurrents in the room.

"Meet today's problem, McCall. As I'm sure you've figured out for yourself, this is Officer D.J. Halloran, recently involved in the shooting of a minor, now on mandatory suspension, and assigned to help you with your project."

"No, sir." Officer Halloran took a step out of her corner, hands clenched into fists, prepared to go five rounds with a contender. "Not me. I'm not taking some civilian with a cop fetish on a tour of the city. If I'm suspended, then I'm going home. I can work on our gang problem from there. I'm going to take apart that neighborhood inch by inch. The kid got that gun from someone, and I'm gonna find out who. Whoever's behind the guns is the one behind all the problems we're having around here."

"No one in that neighborhood will talk to you," the captain said. "You shot one of their kids. Let Lou handle it."

"No!" There was more emotion in that one word than Chris had heard her utter all morning. She took a deep breath and relaxed her clenched fists. "No," she said more calmly. "This is my investigation. I want to be in on the arrest. Whoever thinks they can start up gangs in Lakeview is going down with me on his tail."

"Put a plug in it, Halloran. Lou wants this guy just as much as you do. Let him handle it. Besides, you have no choice." The captain's voice brooked no further argument, and the officer subsided, leaning back against the wall once more, though her hands flexed back into fists. "McCall is the difference between a suspension with pay or without."

"You don't need to do me any favors."

Miller let her sarcasm pass as he rubbed the bridge of his nose again. "McCall writes children's books, and he's a personal friend of the mayor. I want you to help him out for a few weeks. By then the worst will have blown over."

"A friend of the mayor, huh?" If possible Officer Halloran's glare became even more ferocious. "Well, ain't that convenient for you?"

Chris stifled a sigh. He should have known going to the mayor would be a mistake. But his deadline loomed, and he had taken the quickest route to gain the information he needed.

"Fine," she snapped. "I know when I'm beat." She walked to the door and jerked it open, turning back to him with a snarl. "Well, come on." She spoke to him as though he were a recalcitrant dog.

He glanced at the captain, who shook his head and rubbed his nose once more. When Chris looked back toward the doorway Officer Halloran was gone.

He caught up to her at the back "Police Personnel Only" entrance to the station. "Officer?"

She paused with her hand poised against the glass door but did not turn around.

Chris sighed. She wasn't going to make this easy, or much fun.

"I realize you've had a traumatic night. We don't have to get started today. It's no problem if we wait until tomorrow."

She straightened, her hand falling away from the door to rest listlessly at her side. She turned and almost bumped into him. Chris took a quick step back. She looked up into his eyes, and her mouth quirked in the first flash of amusement he'd seen on her face. Not a real smile, but a start. Then, almost as though she realized she'd softened a bit and hated it, the mask of indifference she'd worn since he first saw her settled into place, killing any other expression that might have appeared there in its stead.

"Listen, Mr. McCall, I'm not a happy camper right now, and I'm not going to pretend I am. Not for you, not for the captain, and certainly not for your good buddy the mayor."

She spat the last word, leaving no doubt in Chris's mind that he'd erred in asking his father's oldest friend to intervene on his behalf with the Lakeview PD. But he hadn't allowed himself to be intimidated for a very long time, and he didn't intend to start today. He saw the desk sergeant, Colleen, no longer so busy, pretending not to listen to their conversation. She wasn't very good at pretending, so Chris kept his voice low, though his tone stayed firm. "No, you listen. I have a job to do, and so do you. I'm on a tight deadline with this book. I don't have time to contact another city's force and go through what I've already gone through to get where I am right now, just because you have a problem with me. So, like me or not, we're stuck with each other for the next two weeks, Officer Halloran."

She stuck her hands into the pockets of her jeans, tilted her head to the side, and studied him. Chris stared right back, taking in the way the shadows under her eyes increased the look of fragility upon her face—a look completely at odds with the woman he'd seen thus far.

"You're right," she agreed suddenly, looking as surprised at her own capitulation as he was. "I don't like the situation, or you. But I'm stuck, so you may as well start calling me D.J." Yanking her right hand from her pocket, she stabbed it toward him. "And what should I call you?"

He took her hand and an odd jolt passed between them, making the back of his neck tingle. She frowned and yanked her fingers from his, putting them back in her pocket as though for safety.

"I'm Christian," he said, wondering at the hoarse quality of his voice.

"So are a lot of people, but we're not exchanging religious beliefs. I just want to know your first name."

He laughed. "No, my name's Christian. Most people call me Chris."

"I can see why," she muttered.

"Have you got a problem with my name along with everything else?"

"No, it's just different."

"So's yours. What does D.J. stand for, anyway?"

She turned away without answering and pushed through the glass doors to the street. Chris followed, staying even with her until she stopped next to a red pickup.

"You're not going to answer me, are you?"

"Nope." She unearthed her keys from a back pocket and attempted to insert one into the lock. Her hands shook, and she dropped the bunch to the ground, the harsh clash making her jump.

Chris bent to pick them up, then held the keys out of her reach until she looked at him. "Why not?"

"No one knows my real name but my father, and I intend to keep it that way."

Chris grinned. "That bad, is it?"

He almost got her. Her lips twitched once before she surprised him by jumping up and snatching the keys from his grasp. In a second she had skirted the front of the pickup and jumped behind the wheel. The passenger window slid down, and D.J.'s voice drifted to him as she pulled away from the curb.

"You want to play cop, McCall? Be here. Tomorrow morning. Eight sharp. I'll teach you to play like nobody else can."

"Why is she so cold? If she'd just let him, that young man could brighten up her whole world."

"That young man has his own set of problems."

"For instance?"

"You'll learn Christian's problems in due time.

31

Your job is to teach D.J. to love."

"How?"

"How is your department."

"I meant, how can I teach her anything when I'm up here and she's down there?"

"Obviously you'll get to return to earth for a short period to complete this mission."

Josie clapped her hands in delight. "Wonderful. Then I'll get to know my girl. Won't she be happy to meet her mother?"

Raphael cleared his throat.

"What?"

"You can't tell her who you are."

"Excuse me? I thought you said I couldn't tell my daughter I'm her mother."

"That's right. Your mission is to teach her how to love. If she finds out you're her mother, that's all she'll be interested in."

"How can she not know I'm her mother? She'll take one look at me and recognize me from pictures. She'll hear my name and know it's her mother's name."

Raphael shifted uncomfortably. "I'm afraid not. She's never seen a picture of you or heard you called by the name you prefer. She knows she was named after her mother, but she chooses to use the initials of that name as hers."

"Ed named her after me? He knew how much I hated my name."

"He was grief stricken. That's why he started calling her D.J.—he couldn't stand to hear your true name spoken out loud. Just like he couldn't stand to see your picture and know you were gone. He de-

stroyed every picture, every negative that existed. D.J. has never seen your face."

"I really hate the sound of this. You're describing the actions of a man I don't know."

"Ed is not the issue right now. D.J. is. We don't have all that much time. That's why you've been chosen. He felt that with your connection to D.J. you'd be able to accomplish this mission the quickest."

"Why are you in such a big hurry?"

The bright, ethereal light that shone from Raphael's face dimmed for a moment. Josie shivered, as though a bank of clouds had blotted out the heat of the noonday sun.

"What?" she cried. "What aren't you telling me?"

"D.J. has nothing to look forward to in her life. She takes too many risks. She feels no fear." He raised his head and looked straight into Josie's eyes. "Christian's life is in danger, and soon D.J.'s will be, as well. She must learn to love in order to save them both. That's all I can tell you. If you want to save her, you must agree to these terms. I must have an answer now, Josie." Raphael paused and held out his hand to her. "Will you be D.J.'s angel?"

Chapter Two

D.J. walked into her silent apartment and tossed her keys onto the hall table. In the living room she switched on the television. A game show blared loud music and stupid questions back in her face. With a grimace she snapped the "off" button.

Silence descended once more. After wandering into the kitchen D.J. spent one minute putting her breakfast bowl, spoon, and coffee cup into the almost empty dishwasher; then she completed her tour of the apartment in her bedroom, where she plopped down on the bed and tried to read a law enforcement magazine. After five minutes of seeing the face of the kid she'd shot in front of her eyes instead of the printed words, she threw the thing to the floor and stared at the ceiling in disgust.

If I have to keep thinking about him every time I

turn around, I'm going to scream. she thought.

"This is pretty sad."

At the sound of a woman's voice in her bedroom, D.J. sat up so fast her head spun from the speed.

"A young, attractive girl like you. I would think you'd have plenty of friends, male and female, to spend your time with. You don't need to mope around this dreary excuse for a home the entire day. Get out and do something, and then you won't keep thinking about that poor boy you had to shoot. You and I both know you had no choice."

D.J.'s gaze darted around the room, searching for the source of the female voice.

Nothing. No one.

With great caution she reached for her shoulder holster, where she'd tucked her newly issued sidearm, her usual weapon having been taken for evidence by the first officers on the scene the night before.

"Oh, you don't need that silly thing, dear. Look at all the trouble it's caused you already. Besides, a gun wouldn't do you much good on me anyway."

"Who are you?" D.J. found her voice. "Where are you, and what do you want?"

A giggle sounded, directly above D.J.'s bed. She jerked her head backward, then winced at the pain shooting through her neck at the abrupt movement.

"Oops," the voice said. "I forgot. Rule number 650—materialize for your human being. But only for her."

D.J. watched in amazement as a young woman appeared above her bed, sitting in thin air as though perched upon an invisible tree limb. She looked to be in her mid-twenties, with long, curling black hair, a heart-shaped face, and blue eyes. She wore a long dress that looked to D.J. as though it belonged in the sixties section of a vintage clothing store. The woman's feet, swinging in the air above D.J.'s head, were bare.

"Aah." The woman put her hands out in front of her and wiggled her fingers. "Much better. I knew I'd enjoy having a body again, if only for a little while."

D.J. blinked. She blinked again, harder this time. The woman was still there. A groan issued from her lips as she fell back on the bed, squeezing her eyes shut.

"What's the matter, dear?"

"They told me this would happen, but I didn't believe them. All the old-timers said one day I'd hold too much in, and then I'd snap. But I thought they meant I'd start shooting innocent bystanders. I never thought I'd start seeing imaginary people." D.J.'s eyes snapped open, and she met the concerned gaze of the woman still dangling above her bed. "Or maybe that's the problem with the shooters. Maybe they see imaginary people, too, and they're just trying to shoot them."

The woman frowned. "I have no idea what you're talking about. I'm not imaginary. I'm a very real guardian angel."

D.J. groaned once more and turned over on her stomach. "Oh no, a religious hallucination. Now I've really gone 'round the bend. I don't even believe in God and now I'm seeing angels."

"That's enough!" The woman's voice held shock and outrage. "Turn over and look at me."

D.J. lay still for a moment. Did she need to obey a hallucination? Doubtful. But if there was any chance the delusion would go away by listening to an explanation, then D.J. would listen. She turned onto her back and faced the intruder once more.

"You may not believe in God, young woman, but He certainly believes in you. Not everyone gets a guardian. Be thankful I'm here."

"Thankful I've lost my mind?"

"You have not lost your mind."

D.J. sat up. This was getting too weird. Not only did she see a woman in her bedroom who couldn't be there, but she was arguing with the apparition. She could feel the walls start to close in on her. When her time came to live in a padded room—an imminent situation, from the sound of things— she'd be in big trouble. D.J. did not like being confined. Perhaps now would be a good time for some fresh air.

D.J. got to her feet and headed for the door.

"Where are you going? I'm not done explaining things to you yet."

"I'm going out for a walk. When I get back you'd better be gone. I don't need another bout with the police psychologist." D.J. shut her apartment door behind her. "He already thinks I'm nuts."

Half expecting the delusion to materialize in front of her, D.J. uttered a sigh of relief when she was able to walk down the street unaccosted.

Maybe this suspension would be a blessing in disguise. She could use a rest. Too many nights of dealing with the shady side of life made for days in the loony bin. But what would she do with herself for two weeks? Playing cop with McCall wouldn't take up all her time.

Without conscious knowledge her feet carried her toward the police station a few blocks from her home. She had chosen her apartment because of it's close proximity to the station. Living and breathing her job, D.J. wanted nothing—no snow-storms, broken-down vehicles, or other acts of a God she didn't believe in—to interfere with D.J. Halloran being on the job whenever she might be needed.

"Thought you'd gone home to get some sleep."

The voice, so close to her ear, made D.J. jump and spin around with a shriek. Half expecting to see her imaginary visitor hovering in the air above her, it took D.J a minute to register the voice as male and the owner of the voice as Christian McCall.

"My, aren't we jumpy. Too much caffeine, Hal-loran?"

D.J. scowled. "Too much of you, McCall. Didn't I tell you to meet me here in the morning?"

"I will. I just came back to take a few more pic-tures. I needed Colleen to let me into some of the locked areas. One of the other officers offered to take me out on a call with him." He pointed to the squad car idling at the curb.

D.J. nodded to Lou Clark, behind the wheel. The officer motioned for her to come over.

"Hey, Halloran, want to go with us? We've got a jumper over on State Street. I could use a hand."

D.J. reached for the doorknob before she remembered, then let her hand fall away to hang at her side. "I'm suspended, Lou."

"Hell, I know that. The world knows it, sweet pea. But you're supposed to be working with *him,* ain't ya?" Lou jerked his head toward McCall. "God knows why the captain put you on such an assignment. But he's comin' with me, so you can, too. Hop in."

McCall came up behind D.J. and reached around her to open the door. His forearm brushed hers, and a tingle radiated upward, settling at the base of her neck with a hum. D.J. took a quick step away—a retreat McCall must have noticed but did not comment upon. For that she was thankful. She didn't think she could come up with another snappy comeback to save face right now.

Why did she feel such a strong physical attraction to this man? He was the exact opposite of every man she'd ever been attracted to before. Tall, lean, soft-spoken, with waving black-brown hair and warm brown eyes. Kind of cute in a bookish sort of way. She'd always gone for the macho types, which had gotten her into trouble more often than not. Manly men didn't appreciate smart-mouthed, action-centered women.

"D.J.?" McCall's questioning voice brought her back to the present. She stepped past him, careful to avoid touching him again, and got into the squad car. Just as they pulled away from the curb another man came out of the station, and D.J. craned around her neck to get a better look.

"Think of the devil and he appears," she muttered.

Lou slid a glance her way. "He was inside looking for you when I came out. That's the main reason I figured you'd want to go with us."

D.J. smiled at him. "Thanks, Lou. You're a pal."

"Just so you know, we picked up a guy from Chicago, gang type, selling crack at one of the middle schools. He's in holding now. I'll question him later and let you know what I find out."

D.J. raised her eyebrows. Maybe they'd found another break in the gang activity case she and Lou were working on together in their off time. "Yeah, let me know. I'm sure the gun I faced last night came through the guy we're looking for. The thing was registered in California. How did it get here, for crying out loud?" She kept her gaze on the rear-view mirror outside the passenger window as she spoke, watching the man who'd exited the police station and gotten into the double-parked red Mercedes. When he drove away she let out her breath in a whoosh of relief. He hadn't seen her.

"Your guess is as good as mine, sweet pea," Lou answered her rhetorical question as he often did. "But I plan to find out where all this gang paraphernalia is coming from."

D.J. nodded, still staring at the rear-view mirror, her mind on personal, not departmental, problems. She must really be slipping. If she'd been paying any attention, she would have seen his car when she walked up to the station and run for her life. But she'd been too involved in her other problems to think about the one that kept coming back into her life like an untreated strep infection.

Rich Halloran, first-class jerk, macho creep, and ex-husband of one year. D.J. could think of quite a few other adjectives, but she'd had a bad enough day already without spending more time thinking about Rich.

He must have heard about the shooting and come to rub it in. Most of the other cops on the Lakeview PD—actually, all of the cops except D.J. and Lou—were friends with Rich. He owned a fire-arms and ammunition store nearby and provided great deals to officers of the law. He had gotten the police business because of D.J. and her father's influence, but since D.J. and Rich were no longer married Rich took delight in furthering his friend-ships with the other cops. His macho attitude won him friends in D.J.'s world, and his tales of their relationship increased her image as "Officer Ice."

Rich had taken the divorce to heart and now de-tested D.J. with all the passion he'd lacked in their marriage. D.J. couldn't lay all the blame on Rich. She'd married him because she'd wanted a com-panion, someone to share her life with, someone who could keep the loneliness hunting her in the night at bay. But D.J. had never been able to deal with strong emotions, her own or other people's. That flaw in her character had netted her several meetings with the police psychologist, meetings she would soon be attending again; the Lakeview PD required mandatory counseling following a shooting.

McCall had remained silent thus far, and D.J. twisted in her seat to see if he'd fallen asleep or slipped out the back when she wasn't watching. No such luck. He wrote studiously in a small notebook. At her movement he looked up and smiled.

D.J.'s breath caught. He was downright handsome when he smiled. The warm brown eyes glared with an inner light she envied.

D.J. turned to face front without returning the smile. She saw no reason to encourage him. When two weeks passed she'd be back at work, and he'd be off doing whatever children's book writers did.

"Here we are." Lou pulled to a stop in front of a ten-story office building in the business section of Lakeview. He leaned forward and looked up. "And there he is."

D.J. released her seat belt and got out of the car, looking up toward the top of the building. Sure enough, a man perched on the ledge far above them, arms outstretched as though ready for flight. A sizable crowd had already gathered below, waiting for the show.

"Hey, you, mister," D.J. shouted. The man looked down, whirling his arms a few times to regain his balance. "You're causing a scene. Get off the ledge."

"I think getting off is what he's got planned," McCall said as he unfolded himself from the squad car and stood next to her.

The crowd, most of whom were students from the nearby high school out on their lunch break, began to chant, "Jump! Jump! Jump!"

D.J. let out a harsh breath of irritation. "Just what we need." She turned to Lou as he came around the car and joined them on the sidewalk. "I'll go up. You take care of the riot down here."

"Excuse me." McCall stepped in front of D.J. as she made a move toward the door.

"What?" D.J. snapped, the constant shout of "Jump! Jump! Jump!" wearing on her nerves.

"I've been a crisis counselor for the last five years."

"Figures," D.J. muttered.

McCall ignored her. "I think maybe I should go up with you. I might be able to help."

"Good idea," Lou put in. "Take him up with you, Halloran. Sounds like the boy knows what he's doing."

D.J. scowled. "All right. Let's go before the guy decides to follow their orders." She jerked her head toward the crowd. "Instead of mine."

They entered the building to the continued chant of, "Jump! Jump! Jump!"

As the security guard—a young man in his twenties who looked like he played football for the local college—came toward them, D.J. flashed her badge.

"Oh, good. Never thought I'd be glad to see the cops," he said. "I don't know what to do. They keep calling from upstairs, asking for help. I'm just a rent-a-cop, man. I don't know nothin' about jumpers."

"Relax," D.J. said. "I'll handle it. Where is he?"

"Tenth floor. Office Ten-ten. Department of Revenue. Weird dudes, all of 'em. Suits and ties, briefcases all the time." The guard followed them as they walked toward the elevators, continuing to talk even when the doors started to slide shut. "I guess this one got sick of auditing people's lives, bein' suspicious of everyone and everyth—"

The doors shut with a muffled thump, cutting off the guard midstream.

"What do you usually do in a situation like this?" McCall asked.

D.J. shrugged. "We don't get many jumpers in a city the size of Lakeview. But I've dealt with them before."

"Successfully?"

D.J. didn't answer. She didn't like to remember her failures.

"Thought so."

Anger coursed through D.J. This day wasn't getting any better, and McCall wasn't getting any easier to put up with. She looked at him, her irritation increasing when she saw the superior smile playing about his lips. "If you're so smart, why don't you try talking to him first? I'm not even supposed to be here."

"All right. If you insist."

The elevator doors slid open. D.J. made an elaborate bow, then swept her arm out in invitation. "By my guest."

A group of men and women huddled outside an office down the hall revealed the direction of their quarry. D.J. flipped her badge open once more and followed an agitated woman to an open window.

"I came in to tell Mr. Packard I was going to lunch." Her hands shook as she spoke, and she clasped them together in front of her, the knuckles showing white under the pressure. "And he was out there. He won't answer any of us."

McCall stepped forward. "Do you know if anything's upset him lately? Big changes in his life? That sort of thing?"

The woman's gaze switched to McCall. "W-well, I wasn't supposed to know about this, but . . ." She hesitated, then looked toward D.J., who raised her eyebrows in encouragement. "His wife left him for another man. The only reason I know the story is because the secretary from his old office and I are friends. He transferred here about a month ago. She thought I should know so I could help him."

"I see." The woman returned her attention to McCall when he spoke. "Does he have any other family we can call?"

"Not that I know of. He never mentioned anything personal. Just kept to himself and did his job. I think he was still trying to get over the shock of losing his wife."

"All right." McCall took the woman gently by the elbow and led her to the door. "We'll take care of things now. Just keep everyone out." He gave her a little push, and she stepped into the hall. "Oh, and what's Mr. Packard's first name?"

"Craig."

"Thank you." McCall closed the door in her face.

"Very nice," D.J. observed. "I'm impressed already. You handled the secretary—who wasn't out on the ledge, may I point out—quite well. Now let's see what you can do with the real problem. Sounds like this Packard has had a tough time with the little woman and wants to go visit the angels earlier than he should." The mention of angels reminded D.J. of the woman floating above her bed. She hoped the apparition would be gone when she got home. Otherwise she might be walking a ledge herself before the day ended.

D.J. walked over to the window and stuck out her head. "Lakeview Police, Mr. Packard. What do you say to coming inside and having a little talk with us?"

The man continued to stand on the ledge, the heels of his shoes against the brick building, his toes in open air. His arms remained outflung for balance, pressed to the brick, as well. At least he wasn't looking down, which was always a bad choice under the circumstances. He didn't answer her question, didn't even look her way.

D.J. looked down. The crowd was multiplying, as crowds always seemed to do in such situations. Before too long Lou would have a real problem on his hands. She'd better get this guy in as quickly as she could.

She looked back up and froze. The woman from her bedroom hovered directly in front of her.

"Get out of here," D.J. hissed. "Go away!"

"Not until you get back inside the building. What kind of guardian would I be if I let you climb out on a ledge?"

"This is my job."

"Not today."

Someone grasped D.J.'s hips and jerked her back into the room. A big smile appeared on the angel's face just before she disappeared. D.J. spun around and smacked the heels of her hands against McCall's solid chest. "What the hell do you think you're doing?"

"Getting you out of my way." He released her and

stepped toward the window. "Your ledgeside manner is atrocious. The guy's gonna jump just to get away from your yelling at him."

D.J. breathed a sigh of relief. McCall hadn't realized she spoke to thin air and not the jumper. "Excuse me for wanting to get the guy inside. Let's see how you do."

Before D.J. could stop him, McCall climbed out onto the ledge.

"Hey, get back in here!"

McCall silenced her with a glare. "I know what I'm doing; now back off."

D.J.'s eyes widened, but she did as he said. In truth, she had no desire to deal with Mr. Packard. She had never been good in situations where extreme emotions were involved, and from the looks of Craig Packard such was the case here.

McCall's voice drifted in through the window, and D.J. inched forward, drawn to the sound of peace in his tone.

"So, Craig, I hear you don't want to talk. Hey, that's all right. Some things are just too big to be talked about, aren't they?"

D.J. strained her ears, hoping for some response from Packard. Not a sound. She leaned her back against the wall next to the open window. From such a vantage point she could hear everything and still remain out of sight of the two men. She didn't think McCall would take kindly to any distractions right now.

"Care if I sit down?" No answer from Packard. "Thanks."

"Don't get too close to him, moron," D.J. hissed.

She'd heard plenty of horror stories about jumpers who took caring cops with them for a free ride.

McCall kept right on talking, ignoring D.J.'s warning, though he must have heard her. "I've gotta tell you, Craig, I don't much care for heights. But I would like to hear what's bothering you."

Still nothing. D.J.'s patience slipped a notch. She opened her mouth to order McCall back inside, but when he spoke again the order died on her lips.

"Bad things happen to good people all the time, Craig. It's a sad fact of life. But the strong fight back. I know it sounds trite, but given time just about everything has a solution. I'd like to help you find yours, if you'll let me."

McCall sounded so sincere, D.J. found herself leaning forward to catch a glimpse of his face. How could he care about a complete stranger within a matter of moments? It took her months to loosen up enough to make a friend, and even then she had trouble talking about anything important with anyone. As a result, people often drifted away after a few failed attempts at trying to draw D.J. out of herself.

Craig Packard turned toward McCall with a lost look in his eyes. D.J. caught her breath. The blank look had receded. McCall had made progress. Packard lowered his arms and sat with great care on the ledge next to his companion.

"Who are you?" he asked.

"I'm Chris. Chris McCall."

"Do we know each other?"

"No, but I'd like us to. What do you say we go

inside? I know some people who'd like to help you work through this."

Packard looked down. His skin paled several shades; then he tore his gaze from the street ten floors below. "All right."

D.J. almost fell out of the window at the man's capitulation. What had McCall done that was so wonderful? He'd acted like he cared, and a few seconds later the jumper was eating out of his hand like a tame wolf. Maybe this softer side stuff had its uses.

McCall inched back toward the window, glancing over every few seconds to check on Packard. The man inched along next to him, docile as a newborn lamb. When McCall reached the window he gave D.J. a jaunty thumbs up, complete with a grin, and threw his leg over the sill. With one leg on the inside and one still outside, he helped Packard through the window.

Once inside, Packard sank to the floor, as though his legs could no longer support him. He looked up at D.J. "Guess that was pretty dumb."

She fought the urge to shuffle her feet in discomfort. She never knew what to say to people who looked at her with a world of pain in their eyes. And, in her line of work, there'd been a lot of them.

Thankfully, the door opened at that moment, and several emergency personnel came in. They surrounded Craig Packard, talking to him in soothing tones reminiscent of the one McCall had used, and leading him toward the door. He would have an escort to the Lakeview hospital, where he would undergo twenty-four hours of mandatory observation. The crowd of people in the hallway dispersed as the EMTs approached.

"Hey, Craig," McCall said, still perched on the windowsill. Packard turned around. "I'll come by and visit you. We'll have that talk soon."

The man smiled and nodded, a spark of hope lighting his eyes. D.J. shook her head at the change in the man. She had no doubt he'd be all right now, and all it had taken was a few sentences from someone who truly cared. The taste of failure flooded her mouth. Why couldn't she have been the one to help him?

D.J. spun back toward McCall, her hands on her hips. "How'd you do that?" she demanded.

McCall, who had started to inch the rest of the way inside, pulled back at her loud demand. He wavered backward, off balance. The one leg he'd slung inside the room slid with the rest of him toward oblivion.

D.J. gave a yelp of fright and dove for McCall's arm. Before she could catch him, he flipped forward with a graceful movement reminiscent of Bruce Lee. Where had the guy learned that trick? He came back through the window toward her at full force. Unable to stop his forward momentum, McCall careened into D.J., knocking her to the ground and following her to the floor.

Her breath came out on a whoosh and a grunt. Brother, was he heavy.

"Ouch!" She poked at his shoulder, hard, with her finger and encountered bunched muscle. He might look tall and wiry, but underneath the loose-fitting jeans and baggy University of Wisconsin sweatshirt rested work-hardened muscle. D.J. shoved with her whole hand. "Get off me, you big horse."

McCall shifted, his body fitting against hers in an age-old alignment. He lifted his head and their gazes caught and held. His brown eyes warmed. D.J.'s mouth went dry, and she licked her lower lip. His eyes followed the movement of her tongue. He started to lower his head toward her. D.J.'s lids fluttered closed, and she arched her neck, offering her lips.

A second later she lay alone on the floor, the warmth and hardness of McCall's body removed from hers. D.J.'s eyes snapped open and she sat up. McCall stood at the window, staring out—not down. If not for the rigid line of his back, D.J. would have thought she imagined what had just passed between them.

"What happened?" she asked, cursing the husky, sexy sound of her voice.

"I talked him in."

She'd meant between them, but she wasn't about to admit that now. "I saw. How'd you do it?"

McCall shrugged, the movement emphasizing the tension in his shoulders rather than easing it. Why did he seem so upset now—when he'd succeeded in saving a man's life? "I've had a lot of training. He needed to know someone in the world cared. Hopefully he'll listen to the psychologist at the hospital and get more help. I only wish I could have done more."

D.J. got to her feet. "You did very well. If I'd tried to talk to him, he probably would have jumped. I— I'm . . ." She trailed off and sighed, reluctant to admit her deficiencies aloud. "I don't relate to people very well."

McCall shoved himself away from the window and paced the room without looking at her. "I've been where he is. I know what it's like to be so filled with despair dying looks good in comparison to enduring one more day. When things get that bad you need a miracle to turn yourself around."

Raw pain tinged his voice, and D.J. shifted from one foot to another in discomfort. What the hell should she say to him?

"Aah, I'm sorry. . . . " She floundered to a stop as McCall swung around midpace and glared at her. "You're better now, though. I mean, you seem all right. Not suicidal." She bit her lip. God, she couldn't stop making a mess of this. As usual.

"Don't worry, D.J. I won't fall apart on you. I'm sure all this emotion has been a strain on your logical cop personna." McCall went to the door and held it open for her. "We'd better get downstairs before Lou sends someone after us."

At the mention of Lou, D.J. grimaced. She hoped he didn't get in any trouble for allowing her to come with him on this call. If he did, she'd have to hope she could talk fast enough and hustle hard enough to get him off the hook.

As they stepped into the elevator, D.J. glanced over at McCall. Lost in his own thoughts, he pushed the button for the lobby and stared at the descending numbers on the consol above the doors. With his head tilted just that way, the muscles in his neck stood out. She wanted to reach out and trace them with her fingers, wrap her hand around the back of his neck, and make him finish the kiss he'd run away from only moments before.

D.J. caught her breath and forced her gaze away. Such thoughts weren't for her. She should be thinking about what she would do if the captain found out Lou had invited her along today. She wouldn't stand for Lou getting in trouble. If worse came to worst, perhaps McCall would get Lou off the hot seat with Captain Miller by using his influence with the mayor. She'd even be willing to ask for McCall's assistance, debase herself, grovel, whatever, if she could help Lou. Of all the cops on the Lakeview PD, Lou was the best. He'd always treated D.J. with respect. He only called her "sweet pea" when none of the other officers were around. She couldn't expect him to totally abandon her childhood nickname. Sometimes she was hard put not to call him "Uncle Lou," as she'd done since she'd first met him. Lou Clark was her father's best friend—and had been his partner for ten years. If it hadn't been for Lou, D.J. would never have known anything beyond apathy and disgust.

The only two emotions in her father's eyes whenever he looked at her.

Chris opened the front door of his house and stepped inside. Reaching out, he found the light switch and pushed. Electric sunshine poured down, making him blink.

He couldn't stop the afternoon's events from replaying in his head. The despair in Craig Packard's eyes had called out to the despair that had once haunted Chris during every moment of his life.

He'd been somewhat successful in keeping his despair at bay during his waking hours, but when he slept—well, that was another story.

Then there'd been D.J. with her beautiful, fragile face, her trim athlete's body, her soft, full lips and her soul of ice. He couldn't understand the woman.

She'd driven them back to the station in the squad car, leaving Lou to return with one of the other officers who had arrived on the scene with the EMTs. She'd spoken few words to Chris, and her neglect had been fine with him. He hadn't felt much like talking at the time. But he had sensed her withdrawal, as though she'd put a wall between herself, her emotions, and the rest of the world.

Maybe cops got used to violence and despair so that no matter how much they saw, they took it in stride. Maybe D.J. Halloran was exactly the same as any of the other officers on the Lakeview force. But somehow Chris doubted that. D.J. was different.

Chris set a new disposable camera on the table. He'd dropped off the roll he'd completed earlier at the grocery store film drop on his way home. He tapped the base of the table lamp and the living room sprang to light.

"What the . . . ?"

The room had been ransacked. Books poured out of the bookcase. The couch had been slit open and the stuffing splayed about the room. The entertainment center resembled kindling, with glass from the busted television sprinkled on top like sugar.

Chris turned, heading for the kitchen and the telephone. Blinding pain ricocheted inside his brain, and then the night closed in around him.

Chapter Three

"All right. Where are you?"

D.J. slammed the door of her apartment and stalked through the hallway and into her bedroom. A glance around the room revealed no one hovering in the air.

"Come on," she shouted, returning to the living room. "You're my delusion, and I want you to materialize right now."

"All that shouting, dear. You'll upset the neighbors."

The voice came from the kitchen. Three steps later, D.J. found her quarry making soup at the stove.

The scene pulled D.J. up short. She could see the kettle, steam rising from the simmering broth. She could even smell the soup—chicken something.

How could a figment of her imagination make real soup?

The answer blared in her mind. A figment couldn't.

D.J. grabbed a chair and sat down. The angel looked at her with a smile. "Hungry? Good. Soup's almost ready. I always liked to cook. I must say it's nice to get back to it."

"Wh-who are you?"

"I told you, dear. Your guardian angel. You can call me Josie. And I know all about you. Your name is—"

"D.J."

Josie glanced at her with a frown. "That's not your real name."

"It is now. The only person on earth who knows my real name is my father, and I plan to keep it that way. Just call me D.J."

"Whatever you say, dear. Though it's a shame to deny such a beautiful name."

"Tough." D.J. took a deep breath. She hated her real name. Just hearing it out loud made her flinch. She turned her gaze back to the angel. "Why do you keep calling me 'dear' like you're an old woman or something. You're younger than I am by the looks of you."

Josie shrugged, stirring the soup. "Twenty-four when I died." She sighed, a sound full of sadness and pain. "Dying has a way of aging the soul. I've seen things you couldn't imagine."

"I bet." D.J. rubbed the bridge of her nose with her fingers. Pain pulsed behind her eyes. It had been one hell of a day, but at least she hadn't lost her mind completely. The woman was real—or as real as an angel could be—however real that was. She didn't have the brain power right now to question why she, who denied the existence of God, heaven, and angels, would suddenly believe she had an angel in her kitchen. Perhaps because the opposite side of the coin appealed to her even less. If Josie wasn't an angel—then D.J. was insane.

Another question occurred to her, and D.J. let her hand fall back to the table. "Why me?"

"What do you mean?"

"I mean, why do I rate a guardian angel? I told you, I've never believed in God."

Josie didn't answer right away. She took her time getting out a bowl, ladling the soup, and then placing a spoon into the steaming liquid. She carried the bowl to the table and set the soup down in front of D.J. Taking a seat at the opposite side of the table, Josie put her chin in her hand.

"God believes in you, D.J. He believes in us all. He won't let you flounder along through life if there's a way to help. I'm your help."

"Help for what? Is my life in danger?"

Josie sat up straight. "Eat." She waved at the bowl of soup. "It'll get cold."

D.J. put a spoonful into her mouth. The soup tasted as good as it smelled. "I could get used to this," D.J. said between spoonfuls. "But, as my father always said, nothing good lasts forever."

Josie frowned as she leaned forward once more. "You believe that?"

"Sure. I never saw anything to contradict what good old Dad told me."

"What about love, marriage, family?"

"They definitely don't last forever. You should know that."

"I can still love. I'll love the husband I left behind and my—" She broke off with a little gasp. Biting her lip, Josie glanced at D.J, then smiled a brilliant smile—though the expression did not reach her eyes. "I'll love him forever. My love will never change or die. When he joins me we'll be together for all eternity."

"Oh, please. Don't start that sappy stuff with me. I've had a tough day."

Josie, who had been staring into space with a soft smile on her lips, blinked and focused her gaze on D.J.'s face. "You want to know why you've been given a guardian? I'll tell you. I'm supposed to teach you how to love."

The soup D.J. had just spooned into her mouth went down the wrong pipe. She sputtered, choked, and started to cough. Her eyes filled with tears as she gasped for breath. Josie jumped up and delivered a resounding slap to D.J.'s back.

"Hey," D.J. wheezed. "That hurt."

"Life hurts. Did you want to breathe or not?"

"I guess. Thanks." D.J. pushed away her half-eaten bowl of soup and Josie carried it to the sink. "You're wasting your time, you know," D.J. said softly. "I don't believe in love either."

"I know. That's why I'm here."

"This is ridiculous." D.J. shoved back her chair and got to her feet. "What does God care if I don't believe in love? I'm doing fine. I like my job; I'm a good cop."

Josie turned away from the sink and leaned against the counter. "Life is pretty empty without love. What do you have to look forward to, day after day, D.J.? Going to work, saving the world from the bad guys, then coming home to an empty apartment, waiting for the next night, when you can go back to work and start all over again?"

"It's my life. I like it this way."

"Do you? Do you really? If you ever took the time to look inside yourself, I wonder what you'd find."

D.J. didn't like the way the conversation was headed. A buzzing, like the static of a television after the station's gone off the air, played in her ears, telling D.J. she ran on her final reserve of energy. Serious sleep deprivation lurked just around the corner. She didn't have the brain power left to deal with angels anymore today. "I've had enough of this. Enough of you. I haven't slept for over twenty-four hours. I'm going to bed."

D.J. left the kitchen, slamming and then locking her bedroom door behind her. She went into the bathroom and grabbed her toothbrush. When she looked into the mirror Josie's face stared back at her. She jumped backward with a squeak of alarm.

"A locked door won't keep me out, D.J."

"Don't do that!" D.J. stepped forward and shouted at the mirror. "Get out of there! You're going to drive me insane, if I'm not already." D.J. stalked out of the bathroom, yanking off her clothes and throwing them in a heap in the corner. She tugged on a nightshirt and climbed into bed, turning the lights off with more force than necessary to do the job.

"Maybe you should think about why you're so angry with me." Josie's voice came from the darkness surrounding her. "Good night, D.J. We'll talk again in the morning."

Josie watched D.J. sleep. The girl slept as stiffly as she lived—flat on her back, arms straight at her sides, never tossing or turning. She gave Josie the willies. How on earth had a child of hers ended up this way?

Unable to stand the stillness any longer, Josie lifted one of D.J.'s arms and moved it so the girl's palm lay against her cheek. Then she eased D.J.'s head sideways. The girl mumbled and turned on her side, curling her legs up and cuddling against the pillow.

"So much better," Josie whispered as she allowed her fingers to tangle in D.J.'s short hair.

"Josie." A man's voice called her name.

"What?" She yanked away her fingers and looked up at the ceiling. "She looks like she belongs in a coffin. How can I teach the girl anything when she's such a stiff?"

"Never mind how she sleeps. I want to talk to you. Come to me."

Josie sighed. What could Raphael want already? She'd been on earth a mere day. With a last look at D.J., Josie closed her eyes, concentrated as Raphael had taught her, and went to meet the boss. When she opened her eyes Raphael was directly in front of her.

"What did I do wrong?" Josie asked.

"Nothing. But I've just learned new information I thought you should be made aware of. The threat to D.J.'s life has increased."

"What threat? Since I've known her a boy's been

shot and a man nearly jumped off a building. I'd say she's a threat to everyone else's safety. The girl's a walking time bomb. She only pretends to be cool and collected. If you hit too close to the heart of D.J., she's got quite a temper. I worry about this Christian. He's pretty insightful. He'll set her off for sure."

"Christian McCall is well able to take care of himself. Worry about D.J. She's your problem."

"Well, what's the threat? I'll just tell her in the morning, she'll take care of everything, and I can concentrate on finding her a man."

"I'm afraid it doesn't work that way, Josie." Raphael's face reflected his disapproval.

"What do you mean?"

"I can't just tell you the threat. I can only warn you to be on the alert."

"What?" The volume of Josie's voice made Raphael raise his eyebrows in mild surprise. "You're an archangel, for God's sake."

"Yes, I am. For God's sake."

The quiet reprimand behind the words made Josie pause and take a deep breath. "I just meant, you should know everything."

"I didn't say I didn't know. I just can't tell you."

Josie crossed her arms over her chest. "Who makes these rules anyway."

"Who do you think?"

Josie sighed. She should have known. "Why won't He let you tell me?"

"Because the threat to D.J. is something she must handle on her own. It is part of her life lesson. If the threat was eliminated before she had the chance to

learn it's lesson, she wouldn't become the person she is supposed to be."

"Who is she supposed to be?"

"A happier woman. A wife. A mother."

"A mother? D.J.?" Josie shook her head slowly. "I don't know if that's such a good idea."

"Whyever not?"

"If she doesn't know how to love, how can she be a mother? Having a child is the ultimate act of love."

"I agree. So you'd better get to work, hadn't you? Just make sure she stays alive long enough to learn what she needs to know. Is there anything else you want to ask before you go back?"

"What does Christian have to do with this?"

Raphael smiled a slow, secret smile. "What do you think?"

Josie's eyes widened. "Him? He's the one for D.J.? Oh, I don't think so. She'll eat him alive."

Raphael laughed, a deep, rich sound ripe with amusement. "Hardly. Christian McCall will surprise you. He'll surprise her. What you've got here, Josie, are two lost souls searching for each other. They just need a little help to find their way."

Josie sighed. She wished she could at least tell her daughter who she was. But she couldn't risk hurting D.J. for her own selfish reasons. "All right. But this isn't going to be easy, you know? Those two are as far apart as two people can get from falling in love."

"They're closer than you think. Remember the lessons you learned in your life, Josie. Is anything worth having ever easy?"

Josie closed her eyes, and the face of her husband came to her, as clear as if he was there with her now.

The memory filled Josie's heart, and her throat thickened with love. D.J.'s face replaced her husband's. Though it was hard on Josie not to reveal her identity, she would do whatever was necessary to have some time with her daughter.

"No. It's never easy. But love's worth all the trouble." She opened her eyes and found herself once again above D.J.'s bed. "I'll make sure you get your chance, D.J. I promise."

The phone shrilled, bringing D.J. out of a heavy sleep. She sat straight up in bed, her heart beating a painful cadence of fear.

"Everything's all right, dear." Josie's voice came from above the bed. "Just answer the phone."

D.J. took a second to glare at the interloper, then fumbled on her bedside table for the telephone.

"Sweet pea?" The volume of Lou's voice made D.J. wince.

"Yeah, Lou. I'm here. What's up?"

"Your friend, McCall. He's in Lakeview Hospital."

The last vestiges of sleep fled D.J.'s mind, and she threw her legs over the edge of the bed and stood up. "What happened?"

"Someone broke into his house last night. Trashed the place pretty good. He must have walked in on them. They hit him over the head and took off."

"Is he all right?"

"I brought him down here to get checked over. The doctor says he's got a mild concussion, but he'll live. Anyway, McCall said he told you he'd meet you at eight. Maybe you can just come down to the hospital and pick him up. I've got to get home."

"Yeah. Fine. Tell him I'll be there in half an hour."

D.J. hung up and rubbed her eyes. She'd known McCall was trouble from the first time she'd laid eyes on him. Had that only been yesterday morning? It seemed as if she'd known him for weeks already. She'd certainly had enough of him to last a lifetime.

"Would you like coffee?"

D.J. jumped and yelped at the voice right behind her. She spun around and bumped into Josie.

"Are you still here?"

"Of course, dear. Where else would I be?"

"Don't you have someone else's life to mess up today?" D.J. headed for the shower, with Josie following.

"No. You're the one I've been assigned to. You'll have my undivided attention until we've solved your little problem."

D.J. stopped short at the bathroom door and spun around. "Look, I'm going to tell you one more time: I don't have a problem. I don't believe in love. I'll never believe in it. The people who do believe in love self-destruct in the end. You saw the poor sap out on the ledge yesterday. He's in the Straight-jacket Hotel right now because he believed in love. Not me, honey. No way."

"What about your parents?" Josie persisted, putting her palm against the bathroom door as D.J. tried to close it in her face. "They must have been an example of love for you."

"I don't discuss my parents. Not with you. Not with anyone."

Josie's hopeful expression faded. "Why not?"

"You're the angel; you figure it out."

D.J. slammed the door.

"I'll make coffee, dear." Josie's voice faded as she walked toward the kitchen.

D.J. turned on the shower. "I am losing my mind," she said through her teeth.

She had always prided herself on her cool, calm exterior. Emotions inhibited peak performance and efficiency. Now, in the past two days, she'd met two people who made her lose her temper at every turn. How did anyone endure the exhaustion when they convinced themselves they believed in passion, love, and happily-ever-after? Anger and irritation had D.J. in enough of an uproar to last a lifetime.

After hurrying through her shower D.J. dragged a comb through her short hair in an attempt to yank straight the natural wave, gave up as she did every morning, and finished her toilette by brushing her teeth. Well-worn jeans and a faded sweatshirt combined with high-top red sneakers completed her ensemble. A glance at her watch told D.J. she'd get to the hospital by eight if she left now.

She was anxious to pick up McCall and learn the details of his attack. Her cop instincts couldn't rest even when she'd been put on an enforced vacation. The mystery of the crime would haunt her until she solved the puzzle.

"Wait a minute. You forgot your coffee." Josie's voice stopped her at the door.

D.J. sighed and turned around. The angel had changed clothes, giving up her flowing mumu-type dress for a pair of bell bottoms and a flowered T-shirt. Josie's feet remained bare beneath the belled material of her pants. D.J. had the fleeting mental image of Josie shopping in a heavenly thrift store, complete with garments from every era. Perhaps tomorrow the angel would appear in a toga and sandals. She shrugged. What did Josie's clothing matter? No one could see her but D.J.

"Are you wearing that?" Josie wrinkled her nose at D.J. as she handed her a travel mug full of coffee.

D.J. blinked. Josie was a fine one to be making fashion judgments. "What's wrong with it?"

"Well, since you don't have to wear your awful uniform, I thought maybe you'd like to wear something more feminine." When D.J. continued to stare at her in blank amazement Josie tried again. "A skirt? Or a dress?"

D.J. gave a snort of laughter. "The only dress I have is black. It's my funeral dress. I wear black flats and my one pair of earrings, also black. Why on earth would I want to wear a dress to pick up McCall at the hospital?"

"Well, I just thought . . . He's . . . I mean . . . You and he . . ." Josie spread her hands and shrugged.

"Oh, no. No, you don't. Not him. You're not matchmaking me and that—that—writer. No, sir." D.J. opened the door. "You go right back to your superior, whoever he is, and tell him no way, José."

"Not José. Raphael."

D.J. swallowed the mouthful of hot coffee she'd just sipped, wincing at the burn of the liquid down her throat and into her empty stomach. "Raphael? The painter?"

Josie's lips quirked upward in amusement. "Not

quite. The Archangel Raphael." At D.J.'s shrug she explained, "He's the chief of the guardian angels."

"If you say so. I'm afraid I'm not up on my angel mythology."

"Raphael is hardly a myth, D.J."

"Whatever. You can just tell him to take you back wherever it is you go back to and leave me alone."

D.J. walked into the hallway, closing her apartment door behind her. When she turned around Josie stood in front of her. D.J. leaned back against the door with an exasperated sigh.

"You know I can't leave you, D.J. I can't get what I want until I help you learn what you need."

A glance at her watch made D.J. straighten and skirt around Josie. "We've had this argument already," she said, walking backward as she talked to the angel. "I have to pick up McCall and get to work, such as it is. I want you to stay here. I don't need you hovering over my head all day."

"But I'm supposed to—"

"No buts. Just stay out of my way. I'll talk to you later."

D.J. turned around and almost bumped into her neighbor, Mrs. Stalwerg, who stared down the empty hallway toward D.J.'s apartment door with a puzzled expression on her face.

"Excuse me, Mrs. Stalwerg. I'm late for work."

The sound of the apartment door opening and closing made D.J. flinch. "Dammit, Josie," she mumbled. The angel had materialized in the hallway in front of D.J., but she couldn't return to the apartment in the same way. Oh, no. She had to use the door.

"There's no one there," Mrs. Stalwerg said in an accusing tone.

"No, ma'am. There's not."

D.J. took the stairs to the ground floor two at a time, cursing under her breath all the way. She should have known better than to argue with an angel in public. Not only had she lost her marbles, but everyone in the building would know it as soon as Mrs. Stalwerg recovered her voice.

The ride to the hospital took a mere five minutes. D.J. parked in the back and went in through the emergency entrance. Several of the EMT personnel waved a hello, as familiar with her as she was with them.

The nurse at the desk pointed to one of the examining rooms before D.J. could even voice a question. "Lou said you were taking him with you. Sign this." She put a long, legal-looking form attached to a clipboard in front of D.J.'s face and poked a pen into her hand. "Then he's yours for life."

"No thanks. I'm just taking him for the day."

The nurse looked D.J. up and down. "Sister, if I were you, I'd take him for as long as I could get him. He's a dream."

"More like a nightmare." D.J. signed the paper and handed the pen and clipboard back to the nurse. She turned to walk toward the examining room the nurse had indicated, but the sight of a man coming around the corner made her spin back around. "Speaking of nightmares," she muttered. Her gaze flew around the emergency room, looking for a place in which to disappear. No avenue of escape presented itself. If she'd been a few moments earlier she'd have been safe inside the room with McCall. She had her guardian angel to thank for this. Now she'd have to face—

"Hello, D.J. I've been looking for you."

D.J. unclenched her back teeth, pasted a smile on her face, and turned to meet her ex-husband. "I heard, Rich. What could be important enough for you to chase me down here?

"I came here on some other business. Imagine my surprise when I turned the corner and found my little wife standing there."

"I'm not your wife. What do you want?"

"Tsk, tsk." Rich took a step forward, crowding D.J. against the nurses' station. "You still haven't learned any manners, have you?"

D.J. stood her ground, staring up into Rich's face with the indifferent attitude that always drove him crazy. She wondered how she could ever have found him attractive. Since she now knew what lay beneath the smooth veneer, his black Irish hair and eyes made the coldness inside her freeze colder. When Rich saw she couldn't be intimidated, as usual, he backed away. Despite his expensive silk suit and Italian shoes he was a bully and a thug, through and through. D.J. still couldn't believe she'd actually thought they could have a marriage with a future between them.

"I wanted to make sure you were all right. I read about the shooting."

D.J. rolled her eyes. "Don't insult me, Rich. You could care less about me or my job. Lou told me you were at the station yesterday. What do you want this time?"

"I just wanted to see if you'd sold the stock like we agreed."

"I did. I'm still waiting for the check. When it comes I'll send you your half. Just like I told you the last time you asked me."

"Oh, yeah. I remember now." Rich's voice held a distracted note, and he stared past her left shoulder.

Turning, D.J. looked behind her, half expecting to see Josie hovering in the air. The guardian angel might be worth all the trouble if she gave Rich a few nightmares. Maybe D.J. could get Josie to pay Rich a little visit in the dead of night—just for fun. But there was no sign of Josie—just McCall, poking his head out of the examining room door and looking around the room for her. He smiled when his gaze encountered hers, and the rest of his body slipped through the doorway.

D.J. returned her attention to Rich, intent on making him disappear before she had to perform an introduction between the two men. But her ex-husband had taken care of the disappearing act on his own. Weird. When Rich was on the hunt for money he usually pestered her until she came up with some. It wasn't like him to fade away before he needled her awhile. He'd never forgiven her for calling the police the day he'd finally given into his anger and hit her in the mouth after she smarted off one time too many. Instead of taking the abuse like the good little wife he'd expected her to become D.J. had called Lou and then filed charges. She'd dropped the charges when Rich agreed to a quick and easy divorce. The fact that most of the clients at his gun shop were cops—cops who worked with D.J. and wouldn't appreciate Rich's abuse—had expedited her wishes. Rich had kept his clients, and D.J. had won her freedom.

Thank heaven for big favors, D.J. thought, then frowned at her choice of words. Two days with Josie and the woman had her thanking a heaven she didn't believe existed. The angel definitely had to go.

A hand on her shoulder made D.J. jerk away before spinning to meet whoever dared to accost her.

"Sorry." McCall held up his hands in a gesture of defense. "You didn't seem to hear me when I called your name. Are you looking for someone?"

"No. I mean, yes. Well, just you." D.J. stopped and took a deep breath. She stifled the urge to apologize for throwing off McCall's hand. She could still feel the warmth of his touch, fleeting though it had been, which had set off an answering fire within her. She wanted the warmth back. "Are you all right?" she blurted in an attempt to stop her mind from analyzing any further.

"Fine." McCall reached for her hand. Since the movement so closely echoed her own desires she didn't pull away. He pulled her fingers up to his forehead and placed them against the bump. Her fingertips tingled at the contact. "I've got quite a knot." He dropped his hand away from hers.

D.J. allowed her fingers to remain against his skin. She couldn't stop herself from rubbing her thumb over the raised injury. His eyes snapped up to meet hers, surprise and desire mingling. The sight shocked her, and she dropped her hand with a guilty jerk. "You've got a hard head," she snapped in an attempt to defuse the heated moment between them. "You'll be all right."

McCall stared at her for a moment and D.J. held her breath, afraid he would give voice to the current that hummed between them, despite all her attempts to make it stop. Then he grinned at her, and her lips twitched in response, though she didn't actually let herself smile at him. "Glad to see you're back to your always pleasant self. You must have gotten a decent night's sleep."

"Yeah."

"Me, too. Though I have to say I'd rather sleep in my own way than have sleep forced upon me."

They left the hospital, and D.J. led the way to her truck. Once inside, she turned to McCall. "Lou said your house was ransacked. Do you have any idea why? What turned up missing?"

"Nothing missing that I could tell. I don't need much. I write and draw, travel a bit. My house is pretty bare; just the necessities. The only things to steal would be the television, VCR, and computer. Every one of those items is still there, although the television is smashed into a thousand pieces. Since they didn't break anything else, I have to think that was accidental. Maybe it fell off the entertainment center when they were looking behind it." He shrugged. "I don't know how thieves work."

"Strange," D.J. muttered.

"I thought so, too. I plan to take a better look around tonight."

"No. We'll go over there right now." D.J. started the car and, after getting directions to McCall's house, eased out of the hospital parking lot and onto the street. "If something's been stolen, it's best to find out right away and get the word out. You'll have a better chance of recovery."

"Everything's replaceable except for my drawings and my writing. And I can recreate them if I have to, though they wouldn't be exactly the same."

"Did they trash your office, or wherever it is you work?"

"Lou said the office is a mess. But nothing's ruined. He thought the thieves must have been searching for something. Then I surprised them and got a whack for my troubles."

"I don't like the sound of this. If they didn't find what they wanted, and they thought it important enough to break into your house and conk you over the head for it in the first place, they'll be back."

"Here we are." McCall pointed to a three-story gabled monstrosity on the right side of the street.

D.J. glanced upward, then back at McCall, her eyebrows raised, before she pulled over to the curb. "You live here?"

"Uh-huh. All my life—except for a few years when I lived—a—well—" He broke off and seemed to be searching for an explanation. His lips tightened a bit before he continued. "I lived somewhere else for a while. But I'm back to stay. This is the McCall family home."

He got out of the car and D.J. joined him on the sidewalk, her gaze fixed to the house. It looked like something out of a horror novel—with windows like eyes and green shingles that reminded her of scales on a dragon's back. A fresh coat of white

Lori Handeland

paint plus green trim gave the rest of the house a fresh-faced look, but D.J. could feel the character within.

She adored it. She, who had never lived in anything larger than an apartment in her life, lusted after this monstrous house with all her heart. The place was huge, impractical, probably hell to heat, but she could hardly keep herself from running up the steps to burst through the door and discover what lay on the other side.

"D.J.?" McCall stood at the door, looking back on her with a smile. "You wanted to come here; let's go in."

"Oh, yeah. Sure." D.J. tore her gaze away from the house and tried to hide her eagerness to view the rest. This was McCall's house; his family home, he'd said. There was no way on earth she would ever be able to live here.

McCall unlocked the door and stepped back to allow D.J. to enter first. "The place looks a lot better without all my belongings strewn around," he said. "But that's what you're here to see, I guess."

D.J. nodded and stepped over the threshold. Her breath caught in shock.

The hardwood floors gleamed with fresh wax. The windows sparkled in the autumn sun. Not a chair or book stood out of place.

A giggle like the ringing of Christmas bells sounded from the second floor. D.J. looked up in time to see the flash of a purple flowered T-shirt just before it disappeared.

"Josie," D.J. whispered. "If she wasn't already dead, I'd kill her."

74

Chapter Four

"What the . . . ?"

Chris shouldered past D.J. to stand with his mouth hanging open in the immaculate hallway. He turned to where D.J. hovered just inside the doorway, her gaze focused up the stairs, a scowl marring her features. Chris followed her gaze: nothing but the stairs.

"What are you looking at?" he asked

D.J. blinked. "No one. I mean, nothing. I—ah—I thought you said the place was a mess."

"It was. I didn't think the police would put every-thing back together when they were done."

"Hardly, McCall." D.J. gave a short laugh. "Do you have a cleaning lady?"

"No." He turned around in a slow circle, taking

in the wonder of a clean house. "But I think I'll get one. I kind of like this."

D.J. wandered into the living room, muttering under her breath. Her hands were clenched into fists, revealing an inner anger. What had gotten her so worked up?

Her gaze searched the room, resting on the furniture, the walls, the curtains in turn. Chris followed. Was she looking for a clue the others had missed? It would be hard to learn anything now that the house had been put back together.

"I can't understand how this place got fixed up. I think I'll call the station and ask."

"No!" D.J. spun around. Chris frowned. "I mean, let it go. One of your neighbors must have done you a favor. But if the captain hears a crime scene was cleared before he gave the okay, there'll be trouble. I'll talk to Lou about it."

"Oh, I never thought of that." No wonder she was so angry. He hoped no one got fired over this mistake. "All right," he agreed.

D.J. heaved a sigh that sounded almost like relief. "Do you mind if I look around?" she asked, already stepping toward the hallway.

"No. Go ahead. Though, since everything's picked up, I don't know what you'll be able to learn about the break-in."

"Uh-huh," she muttered and took the stairs two at a time.

By the time Chris caught up with her she stood in his parents' room. When he came in she was looking behind the closet door and whispering under her breath.

"I don't have any animals if you're looking for one."

She jumped and let out a little squeak. "Ah, no. I was just—just looking around. This place is wonderful. You said it's your family home: Do your parents live here too?"

Chris's face tightened at the mention of his parents. People who knew him avoided the subject, conscious of how the past upset him. But D.J. didn't know him. Not at all.

"My parents are dead." He turned and left her standing in the middle of the room.

Chris went to the kitchen and sat down in the window seat of the bay window, overlooking the garden. Why, after eighteen years without them, could the mention of his parents still cause such pain?

His mother had loved this house, lavishing care and affection on every room with graceful abandon. She had planted the wildflower garden the summer Chris turned six, and he had tended it faithfully every year since her death. Dad, a gentle, quiet man who loved his wife and child with his entire heart, had enjoyed being a lawyer, but the true joy in his life had been his family. Chris wanted the same type of family life for himself. He wanted a soul mate to share his days and nights forever. Sometimes the loneliness became almost too strong to bear, but he would settle for nothing less than what his parents had shown him. Life with the one right person could be heaven.

"Hey, McCall. Are you okay?"

D.J.'s voice drifted down the hallway from the living room. Chris took a deep breath. When Captain Miller had said she was a problem he hadn't been joking. There was something irresistible about D.J. Halloran, yet she was the exact opposite of everything he had ever wanted in a woman. Somehow he couldn't see D.J. as the soul mate of his dreams, sharing his work, his mind, his body, bearing his children. The thought of D.J. with children almost made him wince. She'd scare them to death.

The years he'd spent alone had taken their toll, weakening his resolve to wait for the one woman with whom he could share his life and his heart. If he gave in now to the siren call of D.J., all his years of enforced loneliness and celibacy would mean nothing.

"Here you are. Didn't you hear me calling you?" D.J. walked into the kitchen, and Chris turned away from the garden view with reluctance.

"No," he lied. "I didn't."

She stood just inside the doorway, the sun from the window falling across her upturned face and illuminating a rapt expression. She was so beautiful, he wanted to cross the room, take her in his arms, and kiss her upturned nose. Instead, he forced himself to remain seated, watching as she stared upward, her green eyes trained on the plate well that circled the kitchen. "Oh," she breathed, wonder filling the word. "How lovely."

Chris followed her gaze, cataloging the Hummels positioned in the plate well by year of issue, happy to see none were missing. His mother had loved knickknacks such as these.

Chris's perusal stopped and held when he

reached the clock. Ten A.M. And today was . . .

"Tuesday." He jumped to his feet.

D.J.'s gaze snapped toward him. "What?"

"I'm supposed to be somewhere right now."

"I thought you wanted the fifty-cent cop tour."

"Later. Right now I have to go." He headed toward the back door, then paused. He'd thought of the perfect way to get his lusting libido under control. He'd take D.J. with him on his errand. Once there, she'd prove to him she was in no way cut out to be anything more than a helpful addition to his next book. "Why don't you ride along with me?" he asked.

"I can wait here." She gazed out the window at the fading splendor of the wildflowers.

"I'd rather you came along. I can ask you some questions about your job on the way. Then we won't be wasting the morning any more than we already have."

D.J. turned away from the window with reluctance. "All right. Since you insist." She followed him out to the garage.

He handed her a helmet, which she took into her hand as though it might be diseased. "You have a motorcycle?" Her nose wrinkled on the last word.

"Yeah." He went inside and rolled the bike out onto the driveway. After fastening his helmet he turned back to D.J. She still stood where he'd left her, helmet in her hand. "Aren't you going to put the helmet on? Good to be safe."

"I'd rather not get on that thing."

"What?" Chris would have thought D.J. would be just the type of woman who'd relish a motorcycle ride. She lived a dangerous life—why would something as tame as a motorcycle put her off? "Don't tell me you're afraid."

D.J.'s eyes snapped at the taunt. "Hardly. I've just seen what people look like on the pavement after riding one of those."

"So have I. Believe me, D.J., I'm a safe driver. I'll get you there and back in once piece." He held out his hand. "Trust me."

She stared at his hand for a moment, then looked into his eyes. What she saw there must have convinced her, for she put the helmet on her head and climbed on the bike behind him.

"Where are we going?" she yelled over the roar of the Harley's engine.

"It's a surprise," he shouted back.

D.J. put her arms around his waist and fitted her thighs around his. Chris gritted his teeth against the warmth flooding through him at her innocent touch. Her breath tickled the back of his neck, and he twitched his shoulders. Tightening his resolve, he released the clutch and they shot forward, headed toward a place Chris hoped would end his fascination with D.J. Halloran before it raged further out of control.

CINDY'S CASTLE, the sign read. QUALITY DAY CARE LICENSED BY THE STATE OF WISCONSIN.

D.J. climbed off the bike and yanked the helmet free of her chin, running a hand over her smashed hair as she stared at the building in front of them in trepidation.

McCall had brought her to a day-care facility? What was he up to?

She turned to ask him, but he had strode up the front walk toward the door. Little faces pressed against the windows as little hands waved a greeting. D.J. continued to stand by the motorcycle, uncertain of what he expected her to do.

McCall turned with his hand on the doorknob. "Come on. I'm already late for class." He beckoned to her with his free hand. "You can help me. You'll love it."

D.J. placed the helmet on the seat and walked up the sidewalk, which she saw had been painted to look like the yellow brick road.

First it's angels, now it's kids. Why me?

The front door opened and a young woman stepped outside. D.J. stopped short and stared. She had never seen anyone so beautiful or so feminine. Her long blond hair had been braided around her head into an artful crown framing an exquisite face, highlighted by innocent blue eyes. The woman was petite, and the long, swirling floral print of her skirt nearly touched the white, high-topped boots encasing her small feet. She smiled up at McCall, her perfect ivory teeth flashing in the sun. The scent of hibiscus drifted to D.J. on the breeze, and she sneezed, once, violently. The woman's gaze shifted in D.J.'s direction, dismissed her, and returned to rest on McCall with admiration.

"Christian, we thought you'd forgotten all about us." The woman's voice, soft and breathy, hinted at cryptic promises she could share in the darkness of the night. To McCall's credit, he didn't take the bait.

"I'm sorry we're late." He turned to D.J. with a smile, beckoning her once again.

Something, perhaps the way the beautiful vision ignored her, made D.J. step forward and clasp McCall's fingers as though she had every right to touch him. He gave her a startled glance but didn't pull away. He drew her up next to him for an introduction. "D.J., this is Cindy, the owner of the castle. I teach a safety and awareness class for the preschoolers on Tuesday mornings, with a little karate thrown in."

"Karate? You?"

McCall smiled at her skepticism. Cindy jumped in and answered her question. "Christian has a black belt. He's been studying since he was young."

McCall went on with the introductions. "Cindy, I'd like you to meet Officer Halloran of the Lakeview Police Department."

Cindy turned to D.J. with more interest, though her gaze kept coming back to rest on D.J.'s hand enveloped in McCall's.

"She's helping me with the research for my next book, and I asked her to come along today. I thought the children might like to meet an honest-to-goodness policewoman."

"How thoughtful of you," Cindy cooed. "They'll be thrilled." She opened the door and motioned for D.J. and McCall to follow her.

As soon as the woman turned away, D.J. pulled her fingers out of McCall's grasp. He ignored her and walked inside, leaving D.J. no choice but to join him or be left alone on the doorstep. With a longing glance back at the motorcycle, which didn't look half so frightening to her now, when compared with what lay ahead, D.J. stepped into the day-care facility and shut the door behind her.

The front hall stood empty, but the sound of excited children's voices came to D.J. from the room to her right. She stepped around the corner and caught her breath. The room contained children of every imaginable shape, age, and size. At least twenty-five of them turned to stare at D.J. as she slid against the wall toward a chair. As soon as she sat down, they charged.

D.J. sat up straight with a little yelp of surprise. Her startled gaze sought out McCall, who stood watching her with an intent look on his face. What was he up to with this trick?

Twenty-five voices chimed. Little fingers clasped her jeans and held on; one tiny girl in a red and white pinafore and lace-encrusted panties climbed D.J.'s leg and settled onto her lap with a sigh of contentment. D.J. stiffened, staring down at the girl in confusion; then a little face turned up to her with a smile so sweet even D.J. couldn't resist. She reached out and stroked a tentative finger down the smooth cheek. Soft as a cloud. The child grabbed D.J.'s hand and wrapped it around her waist, ensuring a hug.

"Are you really a policeman?"

Looking to her left, she met the curious face of a towheaded boy. He perched his elbow on her knee and stared intently into her eyes.

"Uh—yes. I mean, no. Well . . ." She looked to McCall for help. He'd left the room, along with Cindy and maybe fifteen of the older children, leaving D.J. with the youngest crowd. Another teacher hovered in the hallway, watching to make sure D.J. behaved. She swallowed the lump in her throat and focused her attention back on the boy.

"I'm not a policeman; I'm a woman. We like to call ourselves police officers. Saves confusion."

"Do you got a gun?"

"Not on me. I'm off duty, so I left it at home."

"Aw—you're no fun." He scrunched up his nose in disgust. "I thought we'd at least get to see your gun."

"Guns are dangerous. I don't know if Cindy would appreciate having one in her day care."

"She's no fun neither. Always tellin' us what to do and how to do it. I wanna be a police officer. Then I'll tell everyone else what to do. And if they don't listen . . ." The towhead shaped his hand into an imaginary gun and pulled the trigger of his thumb. "Pow! Right between the eyes."

"Bloodthirsty little cuss," D.J. muttered.

"Did you ever shoot anyone?"

D.J. started. Her mouth opened, then closed. Curious eyes surrounded her, waiting for an answer. She had no idea what to say.

She'd put the shooting out of her mind, burying the memory in that part of her where she buried all incidents in her life requiring an emotional response. She'd learned if she didn't think about things, they went away. She was very good at ignoring anything she put her mind to ignoring. But the little boy's question brought everything back to her in a rush—the cold night, the hot rush of adrenaline, the screaming kid on the pavement.

"Yes." The word whispered past D.J.'s lips, surprising her. "I've shot someone. It was horrible. The most horrible thing I've ever done." Her voice sounded odd to her own ears, and D.J. cleared her throat. When she spoke again, nothing had changed. Unaccustomed emotion still colored her tone. "The reason I do what I do is so little guys like you can be safe on the streets." D.J. frowned at the words. They even seemed sincere. Why did she sound like a greeting card? She'd become a cop to try to make her father love her; then she'd discovered how good she was at the job and had stayed, despite the fact that no matter what she did the sight of her always made her father flinch.

"Read us a story. Please, D.J. Please." D.J. looked down at the eager faces around her. They hadn't noticed her lapse into the past, probably because their attention span lasted all of two minutes. So much the better for her. She didn't need to analyze the complicated reasons for her career choice in the midst of a day-care facility. Especially since the kids could care less why she'd become a cop—they only cared that she was one.

"All right," she agreed to cheers and shrieks. "Bring me a book and then settle down."

The afternoon slipped away as D.J. read books and then started to relate stories about her job— modified versions meant for little ears. One by one the children lay down on the floor and fell asleep until only the towheaded kid stared at D.J. with a rapt expression and begged for "a shootin' story, D.J." The little girl in her arms slept on against D.J.'s chest, a slightly sweaty bundle. Without

Lori Handeland

knowing why, D.J. turned her face to the side and rubbed her cheek along the child's downy head, placing a kiss on the damp brow. A little hand curled around D.J.'s arm and a sigh escaped the child's lips as she rooted closer.

A quiet sound drew D.J.'s attention. With her cheek still resting on the child's head, D.J. glanced up. McCall stood in the doorway staring at her, the expression on his face a combination of want and need and wonder. D.J.'s heart contracted and her breath caught. Though what sanity she still possessed screamed at her to turn away, she found herself caught in the web of Christian McCall's eyes, unable to deny him the sight of her own desire.

Chris couldn't tear his gaze from the scene before him. With sleeping children around her feet, a cherub at her knee, and an angel in her arms, D.J. Halloran looked like an Irish Madonna. How had she done it? He could have sworn she would run screaming from the day-care facility in ten minutes, especially after he'd left her alone with the toddlers. Instead, she had them all sleeping—except for Jimmy, of course—but Jimmy always avoided sleep like spinach soufflé. Chris nodded toward a mat in the corner and Jimmy crawled across the rug to lie down, though his eyes remained wide open and trained on D.J.

She looked more relaxed than Chris had ever seen her—and more beautiful. Any thought he'd had of fighting the irritating attraction between them withered and died. Instead, the seeds of desire grew stronger within him.

D.J.'s eyes shadowed to evergreen as she continued to stare at him over the head of the sleeping child in her arms. In an attempt to break the thick tension hovering in the air around them, Chris smiled and stepped into the room. He stopped next to her chair and bent down to take the child.

"I'll put her down," he whispered. "We should go."

For a second D.J.'s arms tightened on the little girl, and Chris thought she would refuse his offer. Then she gave a sharp nod and allowed him to take the child. The back of Chris's hand brushed along D.J.'s stomach, and the harshness of her indrawn breath echoed in the quiet room.

Chris stood with the child in his arms. "Sorry," he muttered.

Standing, she shrugged off the contact and her reaction to his touch. D.J. tilted her head back to look into his eyes. The angle, combined with the fading light from the windows on the fine bones of her face made D.J. look ethereal. A subtle scent of lavender drifted to him on the drowsy air, and Chris unconsciously leaned toward her.

The light in the hall snapped on. Chris and D.J. both glanced in that direction with a guilty start. The little girl in Chris's arms shifted and sighed, reminding him of all he needed and wanted in life. He stepped away from D.J., lifting his foot over the nearest sleeping child, just as Cindy appeared in the doorway.

"Wow." She surveyed the room. "What did you do to them?" She turned to D.J. in amazement, reluctant admiration in her eyes.

Lori Handeland

D.J. shrugged. "I read them some books, told them some stories, and the next thing I knew they were out. I guess I'm more boring than I thought."

"Must be." Cindy returned her gaze to Chris, smiling at the child in his arms. "Don't you look fatherly." She glanced back at D.J. "Christian just loves kids. Can't you tell? If he could find a woman as good with them as he is, I'm sure he'd settle down and have half a dozen."

Chris gave an inward sigh. Cindy never changed, always angling for a marriage proposal when he'd never even asked her for a date. Though he admired her dedication to her job—and couldn't help but admire her beauty—when he looked at Cindy there was nothing else. No spark, no desire, no slow spread of warmth through his stomach to tell him she was the one. Chris's father had told him how love should be, what falling in love had been like for him and Chris's mom. Chris would wait as long as it took to find his one special woman.

He looked up. His eyes met D.J.'s and held. What he felt for her was going to be a problem—a threat to everything he'd always believed would one day be his. D.J. Halloran couldn't be the woman for him. She lived on the edge of violence. Her life hung in the balance every time she went to work. He could never spend a lifetime loving a woman who's existence could be snuffed out on the whim of a moment. He'd lost the two most important people in his life to such a whim, and he couldn't endure such devastation again. He couldn't live with the threat. God couldn't be so cruel as to expect such a sacrifice from him.

88

"Put her down over here." Cindy's voice interrupted his thoughts, pulling his attention away from D.J.'s green eyes. Cindy pointed to an empty mat near the door, and Chris navigated a path through the sleeping bodies, then leaned down to deposit the girl on the floor. When he straightened, D.J. waited for him at the front door.

They said their good-byes, Cindy holding his hand a bit too long and standing a bit too close. When Chris glanced at D.J., uncomfortable with Cindy's not-too-subtle message, her mouth quirked up and her eyebrows followed suit. She'd gotten the message and it amused her. But by the time Chris followed D.J. out to the bike her momentary amusement had fled, and she'd regained her stiff posture and cool facade, the soft warmth he'd surprised upon her face now a thing of the past.

The trip back to his house took a few minutes. Chris slowed the bike to a stop next to D.J.'s pickup. She climbed off and handed him the helmet.

"Thanks for helping out," he said. "I'm afraid we didn't get much work done."

"That's all right. I enjoyed myself. I've never been around kids. They aren't so bad."

"No, they're not." He glanced up at the house, the shadows from the approaching dusk making the dwelling look even more lonely inside than he knew it to be. "I should at least offer you dinner. For your trouble."

D.J. had drawn her car keys out of her pocket and just fitted one into the lock on the driver's side door. She left the bunch of keys hanging in the lock as she turned to face him. "Don't worry about it. I'll see you in the morning."

"No, really. I'd make you dinner, but I'm not much of a cook. What do you say to Italian—my treat?"

"Are you asking me out?"

Was he? Dates for Christian McCall were few and far between. Not to say he didn't like women; he just didn't get the opportunity to meet many in his solitary line of work. And the ones he did meet hadn't incited his romantic nature. Until D.J.

He pushed that thought away. "Not a date, exactly. Let's call it a working dinner. I can ask you some of the questions I should have been asking you today."

D.J. hesitated, staring at him with suspicion. "All right," she said, drawing the two words out as if she were making the decision as she spoke. "I do have to eat."

"Right." Chris looked down at the sweatsuit he'd changed into at the day-care center to work with the preschoolers. "I'll take a shower and change; then I'll come by and get you in say, an hour? Give me your address."

D.J.'s face froze; then she glanced up and down the street, as though expecting to see someone. She even looked up at the descending night, then shook her head. "I'd rather meet you at the restaurant."

"Why? Do you live with your crazy old aunt or something?"

"Or something," she muttered. "Just tell me where to meet you for my free meal, McCall, and let's get on with it."

Now she sounded like the D.J. he was familiar with: rude and to the point. Why on earth did he like her so damned much?

"Seven o'clock at Lasagne Lovers. Got a dress?"

D.J. rolled her eyes. "Please. Why is everyone so interested in my wardrobe all of a sudden? Just be thankful I'm coming, McCall, and shut up."

With those parting words, D.J. twisted her key in the lock, hopped into the cab of the pickup, and roared off down the road.

By the time she arrived home D.J. had a half an hour to change and get to the restaurant. She barreled through the front door, tossed her keys on the hall table, and made a beeline for her bedroom.

"There you are, dear." Josie hovered over the bed reading, of all things, a romance novel. "Did you have a nice time at the day-care center?"

D.J. stopped in midrush. "How did you know where I went?"

"I'm your guardian angel. I have to know where you are and what you're doing at all times. I'm supposed to protect you."

D.J. crossed the room to her closet. "I thought you were supposed to teach me how to love."

"That, too. If something happens to you, it'll be a little hard to fulfill my mission, won't it?"

"I suppose so. Don't worry; I can take care of myself." D.J. looked up from a perusal of her nearly empty closet with a grimace. "And, by the way, knock off the celestial housekeeping. You're going to get me in trouble."

Josie's blue eyes widened with feigned innocence. "Whatever do you mean?"

"You know exactly what I mean. I heard you laughing at McCall's. You cleaned his house."

"I couldn't help myself. The poor dear would have been days putting such a mess to rights. I accomplished the same thing in a matter of seconds. Where's the harm?"

"I didn't know how to explain it: There's the harm. McCall's house was a crime scene, Josie. Lou could get fired if the captain finds out he allowed the crime scene to be cleared before the investigation was complete."

"Lou didn't allow anything. I did it."

D.J. gritted her teeth. There was no talking to this woman. "And I'm supposed to tell everyone that? Just mind your own business and stay the hell out of mine."

The angel's eyes widened at the ferocity in D.J.'s tone. For a moment D.J. almost felt bad. She probably hadn't needed to be so mean—but she was angry. Josie could become a real problem if she kept sticking her nose into everything.

D.J. turned away from the hurt in the angel's eyes and searched her dresser drawers in the hopes of finding something suitable to wear to Lasagne Lovers. Though the restaurant wasn't fancy, her jeans and sweatshirt were out of the question. She didn't pause to contemplate why she cared what she wore; if she did, she might discover her feelings toward McCall were becoming more than they should be.

"What are you looking for?" Josie's voice came from just behind D.J.'s left shoulder and she jumped, then glanced backward. Josie stood right behind her, peering into D.J.'s middle dresser drawer. Since Josie seemed to have recovered from D.J.'s anger quite well, D.J. swallowed the uncommon apology that had been hovering on the tip of her tongue.

"I wish you wouldn't do that."

"What, dear?"

"Materialize here and there without warning. I'm going to be a nervous wreck, the way you pop around."

"You'll get used to it. You didn't say what you were looking for."

"Something to wear. I have to meet McCall for dinner."

"Lovely." Josie clapped her hands together in delight. "A date. This is wonderful."

"It's not a date," D.J. said through her teeth. "We're working."

"Of course you are. Well, you're right; you can't wear what you have on. Let me have a look." She pushed past D.J. and rifled through the mound of clothes in the drawer.

"Hey, what are you doing?"

"Finding you an outfit. You've got to have something suitable in this tumble of clothes. A-ha." Josie's hand disappeared into the depths and reappeared with a gold shell hanging from her wrist. Turning away from the dresser, she stepped past D.J. without a glance and started to riffle through the closet. Another muffled "ah-ha" drifted to D.J.

"What?" she asked, interested in spite of herself.

Josie stepped back from the closet with a pair of black crepe pants and a gold jacket. D.J.'s eyes wid-

93

ened. She'd forgotten about the jacket and pants, which she'd bought to wear to the wedding of one of her fellow officers, then relegated to the back of her closet the morning after the reception.

Josie held up the outfit with a triumphant grin.

"You'll look wonderful in this, dear." Josie handed her the clothes. After glancing at her watch D.J. hurried to the bathroom to change. Emerging moments later, she moved to the mirror above her dresser and adjusted the shoulder pads on the jacket, then fastened the single button at her waist. The gold and black tones complemented her fair skin and red hair. Even her eyes looked greener against the backdrop of gold.

"Here." Josie held out a pair of dangling gold earrings.

"Where'd you get these?" D.J. put them on, then gently shook her head. The earrings sparkled in the overhead light.

"They're mine. You can borrow them for tonight."

"Thanks." D.J. smiled.

"Now." Josie rubbed her hands together. "Let me help you with your makeup."

D.J.'s smile froze. "Makeup! I hate makeup. Yuck. I always want to scratch my face or rub it off."

"How about some mascara and lipstick? It will bring out your eyes."

"Don't have any."

Josie frowned. "I can't believe that. A young girl without makeup?"

"Believe it. Now reach in there," Josie pointed to

the top drawer on her dresser, "and hand me my Chapstick."

Josie complied, and D.J. painted on what she thought was chapstick with a quick flick of her wrist. Glancing at her reflection one last time, she narrowed her eyes and leaned closer. Then she peered at the tube of "Rapid Rust" lipstick in her hand. "Josie, you did that on purpose."

"Oh, leave it on. You look lovely with just a little color. It won't kill you to wear lipstick."

D.J. hated to admit it, but she did look better. The touch of lipstick made her eyes look brighter and her skin seem almost golden. She shrugged and stuck the tube into the pocket of her pants. "I don't want to look lovely. McCall's going to think I'm trying to seduce him."

"Would that be so bad, dear?"

"What? Of course it would. How embarrassing."

"Why? He's attractive. Single. So are you. Go with your feelings."

"I don't have any feelings."

"Oh, please, don't start. Everyone has feelings. You just keep yours hidden. You're going to make yourself sick if you keep it up."

D.J. tilted her head and stared at her reflection. She did look good. *Pretty. Soft. Feminine.*
Different.

"What the hell?" D.J. asked herself.

Her reflection, along with the angel at her shoulder, agreed.

Chapter Five

She was late.

Chris looked at his watch for the fifth time in as many minutes, then glanced again at the doorway; 7:20 and no sign of D.J. Halloran. Had she stood him up?

Despite being a weeknight, Lasagne Lovers bustled with business. The restaurant, located on a stretch of highway that led from Lakeview to one of the affluent northern suburbs, did a brisk trade with young, urban professionals. Most of the tables were filled with couples, obviously stopping in on their way home from work for dinner after a hard day in separate career pursuits. The repeated reminder of his solitary existence made Chris envious. At table after table surrounding him, a man and a woman shared their day with soft whispers, secret smiles, and the tinkling of glasses raised in toasts to unknown triumphs. Chris forced his gaze away from the sight and sat back in his chair. He took a sip of water and glanced at the door once more.

It was 7:23. Where the hell was she?

"Well, well, well. If it isn't Christian McCall. How long has it been?"

Chris froze at the sound of the deep, sarcastic drawl, then slowly looked up to meet the heated gaze of the man standing next to his table. Old enemies turned up in the strangest places.

"Not long enough, Kirk. What brings you to town?"

Without invitation, the man slid into the seat across from Chris. "I'm in and out with my job. A lot of traveling. A lot of women in every city. You know how it is." His eyes widened in feigned surprise. "Oh, but that's right; you don't know how it is, do you?" He winked, as though they shared a great joke, then motioned for a waiter.

"Jack Daniels, neat," he ordered, then lifted an eyebrow to Chris.

"Nothing for me. I'm waiting for someone."

"Really? A woman?" He took Chris's silence for assent and laughed. "You, McCall? After all these years I'd started to believe you didn't like them."

"I like them fine. I'm just more discriminating than you are."

"I doubt that. Well, I'll just have to stick around and see what you've come up with."

"I don't think so," Chris said. "Say what you have to say and then get lost, Rousseau."

97

Kirk's eyes narrowed, lending his long face a feral cast. His blond hair had begun to gray, and the lines around his hazel eyes were deeper than they had been the last time Chris had seen his foster brother—the time he'd broken Kirk's nose. Chris could still see the lump along the bridge where the bone had cracked. He didn't like to remember his lapse into violence, but Kirk seemed to have that effect on him—always had. The two had detested each other on sight, and their feelings hadn't changed one iota over the intervening years.

"I don't take orders from you, McCall," Kirk sneered. "Never have and never will. You may have beaten me once, but you won't again. Next time I'll be ready for you."

"There won't be a next time, Rousseau. I'm not going to fight you again."

"Fight?"

Both men glanced up at the feminine voice, then stood. Chris's mouth dropped open, and he made an effort to close it before Kirk noticed and made a snide comment. But a quick glance revealed his foster brother to be in the same predicament— stunned by the woman before them.

"I'm sorry to be so late." D.J. smiled at Chris, then glanced at Kirk. "But I can see you found someone to keep you company."

What had she done to herself? The woman before him couldn't be the one who had driven away from his home in a pickup truck such a short time before. Though she wore a simple outfit of slacks and a jacket, the clothes emphasized her trim form, enhancing her distinctive coloring. The golden earrings waving alongside her face brought out the light in her sparkling green eyes. Chris had known she was beautiful—but he had never imagined this.

"Rousseau has to leave."

The waiter arrived and deposited Kirk's drink on the table. Kirk tossed the alcohol back in two long swallows, his gaze never wavering from D.J.'s face. "I'm not going anywhere until you introduce me."

Chris sighed. Kirk was just stubborn enough to do what he threatened. "Kirk Rousseau. D.J. Halloran."

"Halloran?" Kirk raised his eyebrows in surprise. "I've heard that name before."

D.J. frowned. "I'm afraid my name's been on the news and in the papers lately. I'd rather not discuss it."

"Ah, yes." He nodded. "I remember." Kirk held out his hand. "Nice to meet you, officer."

The two shook hands, Kirk holding D.J.'s fingers until she tugged them away from his grasp with a frown. She glanced at Chris in confusion.

"Good-bye, Rousseau," Chris said pointedly. He wouldn't put it past Kirk to start dissecting the details of the shooting, regardless of D.J.'s appeal not to speak of the incident.

Rousseau put his glass back on the table. With a smirk in Chris's direction, he moved to hold D.J's chair for her. When she was seated he leaned down, placing his palms on her shoulders and whispering into her ear.

D.J. tensed at Kirk's touch, and her mouth tightened at his words. Chris took a step forward, fury washing through his stomach in an acid wave. Kirk turned an amused gaze up to Chris before he straightened away from D.J. "Don't get excited." Kirk smiled—the same oily, knowing smile that had made Chris want to bust Kirk's nose in the past—the same smile he'd used when Chris had found his foster brother in bed with the one girl Chris had dated since college. Chris hadn't loved her, but then, neither had Kirk. Still, Chris had cared for the girl and had enjoyed the feeling of being a couple, of fitting in with the rest of the world, if only on the surface. Kirk hadn't known Chris's feelings. He'd seduced the girl just to prove to Chris that he could. Kirk had always seen a competition between them where none existed. Chris had most often ignored any challenge. That day, over five years in the past, Chris had lost his temper and made use of his training to harm someone, instead of for defense, as he'd been taught. Funny, but he'd never felt guilty for bending his principles when it came to Kirk. He'd broken his foster brother's nose before Kirk even got out of bed. Then, while Chris's ex-girlfriend screamed and Kirk shouted obscenities as blood flowed down his chin, Chris had walked out of the man's apartment. He hadn't seen Kirk Rousseau since.

Kirk squeezed D.J.'s shoulders one final time. Chris's lips tightened. Kirk saw the movement and laughed out loud. "I'm going, brother mine. I'm going." Then he turned and walked away, laughing as he went.

"You're no brother of mine," Chris muttered, staring after Rousseau as he exited the restaurant. He returned his gaze to D.J., who watched him with a frown. An attempt at a smile failed, and Chris gave it up to take his seat. "What did he say to you?"

"He said you were no threat to my virtue. You don't like girls. But he does."

"Figures."

"Is what he said true?"

"Yeah. He loves girls. All kinds."

"I meant about you."

Chris leaned back in his chair, studying her. The sudden appearance of his foster brother had unsettled him. He'd been looking forward to a quiet evening of working conversation. Now his mind spun with remembrances of a childhood in the same house with Kirk Rousseau—the boy who had hated him with a desperate passion was now a man. A man who hated him still.

"McCall?" D.J. waited for her answer.

"I like girls." He looked at her and allowed his eyes to tell her what he could not. D.J. blushed and glanced away. "I like them a lot. But your virtue is safe with me, D.J. You don't have to worry that I'll seduce you over dessert."

Even though I might want to, he added to himself.

D.J.'s curious gaze returned to his face. "Why not?"

She sounded almost disappointed, and warmth surged through Chris at her low-voiced question. Instead of answering, he snapped the menu open and stared at his choices without seeing them. "Some things are private, Officer. We'd better order."

Her breath caught in surprise at his cold reminder of their relationship, but when the waiter appeared to take their order her voice was once again as cool as a December wind.

"How do you do that?" Chris asked once the waiter had gone.

"What?" D.J. raised an auburn brow in question.

"Turn everything off. One minute you're angry; the next you're the ice princess. It's like you have a switch inside you marked 'emotion—on/off.'"

"Why don't you ask yourself that question? You did the same thing when I asked you a question. I assume your reasons are identical to mine. As you said yourself, some things are private. My emotions, or lack of them, are my business."

"I didn't say you lacked emotion. You've definitely got a whole lot of anger."

D.J. took a sip of her ice water. "I'm working on that."

"Why?

"Emotions just get in the way of my doing my job. They inhibit decision-making and slow down reaction time."

"You sound like a textbook. Didn't anyone ever tell you there's a difference between your work and your private life?"

D.J. stopped in the act of reaching for a breadstick. She withdrew her hand and put it back into her lap before fixing Chris with a cold stare. "Officers who bring personal problems to the job end up dead. I've seen the truth of that on the streets and on the news. My private life, however, is not subject to discussion. I said I'd come here to answer questions for your book. Let's get on with it."

"That is one of my questions. How do you separate your cop persona from D.J. Halloran?"

"For me, there is no separation. I don't have to worry about bringing my home life on the job. My work is, quite simply, my life."

Chris stared at her. D.J. stared back. She was serious, or at least she believed she was. Her statement should make him happy. It proved beyond a shadow of a doubt that she couldn't be the woman for him—a woman whose job was her all-consuming passion couldn't be his soul mate. But instead of happiness that his dilemma had been solved so easily, Chris felt something else. Could it be dismay?

"Come on, D.J." He found himself leaning forward, a desire to convince her of the error of her ways consuming him. "You have to do something other than work and eat and sleep. No one lives like that."

"Really? What do you do besides work and eat and sleep?"

He sat back, blinking in surprise at the sudden change of tactics. "We aren't talking about me." Even to Chris's own ears, his voice sounded defensive.

D.J. smirked. "Hit too close to home for you, McCall?" She snatched a breadstick and stuck it into the corner of her mouth like a cigar.

"I work with the kids at the day care. I travel. There are a lot of things I do besides work." Chris took a breath before he asked his next question. This one was of more personal concern for him, though he didn't want D.J. to know that. "Next question, Officer: Under what circumstances would you give up your job?"

She bit down on the breadstick with a loud crunch. After chewing and then swallowing in almost the same motion she put the rest of the bread stick on her plate and gave Chris her full attention. "No circumstances exist that would make me give up my *career,* McCall. At least none of my own devising, anyway. This isn't just a day job; being a cop is who I am. Without my job I don't know what—" She broke off, and her gaze slid away from his. She picked up the breadstick and became very interested in chewing once again.

Chris waited for her to finish her sentence. When she didn't he pressed her some more. "You have a dangerous job, D.J."

"Shoot-outs don't happen every night. In fact, they're quite rare—though with this gun problem we've been having, I'm afraid they'll be on the increase. These damn kids keep turning up with guns from all over the place, and we can't figure out where they're getting them. They're starting to sell drugs, choose up sides, take territory. I don't like what's happening one bit." She shrugged. "Once Lou and I discover who's behind the guns and who's tipping these kids off as to where to find illegal substances, we'll put the guy away for a long time, and Lakeview will be a safer place."

"And that's what you want? To make Lakeview a safer place?"

"Of course. This is a midsized town with a small-town flavor. We want to keep it that way. Unfortunately, someone's figured out we're far enough away from Chicago not to compete with their gangs and cause a war. The individual we're after has started to put some kids with no scruples onto some bad, bad business."

Chris watched her face while she talked. He had no doubt she would find the culprit and make Lakeview safe once more for people to walk the streets. But he knew how precarious and delusional safety could be. "What if someone asked you to give up your job?"

She blinked at the change in subject. "Why would anyone ask me to do that?"

"I don't know. Maybe if they loved you, they'd be worried about you."

D.J. laughed and chose another breadstick. "If they loved me, they'd understand me. My job is my life. Without it I'm nothing. No one."

"Did your job come between you and your husband?"

Her gaze narrowed. "Let's get one thing straight right now: I don't discuss my past—especially my ex-husband. Not with you. Not with anyone."

He'd hit a nerve. Interesting; the good officer had secrets in her past. Secrets he wanted to uncover. Secrets that would, in all likelihood, reveal what made Officer Ice so icy.

"Doesn't look to me like you're on very good terms with *your* family, McCall. From what I saw, your brother hates your guts."

He opened his mouth to give her some of his own ground rules on questions about his past, then decided not to. He would never uncover her secrets if he didn't share some of his own. "Kirk isn't my brother. I lived with his family as a foster child. Kirk didn't appreciate the loss of his status in the Rousseau household—the one and only son. We never cared much for each other. Over the years our relationship hasn't improved."

"That explains a lot. What happened to your parents?"

The waiter arrived with their salads at that moment, and D.J. didn't seem to notice the way Chris's breathing increased in tempo. By the time the waiter left he had himself under control once more.

"Enough about me," he said. "Answer another question: Why did you decide to become a police officer?"

D.J. took her time answering. Chris had the feeling she was as reluctant to answer this question as he'd been to discuss his parents. Finally, after chewing and swallowing several bites of a tomato, D.J. spoke. "My father was a cop. Lou's partner, in fact."

"Ah-ha. Is this one of those family tradition things? No Halloran son so, in this day of women's equality, the daughter was elected to follow in her father's footsteps?"

"Not quite."

"Not quite? You have to do better than that, D.J."

Her eyes flashed emerald fire as she placed her fork next to her plate. Despite the deliberation of her movements, the suppressed anger was evident. "I had to take this assignment, McCall, or lose two weeks' pay. That's the only reason I'm here. But I did not agree to discuss my personal life. I don't. Not with anyone. Do you understand?"

Chris followed her example, laying down his own fork and staring into D.J.'s face. "Why not, D.J.? Is it really so bad? At least you had parents. I had no one. Maybe if you talked about what was so awful in your life, you wouldn't feel so angry all the time."

D.J's face drained of color. She stood, her chair sliding backward, tilting and almost falling over with the force of her shove. Without another word, D.J. spun on her heel and left Chris alone at the table.

D.J. burst through the door to the ladies room, her face hot and feverish. A quick glance around revealed she had the room to herself. She turned the cold water on full force and stuck her wrists under the gushing fluid. The coolness soothed her. D.J. took a deep breath and looked into the mirror.

Josie's face stared back.

D.J. straightened so fast, her back gave a painful twinge of discomfort. "Get out of here," she hissed. "I told you not to do that. What if someone sees you?"

Josie materialized next to her, wearing another of her flowing, flowered dresses. "I told you, dear, no one can see me but you."

"What are you doing here?"

"You looked like you needed some moral support. Though, I must say, you're blowing this."

D.J. sighed, bringing her cool hands up to rest against her throbbing cheeks. "Blowing what?"

"This date."

"It's not a date!" D.J. flinched as her angry shout echoed off the tiled walls and floor. "It's not a date," she repeated more calmly.

"Of course not, dear. But really, I don't understand why either of you gets so upset whenever you talk about your family. Honestly, the poor boy practically has a cardiac arrest whenever his parents are mentioned."

D.J. frowned, remembering. "You're right. I wonder why."

"I'm sure I don't know. Though Raphael did mention Christian has some problems of his own. I didn't think to ask what they were. I've got enough to do worrying about all your problems."

"I don't have any problems." D.J. allowed her hands to fall back to her sides, grateful her face no longer felt as though it would explode at any second. She gave the angel a pointed glare. "Except for you."

Josie waved away her anger. "Everyone should have such problems. Do you know how special you are to have a guardian angel? Not everyone rates the assistance."

"Gee, aren't I the lucky one?"

"Sarcasm will get you nowhere, young lady."

"You're acting like my mother."

"That's good because I—" Josie took a deep breath and let it out slowly before continuing. "Because I always wanted to be a mother."

The sadness on Josie's face made D.J. pause at the beginning of another sarcastic comment. She felt small and ungrateful. Josie was, after all, only trying to help.

"I'm sorry," D.J. said and perched her fingertips on Josie's arm. She could feel the flesh beneath the fabric, warm and alive, nothing like she'd ever imagined an angel would feel—if she'd ever imagined it at all. This whole situation just got weirder and weirder. "You died before you could have a child?"

Josie stared into the mirror, a stark, pained look on her face. Her eyes met D.J.'s in the reflection. "I can't talk about my life."

"Why not? What kind of rule is that?"

"My life is over. Talking about it won't change a thing. We have to concentrate on you, not me. Besides, I can't bear to speak of it. What I lost . . . It's too painful to remember."

"See? That's exactly what I've been trying to tell you. Feelings only bring you down. What good are they?"

Josie spun toward her and grasped D.J.'s hand in surprisingly strong fingers. "They're everything. My life would have been worthless if I hadn't had . . ." Josie's voice drifted off, and she stared into D.J.'s eyes earnestly. "I want you to have what I had—a love so strong and wonderful it's life to you."

D.J. yanked her fingers from the angel's grasp. "Why? What difference does it make to you how I live my life?"

Josie turned away, her hand going up to massage her forehead as though she had a headache. Did angels get headaches? "I don't know," she answered. "For some reason I care about you. Call it an angel thing. Call it insanity. But I don't want you to die like I did, lacking the one thing that could make you whole."

D.J. frowned and took a step toward Josie. The

despair in the angel's voice frightened her. If a guardian angel despaired, what was the world coming to? "I don't understand. You said you had a love that meant life to you. What were you missing?"

The bathroom door opened and a woman came in, glancing at D.J. once before her gaze skittered away. *She must have heard me talking,* D.J. thought. The intruder hurried into a stall, and D.J. turned back to Josie.

The angel had disappeared.

"Terrific," D.J. muttered. She glanced in the mirror once again, but the only reflection held there was her own. With a sigh, D.J. left the room. The front door beckoned a few feet away and she headed toward the freedom.

She had no intention of returning to the table. To McCall. To more questions she didn't want to answer and an hour of nicey-nice conversation over Italian food. Lord, she hated dates.

"It's not a date," she said through her teeth and slammed the flat of her hand against the door. It swung open, and damp, cool October air wafted across her face. D.J. inhaled deeply, calmness rushing into her along with the bright, sharp taste of autumn. She stepped onto the porch of the restaurant. The door closed behind her, shutting out the warmth and the clatter of people and dishes. At last she stood alone.

Until Christian McCall unfolded himself from the shadowed corner and walked toward her. D.J. watched him approach, mesmerized by the long-legged grace of the man.

McCall stopped in front of her. "I knew you'd

never come back." His voice was soft, near to a whisper, and the skin on the back of D.J.'s neck tingled in response. "I'm sorry I upset you."

D.J. looked away from his earnest face, out toward the street, where she saw his motorcycle parked at the curb. She was too sensitive about her family. How could McCall know her quirks? She supposed most young people shared stories of their families when they first started to gather knowledge of each other. She and Rich had never gone through the courting stage. Her father had known Rich's parents, their tavern being a frequent cop hangout. When Rich had gotten in trouble as a teen his parents had sent him to live with an aunt in Chicago. He'd spent his youth there, returning to Lakeview in his late twenties on the hunt for a job. The Hallorans, fearful he'd return to the troublesome friends of his teen years, had turned to D.J.'s father, Ed, for advice. Ed had helped Rich to start a weapons and ammunition store and had encouraged the relationship between his daughter and the young man he came to see as a protégé. When D.J. and Rich had married no one had been happier than Ed. Certainly not D.J. The flaw in her character that made her continue to try and please her father, when she knew in her heart there was no pleasing him, had made her life hell on more than one occasion. Marrying Rich had been a major lapse of judgement that had caused her no end of difficulties.

"Come on." McCall's voice drew her away from the painful memories. She returned her attention to him as he jerked his head toward the street. "I'll walk you to your car."

D.J. nodded, anxious to get the evening over with, embarrassed to be so inept at the basic behavior required of a woman of the '90s.

"I'm right there," she said and pointed to her pickup, two cars in front of his bike.

"I see." Chris stopped and rested his hand on the chrome of the bike's nearest handlebar. "This wasn't such a good idea." He indicated the restaurant behind her with a slight movement of his head, keeping his eyes fixed on the blazing lights inside. "I've never been good at this sort of thing. I'm an embarrassment to the male race." He looked into D.J.'s face, his gaze catching hers and holding it. "Can we start over tomorrow? Business as usual?"

His admission so closely echoed her own thoughts, D.J. couldn't help but smile at him. His face softened from its tense mask, and the warmth in his brown eyes warmed her. If she let herself, she might even like this guy.

"Sure," she agreed, putting her hand out for a shake. "Business as usual sounds good to me. Shall we try eight o'clock at the station one more time? Try to stay out of the hospital tonight, would you?"

"I'll try." He took her hand, but he didn't shake it. Instead, McCall linked her fingers with his own and gave her hand a soft squeeze. He released her immediately, so fast D.J. had to wonder at the rush of heat running up her arm. Turning away, he threw a long leg over the bike and adjusted his helmet.

No further words passed between them. He

glanced at her once between the opening in his black biker's helmet, and D.J. tried to smile at him again. But for some reason this time the smile didn't work. The expression wavered as she stared into McCall's eyes and wondered what to do about the tension between them.

He put the bike into gear and roared off into the night. D.J. stared after him for only a moment before the dampness of the Wisconsin night seeped into her bones. Winter wasn't far away. In fact, it had already arrived in the most northern reaches of the state. Someday she would move to Florida, as she threatened to do every January, when the snow started to look dirty and the ice threatened the hips of every little old lady on the street.

D.J. blew her breath out on a sigh and watched the steam float away on the cold night air. She'd never leave Wisconsin. Though she might whine in the dead of winter, the wonder of the four seasons was too good to miss—even when one of those seasons lasted for six months.

Shaking her head, she hurried to the pickup. She turned the heater on full blast before she pulled away from the curb. In seconds her tingling fingers had thawed, and she relaxed against the back of the seat as she pulled out of the parking lot. Brake lights flared up ahead, and she focused on them. McCall's motorcycle rumbled only a few car lengths before her.

Suddenly a black van passed on her left, going at least seventy on the residential highway. D.J. frowned, wishing for her squad car, red light, and siren. Before she could form any other coherent thoughts, the van, which had been gaining on McCall's motorcycle bit by bit, drew even with him, pulled slightly ahead, and then slowed.

Without conscious thought D.J. pushed harder on the accelerator of her truck in an effort to catch up. Her heart thudded faster, and she could hear the rasp of her breath in the closed cab of the pickup.

"Shit," she muttered right before the van cut back into the right lane too soon and clipped the front of the motorcycle, sending McCall and his bike skidding into the gravel at the side of the road.

D.J. slammed on her brakes and pulled over. She jumped out of her car and raced toward the still, black lumps of McCall and his bike. The drone of an engine made her glance up. The van idled several yards away. D.J. squinted into the darkness, waiting for the driver to get out and offer assistance. The back-up lights flared, white against red.

"This man needs help!" she shouted.

The van, which had begun to roll backward to-ward McCall, a little too fast for D.J's liking, jerked to a stop at her shout. The back-up lights went off as the driver shifted into gear and drove away.

She hadn't been able to see well enough in the dark to get a license plate. D.J. took a few steps forward, as if to run after the disappearing van, then thought better of such stupidity. Instead, she ran to McCall and knelt at his side.

He'd been thrown clear of the bike, which was in sorry shape from the looks of the twisted metal. As D.J. reached him, McCall groaned and sat up. Thankfully he'd worn a helmet, heavy wool pants, and a leather jacket and gloves. He would have been scraped to hamburger if not for those items.

D.J. helped him take off his helmet. He looked up at her and shook his head as if to clear it.

"What happened?"

"A van cut in on you too soon, then took off." D.J. stared down the empty road. "Jerk."

"I have to agree with you there," he said, then glanced over at his motorcycle. "Oh, no." He stood and took a step toward the bike.

When he swayed and raised a hand to his head D.J. jumped to her feet to put an arm around his waist. "I think maybe we'd better make a trip back to the hospital."

"No. No more hospital. I'm sure I either have another concussion, or this is more of the same one. I know what to do about those. I just want to go home."

D.J. sighed. From the tone of his voice he wouldn't be swayed. She'd take a closer look at him in the light before she left him alone.

"All right; let's get to my car. I'll call from your house and send someone out for the bike."

"Thanks." His voice faded away on the word, and his full weight pressed against her shoulder. D.J. frowned and hurried toward the pickup. If he passed out, she didn't think she could lift him into the truck. After settling him in the passenger seat she lost no time driving back to McCall's house.

D.J. managed to get him inside and up the stairs to his room. He sat down heavily on the bed, then fell backward.

"I feel bad," he said in wonder. "Very, very bad."

"I should think you would. Conked on the head yesterday, in a motorcycle accident today. What next? Are you sure someone hasn't put a curse on you lately, McCall?"

"I don't know. Have you?"

"Me? Why would I?"

"You're the only one I've ticked off recently."

D.J. bent down and pulled off his shoes. "No voo-doo doll in my pocket. You'll have to look somewhere else."

He sat up with a groan of pain. "I'll just chalk this accident up to an absent guardian angel."

D.J. frowned at his words. Could that be it? Was Josie supposed to be McCall's angel and not hers? The woman seemed kind of flaky. D.J. wouldn't put it past her to attach herself to the wrong person. Although this Raphael guy she kept talking about should know what was going on.

"I'm going to get out of these ripped clothes and take a shower." Chris stood, swaying a bit before righting himself. "Thanks for bringing me home. I'll see you in the morning."

"You'll see me on your couch in the morning. I'm not going anywhere with you in this kind of shape." D.J. frowned at her own words. Now why had she said such a thing? Since when had Christian McCall's health become her concern?

He turned to look at her from the door to the bathroom, his face pale and drained in the harsh overhead light. "Suit yourself. I'm not up to arguing with you anymore tonight. But sleep in the guest room. Two doors down. It's all made up." He turned away and closed the door.

116

Silence descended on the room for a few seconds. Then the sound of the shower drifted to her from beyond the closed door. The thought of McCall in the shower, his tall, toned body naked and wet beneath the heated spray, made D.J. lick her lips against the sudden dryness invading her mouth.

"I am losing my mind," she muttered, and forced the image away as she went in search of the guest room.

Two doors down, she reached into the room and flipped on the light. "Oh," D.J. breathed and stared in wonder. She had missed this room on her tour of McCall's house earlier in the day. Without knowing how, she had stepped into the past. The room looked to be straight out of an English castle, complete with heavy draperies around the bed and a stone fireplace with wood ready for igniting. Antique rugs covered the floor and a tapestry graced the wall in front of her.

D.J. walked around the room, touching the antique lamps, the oak dresser, and the water urn on the nightstand. She sat down on the bed, then fell backwards, sighing in ecstasy at the softness of the overstuffed mattress. The phone, on a small table next to the bed, was the one item out of place in the old-fashioned setting.

Sitting up, D.J. grabbed the receiver and made a quick call to the local garage to arrange for the pick up of McCall's ruined motorcycle. Then she phoned in the accident to the station and left a message for Captain Miller to call her in the morning. Hanging up, she sighed. She could do nothing further tonight. Except . . .

Josie probably was waiting for her at home. Should she call and tell the angel she'd be staying the night at McCall's? She'd never had anyone waiting up for her before. Or did Josie just know where she was all the time? In that case, calling wouldn't be necessary. This angel stuff confused her.

"Josie?" she called, her voice echoing in the empty room. No one answered. D.J. felt silly. What if McCall heard her calling for the angel? How would she explain herself?

D.J. shoved off the bed and went to explore the bathroom. A large claw-footed tub occupied one corner. Though the decor reminded her of the bedroom, antique and beautiful, the plumbing was the best the twentieth century had to offer. She looked longingly at the tub—big enough to soak in for a long, long time—then turned away with a sigh. She was too tired to take a bath. Besides, McCall might need her. If so, she might not hear him over the roar of the water.

A thick, terry-cloth robe hung on the back of the door—so blindingly white D.J. knew without asking that it had never been worn. She undressed and gathered the robe about her. She would just go check on McCall one more time and then—lights out.

Barefoot, she padded down the hall and tapped on his door. After several seconds with no answer she opened it a crack. "McCall?" she whispered.

The warm glow of a lamp dusted the room, and D.J. stuck her head inside. In contrast to the room she occupied, McCall's room had a very masculine decor. Though also antique, the large bed was made of a dark reddish wood that matched the heavy dresser and armoire. The curtains and quilt were navy and tan, sporting an Aztec print that contrasted the sedate nature of the furnishings.

D.J.'s gaze stopped at the bed. McCall slept atop the quilt, his hair still damp from the shower and curling every which way, out of control. D.J. tiptoed through the door and paused at the foot of the bed. His breathing seemed normal, his color not so pale. She couldn't see any new bumps or bruises—just the one on his forehead from the night before. Coming around the bed, she perched on the edge of the mattress next to him.

He smelled of Ivory soap and warm water. He'd donned sweatpants but no shirt, and the muscular strength of his upper body lay revealed to her eyes. He had a great chest, tanned and dusted with curling black hair. D.J. found herself staring at the path the hair made, disappearing into the drawstring waistband of his sweats. The tied bow perched atop his navel, begging her to take the string between her fingers and release the twist.

Her gaze drifted up the length of him, noting his height and breadth. That combination might seem intimidating, but his gentleness of manner made McCall's size and the suppressed power of his toned body all the more beguiling. She had never met a man like Christian McCall.

She reached forward, gently running her fingers through his hair, feeling for a lump. The injury he'd received the night before stood out against his forehead, smaller than it had been that morning but still there. Luckily for McCall, his helmet had protected him from further injury this evening.

McCall muttered something and shifted in his sleep. D.J. yanked her fingers from his hair and jumped to her feet. He turned on his side and settled back to sleep.

"Not bad, hey?" Josie's voice, coming from behind D.J., made her start and turn with a little squeak of alarm.

"Quiet," she hissed. "He's asleep."

"He can't hear me, dear. Only you can."

The angel wore a long white cotton nightdress, her black hair twisted into a thick braid that hung down her back to her hips. She looked even younger in her nightclothes, more like a child than a woman.

"What are you doing here?" D.J. whispered, drawing the angel away from the bed and toward the door.

"You called me."

"You heard?"

"Of course. But I was right in the middle of putting a cake in the oven. I knew you weren't in danger, so I finished up before I came over."

"Cake?" D.J.'s ears perked up. She loved cake. Real homemade cake, from scratch, not the processed, sugar-coated, fake cakes she avoided at the local market. She'd always had a weakness for homemade cakes, ever since Gran had died and her weekly treats had ceased. Cakes just weren't the same if you made them yourself—especially the ones D.J. had attempted. Her mouth salivated at the thought of the undoubtedly heavenly offering on her kitchen counter. Inhaling, she imagined she could smell the chocolate frosting dripping down the side of a still-warm yellow cake.

D.J. sighed and shook her head. No time for pleasure now. She'd satisfy her craving tomorrow. "I just wanted to let you know I was staying here. I don't think he should be alone."

"No, I'm sure you're right. He's been quite accident-prone lately, hasn't he?"

"Yeah. Which reminds me: Are you sure you're not supposed to watch over him instead of me? I mean, I can take care of myself. But he seems kind of . . . Well . . ." D.J. shrugged and looked back at McCall. The sight of him on the bed, looking so strong and powerful and masculine, made the thought of telling Josie he was helpless seem ludicrous. D.J. just shrugged. "You know what I mean."

"Raphael was quite clear on the subject, dear. You are my charge. Christian can take care of himself."

"Well, can't you watch over him too?"

Josie frowned. "I don't think so. So far, whatever powers I have are limited to you. When I concentrate I know where you are, what you're doing. I haven't had any flashes of the future, if that's what you mean. I don't know if I'm supposed to. Perhaps I should ask Raphael."

"Yeah, why don't you ask him? Get the angel rules straight. In the meantime, I've had enough for today. I'm going to bed."

D.J. started to close the door to McCall's room, then hesitated. A glance around her revealed that Josie had already disappeared.

She tiptoed back into the room. Taking a blanket

from the back of a chair, she spread the covering over McCall's sleeping form and tucked it under his chin before she left the room.

Since she usually woke up several times during the night, D.J. planned to check on McCall during those hours when she couldn't sleep. Surprisingly, the first time she awoke after she lay her head on the overstuffed pillow and cuddled into the fluffy quilt, bright sunlight shone into the window, indicating the lateness of the hour. Weird. That made two nights in a row she'd slept straight through without waking.

D.J. showered and dressed in a hurry, grimacing when she put on the same clothes from the previous evening. First stop her apartment, for more appropriate working clothes.

A quick search of the house didn't turn up McCall, though the full coffeepot indicated that he lurked about somewhere. Helping herself to a cup, D.J. drifted toward the front of the house. Through the bay window in the living room she glimpsed McCall on the porch, reading the paper.

The screen door squeaked as she opened it, and he looked up. The remembrance of how she'd seen him last, half-naked and sprawled across his bed, of how she'd run her fingers through his hair and imagined touching more, made D.J. duck her head and take a gulp of coffee instead of returning his easy smile.

"I hope you slept well."

"Yes." D.J. took a step out onto the porch, allowing the screen to bang shut behind her. She leaned against the wall of the house and stared out at the neighborhood. Across the street, two children rode their tricycles up and down a driveway. On the sidewalk a woman walked by with her dog. McCall lived in residential heaven. D.J. was astonished to discover she loved it. Glancing at McCall, she caught him watching her watching the neighborhood.

"I should apologize," she blurted out.

"Really? Why?"

McCall was continuing to observe her closely. He had beautiful eyes. So expressive. And they saw too much. D.J. resisted the urge to fidget under his scrutiny. "I meant to check on you during the night. That's why I stayed here. I'm not a good sleeper, and I often wake up several times every night. But last night I slept straight through after I left your . . ." She trailed off, realizing what she'd just admitted. She looked over to see if he'd noticed her slip.

He grinned. "Thank you for covering me up."

D.J. shrugged. "No big deal. If you're sick, I have to put up with you longer."

"Uh-huh." He reached down and grabbed a white bag from the floor next to his chair. "Doughnut?"

D.J. straightened. She loved doughnuts. "Where'd you get these?" She glanced inside the bag and withdrew a cruller, her favorite kind.

"I got up early, so I went out, bought breakfast, and picked up the pictures I took at the station the other day." He held up a slim envelope that presumably contained the photos. "We can look at them when you're done."

D.J. nodded, her mouth full of cruller. She took a sip of coffee and leaned back against the house.

Closing her eyes, she savored the ecstasy as the two tastes combined—too sweet and too bitter—just right.

"If you're going to look like that, I'll have no choice but to kiss you."

D.J.'s eyes snapped open. He stood in front of her. How had he moved so quietly and so fast? She licked the sugar from her lips in a nervous gesture. His gaze followed the movement of her tongue, and he took a step forward. D.J. wanted to take a step away, but her back was against the wall, literally.

He stopped, so close she could feel the heat from his body brush her skin. Keeping his gaze locked with hers, he took the empty coffee cup from her hands and tossed it over his shoulder.

"Plastic," he whispered, the ordinary word erotic on his tongue.

D.J. couldn't move. She didn't want to. He must have sensed her acquiescence, for his lips curved upward in a small smile, and he placed the palms of his hands on either side of her head as he leaned forward.

His large body blocked her view of anything but him, and his closeness overwhelmed her senses, but the sound of a car being driven too fast down the suburban street still penetrated her consciousness. She was too much a cop not to notice. Just as Christian's lips grazed hers, she heard a muffled pop. A chunk of wood nicked her cheek.

She grabbed McCall by the shoulders and yanked him sideways to the floor. D.J. followed him down onto the wood planks of the porch.

"Hey, I'm not that kind of guy." He laughed, obviously unaware of the danger.

"Shh!" D.J. duckwalked over to the front of the porch and peered over the top. The street lay deserted.

She stood. Could she have imagined the sound?

Turning, she stepped over McCall, who continued to lay on the floor where she'd thrown him, staring at her with confusion in his eyes. Thankfully, he remained silent and did not pepper her with questions she had no answer for yet. She hadn't realized until just that moment how much she admired a quiet man.

D.J. leaned forward and squinted at the wall of the house she'd been leaning against only seconds before.

No, her imagination wasn't working overtime. She might see and hear angels, but she knew a gunshot when she heard one.

And the proof lay in the neat bullet hole through the side of Christian McCall's house.

Chapter Six

D.J. stared at the bullet hole in the wall and thought back over the past few days: the break-in; someone searching for something—a something they couldn't find; McCall hit on the head when he surprised the thief, injured, but not killed.

Then last night: the motorcycle accident. D.J. saw again the black van idling a few feet away. The back-up lights flared to life, she yelled for help, and the culprit drove away.

Had the driver been planning to back over McCall instead of coming to his aid? Had the accident not been an accident at all, but deliberate? Had her shout for help warned the driver of her presence, causing him to flee?

Neither of the occurrences would have made her think twice, since they seemed unrelated—one incident an interrupted theft and the other an accident. But a drive-by shooting in this gingerbread-house neighborhood combined with the other two happenings made D.J. come to a single conclusion: McCall wasn't accident-prone. He wasn't having a run of bad luck. Someone wanted him dead.

She heard him get to his feet and move two steps closer until he stood directly behind her. The warmth of his body called out to hers, and despite the severity of their situation she found herself remembering the kiss they'd almost shared only moments before. To stop the traitorous reaction of her body, D.J. turned around and shoved McCall in the shoulder.

"What's going on here?"

He ignored her, bending to peer at the bullet hole with a curious frown. "Is that what I think it is?"

"You betcha, buster. I want to know why someone's trying to kill you."

"Kill me?" He continued to look at the bullet hole, putting his forefinger into the indentation, and then shaking his head in amazement. "Why do you think someone wants to kill me?"

"Do you have many drive-by shootings around here? I doubt it. Combined with the black van that ran you off the road last night and the knock you took on the head the night before, in my professional opinion someone's trying to kill you."

He glanced over his shoulder with a frown. "Then why didn't they kill me that first night? I was alone, and after they hit me I was out cold."

"I don't know, but I intend to find out. They almost got me this time."

The rumble of a car from the street made D.J. start. She grabbed McCall's arm and yanked him with her into the house. "Sit there." She pointed to a chair out of range of the windows. He complied without argument.

Locking the door behind them, D J. drew the living room drapes, then moved to the side of the window and peered through the gap between the material and the wall and the window seat.

Just as she'd suspected, a black van crept down the street in front of the house. When it pulled even with the window D.J. strained her eyes to see the driver. But the tint of the glass sabotaged her effort.

Since the porch was now empty, the van drove off in a puff of exhaust. This time D.J. looked for a license plate. There wasn't one.

"Same van as last night?"

McCall's voice right behind her ear made D.J. jump. "Quit sneaking up on me! You're as bad as . . ." She trailed off. She didn't need to explain about guardian angels right now. Right now she needed to call her captain.

She pushed past McCall and headed for the phone. He grabbed her arm, jerking her back to face him.

"Was it?" he repeated his earlier question.

"Yes, the same one, as far as I could tell." She tugged on her arm and he released her. "You know whoever it is will be back."

McCall turned and looked toward the window. "Yes, I suppose they will. I wonder what they want."

"You sit down and think while I call Captain Miller. Where have you been? What have you done? Who have you talked to? Think about those questions, and write down everything you can remember. We have to figure out what's going on or we won't know how to fight them."

D.J. went to the kitchen, her mind turning the problem over and over, searching for an explanation.

They searched for something. Something McCall had. But whatever they wanted hadn't been in the house when they ransacked the place and hadn't been worth killing McCall then to obtain. But now it was.

Why?

D.J. dialed the station and was put through to the captain. She explained the situation, along with her theories.

"Get him out of town, Halloran," Captain Miller barked.

"Huh? Me? I'm suspended."

"Consider yourself reinstated." He broke off and mumbled something to himself.

"What was that, Captain?"

"I don't know why I'm bucking the system for you, Halloran, but something tells me to put you on this assignment. Don't ask me why. Call it a whim."

D.J. pulled the phone away from her ear and frowned at it in confusion. *A whim?* The captain wouldn't know a whim if it flew up and tapped him on the shoulder. Come to think of it, he'd been acting strangely ever since the morning of her suspension. Almost as if someone was pulling his strings from above. D.J. sighed. She knew only one string-puller who answered that description.

Josie. For some reason, the angel had been putting ideas into Captain Miller's head. But she would deal with her guardian's interference later. D.J. put the receiver back to her ear in time to hear the rest of her instructions.

"You know, McCall, the situation. Try to figure out what's going on. But right now just get him the hell out of there. Call in when you've got him safe and out of the way. Hell, all I need is for the mayor's buddy to get offed while he's working with us." The captain hung up without saying good-bye.

A movement in the kitchen doorway made D.J. glance up. McCall held out a piece of paper to her. "This is all I can think of right now."

"Keep thinking. Bring that," she nodded to the paper, "and whatever else you need. We're getting out of here."

"Where are we going?"

"Away from Lakeview. Until we can figure out what's going on, I've been ordered to take you away from the danger."

"For how long?"

"However long it takes. Now get packed. I don't trust them not to come back for another shot at you."

McCall nodded and went to do as she asked. Half an hour later they pulled to a stop in front of D.J.'s apartment. As far as she could tell, no one had followed them.

"I've got to get my service weapon, more ammunition, and some clothes." D.J. glanced around, frowning at all the people milling around on the sidewalk. She'd never noticed how crowded her neighborhood was until she'd spent a little time in the peace of McCall's. "You'd better come up. I don't like the idea of you staying down here alone."

He shrugged and followed her into the building. D.J. remained on the alert all the way to her apartment. Whoever was stalking McCall must know by now that she had stayed the night with him and could easily have staked out her apartment. But she saw no one in the hall. When she opened her front door Josie stood waiting just inside.

D.J. stopped short. McCall bumped into her back.

"Am I supposed to wait outside?" he asked dryly.

"Ah, no. Come in." D.J. cast a warning glance at Josie and the angel grinned. "I'll be right out." She motioned for Josie to follow her and walked into the bedroom. The angel, and McCall, followed. "No, stay here," she said to McCall.

"You nodded for me to come with you." He frowned. "Didn't you?"

"Not you. I mean, no. Just go in the living room, and I'll be out in a second."

D.J. turned away and shut her bedroom door in his face. She leaned back against the wood and let out a long breath. Josie appeared in front of her.

"You've had quite a morning, haven't you, dear?"

D.J. scowled and marched into the bathroom. Josie followed, and she shut the door behind them, then turned on the water full force before speaking to her angel.

"I thought you were supposed to be my guardian angel."

"I am."

"I almost got shot this morning. Where were you?"

"Oh, no. You weren't in any danger. They're after Christian."

"I don't think they care who they're after. Bullets have a way of hitting the wrong people all the time."

Josie raised her eyebrows. "Why do you think that one missed?"

"You?"

The angel nodded.

"Oh." D.J. shrugged. "Sorry. I guess I should thank you."

Josie waved her hand. "That's my job. Now, what is this I hear about us going away?"

"Oh, no. Not *us*. Me and McCall. You're staying here."

"I'm afraid I can't do that, dear. If you plan on staying with Christian, I'll have to go wherever you go. You'll be in danger."

"I thought you were supposed to teach me how to love. Can't you just back off until I'm done with this mess?"

"How can I? If you get killed, then I'll have failed on two counts. I don't think Raphael will be very happy. And believe me, you don't want to make him unhappy."

"I can't believe this," D.J. muttered, turning away to stuff toilet articles into a makeup bag. "Personally, I don't give a hoot if Raphael's happy or not."

"Well, I do. If I don't accomplish what I'm supposed to with you, I'll never get to—" Josie broke off and bit her lip.

"What?"

"Never mind."

"No, what? You won't get into heaven? What's he threatening you with? And since when does an archangel make threats?"

"You don't understand. I'm not supposed to distract you with my problems. Everything will work out for everyone if you'll just cooperate."

"Cooperate and fall in love? No way. I don't want any part of love. Go back to Raphael and get another assignment." D.J. turned off the water, jerked open the bathroom door, and went into her bedroom. She yanked a small suitcase from under the bed and threw clothes in pell-mell. She half expected Josie to continue the argument, but when she looked up the angel was no where in sight.

"Good, maybe she's gone back to her pain-in-the-butt archangel. She's got to make him see reason," D.J. muttered as she snapped her suitcase closed.

"D.J.?" McCall tapped on the door. "Who are you talking to?"

"No one," she called. "I'll be right out."

Between the two of them, they're going to drive me insane, she thought as she hoisted her suitcase off the bed and headed for the door.

That is, if I'm not already there.

Chris stared out the window, watching the panorama of colors inherent in a Wisconsin autumn pass them by. D.J. drove, headed northwest on Interstate 94. When he'd asked her where they were going she'd ignored his question.

In fact, she'd ignored all his questions since they'd left her apartment over four hours before. Just outside of town she'd stopped and rented a Ford Explorer, leaving her pickup in the parking lot of the rental place. Chris had made no comment, just hauled their stuff from one car to the other and climbed into the passenger seat once more.

Chris slanted a glance toward the driver. She drove with determination, her jaw set as she watched both the road and her rear-view mirror with equal interest. She would protect him—but at what cost to herself?

Having his life threatened wasn't a new situation to Chris. But since the last time he'd made sure he would be prepared should the situation ever arise again. Though he might not look the part, Christian McCall had trained himself for every eventuality. The problem was, whatever he had done or seen that had caused his life to be targeted for extinction could just as easily be something D.J. knew, as well. D.J. was tough and could probably take care of herself without his help, but he had no guarantees she would be safe if he left her alone.

D.J. flicked on her directional signal and left the interstate. She pulled into a hotel amid a plethora of other hotels and restaurants lining a service drive next to the freeway.

Turning off the motor with a flick of her wrist at the ignition, D.J. turned to Chris, speaking in what he'd come to think of as her Joe Friday voice: *just the facts, ma'am.* "We weren't followed. This is Outgamie, a big enough town to hide in, and the hotel's right on the freeway in case we have to leave quick. Down the road, just on the other side of a little puddle they like to call Lake Dell, we can get off the freeway and disappear into the back roads. I've driven around here since I got my license and I know them all. No one will catch us if I don't want us to be caught."

"You've convinced me," Chris said. "Let's check in."

He opened the door and put one foot onto the pavement. Her voice stopped him from going any farther. "Hold on; I'm not done. What was your mother's maiden name? We'll use it to register as husband and wife."

He turned back to her with a smirk. She blushed, and he nearly laughed out loud. D.J. might pretend to be tough, but she embarrassed real easy. "Walters." He got out of the car.

She did the same on the other side and followed him around to the back to get their luggage.

"Fine. We'll register as Mr. and Mrs. Walters, from Chicago. If anyone's curious, we're here to visit your brother. We'll ask for adjoining rooms. Since we'll be staying a week, we'd like the extra space. Got it?"

"Yeah, I got it." But he didn't like it. Chris pulled his suitcase and his laptop out of the car, waiting while D.J. shut and locked the vehicle. The thought of staying for an indefinite period of time in the same room, adjoining or otherwise, with D.J. Halloran had set his insides twirling. He was far too attracted to her to be exposed to such temptation. Though he'd sworn to keep his distance, he'd been unable to hold to his vow. His attempt to prove to himself she couldn't be the woman for him by exposing her to children had backfired in his face. The kids had loved her, and from the look on her face when he'd come upon D.J. with the little girl sleeping in her arms, she'd loved them right back.

This morning, when she'd appeared at his doorway after sleeping in his house, his heart had contracted at the sight of her tousled beauty. She'd seemed uncomfortable and just a bit shy. He liked her that way—though her tough facade intrigued him too.

Hell, he might as well admit it to himself: Everything about D.J. Halloran made him half crazy with desire.

His celibacy had never been much of a problem before. Sure, he'd become frustrated, but all he had to do was remember the life his parents had lived in contrast to the anger and hate he'd witnessed in the home of his foster family. He would have what his parents had no matter what the cost to himself. He wouldn't give in to his desires and ruin his life and D.J.'s.

Silly and stupid and chauvinistic as it might be, he wanted to spend his life with a woman who valued family as much as he did. He didn't want a career woman, especially one with a job as dangerous as D.J.'s. After the loss of his parents to violence he couldn't survive the loss of a wife to the same horror. D.J. had admitted her job was her life—her dream. His dream lay in discovering the woman who would fill the empty places inside him with love. He had a feeling D.J. didn't even believe in love.

D.J. completed their registration and led the way down an inner hall toward their rooms. She unlocked the first door, stepped through, and twisted the bolt on the connecting door. After dropping her suitcase on the bed she went back into the hall. Seconds later the other connecting door opened, creating a window between the two rooms.

"Do you care which side you take?" D.J. poked her head through the opening. "They're exactly the same."

Chris walked through to the other room and placed his laptop on a table between two chairs. "This is good."

"Suit yourself." She went through to the other side, and Chris heard her unpacking. He did the same. As he opened the zipper on his laptop, a piece of paper fell out. It was the list he'd made for D.J. that morning—the list of what he'd done and who he'd seen, and who might hate him enough to kill him.

"D.J.?" he called just as she came through the door.

"McCall, where's the list I told you to write?"

He held up the paper. She snatched it from his hand and bounced onto the bed.

After a moment she looked up at him with raised eyebrows. "You lead a boring life, McCall."

"I told you." Chris leaned against the dresser. He curled his fingers around the edge and fought the urge to sit next to her on the bed. Sitting close to D.J. could be a big mistake.

"According to this, you just finished working on a circus book. You've been at the Circus World Museum in Baraboo and down in Florida at the Ringling winter quarters." She looked up at him again. "Piss anyone off at the circus?"

He laughed at the thought. "It's kind of hard to make circus people angry. They're funny that way. With so much joy and color and happiness around them, I don't think they could be nasty if they tried. Besides, all I did was walk around, take pictures, and ask questions about their work. People love to talk about their work. I've never had a problem until . . ."

You, he thought.

She ignored the way his sentence floundered and died, continuing to read over the paper in her hand. "The only person who doesn't like you is your brother, Kirk."

"He's not my brother," Chris said through clenched teeth.

"All right, all right. I forgot. Boy, you're touchy. I could tell you two didn't care for each other, but what possible reason would he have for killing you?"

"None. He could have killed me countless times if he'd wanted to. I lived with him for six years. He hates my guts, but not enough to kill me."

"Then why did you write down his name?"

Chris shrugged. "Kirk is a bit on the edge. I don't know. I guess I could be wrong about him wanting me dead, though I don't know what possible reason he'd have for killing me now."

"Hmm. You'd be surprised at how little of a reason some people need. I'll have him checked out. What about the people you work with?"

Chris pushed away from the dresser and took a short walk around the room. "My editor, my agent. That's all. They make too much money from my books to kill me off."

"No contract hassles lately?"

"Never. I write and draw; they buy. Everyone's happy."

"My, my, don't you have a gingerbread-house life, McCall. Everyone loves you and you love everyone. Except for your brother." She held up her hand, staving off his automatic denial. "Your foster brother. Sorry. What about your foster parents? You haven't mentioned them."

Chris stopped in his pacing. *Mr. and Mrs. Rousseau.* He had never thought of them as anything else. They had never asked him to call them Mom and Dad—not that he would have. Oh, sure, he could have called them Dave and Carol; in fact he had when he spoke of them to his teachers or friends. But to their faces and in his mind he always called them Mr. and Mrs. Rousseau—the people who had taken him in for the money.

D.J. waited for his answer. She stared at him, curiosity in her eyes. He had to say something.

"They took me in. Someone had to. I was grateful."

D.J. frowned at the lack of warmth in his tone. "Really? You don't sound grateful. You have no other relatives?"

Chris closed his eyes and leaned his head back, turning it from side to side to try to ease the sudden

139

tension in his neck that the memories had caused. "No. My parents were both only children. Their parents were dead. I had a great-aunt, but she was past the age where she could raise a twelve-year-old child. No one wanted me. No one but them."

He opened his eyes and glanced at D.J. A soft look had stolen over her face, one he'd never seen there before. He recognized the look. He'd seen it on people's faces all his life, whenever they heard about his past.

Pity.

God, he hated pity.

"Stop," he commanded, his soft voice laced with anger.

"What?" Her eyes widened in surprise.

"Feeling sorry for me. So my childhood wasn't anything to brag about after my parents died. I lived through it. I survived."

"Don't we all," she muttered and lay back on the bed, staring at the ceiling.

Chris didn't care for the feelings stealing over him at the sight of her reclining on his bed. He would never be able to stop his mind from remembering her just like this—or perhaps a bit differently. Still upon his bed, but naked and staring into his eyes as he moved over her and—

"The point is," he blurted, forcing his mind away from the image. D.J. sat up and stared at him, waiting. "The point is," he repeated, "there are kids who've had worse foster families than I did, and kids who've had better. The Rousseaus took me in, fed me, clothed me—for a price—and when I was old enough to leave I left. They would have no reason to kill me. They never cared for me enough to warrant violence." His voice sounded as dead as he felt inside whenever he thought of those lost years between his parents' death and college. In college he'd found another reason to survive—bringing his stories and his drawings to children throughout the world.

"Have you seen them lately?"

D.J.'s question brought him back to the subject at hand. "I haven't seen them since I moved out of their house the day after my eighteenth birthday. I packed my things, drove to Madison, entered college, and never looked back."

"Nice guy."

"They were paid to take care of me. The money was all they wanted. They were happy to see me go, Kirk most of all. Then they got another kid to take my place. The money stayed the same no matter who slept in the extra bed."

D.J. remained silent for a long time. She continued to look at the paper in her hands, as if willing the words printed there to tell her a secret. Finally she crumbled the paper into a little ball and tossed it into the wastebasket. "Two points," she said, then glanced up at Chris. "Maybe your life wasn't so gingerbread house after all, McCall. I apologize."

"Don't. People who've grown up with both parents always want to apologize to me for my lack of them. An apology doesn't help."

"No, I suppose it wouldn't. But, just for the record, I never knew my mother. She died in childbirth. And my dad was no prince of a father."

"In childbirth? Isn't that rare?"

"Yeah, though less rare in the sixties than it is now. They lived in the boondocks, and my mother started hemorrhaging. She bled to death before my dad could get help. I guess I wasn't breathing either, so he had two emergencies to deal with." She stopped abruptly and rubbed her forehead with her fingers. "But you don't need to hear all the gory details of my life."

Chris crossed to the window, pulling the curtain aside to glance out. He had a prime view of the parking lot. The Explorer they'd driven from Lakeview sat alone in an aisle of empty parking places. "I suppose most people say they're sorry when you tell them your story. I won't. I know how useless words are."

"Yes, I can see how you would." Chris heard her stand and cross the distance between them. His body called out to hers, but he refused to turn around. He could feel her standing right behind him. If he turned, he'd take her into his arms, and they'd end up back on the bed she'd so recently vacated. But if he did that, it would be for all the wrong reasons. The loneliness he'd lived with for most of his life seemed so much worse since he'd met D.J. Since he'd shared part of his past with her and learned of the similarities in their lives, a kinship had sprung up between them that could endanger all he held dear.

"What happened to your parents?" she whispered.

He stiffened. Caught off guard by the question, long-suppressed memories crashed through his brain like the surf against the rocks of Lake Michigan's shore. The night, the terror. Then the gunshots and the screams.

"I won't discuss them," he said. "Not with you. Not with anyone."

He'd expected her to argue, but after her first shocked intake of breath at the coldness of his tone she didn't say a word. He continued to stare out the window without seeing anything until she shoved, hard, against his shoulder and pushed her way in front of him.

"What is it?" Chris tried to get his place back, but D.J. wouldn't budge.

"Get away from the window," she hissed.

Chris ignored her and looked outside. A black van eased through the parking lot, pulling into the space next to their rented truck.

"This is impossible," D.J. mumbled. "No one knows where we are. No one followed us."

She patted her jacket, an absentminded movement to check for a shoulder holster, obviously in place and full of a semiautomatic weapon. "Get in the bathroom," she ordered.

"I don't think so."

She didn't even turn around at his revolt, just continued to stare out the window. "Who's in charge here? Do what I tell you if you want to stay alive. I don't know how many of them there are."

"There's no way on this earth I'm hiding in the bathroom."

D.J. shot him an exasperated glance. "Listen, McCall, I don't have time to argue with you. I need you out of the line of fire so I can think straight. If you're standing in the middle of the room making a perfect target, what good are you doing?"

"Give me a gun and I won't be a target."

D.J.'s mouth fell open. "You know how to use a gun?"

"Of course. Why wouldn't I?"

"You just seemed like the peace-loving type."

"I am, but I know what to do with a gun. I assume you have a spare."

She nodded, returning her gaze to the black van, which continued to hover like a great black bat in the parking lot. Whoever sat inside was in no hurry to come after them.

"Maybe we should just get out of here," she mused.

"And maybe they thought of that, and there's someone outside just waiting for us to bolt. The way the van's idling out there makes me think it's the getaway car."

"Yeah, you're probably right." D.J. pulled her gun out of the holster. "I hate being a sitting duck."

Chris didn't like it much either, especially since he recalled in vivid detail what staring at the business end of a firearm felt like. "You keep watching the van. Where's your other gun?"

"My suitcase. Clip's in the side pocket." She kept her gaze focused on the van. "Stay away from the window."

"Goes without saying, Halloran." Chris left her to her job and went into the adjoining room. She hadn't finished unpacking and the gun, an older model .9 mm than the one she wore in her holster, rested underneath her clothes still inside the suitcase—directly beneath her underwear.

144

D.J. Halloran wasn't one for frilly panties, not that Chris had ever imagined she would be. Plain white cotton briefs for her, with serviceable bras, also white cotton. Jeans, flannel shirts, and a pair of long johns rounded out her ensemble, with some T-shirts and sweat socks on the side. Irritated with himself for cataloguing her private items, Chris slapped the top of the case shut before checking the .9 mm and the clip.

Ready to rock, as he'd known it would be. D.J. Halloran wouldn't go on a job without a working back-up firearm. It must be a sin in the good little cop's handbook.

Chris had just snapped the clip into place when D.J.'s voice came from the other room.

"McCall, you're not going to believe this. Get in here."

He spun around and sprinted through the connecting door, taking one leap onto the middle of the bed and landing in a crouch on the other side.

She stared at him, her eyes wide and full of mirth. Then she burst out laughing. "Very impressive, McCall. Who do you think you are?" She gave a final snort of laughter. "Batman?"

Chris frowned. As a kid he had pretended to be Batman. He'd found the similarities between himself and the Caped Crusader numerous. Funny how D.J. had honed in on the same idea.

"I thought you needed me." A roll of D.J.'s eyes revealed what she thought of that statement. Chris sighed and ignored her sarcasm. "What happened?"

"Look." She pointed with her gun out the window.

Lori Handeland

Chris peered past her just in time to see an elderly man open the back of the van and assist his wheel-chair-bound wife out with an electric chairlift.

"I should have seen the handicapped license plates and realized it wasn't the same van," D.J. admitted. "But I guess I'm a little jumpy."

A knock sounded on the door, and D.J. started with such violence that the top of her head bumped against Chris's chin. His teeth clicked together, missing his tongue by a centimeter. She hadn't been kidding when she'd said she was jumpy. He turned and grasped her wrist gently, steadying the gun she'd aimed at the door.

"Relax," he whispered in her ear. "We wouldn't want you to wound the maid. Let's see who's knocking before we shoot them."

He lifted his mouth away from her ear and turned his attention back to the door. "Who's there?"

No one answered.

Chapter Seven

D.J. didn't care for the way her heart pounded in her throat. She'd always excelled at this type of crisis situation in the past, never becoming upset or losing her nerve. She'd even been considering a move from her current position on the street to a crisis reaction team.

But now she wasn't so sure. Here, in this hotel room, she tasted fear—a metallic flavor she detested—at the back of her mouth. She'd never had this happen to her before. But then, she'd never been responsible for another person's life before. In all the other crisis situations in which she'd been involved, she'd only had to worry about herself and the bad guy.

D.J. swallowed, once, hard. The taste remained. She ignored it and tugged on her arm. When

McCall released her she moved out of his reach. After glancing at him to make sure he stood out of harm's way D.J. forced everything from her mind but the job at hand and inched toward the door.

The tinny taste disappeared from her throat after another swallow, and D.J. relaxed a bit. Standing just inside the bathroom to avoid being in the line of fire from the door, she repeated McCall's question—louder and with more force. "Who's there?"

"It's just the maid, dear. Relax and open the door. But put away the gun first, or you'll scare the poor child to death."

Josie.

D.J. looked up. The angel didn't hover overhead, though her voice issued from that direction. "Where are you?" she whispered.

"I'm outside the door, watching your very dangerous-looking maid as she prepares to knock again."

"Why didn't she answer me?"

"She's got one of those headset thingees the young people like to wear. Whatever she's listening to, it must have a beat—because she's dancing to it."

"Kids." D.J. left the protection of the bathroom to open the door.

Just as Josie had predicted, a young woman, perhaps seventeen or eighteen, stood next to a cart just outside the door. She swayed and dipped to an unheard beat as she piled towels into her arms. When she turned back toward the door and saw D.J. she smiled. Without a word the girl handed D.J. extra towels and bopped on down the hall.

"Thanks, Josie."

"Any time, dear."

The angel hadn't made herself visible, so D.J. couldn't be certain Josie had left. Before she could ask, McCall came up behind her.

"Who are you talking to?"

Hell's bells. I forgot all about him.

D.J. stepped back inside, taking her time as she closed the door. What was wrong with her mind? In the past she'd always been able to compartmentalize her thoughts, staying aware of hidden dangers while she dealt with other problems head on. How could she have forgotten about McCall while she dealt with the maid and with Josie?

Spinning away from the door, D.J. nearly ran into him. He stood too close to her in the cramped hallway. "I—ah—no one. Just me, myself, and I." She gave a little laugh and shoved the extra towels into McCall's hands. Then she pushed past him, intent on reaching the open room and putting some space between them so she could think with a clear head. Everything was happening too fast, and for the first time in her life she couldn't seem to think on her feet.

Taking a deep breath, she took stock of her reactions. Her heartbeat had returned to normal. She would examine her unprecedented panic attack later if she could find some time alone. Right now she needed to pacify her roommate.

After placing the towels in the bathroom McCall followed her into the bedroom, a puzzled frown on his face. Before he could ask another question, D.J. spoke. "The maid brought extra towels."

McCall raised his eyebrows. "I saw."

"She—ah . . . She didn't hear us calling because she was listening to her Walkman. I don't know why she knocked if she couldn't hear an answer, but hey"—D.J. shrugged—"I'm not a maid. What do I know?"

She headed for her own side of the room. McCall stepped in front of her.

"Where do you think you're going?"

"I need to finish unpacking; then I'll go and get some food. I'm starving. Aren't you?" She didn't wait for an answer, but plunged ahead, trying to distract him from asking more questions she didn't know how to answer. "We should eat in our rooms as much as possible. Oh, and I need to call Captain Miller."

When she moved to step around him McCall took a step in the same direction, blocking her path.

"What?" She looked up at him impatiently. He smiled, and D.J. stopped breathing for a moment. His smile did funny things to her insides.

"You didn't answer my question, D.J."

Her mind had gone blank as she stared into his eyes. She found herself wondering what might happen if she touched his hair when he was awake. He had nice lips, full but masculine. Sexy as hell. Would they feel as soft as they looked if she touched them with her own?

"D.J.?"

"Huh? Oh, your question." D.J. forced herself to look away from McCall's lips. As soon as she did, sanity returned. What was the matter with her? She'd never mooned over a man in her life. She couldn't see one thing in Christian McCall that would make her behave so out of character. "Yes, I did. I *did* answer. I was talking to the maid."

"No, before you opened the door. You were muttering under your breath; then you said, 'Why didn't she answer me?' "

"Oh, that." She laughed, and it only sounded a bit forced. "I told you, I was just talking to myself. I—ah—I heard her singing. Yeah, that's it. I heard her singing and knew it was the maid. So I just wondered out loud why she didn't answer me." D.J. tilted her head back and smiled up at McCall, pleased beyond measure with her explanation—not too bad of a lie under the circumstances.

"I see. Do you talk to yourself a lot?"

This time when D.J. moved past him McCall let her go. She turned at the doorway. "I live alone. So do you. Don't tell me you don't talk to yourself on occasion."

"I might. But I'm reasonably sure I don't listen for an answer, the way you do."

The teasing smile on D.J.'s face froze. She had no quick comeback for his too accurate observation, so she let the words hang in the air between them and made a hasty retreat to her side of the room.

Josie waited above the bed. D.J. scowled at the angel. Josie smiled back, her serenity in place.

"Close the door, dear. Unless you want him to think you're totally insane."

D.J. turned her head. "I'm going to shower and change before I go out," she called, then shut and locked the connecting door before McCall could respond.

"I thought I told you to stay home," D.J. whispered.

"What you tell me and what I do are two very different things."

"You cannot hang around here with us. We're living on top of each other. I don't know how long we'll be here. He's bound to suspect something's up."

"So?"

"What do you mean, 'so?' " The volume of D.J.'s voice rose threateningly, and Josie put her finger to her lips in a shushing movement as she glanced toward the connecting door. D.J. scowled but took the warning and remained silent.

"I mean," Josie said patiently, "so what if he suspects something? What's he going to suspect? You have a guardian angel? Even if he did suspect you were talking to an otherworldly being, I doubt he'd say so. Besides, he can't hear or see me. What's the problem?"

"I can hear and see you. You're going to drive me crazy. Both of you. I just want you to go away. Right now."

D.J. marched away from the angel, went into the bathroom, and slammed the door behind her.

"And you'd better not appear in here. I'm in no mood," she shouted. When D.J. turned to look at the mirror the only reflection peering back at her was her own.

Josie sighed as D.J.'s shout faded away, and the sound of running water replaced it. Her daughter was more trouble than Josie had ever imagined anyone could be. When she'd agreed to help D.J. Josie had believed a little push in the right direction would be all the girl would need to fall in love. After all, D.J. had inherited half of Josie's genes, and Josie had always been a romantic soul. So had Ed, for that matter. Josie could hardly believe her husband had become a police officer. Not that there was anything wrong with him being one, but he'd always seemed more of the "living off the land" type. As Raphael had warned her, the Ed she'd fallen in love with had died with her. The thought caused a burning sensation to throb just below her heart. D.J. looked a lot like her father; though her hair was dark red and Ed's had been strawberry blond, the resemblance was there and constantly reminded Josie of the man she still loved with all her heart. She wished she could see her husband, but with D.J.'s present situation, it didn't look as if she'd have time to visit her dad anytime soon. If she ever did. There seemed to be an estrangement between the two of them that tore at Josie's soul.

With effort, Josie pushed away the pain. Right now she needed to concentrate on her immediate problem, which was her daughter's attitude. The girl had definitely inherited her smart mouth and sarcastic attitude from her mother. Funny, Josie had always thought those traits were due to nurture instead of nature. Looked like she'd been wrong, which only made her mission all the harder to complete.

Why was D.J. resisting her attraction to Christian? For that matter, why was he resisting his attraction to D.J.? He needed her just as much as she needed him. They were both proving extremely stubborn, and

Josie was at a loss. What should she try next to get these two lost souls to come together?

She'd been on earth three days and made very little progress.

Josie stared at the locked connecting door. Then her glance lit on D.J.'s full suitcase. She smiled.

Drastic measures seemed to be called for in this instance. Raphael wouldn't let her stay on earth forever. D.J. might be mad—but, in the end, she'd understand Josie had known what was best for her all along.

With a giggle, the angel disappeared.

Chris unloaded the weapon, as familiar with the process as he was with putting on his socks. He'd taken gun safety courses along with martial arts. He practiced on a firing range at least twice a month and knew guns as well as he knew karate. With every step toward self-defense, Chris had taken another step away from the terror haunting his dreams. He had been helpless once, but he would never be that way again.

After placing the weapon beneath his socks in a drawer he put the clip in his pocket. Then he tried to work. But the sound of D.J.'s angry voice in the other room interrupted his train of thought. He considered knocking on the connecting door, but when he heard no further outbursts Chris returned to work.

Five minutes spent staring at the blinking cursor on his computer was enough for Chris. He switched off the machine with a curse. He could think of nothing but his situation—and D.J.

From the first day he'd wondered at her apparent

lack of emotion following the shooting of the Lakeview teenager. Perhaps her cool facade merely covered up the deeper pain she hid inside. Ever since they'd left Lakeview she'd been on edge. After her reaction to the black van and the maid's arrival, not to mention her odd habit of talking to herself as if she expected an answer, Chris had to wonder if D.J. perched on the verge of a breakdown.

And if she did, what then? He could hardly take her back to Lakeview and check her into the seventh-floor psychiatric wing at Lakeview General. She'd be an easy target there for whomever stalked them. The nurses weren't trained to protect her—he was. He wasn't even sure if the police could be trusted. This entire mess had started the day he'd walked into the Lakeview Police Department.

He had no way of knowing for sure if he had guessed wrong and D.J. wasn't a target. But unless he could be certain of her safety, he would never leave her to face an unknown enemy alone.

Chris shoved the pillows on the bed into a backrest, grabbed the television remote control, and began to flip through cable channels. Instead of watching the changing screen, he stared at the locked door separating him from D.J. He hated that door. He wished it stood open so he could see her, or at least hear her.

Almost as though his thoughts had turned into actions, the lock turned and the door swung open. Chris dropped the remote and sat up, waiting for D.J. to come into the room.

He frowned. The door hung halfway open. Silence ensued. No one came through the opening because no one was there.

Swinging his legs to the side of the bed, Chris stood and walked toward the open door. He peered through to the other side. His breath caught in his throat. He needed to back away but found he couldn't.

D.J. stood with her back to him as she searched through her suitcase for clothes. Her russet hair, gleaming with moisture, curled wildly about her head. The white towel wrapped around her naked body reached from her breasts to the curve where her buttocks met her thighs.

She bent forward to pick up a shirt, and the towel rode higher, giving him an enticing glimpse of a taut but round derriere. Chris clenched his teeth and fought the urge to step into her room and touch what he should not see. His fingers curled around the doorjamb.

D.J. straightened with a shirt in her hand and dropped the towel. His fingernails dug into the wood. She raised her arms to pull the green thermal shirt over her head. The muscles of her shoulders and back flexed and relaxed. She reached for a pair of white cotton underpants and slid them up her long legs.

Then she turned and saw him in the doorway. She froze, her eyes widening with shock, her face paling a shade. Her breathing quickened, drawing his glance to her chest. As he watched, her nipples, unhindered by any undergarment, hardened to peaks beneath the clinging material of her shirt.

He didn't know when he moved, but suddenly he stood before her, the steamy heat emanating from her shower-kissed skin warming the cold, lonely place within him. She didn't turn away. She didn't say a word. Instead, she tilted her head back to meet his eyes, and her lips parted on a sigh.

"Christian," she whispered, speaking his given name for the first time.

Lust roiled through him, new and frightening. He closed his eyes against the promise on her lips and tried to turn away. She was a temptation he couldn't afford, stirring feelings he didn't understand. Then her lips met his, and any thought he might have entertained of leaving her untouched fled.

Nowhere else but their joined lips did they touch, yet the desire coursing through Chris made his legs shake. He grabbed onto her shoulders for support, then found himself fascinated with the contours of her bones and the softness of her skin. His thumbs rubbed over and around her collarbone, fingers resting at the base of her neck. He tilted her head to kiss her more deeply, stroking her open lips with his tongue, taking her moans of pleasure into his mouth.

The remembrance of her nipples springing to life at a mere glance made his fingers ache to touch. His palms moved from her neck to her breasts, cupping their fullness, unfettered beneath the shirt. His thumbs stroked over the buds and, incredibly, they tightened further. He wanted—no, he needed—to take them into his mouth and suckle them like a hungry child.

D.J. had just wrapped her arms around his neck, drawing him toward the bed, when his own thoughts brought Christian up short.

What on earth am I doing?

He'd sworn to avoid such a situation. D.J. was poison to him. He hadn't waited all these years to find the woman he would spend his life loving to ruin his dream with a casual affair. The certainty an affair was all D.J. would ever want from him made Chris equally certain an affair would be all he could ever give her—and he needed so much more than that.

He pulled away, reaching up to unclasp her fingers from around his neck. D.J.'s eyes drifted open, and she smiled at him, tightening her fingers upon his. Chris's heart turned over at the innocence of her expression. Her lips were swollen from his kiss, her hair a halo of red, curling fire about her head.

Dear God, she's so beautiful. Why does doing the right thing have to be so damn hard?

His expression must have alerted her to the direction of his thoughts, for D.J. stiffened and pulled her fingers from his. "What's the matter?"

"Nothing." He turned away and retraced his steps to the door. "I'm sorry. That shouldn't have happened."

She stared at him for a moment, shock evident on her face. Then the cool mask he'd come to know so well fell into place, and her eyes narrowed with anger. "It was a kiss, McCall." He flinched at the sarcasm she put into his last name, remembering how she'd whispered "Christian" just before she'd kissed him. "You don't have to act like I assaulted you. You're the one who was playing 'Peeping Tom.'"

He stopped at the opening between their rooms and leaned his hand against the wall. He didn't look at her. He'd hurt her, embarrassed her, so she'd struck back. Still, the way she could turn off her softer emotions and become "Officer Ice" in the blink of an eye proved to Chris that D.J. could never be the woman for him. He could deal with honest emotion, but when she shut everything off like a power switch he didn't know what to do.

"You opened the door," Chris told her, startling himself with the coldness of his own voice. "Not me. What are you trying to pull, D.J.?"

Chris sensed D.J.'s growing fury, though her voice revealed no such emotion. "The last time I touched that door, McCall, I locked it. I don't know what *you're* trying to pull. I'm not so hard up for sex I'd lower myself to seducing you. Now, if you don't mind, I want you the hell out of my room so I can put on my pants. Then I'll go and get us some dinner, and when I get back you can just stay on your own side of the room. For the rest of this assignment. Is that clear?"

"Crystal, Officer." He began to close the door behind him.

"Josie, if you ever pull a stunt like that again, I won't be responsible," D.J. said.

Chris opened the door. "What?"

"Get out!" she screamed and threw her shoe at him.

Chris yanked the door shut. Her hiking boot hit the other side with a thud. Well, at least she'd shown some emotion. Fury was better than nothing. Chris snapped his lock to the right, but it was a long time before he moved away from the door.

D.J. marched down the service drive, long angry strides eating up the distance between the hotel and the nearest fast-food restaurant.

She had never been so embarrassed in her life. When McCall had kissed her she'd lost all sense of herself. Of who and what she was, what she wanted, what she believed. She'd only wanted him to keep kissing her—to keep kissing her and more. Then he'd pulled away, leaving her perched on a mountain of need she didn't understand. His face had revealed shock, confusion, and something else—a touch of panic D.J. understood very well. She understood McCall's panic because she experienced the self-same emotion whenever she examined too closely the things he made her feel.

D.J. stopped in front of the golden arches and stared at the garish characters that composed the slides and swings of an outdoor playland. Children tumbled and shrieked while their parents ate and watched. The bright primary colors of the children's jackets merged and blended with the colors of the playland as D.J. pondered the mystery of Christian McCall.

Something was very wrong with that man. In her world when a woman kissed a man like she'd kissed him, they ended up in bed. Although such an action would have been a mistake of epic proportions, at the time she would have fallen into bed with McCall gladly.

"What's his problem?" she muttered.

"Good question, dear."

D.J. glanced up. Josie sat on top of the fence separating the playland from the rest of the world. D.J. looked around. No one stood near enough, this time, to hear her talking to herself.

"I don't suppose you have any answers?" she asked the angel.

"I'm afraid not. I wish I did. But I'll see what I can discover. That young man is not cooperating with any of my plans."

"Which reminds me: When I lock a door I mean for the door to stay locked. Don't ever open one on me again."

Josie waved away D.J.'s protest. "I know what I'm doing, dear. Just relax and let me handle everything."

"No. You stay out of my work. That's what I'm doing here: work. I'm protecting McCall. I don't need to sleep with him and screw up my mind."

"The way things are progressing, you don't have much chance of sleeping with him. Christian's being very stubborn. A beautiful young girl like you, alone with him in a hotel room." She shook her head and made a "tsking" sound. "I just don't understand him at all."

"That makes two of us."

"There must be something in his past we don't know about. Raphael told me Christian wasn't my problem, but he's being so difficult." The angel looked up at the sky, tilted her head in thought, and then returned her gaze to D.J. "You'll be all right for a while, won't you, dear? I'm just going to take a little trip." She pointed upward with one finger.

"Please," D.J. said. "Go ahead, In fact, tell your boss to give you another assignment. Go help someone who cares."

Josie frowned. "You're not an easy young woman, are you?"

"Whoever said I was? If you want someone easy, go somewhere else."

"Oh, no, dear. I'm enjoying myself. In fact, I'll let you in on a little secret." Josie floated down from the top of the fence and hovered above D.J.'s head. She smiled and put her finger to her lips. "When I was a child," she whispered, "I was even more difficult to get along with than you are. Can you believe that?"

With a giggle, the angel disappeared.

"I believe it," D.J. muttered as she walked toward the restaurant. "Boy, do I believe it."

The first thing she saw when she entered the building was a pay phone tucked into a back corner near the rest rooms. She needed to make a call—a call she wanted no one else to hear—particularly McCall.

After digging the required coins from her pocket and depositing them in the slot, D.J. dialed. A recorded message answered her call. Relief flooded through her. She wouldn't have to talk to him; this must be her lucky day. At the tone, she spoke. "I just wanted to let you know I'm out of town on an assignment, so I doubt I'll be calling you Sunday night. I'll get in touch when I get home." She paused for a moment, but there was nothing else to say. There never was. " 'Bye, Dad." D.J. hung up.

Despite the estrangement between herself and

her father, D.J. continued to call him every Sunday evening—and she'd continued to call him "Dad," though he probably would have preferred she call him Ed. The streak of mulish stubbornness within her refused to give him the satisfaction. He'd probably prefer she didn't call him either, but her father was the only family she had left, and she felt a responsibility to keep in touch. Their conversations usually lasted all of five minutes. She would tell him about her work, he would give her advice, then they would say good-bye. Often the machine would answer when she called. Since she always called on Sunday evenings, she'd know her father did not want to speak to her that week. She'd come to understand that during certain times of the year her father couldn't bear to hear her voice—days coinciding with important dates during his life and her mother's—anniversaries, birthdays, death days. When D.J. and her father had occupied the same house he would lock himself into his room on those days and drink himself into a stupor. She supposed she should be grateful he'd bothered to lock her away from his despair, though she'd absorbed it all the same. But she'd never been able to feel anything beyond anger over his selfishness. D.J. had lost her mother, and his refusal to utter the woman's name, or speak of his wife in any way, had robbed D.J. of the chance to know her mother. No pictures survived. He had torn every photo of his wife into shreds and cut up every negative the day after he'd lost her. D.J. had no earthly idea what her mother had looked like, though the way her father flinched whenever he looked into D.J.'s face made her think

163

she must resemble the woman who had given birth to her.

"May I take your order?"

D.J. glanced up, her memories fading at the sight of the elderly woman behind the counter. She ordered a meal, making sure she picked the least appetizing item on the menu for McCall—a petty revenge, but all she had at the moment. Then she juggled the bags of food and two drinks all the way back to the hotel.

The door between her room and his remained closed, probably locked. She didn't hear a sound from the other side. Could he have fallen asleep so early in the evening? And if so, should she wake him?

D.J. shrugged; he'd have plenty of time to rest before this mess ended. There'd be little else to do but sleep and watch television in the hotel room. She knocked on the connecting door. Seconds later it gaped open.

He wore gray sweat pants and a white, tank-style T-shirt. He must have been exercising, because the shirt clung to his chest enticingingly and his hair curled in damp tendrils against his brow.

D.J. bit her lip. She liked him this way—too much. In an attempt to ignore her fascination with his body, D.J. looked at the floor. McCall's feet were bare, which reminded her of Josie. The angel hadn't returned from her talk with Raphael. Perhaps D.J.'s hope would be answered, and Josie would be assighed to ruin some other poor soul's life.

"What is it, D.J.?"

She looked back up to meet his eyes. He stared

at her without expression, and D.J. fought not to blush at the remembrance of what had passed between them not so long ago. He held the door partway closed, leaning against the side, as if he was afraid she'd invade his domain.

She held up his bag of food without a sound, not trusting her voice to speak in the detached tone she desired. He took the bag with a nod of thanks and looked inside.

"Thanks; this is my favorite thing on the menu. How'd you know?"

"I didn't," she growled. Trust McCall to ruin her petty revenge.

He shrugged, the movement making the muscles in his arms and neck flex and release. She stared, fascinated at the play of his skin against his bones. But when he began to close the door in her face she came out of her trance just in time to stick her foot into the opening.

"No." She cleared her throat, horrified at the breathiness of her voice, which made her sound like an actress in an X-rated movie. McCall's eyes narrowed, and his fingers tightened on the door. When D.J. spoke again she was pleased to find her voice was back to normal. "Leave the door open. I can't hear what's going on in your room with it closed."

McCall's fingers relaxed, then flexed away from the door. He raised his eyebrows. "What do you think you're going to hear, Officer?"

She chose to ignore his suggestive tone and the emphasis he placed on the use of her title. "I'm supposed to be protecting you. I need to hear and see

165

you to do my job effectively."

He shrugged. "However you get your kicks. Listen away."

He returned to his side of the room, and D.J. did the same, sitting on her bed so she could spread her hamburger and fries out before her.

She wrinkled her nose in distaste at the food. What had smelled heavenly inside the restaurant looked unappealing in the bright light of her hotel room. After the fiasco with McCall, and then the phone call to her father and the memories the call had engendered, D.J.'s desire to eat had fled.

She leaned back against the headboard and reached for the telephone; time to check in with Captain Miller.

A different voice answered the phone at the station than the one D.J. had expected. "Colleen, why are you answering the phones?" D.J. asked the day desk sergeant.

"Oh, D.J., the captain's been asking me every other minute if you've called. Where are you?"

"Out of town." Colleen hesitated at D.J.'s evasive answer, and D.J. didn't elaborate. Colleen had always had a soft spot for Rich. Since the first time Ed had bailed Rich out of the Lakeview jail, Colleen had been like an older sister to the kid she'd seen as a "poor lost soul." Though D.J. doubted the woman would tell Rich where she'd gone, D.J. wasn't taking any chances. She had enough headaches with McCall; she didn't need more from her ex-husband. "Since the captain's so hot to talk, better put me through right away, Colleen."

Colleen hesitated again, as though she meant to

argue. What Colleen could have to argue with her about, D.J. had no idea. Then the line clicked, and seconds later the captain bellowed into the phone. "Where are you, Halloran?"

She winced. "Captain, the phone works fine. You don't have to shout just because I'm not in the same room with you."

"Just tell me where you are and don't be a smart ass."

The level of his voice still rivaled a sonic boom. D.J. sighed and gave up. "Outgamie," she told him, and repeated the phone number and address of the hotel. "Have you found anything out?"

"Nothing. Your friend McCall is squeaky clean. There's no reason anyone would want to kill him that I can see. Are you sure about this?"

"Yes. Both times McCall's almost been killed the same black van has been involved."

"License plate number?"

"No plates."

"Hmm. That's suspicious. Well, you keep on it, Halloran. Don't let that boy out of your sight."

"Great." She lowered her voice. "How long am I going to be stuck with him?"

"As long as it takes. I did find out that the mayor is practically his godfather. McCall's dad and the mayor have been buddies since high school. My ass'll be in a sling, and yours will be too, if anything happens to McCall. Don't screw this up, Halloran. You're in enough trouble already."

The line clicked again and D.J. frowned, looking at the phone. She wasn't anywhere near the disconnect button. "You there, Captain?"

"What? Yeah, yeah. I'm on this damn cellular phone. As far as I'm concerned, give me a good old stationary telephone. These things aren't worth crap."

D.J. shook her head. The captain never changed. Anything new always threw him into a fit. Modern technology made him crazy. He'd be happiest if cops still walked the streets with nightsticks and typed reports on manual typewriters.

"Well, you know where to fine me," D.J. interrupted the captain's continuing tirade. "Have Lou try to stir something around. He's best at getting people to talk. Send him over to McCall's foster parents' place. If he digs up anything, he can call me here. And tell him to keep me updated on the other case. I'm sick of running into fourteen-year-olds with better firearms than I've seen in my dreams. I want to put a stop to this as soon as I get back to town."

"We all want it stopped. Gangs and guns make my ulcer burn. And so does the mayor."

"I get the message. I'll stick to McCall like he's a helpless little puppy dog. He'll be safe with me. Don't worry."

"Worrying is my job."

"Just tell Lou to call me, all right?"

"Yeah. I do know what I'm doing, Halloran. You don't need to give me step-by-step instructions." The phone crackled again, and D.J. said good-bye amid the captain's curses. She had wanted to ask if Captain Miller knew the story of McCall's parents, but with McCall in the next room and the captain still swearing about the useless, newfangled

168

phones, she couldn't bring up the subject. Maybe Josie would learn something.

D.J. swore under her breath, repeating some of the captain's more colorful curses. She must be getting desperate if she was counting on an angel's information to do her job. If she wasn't careful, she'd even start taking Josie's advice to the lovelorn. Then she might as well believe in heaven, because hell on earth would be too real.

•

Chapter Eight

"Josie." Raphael smiled at her. "Good work with Captain Miller. It was a stroke of genius to make him remove D.J.'s suspension and send them off together."

She ignored his praise, impatient to return to earth and to D.J. "Things are not going well at all." She allowed her frustration at the situation to leak out on a long, heartfelt sigh. "This is taking much longer than I'd thought."

"Success is never easy, Josie."

"I understand that. I really think if you'd let me tell her who I am, she'd listen to me better."

"No. That isn't possible. We have our rules, Josie. You agreed to abide by those rules when you accepted this mission."

"I know. But that was before I realized how hard

it would be to be near her and not have her know who I am. It's killing me inside."

"I'm sorry. I know this is hard for you, but you have to do what's best for her. Taking into account the small amount of time we have to save her, such a revelation could be disastrous."

"Can I tell her once she's learned how to love?" Raphael frowned.

"Please." Josie put everything she had into that one little word.

Raphael sighed. "I'll ask." He raised his hand to stop her excited reply. "That's all I can do. It's not usual procedure. We'll see."

Josie decided not to press her luck. She'd made progress. She'd let it go at that. For now. "You told me Christian had problems of his own."

Raphael's eyes widened at the sudden change in subject, then narrowed in suspicion. "I did."

"You never told me he would cause as much trouble as my daughter. How am I going to teach D.J. anything if he won't cooperate?"

"What do you mean?"

"I mean every time they get close to making love, he freezes up and walks off. I've never seen a young man with such self-control."

"Hold on." Raphael took a deep breath as if for strength. "Let me get this straight: You've been trying to get them into bed?"

"Of course. What else?"

Raphael let out a groan and put his hand to his forehead. "You're supposed to be teaching her how to love. This is your daughter we're dealing with here. What do you think you're doing?"

Lori Handeland

"I know she's my daughter. That's why I want her to be happy. I'm just doing what you told me to do." Josie frowned, puzzled.

"No wonder you're having such a problem. Sex isn't love. First D.J. has to learn to love, truly love someone, before she can understand making love and sex are two different things."

"I know that."

"You do. But D.J. doesn't. That's part of her problem. To D.J., making love and having sex are one and the same, and she doesn't like sex much. As for Christian, he won't sleep with a woman unless he loves her."

Josie closed her mouth, which had fallen open at Raphael's last statement. Could he be serious? "You mean to tell me he's only slept with women he believes himself in love with? No wonder he's so uptight."

"No, that's not what I meant. He's never slept with any woman. Christian's waiting for his one true soul mate."

Josie's eyes widened. "You can't be serious."

"I'm always serious. Especially about something so important."

"I can't believe what you're telling me. From what I've seen since I've been back on earth, sex is everywhere. It's the 'in' thing. We had free love in our day, but nothing like this."

Raphael sighed. "To our dismay, you're right. Sex has become a commodity to some. But, thankfully, not to all. Christian is one of those who has kept his principles intact despite all the odds against his doing so."

Josie shook her head, still amazed. "You're telling me in this day and age the guy's a virgin? He's thirty years old, for crying out loud."

"I'm well aware of how old he is. I don't think you need to ridicule the young man for sticking to his beliefs. He's a rarity, not an oddity."

"I agree. You just surprised me." Josie shook her head again. "He's blowing his chance. His soul mate's right in front of his nose."

"He doesn't know that." Raphael sighed. "Perhaps I was wrong in keeping Christian's past from you. He doesn't want anyone to know. He won't discuss it. But I'll show you. As long as you don't tell D.J.; Christian must share this part of himself with her willingly before he can let go of his pain."

"All right. I promise." An easy concession on Josie's part, since a revelation about Christian's past was what she'd been angling for all along.

"Watch, Josie. Watch. See. Learn."

Josie did as she was told and felt herself become a part of another world, another past, another life.

"Dad, it's my birthday. Please, please, please. I want to go to a movie. Take me to see *Star Wars*. All the kids are talking about it at school. Everyone says it's great."

Brian McCall watched as his twelve-year-old son danced with excitement. He glanced over at his wife. They smiled the secret smile two people very much in love used to communicate. Marianne raised her eyebrows and tilted her head. Brian put his hand out toward her, palm up in invitation. She ignored the hand, launching herself into his arms instead. He caught her, swinging his wife around in a circle before setting her feet back on the floor.

After kissing Marianne amid a serenade of groans from their son, Brian lifted his head and smiled down into his wife's face. "What do you say? A movie, popcorn, soda, then pizza afterward?"

"If that's what the birthday boy wants," Marianne looked over her shoulder to smile at their son, "then that's what the birthday boy gets."

Chris let out a whoop of joy, and his parents laughed out loud and kissed each other again.

Brian broke the embrace. "If we're going to have our big night out, we'd better get going. Find your coat, Chris."

Chris took off at full speed toward the front closet. He stopped just outside the kitchen doorway, sliding a few feet on the polished wood floor. When he turned his parents stood within each other's embrace. The spring sunlight streamed through the window, catching them in its beam. His father saw him watching and lifted his cheek away from where it rested on the top of his mother's head.

"We love you, Christian. Always remember how much we love you. That will never change."

Chris nodded. His parents constantly held hands, hugged, kissed. Sometimes all that mushy stuff could be kind of embarrassing for a twelve-year-old boy, but, in the end, such a wealth of love reassured a child. The world might be in turmoil, but in the McCall household everyone loved everyone else.

Brian left his wife and walked over to kneel beside Chris. He put his hands on his son's shoulders and stared into Chris's eyes. Chris stared back, straightening his spine with importance when he recognized the seriousness in his father's gaze. They'd had these talks before. Man talk. Important stuff. Chris idolized his father. Whatever Brian McCall said must be the truth. How could it be anything else when Dad said it was so?

"I hope someday, Chris, you'll find a woman just like your mother." He threw a grin over his shoulder to his wife, who smiled back, her eyes moist with love for them both. Brian turned to his son with a wink. Marianne's penchant for happy tears was a source of amusement for both of them. He continued, "Someone who can make your life as full as mine. Nowadays, you might start to believe marriage is a thing of the past. But don't. Always remember what we have here and don't settle for anything less."

"I won't, Dad. I promise."

An hour later the three of them sat inside the darkened theater, Chris between his parents, their arms resting along the back of his seat as they held hands. It was his best birthday ever.

When the movie ended they walked down the quiet streets of Lakeview toward the pizza parlor. Being a Wednesday night, most people had gone home in preparation for another workday. But tonight the McCalls celebrated, and bedtime could wait another hour.

Chris skipped ahead of his parents, humming the theme from *Star Wars* loud and off key. His parents laughed and held hands, strolling along behind him. The lights of the pizza parlor beckoned at the end of the street—the only lights shining on the block. Until, inside a doorway as they passed, a match flared.

Chris started. He stopped humming, amazed that he hadn't seen anyone lounging against the building. Now that he looked, he could distinguish three teenage boys leaning against the wall, smoking and watching them. Dressed in jean jackets and baseball caps, all three looked like everyday teens. In the darkness their features were indistinct, but even so Chris did not like the way the three were staring at them.

He reminded himself that this was Lakeview—a city where the citizens did not fear walking the streets. He had never been afraid in Lakeview before; he did not need to be afraid now. Anyway, his parents were with him. Nothing bad could happen if they were all together.

"Chris." His father's voice beckoned, and Chris took the few steps backward until he stood at his parents' side. Brian grasped his hand in strong fingers, and they walked on, passing the young men.

Chris felt rather than saw the three boys fall into step behind them. He focused on the lights of the pizza parlor ahead and held his breath. They would be inside soon—safe, warm, happy once more. He had nothing to be frightened about. Today was his birthday, his best birthday ever. Tomorrow he would tell his friends about the three hoodlums, and everyone would laugh. Maybe he'd even make up a story about the incident, where he was the hero, of course. He liked making up stories. His teacher said he was very imaginative.

One of the youths spoke. "That's far enough."

Chris glanced up at his father, who ignored the words and kept walking.

Suddenly one of the boys clamped a hand on Brian's shoulder and spun him around. Another grabbed Marianne, and the third grabbed Chris.

"No!" Chris shouted as he reached for his parents. A hand slapped across his mouth, crushing his lips against his teeth. He tasted blood, warm and metallic, on his tongue.

"Shut up, kid. Just shut the hell up."

Chris did as he was told. He didn't like the sound of that voice.

The teenager who held his mother also put a hand over her mouth. The third boy pulled a gun from his jacket and pointed the weapon at Chris's father.

"Hand over the wallet, Pops. Then we'll be on our way."

Brian withdrew his wallet and tossed it toward the youth. The kid smiled and caught the leather billfold in midair. "Thanks." Opening the wallet, he glanced inside. "Thanks a lot." He motioned with the gun. "Now the watch, the ring." A glance toward Marianne. "Hers, too."

Brian didn't take his eyes from the youth who led the trio. "Give him what he wants, Marianne."

Chris's breath came in hot, hard gasps of fear against his captor's hand. He watched, wide-eyed, as the kid released his mother so she could remove her jewelry.

Her watch and necklace came off with ease— dainty gold chains lit with diamonds. Chris recalled his mother's cry of delight when she'd opened the box containing the matching set on her last birthday—her thirty-second. She tugged on her wedding ring, eyes filling with tears when the gold and diamond band wouldn't come off. She glanced at Brian. "I haven't taken this off since we were married. It's stuck." Her voice wavered on the last word.

The leader reached in his pocket again, this time removing a knife. At the press of a button, a long blade appeared. "We can cut off the finger. Will that make it easier?"

Brian took a step forward. "Are you insane? Just give her a minute. She's had the thing on for over twelve years."

Marianne licked the flesh around her finger, desperately working the metal against her knuckle. The kid hovering in the background grabbed Marianne by the hair and yanked her head back. "If we can't have the ring, we'll have something else. But I get to go first." As Chris and his father watched, horrified, the youth ripped Marianne's blouse down the front and groped inside, settling his hand on her breast.

With a roar of protest, Brian launched himself toward his wife. A shot rang out. Time slowed as Chris's father jerked once. Then he fell forward, grasping his wife's skirt before he slid to the ground at her feet.

The silence that ensued in the moments following the shot echoed louder than the loudest thunder in Chris's ears. Then came a roaring to rival the winds before a tornado, and finally a stillness settled in—the quiet before the worst of the storm hit.

The youth who'd held Marianne stared in shock at their leader. When Marianne jerked away from his grasp he let her go. She fell to her knees next to her husband, turning him over. His eyes stared, sightless, into her own. Her sob of horror echoed Chris's silent scream of agony.

Marianne looked up at her husband's murderer. Chris had never seen hate before, but he saw it now on his mother's face. He knew what she meant to do. He tried to cry out for her to stop, but his mouth remained covered by his captor's sweaty palm, and he could say nothing. He could do nothing.

Marianne screamed her husband's name as she dove for the gunman. Another shot exploded, this one finding its mark in Marianne's chest. Scarlet bloomed in the middle of her pretty pink blouse. Her gaze searched for Chris. Their eyes met. He saw her love for him mingling with her fear. She crumpled at the feet of her murderer.

The gunman turned toward Chris. Slithering shadows moved across the youth's face, obscuring his features. But Chris could see his own death reflected in those too-bright eyes.

"Shit, Dickey, what did you kill them for?" the kid who held Chris shouted. "We're in for it now. You said no shooting. You said we'd only use the gun to scare 'em."

"Shut up and get away from him." The murderer's voice was as cold as his eyes. The kid who held Chris went still, then very slowly released him and stepped away. Chris stumbled forward a step, his legs wobbly. Harsh, terror-stricken pants rasped from his mouth, too loud in the sudden, death-shrouded stillness.

Dickey stared into Chris's eyes, and Chris held his breath, waiting for death. He squinted, trying to decipher the identity of the murderer, but the night and the baseball hat on Dickey's head showered the youth's face with shifting shadows. Chris could see nothing beyond the glint of eyes, then the flash of a smile. "Close your eyes, little boy. Listen to the tiger's roar and dream of better things."

Chris frowned. What was he talking about?

"Dickey, if you're gonna do it, do it. Quit yappin'."

"Shut up. Killing someone like this calls for a little ceremony. I think I'll use that line with all my victims. A little ritual. I like rituals."

Nausea threatened Chris. The guy was insane—a cold-blooded killer who talked about ceremonies and rituals over the dead bodies of his victims.

A siren wailed in the distance. The gunman's gaze flicked in the direction of the sound, then focused once more on Chris. The threat in his eyes strengthened. Chris focused his gaze on the hand holding the gun. The finger on the trigger tightened. Chris bit his lip and closed his eyes as he'd been told. The fear that had choked his throat left him. He would go to his parents now. Everything would be all right once more.

"What the hell's goin' on out here?"

The voice came from the pizza parlor at the end of the street. The gun exploded. Chris flinched, but no pain followed. A small sob escaped his throat.

"Listen for the tiger, little man. He always comes back."

The voice made him shiver. Footsteps retreated. Chris opened one eye, then the other. He took a deep breath.

He was still alive.

Alone on the deserted street he stood. Alone but for the bodies of his parents in two heaps on the sidewalk.

Josie blinked and the scene disappeared. Her chest ached from the agony within her. While observing Christian's past, Josie had been able to feel every emotion experienced by the participants in the action. She'd identified with the love of Marianne and Brian for each other, reveled in the love of the elder McCalls for their son and his for them, and been sickened by the cold hatred and calculated cruelty of the young men who had ended the lives of two shining souls.

Exhausted from the trauma, Josie looked up in mute appeal to meet Raphael's sad gaze. Tears ran unchecked down their cheeks.

"Do you see now why he is as he is?" Raphael asked. "He's made his parents' love into the icon for his own life. One of the last things Christian's father asked of him was that he wait for the right woman. The boy's perfect family life was torn asunder in a horrid and violent manner. He's been searching for a return to such stability ever since that night."

"How horrible. The poor child."

"Christian might have gotten over the incident more easily if he hadn't been placed with a foster family who only proved to him what marrying someone without love can do to you. The Rousseaus married because Carol became pregnant. They had noth-

ing in common. They were too young. They made everyone around them miserable—each other, their son, and their foster son."

"All right, all right. I've heard enough. What do you suggest I do now?"

"First of all, cease the sexual matchmaking. It won't work. When they fall in love making love will follow naturally. Forcing the issue will only make Christian berate himself for his weakness. And D.J. has had enough loveless sex in her life."

"What do you mean? She doesn't seem the kind of girl to sleep around."

"She isn't. But she married a man she thought would please her father. A man as incapable of love as she's always been. Their marriage was a disaster. I'm surprised she has any capacity for passion left within her."

"I can understand God wanting D.J. to learn to love. What I can't understand is why He didn't help her out before she became so far gone. And why didn't He do something about Christian's problems before now? Why let things get so messed up and then try to fix them?"

"Josie. Josie. You're still looking at the situation with your human heart and mind. God has His reasons for everything, reasons we don't understand until the time is right. There are life lessons to be learned, and once they are learned a life can progress. D.J. and Christian would not be the people they are, the two people who are meant to be together, if they had not had the experiences that made them so. Yes, their lives up until now have been sad, but they can be-

*come so much more as a result of that sadness. Do
you see what I mean?"*

*"I think I do. Everything that happens in our lives
is meant to contribute to the person we become. My
dying was necessary in some way to make D.J. and
Ed into the people,"* her voice broke and she paused,
swallowing the lump in her throat that had appeared
at the remembrance of all she'd lost, *"the people they
were meant to be,"* Josie finished on a whisper.

Raphael took Josie's hands into his. Peace flooded
her at his touch. All her concerns and worries fled for
a moment, and she uttered a small sound of contentment.

"So nice," she murmured. *"How do you do that?"*

*"It's a gift. One you'll have as well, eventually.
Now, I think you'd better go back. I can see that you
understand the universe a bit better than when you
came to me. But remember, time doesn't move here
as it does on earth. Midnight has arrived. D.J. needs
you. Her dreams—they are not good ones. Go and
give her some of the peace I've given you."*

"Yes. I will. Thank you."

When Josie opened her eyes she stood next to
D.J.'s bed. The girl tossed and turned, twisting her
legs tighter and tighter in the sheets. The way she
slept tonight was a far cry from the way she'd slept
the first night Josie had watched her. Then D.J. had
been as still as death. Now she mumbled and
sweated and moaned, as if in pain.

Josie floated down and sat on the side of the bed.
Reaching out, she smoothed her fingers across
D.J.'s damp brow. "Poor baby," she whispered. "It's

all right. I'm here. Nothing will hurt you while I'm here."

Josie's eyes prickled with tears. How many times had she imagined saying just those words to her baby? Instead, she said them to a twenty-eight-year-old stranger. Her daughter, to be true, but a woman with a soul that mystified Josie as much as Josie's would mystify D.J.'s. Despite all the drawbacks and secrets in their relationship, it felt good to be needed. And though D.J. might deny it, right now she needed Josie.

Josie continued to stroke D.J.'s brow, but the girl did not quiet. Though reading her charge's mind wasn't allowed, Josie did recall another option from her crash course on guardian angelhood. If she couldn't stop D.J. from dreaming, she could at least replace the nightmare with a good dream—a dream that might help her charge see the possibilities in her future. D.J. could use some hope.

Touching her palms to the sides of her daughter's forehead, Josie concentrated. D.J. gave a murmur of distress before her face relaxed; she sighed, and then quieted into a peaceful slumber.

D.J.'s nightmare was always the same. She stood alone in a great, dark cave. The air around her pulsed with night. Scuffling sounds from the ceiling and the floor announced the presence of rodents, both winged and four-footed. The steady drip-drip of water grated on her nerves, along with the dampness seeping into her bones.

She stumbled forward, trying to discover the way out. If she had gotten in, there had to be a way out, a reasonable voice inside her head told her in an attempt to keep the panic at bay. But her hands, outstretched in front of her, met wall upon damp, mossy wall.

When she tilted her head back more blackness met her straining gaze. When she shouted her own voice echoed back.

"Help me, help me, me, me, me."

The loneliness she'd carried inside her all her life became a tangible force within the cave. She understood, in the part of her mind separated from the dream, how her subconscious had personified a hidden fear of dying alone into a closed-in cave where she would, in fact, die alone, forgotten and unmourned.

But tonight, just after the first rush of despair came upon her, the dream changed. D.J. shifted and made a small sound of distress, which the detached, rational part of her mind heard and stifled. Instead of her voice echoing back as it usually did when she called out in fear, another voice answered her call.

"Here. Come this way."

D.J. turned and frowned into the shaft of light from a tunnel. She took one cautious step forward, then another. As she neared the source of the light, she saw a man. He held out his hand to her.

"Come on, D.J. We're waiting for you. The picnic's all ready, and the kids are hungry."

I have lost my mind. But this is a whole lot better than the way the dream usually ends.

D.J. took the remaining steps through the dark tunnel and emerged into the bright sunshine of a

Wisconsin summer day. She blinked, trying to adjust her eyes to the sudden change in light, then stared in amazement at the scene before her.

A field of wildflowers in full bloom—white, purple, green, orange—stretched out before her. In a small clearing blanketed with grass lay a red-and-white checkered tablecloth. On the cloth sat a picnic lunch and three children—two boys with dark hair full of cowlicks that stuck up every which way and who looked to be about six and five years old and a baby girl with red hair. She was just old enough to crawl, and at the sight of D.J. she made a noise that sounded suspiciously like "mama" and put her knees into high gear, bringing her to D.J.'s feet in seconds. Once there she plopped her padded bottom onto the ground and reached up in supplication. The two-toothed smile on the child's face broke D.J.'s heart.

Confused, she looked around for an explanation to this disturbing dream. Her eyes fell on the one person she recognized.

McCall.

He leaned against the rock wall at the entrance to the cave, smiling at her with an expression on his face that she couldn't fathom. The baby yanked on her shoelace and let out a squall of protest. D.J. looked down, and the child held up her hands once again in mute appeal.

"Honey, you'd better pick her up. You know how she is when she doesn't get her way. Her temper's just like yours."

Honey?

D.J. looked back at McCall with a frown. Before

she could question him, the child at her feet started to scream. Without a second thought, D.J. bent down and lifted the little girl onto her hip. The ear-piercing shrieks ceased.

"Mom, can we eat? We were waiting forever and ever for you to come out of the cave."

D.J.'s head snapped to the left to stare in amazement at the two boys sitting on the tablecloth. They both returned her gaze with angelic innocence. She glanced behind her. There was no one there but McCall. No, they had called her, D.J. Halloran, Mom.

What is going on here?

"We'd better eat now, honey." McCall came up behind her and put a palm against the hollow of her lower back, urging her forward. "You were in there a long time. What did you find?"

Before she could answer the little girl started tugging at her blouse. D.J. looked down in shock. "Wh-what's the matter with her?"

"What do you think? She's hungry too. Why don't you sit down and nurse her. I'll feed the boys."

"Nurse her!" D.J. heard the panic in her voice. This dream was getting too weird. "I can't nurse her."

But even as she said the words an odd burning and tightening occurred in her breasts, then a wetness soaked her bra. She looked down, amazed to find her midsized chest had expanded at least two sizes larger than normal, and she could feel herself growing bigger with every second that the child in her arms cried and nuzzled her aching breasts.

187

"Wake up, D.J.," she muttered to herself. "You've *got* to wake up."

And though a tiny thread of panic lodged deep inside, D.J. found she liked the weight of the baby in her arms; she liked the way the child clung to her. When the boy had called her "Mom" a spark of wonder had blossomed in her heart, and the warmth in McCall's voice when he'd said "honey" made her ache in the deepest part of her soul.

But this dream wasn't real—could never be real. Believing in the dream would only cause more heartache than she could bear. She had to end this now. How could she get back to her world?

D.J. glanced at the mouth of the cave. Must she leave this happy scene full of life and promise and journey back through that cold, damp loneliness once again to find her way out?

"No!" she shouted, and sat up with a jerk.

She existed in the darkness. *Alone.* A tiny hiccough of a sob came from her lips, and she put her hand up to stop any further sound from escaping.

The bed dipped as someone sat next to her. She let out a gasp of shock. Her mouth opened, but no words would come out.

"D.J., are you all right?"

McCall. She sighed in relief. He was still here. Confusion snared her. Where was here?

"I—I—I had a dream." Her voice sounded odd—breathy, frightened, almost childlike.

"It's all right. I have dreams all the time. They aren't real."

True. The dream couldn't be real, could never be real. Not the terrifying dream of the empty cave, or the wonder of the family she'd imagined—a family with this man.

Without knowing why, she leaned against him and pressed her damp face to his bare chest. He stiffened for a moment, and she feared he would push her away again. Then the strange hiccough of a sob came out of her mouth once more, and his arms encircled her, pulling D.J. closer.

"Don't worry. Whatever you dreamed is gone now. It can't hurt you here." His whisper stirred her hair; then his hand smoothed down the back of her head, lingering at her neck. Long fingers stroked bunched muscles, kneading away the tension. A contented sigh fluttered from her mouth. "What did you dream, D.J.? Tell me."

She could never tell him about the dream from which he'd woken her. How mortifying to imagine having children with a man who wanted nothing to do with her! She'd keep such a secret to herself. Forever. But the rest . . .

"A cave," she blurted, the tension he'd so recently smoothed away returning full force. McCall began to rub her neck again as he made soothing sounds of encouragement. "It's dark and I'm all alone. I can't get out. There's no way out. I'll die alone."

He nodded, the movement of his head rubbing a beard-roughened cheek against D.J.'s forehead. Though the scrape hurt a bit, she didn't pull away. He felt too good to give up just yet. "Do you dream the same dream a lot?" he asked.

"Yes. Ever since I was a child."

"I dream, too. Though it's not a cave. It's a dark

street. And I'm not alone. Not until the end, anyway."

The despair in his voice reached D.J. through her misery, and she lifted her head away from his chest. Where before the room had been shrouded in darkness, she could now make out the shadow of his face in the encroaching light that spilled from the doorway of his room into hers. Christian stared straight ahead, lost in a memory. Despite his earlier rejection, D.J. couldn't stop herself from touching him.

Reaching up, she cupped his cheek in her hand. His gaze shifted toward her, eyes glinting in the small shaft of light.

She leaned forward. Her lips met his in a gentle, sweet kiss of understanding. Her fingers tangled in his short, curling hair, urging him closer.

They had shared an embrace of passion, but this embrace held so much more—warmth, need, the desire for a human connection in a frightening and lonely world.

She had meant to soothe him as he'd soothed her. But when she removed her lips from his he rejected her retreat, taking her by the shoulders to urge her back onto the pillow. For a moment she stared at his silhouette, his taut body outlined in the yellow electric light. Then his lips met hers, and the tender embrace of moments before became a mere memory.

Chapter 9

The long T-shirt D.J. had donned over her white cotton briefs would have reached to midthigh if she'd stood up. But in the aftermath of her twisting and turning nightmare, the shirt now rested at the edge of her underwear. When Christian's hands touched her legs he encountered bare flesh.

His palms skimmed up her tingling thighs, pausing at the elastic encircling her legs. He slipped a finger under the material, and then his hand cupped her buttock. D.J. groaned into his mouth, her lower body arching toward him. But he held himself away from her, allowing only his hands and his mouth to touch her flesh.

D.J. explored the contours of his chest and back, her fingers running up and down the defined muscles. When her search encountered the waistband of his sweatpants she reached around to the front and yanked the string free as she'd wanted to do—had it been just last night?—when she'd watched him sleep on his own bed. He made a small sound of protest as she eased the material down his hips, then started to move away.

"No. Let me touch you," she whispered against his mouth.

He hesitated. When the tension in his arms relaxed she took the release for acquiescence and reversed their positions, pushing him onto his back and rising up next to him. She slipped the sweat pants from his long, muscled legs and ran her fingers up the sides of his thighs, marveling at the contrast between the hair-roughened skin on his legs and the sensitive skin of her palms. A sudden desire to remove all the barriers between them consumed her. D.J. sat back on her heels and yanked her T-shirt over her head. She leaned forward, placing her palms on either side of his head. Then she kissed him as the tips of her breasts brushed back and forth against his chest. His muscles flexed and hardened, the hair on his chest soft and warm. She wanted to curl herself against him and snuggle ever closer.

Though he returned her kiss, Christian held himself very still, his arms at his sides, as though afraid to touch her. She broke away from his mouth and sat up. Where before she had used her sense of touch to explore him, now she used sight. Her gaze traveled down his body. Beautiful, just as she'd imagined.

No, she couldn't have imagined this. His tall form

was lean and taut—near perfect in its musculature. No slouch in the fitness department herself, she recognized a body honed through hours of physical labor.

He continued to lay so still, D.J. experienced a moment of unease. With a naked woman in bed, most men wouldn't lie passively while she examined him. Perhaps he didn't want her as much as she wanted him.

Her gaze lowered. She smiled. He might say he didn't want her, but his body couldn't lie.

She reached out a hand to touch him, then stopped. Hesitant. Almost shy. Her experiences with sex had been near clinical renditions of the act with no emotion, and even less passion, involved. Tonight, however, she felt an all-consuming desire to make this man experience pleasure at her hands. Unfortunately, she had no idea how to accomplish her goal.

She looked at his face, hoping for a hint. His eyes were closed, his jaw clenched. She allowed her hand to fall back to her side, but on the way her fingertips brushed the side of his thigh. He jumped as though she'd struck him.

With a groan and a curse, he grasped her upper arms, pulling her across his body as he kissed her with a combination of passion and panic. She understood his confusion. She wanted him to stop— and she wanted him to go on and on. Fitting herself to him, she nestled his hardness between her thighs. He throbbed against her aching center, enticingly hot where she'd always been cold. No longer would she be alone in the night if she had this man beside her.

He rolled suddenly so she rested on her back with him lying between her thighs. Lowering his head, he nuzzled his mouth against her ear, muttering a word that sounded like "baby" or "honey." She had a sudden flash of her dream—three children with this man. She wanted him—she wanted this. But the other? She wasn't so sure. Her own version of panic threatened, and D.J.'s eyes snapped open. She grasped his upper arms, feeling the bunched muscles beneath the smooth skin. Curling her fingers into his flesh, she squeezed hard to get his attention.

"Wait," she said. "Do you have something?"

His mouth moved against her neck once more. Half kiss, half response. The muffled word floated toward her ear. "What?"

"You know. Something. I'm not on the Pill. I haven't had any reason to be—until now. But we do have to think about transmitting. Although I haven't been with anyone since Rich, and I haven't slept with him for over a year." His continued silence made D.J. nervous. Her unease with the situation left her babbling, though she was quite proud of herself for remembering to take care of such a matter in the heat of the moment. Maybe she wouldn't make such a bad '90s woman after all.

"Transmitting?" His voice had thickened with desire and confusion. His body lay heavy upon her, having resumed the earlier deathlike stillness.

"Diseases. V.D., A.I.D.S.," D.J. recited. "Or any number of other things I don't know about. Pregnancy isn't the worst thing you can catch nowadays."

Christian took a deep breath. Since his chest still pressed against hers, the slight shake within shook D.J. too. Then he rolled away from her and stood. D.J. started to shiver at the loss of his warmth. She yanked the thin hotel blanket over her nakedness and lifted her head to stare at him. "What's wrong?"

He barely paused in the act of yanking on his pants. A short bark of laughter came from the shadows surrounding him. "D.J., you sure know how to ruin the moment, don't you?"

Icy mortification flooded her veins. She had given more of herself to this man in the last hour than she'd ever given anyone in her life. Then he had turned away while her body screamed for his and had the nerve to say *she* had ruined the moment.

When unsure of her emotions D.J. fell back on anger, and when she was angry she struck out with the best weapon in her arsenal—her sarcastic mouth. "I'm just trying to be a responsible adult here, McCall. In typical male fashion you think with the part of your anatomy that might have a name but doesn't have a brain. In the nineties, consenting adult sex begins with a condom."

"Well, between us there isn't consent, and therefore no need for a condom."

"Five minutes ago we had plenty of consent."

"Five minutes ago you hadn't opened your mouth and reminded me of all the reasons we shouldn't be in bed together."

"What reasons?"

"Just two, D.J." He turned and walked to the door

connecting their rooms. Before he disappeared inside McCall turned back to her. "Only two. I want too much, and you want too little."

With those final words he left her. Seconds later she heard the security chain on his outer door rattle, then the door opened and closed.

D.J. sat on her bed, alone in the darkness once more, and tried to figure out where she had gone wrong.

Chris walked out of the hotel into the damp autumn air. Though it was the middle of the night, cars whizzed by on the freeway. The cheery neon of the fast-food joints and hotel chains lining the service road made the darkness of the night an illusion.

He had to get away from her. She would drive him crazy. His body ached with unfulfilled need, and he was more on edge than he could ever remember being in his life.

Do it. You want her. She wants you. Why are you killing yourself like this?

Chris gritted his teeth and tried to ignore the voice in his head.

This is the '90s, pal. You're acting like an escapee from the Victorian era. Look, there's a drugstore. Buy some condoms and get your butt back to the hotel. You'll feel better in the morning. I guarantee it.

But Chris knew he wouldn't feel better in the morning. Maybe his body would no longer be on fire, but his mind would still be in turmoil. He'd made a promise to his father, a promise to himself. He couldn't break such a promise at this late date.

Maybe she's the one. And you're blowing it. You'll be a virgin for the rest of your life. Is that what you want? What are you, some kind of sexual freak? Or are you a man?

"Shut up," Chris hissed under his breath. "Please, just shut up."

D.J. couldn't be the woman for him. If she was, he'd know; he'd feel in his heart and soul a joy and a peace. He'd be happy and so would she. He wouldn't be so torn up with confusion he couldn't think straight.

He couldn't work. He couldn't sleep. He was a mess.

The cold night air and the brisk pace he'd set served to release some of the pulsing tension within him. Chris glanced around to discover that he'd left the flashing lights far behind. Dark, empty storefronts and equally empty parking lots lined the edges of the highway. In a few hours this area would be a beehive of activity, but right now it slept the sleep of the "closed at five." The residential neighborhoods he could just make out in the distance rested undisturbed, as well.

Chris stood at the top of a long highway, in the midst of the true darkness that lived away from the artificial world near the freeway. He turned and looked back at the other world—the world where D.J. lived. In a way she reminded Chris of those lights blinking and shimmering below him: hard and bright and so beautiful she hurt his eyes to look at her for long. But was she as fragile and brittle on the inside as the glass bulbs that gave birth to the light? He'd seen glimpses of a softer D.J., and those tantalizing glimpses of the woman denied haunted him.

There would be no answers for him tonight. He'd walk a while longer, until he was sure she would be asleep when he returned. Tomorrow he would call the mayor and make certain D.J. stayed out of Lakeview on another assignment—real or fictitious—while he returned and took care of his little problem on his own. He could take care of himself, and once D.J.'s scent, D.J.'s voice, D.J.'s damnable presence no longer confused him, he could discover the identity of the person who wanted him dead.

Chris turned away from the blinking lights below, a sigh upon his lips at the thought of what D.J. would do when she learned he'd gone over her head to the mayor. She'd skin him alive.

The sigh hitched in his chest when he saw them.

Three shadows in the shapes of men walked toward Chris at a steady pace. They walked three abreast, strung out across the deserted highway like gunfighters in a scene from an old western. Since they approached from the opposite direction of the freeway, Chris wouldn't have thought anything amiss. They hadn't followed him from the hotel. They couldn't be looking for him.

But something in the way they walked revealed the truth of his delusion. They *were* looking for him.

And they had found him.

Alone. With no protection beyond his own wits and body.

He had prepared himself for this moment since the nightmarish night of his twelfth birthday. The time had arrived.

Chris took a deep breath and waited.

*   *   *

D.J. lay in the empty, cold bed and stared at the ceiling. She should go and look for McCall. She didn't like him out of her sight. But for some reason she couldn't bring herself to get up and go looking for trouble. And "trouble" had to be Christian McCall's middle name.

Instead, she turned onto her stomach and pulled the pillow over her head with a moan. Her body hummed with unfulfilled desire, a situation she'd never had to deal with before—and had no idea how to deal with now.

The pillow flew from her head. D.J. flipped over. "McCall, I—" The words froze on her lips at the sight of Josie hovering above the bed. The angel drew back her arm and launched the pillow at D.J.'s face. D.J. caught the missile before it connected with her nose. "Hey, what are you doing?"

"I can't believe you blew it again. Honestly, don't you know anything about romance? How could you bring up diseases in the middle of making love? Babies I can see. That's kind of romantic, though I must admit just the mention can turn some men off, though I doubt Christian's one of them."

Josie paused in her tirade to take a breath, and D.J. took the opportunity to break in. "You were watching?" She sat up, grabbing for the bedspread when the covering slid down her bare chest. She clutched the material up to her chin, in no mood to argue with an angel while buck naked. "Listening? Hell, Josie, I didn't know you were a voyeur."

"Watch your mouth, young lady."

"Don't call me 'young lady' in that tone of voice.

199

I'm older than you are." She sounded like a teenager, but she couldn't help it. The thought that Josie had been observing her private moments with McCall made her want to hit something—or someone.

"You might be older in years but not in brains." Josie sighed and floated down to sit on the foot of the bed. "Of course I wasn't watching you two. I'm your guardian. I just know these things. Don't ask me how. I just do."

Somewhat mollified, D.J. nodded. Then the angel's original statement returned to her mind. "You said I was blowing it. What am I blowing, Josie?"

"Your life, dear. I'm honestly starting to despair of ever teaching you a thing."

"Good. Despair away. It's been nice being haunted by you. Now go bug someone else."

Josie sighed and bit her lip. She looked heavenward, as if asking for patience, then returned her disgruntled gaze to D.J. "I'm not a ghost. I've explained what I am to you."

"You're dead and you're on earth. To me that spells G-H-O-S-T."

"I can spell as well as you can, dear. Try A-N-G-E-L. Ghosts are spirits of the dead. They haunt people and places, usually to right a wrong done to them during their life. They're caught between heaven and earth. I'm a guardian angel. I've been sent to a specific person. You. For a specific reason. I can't go anywhere until I teach you how to love."

"I can't love," D.J. shouted. "I don't believe in love. Maybe all I want is some nice, consenting adult sex. I keep hearing about it, and I want it. Why is everyone being so difficult? It's not like this is something new in the world. Everybody does it."

"You're mistaken. Not everybody does it. And not everybody should. Didn't you learn anything from your marriage?"

D.J., who had hung her head over the side of the bed as she tried to discover the whereabouts of her underwear in the semidarkness, went still at the mention of her marriage. She sat up with a jerk. The bed creaked in protest. She scowled at Josie. "What do you know about my marriage?"

"I know everything about you, dear. You married Richard Halloran because you were intent upon pleasing your father. Since Rich seemed unemotional you believed the two of you would make a good match. Rich acted cold, but he also had a whole lot of anger inside, just like you do. You can't be as emotionless as you pretend with all that fire bottled up inside."

D.J. held up her hand. "I don't want to rehash my marriage with you. It's over."

"The marriage might be over, but the scars you received from the experience are still there. You still have no idea what the difference is between having sex and making love."

"There is no difference. Making love is just a fancy name for sex. One I prefer to avoid."

"If you'd ever made love you'd realize how incredibly stupid you sound."

Angel flared within D.J. She was sick and tired of Josie pointing out all her failings—traits D.J. didn't consider to be so bad. Until this angel had showed up, she'd even felt pretty good about herself on occasion. Now, between Josie and McCall, D.J. didn't know what to think.

"If I'm so stupid, then why do you bother with me?" D.J. growled.

Josie reached over and patted D.J.'s feet through the thin bedspread. D.J. jerked her toes away from the angel's touch, not in the mood for comfort of any kind. Josie's eyes gave a flash of pain before she turned her face away to stare out the window. "You're not stupid, D.J., just misguided. I'm here to guide you."

"All right. Let me have it."

"What?" Josie jerked her head in D.J.'s direction to stare at her in surprise.

"You want to talk, I'll listen. Since ignoring you isn't making you go away, maybe hearing you out will do it."

The hope on Josie's face retreated when a reproving frown took its place. "I don't deserve your attitude. I'm trying to save you from an eternity of unhappiness. The least you could do is appreciate me."

D.J. swallowed, guilt flooding her. Josie was right; she was being a snot. But her body still clamored for McCall in a way that grated on her nerves. No man had ever had this effect on her. She wanted these unknown feelings to stop—but she didn't know how to make them obey her command. She'd tried to shut off her emotions, as she'd done all her life. But every time he touched her she couldn't think, she could only feel. Her lack of control frightened her. And when she was frightened she struck out with her cultivated "tough cop" attitude. The only problem with that attitude was, Josie didn't buy it.

"I'm sorry," D.J. said. "I'm sure you'd rather be in heaven than in an Outgamie hotel room with me. I suppose your loved ones are all there waiting for you, and I'm throwing a stick into the works."

"Not exactly," Josie said, and the sadness in her voice made D.J. curious.

"Well, what exactly? Tell me, Josie. What's heaven like?"

"I wouldn't know. I'm not allowed to go there until I'm done with you."

"You're kidding."

"No, I'm not."

"That sounds suspiciously like blackmail to me. It's not your fault I am the way I am. How can He withhold Heaven from you?"

"He can do anything He wants. That's why He's God." Josie brushed her palms together as though washing her hands of the topic. "Now enough about me. My life is over, and I'm not allowed to burden you with the details. Let's talk about you. Raphael pointed out that I've been going about this thing with you and Christian all wrong. Getting you two into bed isn't going to work."

"No kidding. He's more screwed up than I am."

"He has good reason."

D.J. glanced up sharply at Josie's words. Her eyes narrowed as she studied the angel's face. Josie knew something—and she wasn't sharing. "What? What do you know about him? Tell me."

"I can't. Christian's secrets are for Christian to share."

"You know them."

"Raphael works on a need-to-know basis. I needed to know. You, however, do not. Just suffice it to say, Christian needs you as much as you need him."

"I don't need anyone," D.J. interrupted.

Josie ignored her. "Falling into bed before you're in love will just make things worse for the both of you."

"I don't know if I agree with your reasoning, but I do know if I have to endure any more rejection, I just might swear off men for good." D.J. leaned her head back against the headboard. Her body had relaxed from its humming awareness while she spoke with Josie. She had even begun to enjoy herself. She had never had a sister, or a close girlfriend, or a mother to talk with. She'd always disparaged the idea of girl talk as an unnecessary waste of time for a woman who knew her own mind. It was easy to look down on something she'd never experienced. But after one hour of girl talk with Josie, D.J. could see its advantages. She felt a hell of a lot better than she had before. Though Josie could be a pain, D.J. liked her. She was at ease with the angel, as she'd never been with anyone else. Perhaps because no matter what she said, Josie wasn't leaving. Kind of like the unconditional love between parent and child that D.J. had read about in Psychology 101. That kind of assurance worked wonders on D.J.'s usual shyness in making friends. Josie appeared younger in years, but in her eyes and her voice lay a wisdom D.J. wished to explore further.

Josie's remark about not attaining heaven if she

didn't teach her charge to love made remorse flood D.J. She didn't like the feeling of responsibility Josie's comment gave her. How could she make Raphael understand they'd given an angel mission impossible?

"Josie? I hate to ruin your mission, but I truly don't believe I can love. I've never loved anyone; never wanted to."

Josie fixed her with a penetrating gaze. "What about your father?"

D.J. hesitated, then shrugged. What could telling Josie hurt? "You must know my mother's dead." At the angel's nod she continued. "My father—he—I—we—" D.J. rubbed her eyes, which ached in an odd, burning way. "We don't get along. We barely speak. The sight of me is so painful for him; I don't think he's looked directly at my face for . . . I don't know." She paused, thinking back, then glanced at Josie. The angel's face held no pity, only concern. "I can't remember him ever looking me straight in the eye."

"Why?" Josie whispered.

"I must look like her. My mother. That's the one reason I can think of, though I don't know for sure. I've never even seen a picture of her. He destroyed them all when she died. Gran said when my mother died my father died too."

Josie nodded. "I see. I must admit, your father's behavior baffles me. I might have behaved the same way if I'd been left on earth without the man I loved, but if I'd had a child to care for, I would have had a very good reason to go on living."

D.J. didn't want to talk about her father's problems. Ed was who he was, and there would be no changing him now. Now would be too late anyway. To direct the angel's attention away from any further questions about her father, D.J. asked about love—an angel's favorite topic—or at least her angel's. "How did it happen? Falling in love, I mean? So many people think they're in love, then in a blink of an eye they hate each other and it's over. So few find the kind of love you read about in fairy tales. The ones I've known who believe they've found a fairy-tale love end up agonizing forever over the loss of their one special person—either because of death or because said person didn't feel the same way about them. I couldn't stand to live the rest of my life in such pain. I watched my father live like that for too long." D.J. glanced at Josie just in time to see the angel wince. When Josie saw her looking she gave D.J. a brilliant smile that somehow didn't reach her eyes. Why did her father's neglect bother the angel so much? She began to ask, but the angel jumped into the silence and answered D.J.'s question, effectively cutting off any further queries.

"The reason so few people end up so happy is because they don't wait for the right one."

D.J.'s natural skepticism rose at Josie's confident statement. "You expect me to believe there's one right person for everyone?"

Josie shrugged. "There was for me. There is for you. Do you want to be happy or not?"

D.J. could see she would get nowhere arguing theory with the angel. Instead, she asked a question that had been foremost in her mind since Josie had crashed into her life with promises of happiness if she could only learn a simple lesson in love. "How do you know when you've found the right one?"

"You know. In your heart and your soul, you just know. There's no confusion, no question."

"Well, I'm confused and I have a lot of questions. So I guess I don't have to worry about love for a while, especially with McCall. Right now I need to keep him from getting his head blown off." D.J. sat up with a squeak of alarm. She stared at the doorway, her eyes widening in dismay. "McCall! He went outside." She jumped out of bed and got down on her knees, forgetting her nakedness as she searched under the bed for her underwear. "I told the captain I wouldn't let him out of my sight. What's wrong with me?" She located the item and hopped back and forth from foot to foot as she put the briefs on. "I'm supposed to be protecting him, and here I sit yapping with you. Where's my brain? If he gets killed, I'm gonna be out of a job."

"If he gets killed, you'll have a lot more problems than losing your job. Hold on." Josie raised her hand for silence. She tilted her head as though listening to a voice no one else could hear. "Yes, he is having some difficulty. Perhaps you should go out and give him a hand."

Fear thundered through D.J. in tempo with the accelerating beat of her heart. Why had she let him go outside on his own? McCall was her responsibility. What kind of cop was she?

She grabbed the closest items of clothing available, shoved her feet into her tennis shoes without socks, and snatched her service weapon from the dresser, snapping the clip into place as she raced out of the hotel room without a backward glance.

D.J. stopped short in the parking lot and stuffed her gun into the waistband at the back of her jeans before pulling her softball league jacket down over the bulge. She had no idea where he'd gone. Their car remained in the same place. Since she possessed the single set of keys, its presence there created no surprise.

"Where is he?" she asked.

No answer.

"Dammit, Josie, you can't tell me he needs help and then let me stand here wondering where he's gone while he's hurt or killed or both. Where is he?" The last words rose to a shout, echoing back to her from the asphalt and bouncing off the silent parked cars.

"Relax, dear. The way you're acting, you'd think you cared about him."

D.J. looked up but saw no sign of the angel. Lucky for Josie. D.J. heard the smile in her angel's voice, and if she had to see the expression right now, she just might detonate. "Just tell me where he is and then get lost."

"I'll be happy to, dear. He's at the top of the highway. Turn around. Over there, on the hill."

Turning, D.J. squinted into the fading darkness. She could just make out milling figures at the top of the indicated hill. Too many figures from her point of view. McCall was outnumbered and unarmed. D.J. began to run.

Though she was in good shape, fear made her breath come in harsh, fast gasps. She reached the base of the hill and glanced upward. Four figures, she saw now. Three against one. But not for long.

She took a deep breath, in through her nose and out through her mouth, to steady her racing heart. She couldn't just charge up the hill and burst onto the scene. If they saw her too soon, she'd end up with a hostage situation on her hands.

D.J. glanced around, searching for a way to approach the altercation without being seen. A strip mall lined one side of the highway, deserted in the dawn's early light. If she approached by way of the alley behind the stores, she would come out behind the men. D.J. ran, across the parking lot, around the corner of the building, and up the garbage can–strewn alleyway.

She reached her destination and peeked around the corner. Her hand went to the gun that had chafed a sore spot in the hollow of her back. Her fingers froze on the grip. D.J.'s mouth dropped open in shock as she absorbed the meaning of the scene before her.

Two of the men lay on the ground, unconscious. The third circled McCall. Though the sun still hovered below the horizon, it provided enough light to cast a grayish glint off the long, hooked hunting knife in the man's hand. She'd seen such knives at her father's hunting lodge, the blade specially curved to gut a dead deer with a flick and jerk of the wrist. The image made her cringe.

D.J. drew her weapon and stepped out from behind the building. The attacker glanced her way. The second his attention wandered, McCall's leg shot out. The knife flew through the air. The weapon hit the ground, its metallic clatter amplified by the tense silence. The man stared at his empty hand in surprise. He looked up just in time for McCall's fist to connect with his chin. He staggered backward, then shook his head once. Though wobbly from the blow, he stepped forward and swung. With a move so graceful as to be choreographed into a ballet, McCall ducked the man's outstretched arm. When he arose his right elbow caught the attacker's chin with a bone-cracking smack. The man fell to the pavement, as unconscious as his companions.

McCall stood for a moment over the fallen bodies. His back moved up and down while he labored for a full breath. He drew air into his lungs on a long, even inhale, then blew out a slow stream before turning to face D.J. His gaze rested once on her drawn gun, then flicked up to meet her eyes. His face remained as blank as the faces of the unconscious men littering the pavement.

"What the hell was that?" she asked.

"*Mawashi-geri.* Then *mawashi-zuki.* And to finish off, *kagi-zuki.*"

"In English, McCall. What have you done?"

"Roundhouse kick, roundhouse punch, followed by an elbow thrust." He put his heels together, arms straight at his sides, and bowed low in her direction before straightening to meet her gaze once more. "Karate," he said, putting a foreign twist to the word. He glanced down at the three bodies, and some of D.J.'s own shock was reflected upon his face. "It works." When he looked up at her again a delighted grin split his face. "Imagine that?"

Chapter Ten

Adrenaline bubbled in Chris's veins. All his years of preparation had been worth the effort. The three men on the pavement at his feet had intended to kill him. They hadn't told him why they sought his death, only that they meant to accomplish such an end.

When he'd first seen the three striding toward him through the darkness a shaft of panic had entered his chest and scrambled his thinking. Fear for D.J. overrode all his years of training. The reiteration of the fact, mumbled over and over under his breath, that they approached from the opposite direction of the hotel, had calmed Chris and enabled him to prepare for whatever might come. For the moment at least, D.J. remained safe.

Now she stood before him, shock upon her lovely

face and a gun in her hand. Chris walked forward and pried her fingers from the cold metal, clicking the safety into position before he handed the weapon back to her.

"You did this?" She inclined her head toward the three unconscious men.

Do you see anyone else around? The thought flitted through his mind, but one look at her stunned face made Chris bite back the sarcasm. Just because she couldn't seem to grasp the fact that he wasn't helpless shouldn't make him so angry.

"Yeah, I did it." He shrugged, the adrenaline fading and a seeping lethargy taking it's place. "I told you I had a black belt. Remember, at the day-care center?"

She turned wide green eyes on his face, and her brow creased as she thought back. "You said you were teaching safety and awareness. I thought you meant scream at the sight of strangers. Don't get in anyone's car. That kind of thing."

"Well, all of those, too. But a little karate helps."

"I'll say." Her gaze slid past him again to rest on the three men. She gasped. "The knife. Why the knife?"

"They weren't too talkative, but they did mention the need for silence and speed. I got the impression that they wanted to get rid of me, move on to you, and then get out of town before the sun came up."

"You mean this wasn't a robbery attempt?"

"They never asked for anything. They just came at me."

"Hell's bells," she muttered and tucked the gun into the waistband of her pants. She reached out

212

and grabbed his hand, tugging him along with her
as she started back toward the hotel. "I don't know
how they found us, but we've got to get out of here."

*Leave? With the answer to my questions lying at
our feet?*

Chris pulled his hand from hers and hung back.
"I don't think so, D.J."

She spun toward him, fury on her face, and
snatched at his hand again. When he refused to
move she let out a groan of irritation. "McCall,
those guys meant to kill you. That means whoever's
been trying to kill you knows where we are. Maybe
it's one of them, or maybe they were sent by that
person. Either way, I want to go back to the hotel
and get the locals over here to lock them up."

"Why not question them now? You've got a gun.
I bet we can make them tell us what we want to
know."

D.J. smacked her palm to her forehead. "Jeez,
McCall, why didn't I think of that? Let's rough 'em
up. They'll sing like canaries." She shook her head
in disgust. "You've been watching too many Bogey
movies. Did you ever hear of Miranda? The right to
a lawyer? The Fifth Amendment? You can bet those
guys have. They won't tell us one damn thing." She
swept her arm in a circle, indicating the stores
around them. "This might not look like much now,
McCall, but pretty soon this area will get a whole
lot busier. Do you want to explain to the concerned
citizens of Outgamie why we're questioning suspects in the middle of the highway? I certainly
don't. And, a final point for thought: This is not my
jurisdiction. I'm not taking any chances of violating

213

these creeps' civil rights or the statutes of this city. I want them behind bars so I don't have to continue living with *you* for the next decade." She turned and started down the road. When she sensed he wasn't following she stopped. "McCall," she shouted, her temper on the fringes of explosion, "let's go!"

He couldn't resist teasing her one more time. She liked to pretend she was always cool and unemotional, but he knew better. "Maybe I should stay and make sure they don't wake up and take off?"

"No way. No sir." Shaking her head, she walked back toward him until they stood toe to toe. Looking up into his face, her eyes snapped sparks. "You were lucky once, but I'm not leaving you out here to play Batman any more. You're coming with me. I don't want you out of my sight again until this is all settled." She glanced at the three men once more. "They look like they're out for the count. Now come on, McCall, or I'll use this gun on you."

"You're the professional," he said, and started down the hill.

She stood gaping at his sudden acquiescence but recovered her composure quickly and hurried to catch up with him. "Did they say anything to indicate why they wanted to kill you?" she asked, her shorter legs taking two steps to meet his one long stride.

Chris glanced at her. She had returned to her "tough cop" persona—cold voice, stiff manner, all business was D.J. He didn't have the heart to tell her she'd buttoned her blouse crooked, neglected to zip her jeans, and forgotten to put on any socks. He found the way her hair stuck straight up on one side and lay flat to her head on the other endearing—almost as endearing as the fact that she'd obviously run straight from her bed to rescue him.

"McCall." Impatience laced D.J.'s voice.

"Ah, no. They didn't tell me why, or if they'd been sent or were acting on their own." She opened her mouth to ask another question, but he kept speaking right over her attempt. "And no, I didn't recognize any of them. But they did know my name."

Her eyes narrowed in speculation. "Interesting. What, exactly, did they say to you?"

"They said, 'McCall, it's time to die.' Short, sweet, to the point."

"And then you kicked the crap out of them."

"Something like that."

"Hmm." She looked him up and down. He could tell by the tone of her voice that his ability had her impressed, albeit reluctantly. But he'd never hear D.J. Halloran praise him out loud. He'd heard all the good she had to say to him in one small "hmm."

They continued to walk down the deserted highway while D.J. thought out loud. "I'm sure no one followed us. I don't know how they could have. I only called Captain Miller, and since he's scared to death you'll get killed and screw him up with the mayor, I don't think he's a suspect." She shook her head, biting her lip in concentration. "I told him to have Lou call me. But he hasn't, though that was only a few hours ago. Lou would never hurt me. So he's not a suspect either. But someone I've trusted with too much information is." She ran her fingers distractedly through her short hair, making it stand up on end even worse than before. "I just can't understand how this happened. I can't think straight anymore. If I could think for a minute, there's something about this that smells all the way to heaven."

"Don't worry about it right now. I'm fine. You're fine. We've got the three guys. This will all be over in a few hours, and we can go back to Lakeview."

"Uh-huh," D.J. responded, though from the absent wave of her hand in his direction, Chris figured she hadn't heard a word he said.

They reached the hotel parking lot, and D.J. came out of her trance. "Catch, McCall."

He brought his hand up and caught the car keys she flipped toward him just before they sailed past his head.

"Not bad. Maybe you aren't so helpless after all. Bring the car up to the front. I'll throw our things into the suitcases, make a call, and be right out."

Without waiting for his reply, D.J. turned and disappeared into the hotel.

She no longer thought he was helpless. Was that good or bad?

Chris shook his head and laughed to himself. If D.J. only knew. Christian McCall had spent a lifetime making sure he would never feel helpless again. And it looked as though he'd been right to prepare himself.

Because someone with long reaching power wanted him dead—and he had no idea why.

"I told you he could take care of himself, dear."

Josie's voice came out of the air above D.J.'s head as she strode down the hotel hallway toward her room. D.J. didn't bother to glance up before she answered.

"You were right. But if you knew he could take care of himself, then why did you send me out there?"

"You're such a practical girl. I might say Christian could take care of himself, but I knew you'd never believe me until you saw him in action."

"Since you know so much, why don't you let me in on who's trying to kill him and why? It would save us all a lot of trouble."

"I'm afraid I can't, dear. As I told you before, Raphael tells me things on a need-to-know basis."

"Well, I think the identity of a killer falls in the category of things we need to know."

"What you think and what is the truth are two very different things. I can warn you of imminent danger to yourself, but I often don't know of such danger until the second before it happens."

"What about danger to McCall? You warned me he was in trouble."

"I'll only have a premonition if danger to him will represent a danger to you."

D.J. paused at her door and drew the keycard from her pocket. "What was the danger to me tonight?"

"If Christian hadn't disabled those men, if they'd hurt or killed him as they'd planned to, their next stop was this hotel room to take care of you."

"Me?" D.J. paused in the act of putting the keycard into the lock. This time she did glance upward toward the sound of Josie's voice, though Josie was nowhere to be seen. Now that the angel mentioned

217

it, McCall had brought up the same point, but she'd been too preoccupied at the time to pick up on the information. "Why me?"

"I don't know. We need to find out."

"Great. This sounds like just my luck. My life's in danger but my guardian angel can't tell me who wants to kill me. No, sir. Because the archangel imparts such information on a need-to-know basis." D.J. put the keycard into the lock. The door inched inward at her touch. "Dammit, Josie, you don't even use the door. Why is this open?"

"Get down!" the angel shouted.

Years of training made D.J. hit the floor a second before the door exploded outward. Without thinking, she reached for the gun at the small of her back, yanked the weapon free of her waistband, and rolled to the side of the doorway. A quick glance showed a hole the size of a fist in the middle of the door—right where her chest had been just seconds before.

"Son of a . . ." A movement at the end of the hallway caught D.J.'s attention. The hotel clerk peeked around the corner. "Call the police," she shouted. He disappeared. D.J. hoped he meant to comply with her request and not hide under his desk. She glanced up and down the hall, then breathed a relieved sigh. So far, no one had opened his door and peeked into the hall, saving her the trouble of ordering them back into their rooms. Either the hotel was empty, or the guests had the good sense to stay inside at the sound of gunfire.

The angel materialized in front of the door, leaning down to peak through the hole. "Get back," D.J. hissed. "Are you nuts?"

"I hardly think I'm in any danger, dear, since I'm already dead." The angel continued to squint through the hole.

"Who's in there?"

"I can't see anyone, though the room is a mess." She tensed and took a step closer to the door. "Oh, there, someone just moved toward the window. Too dark to see who it is." She turned her head to look at D.J. "What are we going to do now?"

"I don't suppose you want to go in and bonk the guy on the head to avoid danger to my person?"

Josie tilted her head to the side, as though considering the question. "I'd like to, dear. But I'm afraid my options on earth are somewhat limited. Imminent danger is one of the requirements for that type of help."

"Figures," D.J. muttered. "Well, in that case, I guess I'd better sit tight until the cavalry arrives. The guy's cornered."

"D.J.?" McCall's voice came from the end of the hallway. She jerked her head in his direction. He stood, silhouetted at the end of the hall. As she glanced his way, he began to walk toward her. Panic filled her chest, closing off her air. She shook her head and waved for him to go back the way he'd come.

"I heard a weird noise in here. Kind of like a gunshot. Is everything all right?" He continued to advance, despite her frantic waving.

"You'd better do something, dear."

"Back off," D.J. snapped to both the angel and

McCall. To her joy, they both listened. Josie disappeared and McCall stopped short. Unfortunately, he didn't shut up.

"You said we had to get going. Now here you are sitting in the hallway. What's the matter? Are you sick?"

The intruder in their rooms had to have heard them talking. D.J. put her finger to her lips and McCall stopped yapping. In the ensuing silence, the latch clicked on the door to McCall's room. D.J. turned toward the sound, coming up on her knees and putting the gun out in front of her in a straight-arm stance.

"Police," she shouted. "Throw out your weapon and show me your hands."

In answer to her command the door slammed shut. D.J. got to her feet and leaned back against the wall. She felt more in control on her feet than on her knees, but she still had no idea what to do. She and McCall were in the hall. Someone with a very big gun, who wanted to kill them, inhabited their rooms, and the police were nowhere in sight.

"What's going on?" McCall's voice right next to her ear made D.J. yelp in fright.

She turned her head to glare at him. "Don't do that. Why didn't you stay out of the way?" She glanced at the door with the hole in it. "Jeez, McCall, you walked right through the line of fire. Are you a total idiot?"

"I didn't think so until you started telling me I was every other minute."

The sound of breaking glass shattered any attempt at conversation, and D.J. shoved McCall aside. "Stay away from the door," she ordered as she pushed open the door to her room. When no bullets answered the action D.J. took a deep breath and dove inside.

The large window overlooking the parking lot sported a gaping hole. As far as D.J. could tell, the room now stood empty. She got up and sprinted to the ruined window, then peeked outside. The sun limped over the horizon, gracing the parking lot with enough light to reveal its emptiness.

"Stay here," she shouted to McCall and vaulted through the broken window. Just as she landed on the ground, a black van screeched into the parking lot. "Hell's bells," she muttered, searching for a place to hide. The Explorer parked at the front entrance was the only cover available, and the car sat too far away to reach before the van came upon her.

I won't go down without a fight, she thought, and planted her feet astride. She brought the gun up, arms straight out in front of her, and fired ten shots in rapid succession at the approaching van.

The driver fired back, but he couldn't shoot and avoid her fire at the same time. D.J. heard four shots from the van's driver before he began to zigzag through the lot in an attempt to avoid her more accurate fire. One shot shattered the back window, three others made neat holes in a side door, and the rest didn't find their mark. The van fishtailed out of the parking lot and accelerated up the street. Frustrated, D.J. fired her remaining six shots at the rear of the van, even though the vehicle had moved out of range.

A thunk next to her foot made D.J. jump into the

air like a frightened cat. The catch of fear in her indrawn breath produced a hitch in her side, but she bit down on her lip and ignored the small pain. She swung her empty gun toward the sound and encountered a lethal-looking suitcase. Another landed next to the first with an identical thunk. When she relaxed another twinge of pain, this time from her shoulder, made D.J. wince. She rolled her neck against the tension and turned toward the window. McCall climbed out, laptop computer case slung over his shoulder.

"What do you think you're doing?" she demanded.

"I'm gonna toss this stuff in the car so we can get out of here." He grabbed the two suitcases and did as he'd said.

"Where do you think we're going? The locals should be here any minute. We'll have questions to answer."

"If they were coming, they'd have been here already. We don't have time to decipher the delay." He stood at the passenger door and nodded in the direction of the highway they'd walked on earlier.

Three figures approached at a run. As they watched, the black van stopped to pick up the men. Then the vehicle turned around and headed back toward the hotel like a metal tarantula on the prowl.

"Shit," D.J. swore and headed for the truck. She yanked a full clip from the pocket of her jacket and reloaded the 9 mm as she ran. "Those guys are starting to bug me."

She jumped behind the wheel. Before McCall had

his seat belt buckled she sped toward the freeway. A glance in the rear-view mirror revealed the black van in pursuit. Traffic on the service road had picked up with the advent of daybreak. D.J. ignored traffic signs and speed limits in her attempt to get onto the freeway and away from their pursuers. She zigged into the right-hand lane, then zagged back into the left. The van followed her every move. Horns blared in protest of their tactics. D.J. bit her lip and pushed the accelerator lower. "If I can just get onto the back roads, I'll be able to lose them in no time."

McCall threw a glance back over his shoulder. "Are you sure? They seem to have as little regard for traffic laws as you do."

"Don't whine, McCall. They'll kill you for sure. With me you've got a fighting chance." She reached the entrance ramp to the freeway. The road in front of them lay clear, so she pushed the accelerator to the floor. The speedometer jumped to ninety-five. Once merged into the sporadic traffic, D.J. continued her in-and-out method of driving with the black van not far behind.

"At least they're not shooting at us," she said.

"Wouldn't shooting be dangerous in all this traffic?"

"I don't think they care."

As if in answer to her observation, the back window of the Explorer exploded inward in a hail of glass.

"Get down!" D.J. shouted and shoved McCall's head into her lap. "Stay down." She squinted into the rear-view mirror. One of the men hung out of

223

the van's passenger window. He tried to sight on their truck through the scope of a hunting rifle. But the movement of the van didn't allow him a clear shot. The gunfire had caused most of the traffic around and ahead of them to pull over or fall back. A pickup right in front of them slowed, the driver craning his neck in a frantic attempt to see where the shots hailed from. D.J. jerked the wheel to the left to avoid a collision. Another blast of gunfire made her duck in reflex. The rear tire of the pickup popped, and the truck skidded off the road, coming to a stop in the ditch.

"Sorry," she muttered, jerking the Explorer back into the right lane. D.J.'s arm yelped in pain at the movement, and sweat tickled a trail between her breasts. Too bad she didn't have time to take off her jacket. What had been a necessity for warmth during her trip out into the night searching for McCall had become a liability with the advent of day. D.J. removed her hand from the wheel long enough to swipe at her brow.

Odd; her skin felt cold. How could that be when her forehead dripped with sweat?

"What's happening?"

D.J. shifted against the awkward weight of McCall's head in her lap. When he moved as if to sit up she shoved him back, none too gently.

"They're shooting at us, idiot. I'm almost to the lake. On the other side I'll exit and lose them. I don't need to worry about you getting your head blown off as well as my own. Just stay the hell down."

The warning in her voice must have reached him because he subsided without argument, remaining half in his seat and half in hers. Though the weight of his head made her legs cramp uncomfortably, his solid presence comforted D.J. in some indefinable way.

A glance behind revealed the black van inching up on their left. D.J.'s lips curved into a smile. She had them now. Spying her exit, D.J. pushed down on the accelerator once more.

"I thought we were getting off. Why are you speeding up?"

"Mind your own business, which is keeping your head down and your mouth shut, and let me handle this."

As she'd hoped, the van also increased its speed, moving up on her left. The man who had shot at them before again leaned out the passenger window, rifle in tow. D.J. eased off the gas a fraction to allow the van to creep forward until the vehicle rode even with the Explorer's rear bumper.

The exit loomed to the right. The rifle holder to the left took aim at the back of her head. D.J. waited until the last possible second, then yanked the wheel to the right. The window directly behind the driver's seat erupted inward, and glass rained across the back seat. The rental company wasn't going to like this.

McCall started at the explosion, the back of his head bumping against her pelvic bone. D.J. hissed in pain.

"Stay," she ordered, and he did.

The Explorer bounced over the grassy median and roared down the exit ramp. The black van continued straight on the highway.

Lori Handeland

D.J. didn't look to see if the driver hit the brakes and turned to come after them. She punched the gas, leaned into the turn, and shoved McCall off her lap.

He sat up, moved over, then turned and frowned at the empty hole where a window had once been. "A little close, don't you think?"

"In guns, close is dead or injured. We're both fine, so I wouldn't say it was close."

"Oh, well, that's a relief. You had me worried."

She ignored his sarcasm and kept driving.

"Where are we going?"

D.J. sighed. She'd hoped to avoid it, but they had nowhere else to run now. In the back of her mind she must have been planning to go there all along if things got too bad. Otherwise why had she driven north in the first place? She had sworn never to set foot in her father's hunting lodge again, but now she had little choice. At least he wouldn't be there to ruin the peace and beauty of the place, as he'd done on every occasion they'd spent there together in the past.

"We're going to . . ." D.J. began, then stopped and frowned.

Her voice sounded funny. Like a tape player with a waning battery—slow, slower, slowest.

"What's that?" McCall's voice sounded the same as hers, as though he were speaking from the midst of a thick, syrupy fog. She glanced at him. He wavered before her eyes. She blinked and turned back to the road. The yellow line slithered like a snake, and she jerked the wheel in an attempt to follow the shifting path of the asphalt.

"Hey, D.J., stop the car!" McCall's voice drifted to her through a long tunnel. But she still had enough sense to move her foot from the accelerator to the brake. Her leg weighed a ton, and when she planted her boot on the brake pedal the car jerked and bucked.

"D.J.!" McCall shouted her name. When she looked at him he pointed to her blouse. His mouth moved. "What happened?" But no sound came out. She looked down and her eyes widened.

Blood.

The entire front of her blouse bled red. Sweat hadn't been trickling between her breasts. The tickle of liquid had been a river of blood.

D.J. looked at McCall once more, but he wasn't looking at her. Instead, he grabbed the wheel from her slack hands and twisted it to the right. They slid to a stop on the gravel lining the side of the road.

The world spun faster and faster, until her stomach rebelled at the speed. Somehow McCall had gotten her to lay her head in his lap as he'd laid his in hers. Had that been moments or hours ago? She stared at his concerned face and watched the blackness close in on her from every corner. Just before the dark curtain met and obliterated the world from her consciousness, D.J. motioned McCall nearer.

"Isadora," she whispered. "Take me to Isadora."

Chapter Eleven

"Isadora?" Chris stared at D.J.'s still, white face. "Who's Isadora?"

She didn't answer, just continued to lay in his lap, too quiet for his comfort. He'd give anything to have her swear at him, call him an idiot, a moron, or even helpless. The patch of blood on her powder-blue blouse glistened in the sun shining through the front window of the truck. Fear lay at the back of his throat, and Chris swallowed against a rush of panic. D.J. needed him now and he wouldn't fail her.

With extreme care Chris lifted her and removed her jacket. Once the coat was out of the way, he could see the bullet hole in her blouse. He held the jacket up, but couldn't see a bullet hole. She must have been shot back at the hotel when the van careened through the parking lot, spraying bullets in her direction. While she'd returned the fire, her jacket had moved aside enough not to be hit by the bullet that pierced her shoulder just below the collarbone.

Chris yanked the shirt open, splaying buttons onto the floor of the truck. A small, ugly hole marred the smooth skin of her left shoulder directly below the collarbone, matching the location of the bullethole in her blouse. Her skin was covered in blood, but for now it looked as though the bleeding had stopped.

Chris turned D.J. so he could look at her back. Smooth, silky skin. The bullet had not gone through. That could mean trouble.

The sound of a car coming down the road toward them made Chris tense and grab for D.J.'s .9mm, which had fallen behind her on the seat. The car continued past without slowing, and he breathed a sigh heavy with relief before putting down the gun. The incident reminded him that they had more problems than D.J.'s injury. The black van would be after them again soon.

With as much speed and care as he was capable of in the situation, Chris moved D.J. to the passenger seat and got behind the wheel of the Explorer. He had to avoid their pursuers, find a town, and then a hospital. Perhaps he should return to Outgamie; there had to be a hospital there. But did he dare risk returning to the freeway and running into the men who wanted them dead?

D.J. moaned, and Chris turned toward her. "D.J.?"

"Huh?" She tried to sit up, then drew in her breath on a hiss of pain and lay back against the door. "Wh-where are we?"

"I don't know. You're shot. I'm going to take you to a hospital."

"No. No hospital. Too easy to trace us there." She put her hand to her forehead and pressed, as though she was trying to draw her thoughts forth. "Isadora. Go to Isadora. Stay on this road. About ten miles—turn left. Then right on Going Road. There's a doctor. A friend. He'll help us."

"Isadora is a doctor?"

But D.J. had passed out again, and Chris's question went unanswered. He didn't like the growing paleness of D.J.'s face. A fresh wet patch on her blouse told him her movements had caused the gunshot wound to bleed again. Chris gritted his teeth and tightened his fingers on the wheel to keep from gathering her into his arms. He had no time for that now. He had to drive.

Chris put the car into gear and sped down the two-lane highway. The colors of autumn hummed in the trees lining the road—red, yellow, orange. He'd always loved this time of year. The air smelled crisp and fresh, and the sky shone blue and white. He never felt more alive than during a Wisconsin autumn. But right now the life of nature contrasted with the terrible fear of death lodged in his chest, and Chris ignored what he would usually relish.

He had to get to Isadora, or he might lose D.J. Chris drove down the highway, his panic increasing with every mile that rolled beneath their wheels with no sign of civilization. He could keep driving for hours and never find what he sought. What if he'd misunderstood D.J.'s ramblings and taken the wrong road? He could be driving them into the middle of nowhere. If D.J. didn't die from her wound, they'd both die once the members of the black van club caught up with them.

Chris smacked his fist against the dashboard in frustration. "Where the hell is Isadora?" he shouted. Then, more quietly, almost a prayer, he whispered, "Where is Isadora? Please, get us there."

The Explorer rounded a curve; a sign flashed by the car.

Isadora—5 miles.

His racing brain took a moment to register the meaning of the sign. Then Chris sagged in relief. Isadora was a town—a town just five miles up the road. In Isadora lived a doctor.

He wouldn't lose her. Not yet, anyway.

The knowledge calmed Chris enough to allow the near mind-numbing panic to abate. He saw D.J.'s point now: Emotions could get in the way of performance. He'd been so scared for a moment there, he hadn't been able to see straight, let alone think clearly.

Their car crested a hill and sped down the other side into the midst of small-town America. Post office, general store, café, bank.

"Where's the doctor's office?" he muttered, easing off the gas and applying the brakes.

The locals on the street stopped to stare at the shot-up condition of the car. Chris ignored them, his gaze searching for a doctor's shingle.

"Liquor, gas, Isadora *Daily News*," he read. "Maggie's Café, Isadora Bank and Trust. Come on, come on. Where's the doctor?"

When he reached the end of main street with no sign of a doctor's office Chris stopped the truck and rolled down the window. Several men of retirement age or older stood in front of Jerry's Hardware Store, staring and pointing at the shattered windows of the Explorer.

"Where's the doctor's office?" Chris shouted.

"Doc Franklin?" asked one of them—an ancient, grizzled string bean of a man with a smoke-roughened voice and skin resembling high-priced alligator shoes.

"Whoever. I need a doctor. It's an emergency."

The man pointed a long cigarette-stained finger up the road. "Down there, maybe half a mile. Doc Franklin has an office at the back of his house. Can't miss it, son. Big sign out front says, 'Doctor Franklin.'"

"Thanks." Chris tore out of town in a spray of dust. Just as the man said, a half mile away stood a large wood sign with hand-painted lettering announcing the doctor's office.

Chris turned into a long gravel-coated driveway. The Explorer fishtailed, then righted itself, spewing stones and dust every which way. He came to a screeching stop at the front of the house and glanced at D.J. She had slid downward on the door until her head rested against the armrest.

"D.J.?" he called, hoping she would open her eyes and alleviate some of his fears.

She didn't move. The only indication that she still

lived lay in the slight but steady rise and fall of her chest.

Chris jumped out of the car and ran around to the passenger side. He eased open the door and caught her head before it lolled off the seat. When he lifted her into his arms her head hung over his arm, frighteningly lifeless.

He turned, and as he raced up the steps of the log cabin the door opened. A young man, with hair as red as D.J.'s and eyes as blue as the sky in winter, stepped onto the porch. He looked to be in his late teens or early twenties and wore the costume of the north—jeans, flannel shirt, and huge high-topped boots. The welcoming smile on his lips froze at the sight of Chris with D.J. in his arms.

"D.J.," he breathed, staring at her still face in horror.

"She's been shot," Chris said.

The young man's gaze flicked to Chris, then back to D.J. He motioned toward the door. "In here," he said, leading the way through the house to a medical office in the rear. "Put her on the table."

Chris complied, then stepped back, waiting for the young man to call the doctor. To his surprise, the kid pulled on plastic gloves, grabbed a stethoscope from the counter, and approached D.J. himself.

Chris stepped in the way. "She needs the doctor. Right now."

The young man glanced up at Chris and frowned. "I realize that. If you'll just get out of my way, the doctor will help her."

"You?"

"Yes, me. You must want to help her if you brought her to me, so get out of my way and stay out of my way. If you're squeamish, go far away, because if the bullet's still inside, I'm going to have to get it out of her shoulder before she bleeds to death."

Chris hesitated. He hated turning D.J. over to anyone, but she needed a kind of help he couldn't give. He moved aside reluctantly. "I looked for an exit wound on her back, but there wasn't one."

"Damn," the doctor muttered as he shouldered past him to lean over the table, blocking Chris's view of D.J.'s face. He could still see the rest of her, blue blouse caked with blood, pale skin stained by rivulets of rusty red. For some reason the sight made Chris sick, though he'd never been bothered by blood before. Perhaps he was having a reaction to all that had happened to them that day—and the clock didn't even read 9 A.M. Or perhaps he was just disgusted with himself. D.J. had been hurt while trying to protect him. She could have been killed, and he'd need to look no further than the mirror for someone to blame. He should never have allowed her to stay with him once he knew of the danger to their lives. But he'd been so certain he could protect her.

Look where your conceit got D.J., smart guy. Flat on her back and bleeding in a backwoods doctor's office.

"She's lost a lot of blood, but I think she'll be all right as soon as I get the bullet out and stitch her up." The doctor turned toward him. He frowned and tilted his head to study Chris. "You don't look so good yourself, buddy."

"I'm fine. Just take care of her."

"I will. I'm going to give her some Demerol."

"No anesthetic?"

"I don't keep it here. If someone's that bad, I have to transport them to the hospital. Anyway, with the blood loss it wouldn't be a good idea to completely anesthetize her. The Demerol will put her out long enough for me to dig around in her shoulder. Thank God she's already unconscious or I'd have a fight on my hands. She hates needles." The doctor nodded at the door leading back to the main house. "Maybe you should go out there. I don't need you passing out and getting a concussion when you hit the floor."

"No thanks; I already have one of those." Chris glanced back at D.J. The sight of her lying so quiet and pale made him wince. He couldn't stand to see her this way. D.J., so full of life, try as she might to deny it, had almost lost her life because of him. Chris looked at the doctor and found the young man studying his face with interest. Cowardly though his actions were, Chris took the doctor's advice and, after one final look in D.J.'s direction, left the room.

D.J. heard male voices in the distance. She knew both those voices, and they soothed her. She had nothing to fear from either of these men. They would take care of her.

A slight prick in her arm made D.J. struggle toward wakefulness. But the effort became too great, and instead she fell back into the soft, fluffy darkness.

In the darkness, Josie hovered.

"Am I dead?" D.J. asked. She lay on a metal table in the midst of a peaceful stillness.

Josie's bare feet swung above her, back and forth, back and forth. The angel looked down and smiled. "No, dear. What kind of guardian angel would I be if I allowed you to get killed?"

"Unless I miss my guess, I've been shot. Aren't you getting a little lax in the protection department, Josie?"

"No. I told you, I'm informed of imminent danger to your life, nothing else. Remember, I warned you to duck at the hotel. That shot would have killed you. This injury isn't life-threatening, and it's brought you and Christian closer together."

"How do you figure?"

"Well, right now he's agonizing over your being hurt. Pretty soon he'll start to think about what his life would be like without you in it. Then it's a short step to wanting you to be in his life forever."

"Oh, please, I'm gonna throw up. Forever? Nothing lasts forever—except maybe Twinkies. For sure not relationships."

Josie sighed. "You're being difficult again. I thought we'd made progress last night. Why can't you at least try to see my point of view?"

"Why should I? I didn't ask for your help. Just because you're a sap doesn't mean I have to be one. I'm not going to ruin my life and McCall's by believing in something that doesn't exist. What's between him and me is lust, pure and simple."

"How would you know about lust? Have you ever felt lust before? Maybe it's love and you're just calling it lust. Did you ever think of that?"

"No. Because I don't believe in love. Therefore, what I feel for McCall is lust. But he doesn't find me attractive enough to have sex with, so the itch isn't getting scratched. That only makes the need worse. For me, anyway."

"You are so frustrating. I thought we'd cleared up your misconceptions about sex and love last night." Josie bit her lip and closed her eyes. "What can I do to make you understand what you're missing?"

D.J. was frightened—a new emotion for her, though she seemed to be experiencing it quite a bit lately. She didn't like it. Besides the fear, she ached. She was dizzy. She didn't want to talk. "There's nothing you can say," she snapped. "So go away."

Josie opened her eyes and squinted at D.J. "Do you really want me to?"

D.J. opened her mouth to say "yes," but something stopped her. In truth, she'd started to enjoy Josie's hovering habits. And the angel had saved her life on two occasions. D.J. could see where having a guardian angel paid off, especially on this assignment. But all Josie's talk about love and forever was driving her nuts. Unfortunately, since teaching D.J. to love was Josie's mission, D.J. didn't think she'd be able to get the angel to shut up on that score.

"All right," D.J. admitted. "You have been kind of useful so far. It'd be nice if you stuck around until I figured out who's after McCall. But you've got to stop this matchmaking. Even if I did plan to go against everything I believe in, I wouldn't choose McCall to fall in love with."

"You see?" Josie clapped her hands, then pointed one finger at D.J. "That's part of your problem right there."

D.J. frowned at the angel. "What problem?"

"You don't choose who you fall in love with. Love chooses you."

A new concept, which D.J. hadn't considered before. "How so?"

"Have you ever heard of love at first sight?"

"Oh, please." D.J. rolled her eyes. "Yeah, I've heard of it. In movies, books, and songs. No one with half a brain believes love at first sight exists."

"Oh, really? I have a whole brain, Miss Smart Mouth. And I fell in love at first sight. If two people are open to the experience, they feel the connection the first time they set eyes on each other. Others may find their one true love, but it takes longer to realize the truth of the relationship if they aren't open to understanding such a truth."

"I don't think I'm open to any of this. I never will be."

"Yes, you will. Stop drowning your feelings in sarcasm."

"I have no feelings."

"You're wrong. Remember your dream? The one about Christian and the children?"

D.J. lay very still on the table as icy cold awareness flooded her. She'd known from the outset that something had been strange about her dream. "You did that?"

"Of course. I wanted to replace your nightmare

with happiness. And you felt it, didn't you? The joy, the love, the promise of the life that could be yours if you'd let yourself believe."

Josie had hit too close to the truth, and D.J. was scared. And when she was scared sarcasm soon followed. She tried to sit up on the table but found she couldn't. In this world, a place half dream and half reality, she might have control of her mouth, but control of her body rested elsewhere. She settled for using her mouth to the best of her ability. "Who do you think you are, messing with my mind?" D.J. shouted. "Just stay out of my head."

The angel merely blinked and stared at her. "Why would I want to do such a thing, dear? It's your head that's messed up. The rest of you would work just fine if you'd only quit listening to your brain and start listening to your heart."

Fury, hot and blinding, shot thorough D.J. She opened her mouth to retort, but found she could no longer speak. The fear returned.

"That's all right," Josie soothed. "You don't need to be afraid. I'm right here, and Christian's on the other side, waiting for you. The drug is wearing off now. We'll talk when you feel better. I need to go have a few words with Raphael. But in the meantime, I want you to feel something. Remember the feeling, D.J. You could experience this every day of your life."

As the soft, fluffy blackness closed in around D.J. once more, the angel floated down until she hovered right above the table upon which D.J. lay. Reaching out an elegant, pink-tipped finger, Josie traced a path across D.J.'s forehead.

Lori Handeland

"If love doesn't exist, then explain this."

A rush of emotion hit D.J. with the force of an ocean's wave. Pleasure-pain. Icy-heat. A thick, spreading force through her stomach and chest. Joy exploded in her mind, and she caught a glimpse of heaven as her angel's voice came to her once more, then faded into a void.

"And it only gets better when you give it away."

Total silence surrounded D.J. The void was her and she was the void. Then, out of the nothingness, came a sound. She went toward the noise. It became louder and louder until it filled the silence all around her.

A moaning, like an animal in agony, reached D.J.'s ears. Her eyelids were too heavy to lift, and for some reason tears streaked down her cheeks, wetting her neck in an irritating flood.

The sound came again, and she was shocked to discover the pained voice to be her own.

Agony sifted through her shoulder when she attempted to move. Reality burst upon her as she recalled where she'd been before unconsciousness had taken over her world.

"Where?" Her voice still sounded like a feral cry, but at least the word made sense.

"D.J., relax. You'll be all right now. The bullet's out."

She recognized the voice. But the owner's identity lay somewhere in the foggy recesses of her mind. She could trust the owner of the voice—that much she knew—and she relaxed, as he'd ordered. Just before the darkness took her away once more, a name surfaced.

"Christian?" she whispered, and the sound of his name in her hoarse, pained voice followed her into the now silent void.

"Is your name Christian?"

Chris looked up from a studied perusal of his fingernails and met the gaze of the young doctor. Hours had passed, or perhaps centuries, while he waited for news of D.J. He'd cleaned her blood from his hands, though reddish-brown stains still marred his shirt and jeans. He'd left his clothes alone; bloodstains were the least of his worries. He sat up straighter, hope filling him at the lightness in the doctor's eyes. "Yes, that's me."

"She asked for you."

He started to get to his feet, but the man waved him back onto the couch.

"She's sleeping now. You can see her in a minute. I just thought you might want to know, she asked for you before she went under again."

Chris clamped down on the happiness that flooded through him at the doctor's words. She'd probably wanted to know where he was so she could belt him.

"She'll be all right?"

"Yeah. Penetrating wound. You were right; the bullet didn't go through. I got it out—nothing major nicked, as far as I can tell. She should sleep until she wants to wake up. She'll be sore and, knowing D.J., cranky as hell. But she'll live." The doctor crossed the room and sat in the chair, facing Chris.

"You know her well then, Doctor—a—" Chris strove to remember what the sign out front had said

241

this young man's name was.

"Franklin. But you can call me Dan. Any friend of D.J.'s . . . Well, you know the saying. And your Christian."

"McCall. Call me Chris."

"Christian McCall? The children's writer?"

Chris glanced up in surprise. Only a rare adult recognized him by name.

Dan nodded at the miniature table and chairs in the small waiting room outside his office. Chris's latest work to hit the stands, a book about rodeos, sat on the top of a stack of books. "A lot of my patients are children. Your books help to take their minds off the imminent doctor's visit."

"I'm glad."

"In answer to your question, D.J. and I have been friends since we were kids." He pointed at his burnt orange hair. "Carrot tops have to stick together. But don't let D.J. know I said that; she insists her hair is russet." Franklin's wrinkled nose showed what he thought of D.J.'s assessment of her hair color.

Chris ignored the doctor's final words, zeroing in on his first sentence. "Friends?" He turned the word over in his mouth and found he didn't care for the thought of D.J. and this pleasant-faced, talented young doctor being friends. "I didn't think she had much time for friends."

"She doesn't. But we've known each other too long to let time, distance, or anything elsc stop us. We grew up together."

"Playing doctor?"

Dan laughed, a deep, rich sound that appealed to Chris despite his irrational irritation with the man.

"At times." Dan narrowed his eyes and focused a speculative look on Chris. "I take it you don't approve."

"I have no right to approve or disapprove of anything in D.J.'s life."

"Uh-huh. Right. Tell me, has she let you in on her real name?"

Chris frowned. "What does her name have to do with anything?"

"Has she?" Dan persisted.

"No way."

The look of interest on Dan's face faded to disappointment. "I see."

"What do you see? What is her name?"

"I wouldn't know. I've been closer to her than anyone in her life, as far as I know. She has no kind of relationship with her father. A crying shame, considering she's been without a mother, too. But she never told me her real name either. I always imagined if D.J. ever let down her guard enough with someone to reveal such a secret, that cold heart of hers might thaw a bit."

"She was married. Didn't she have to put her real name on the marriage license?"

"She had her name legally changed to D.J. a long time ago, when she was still a kid. I never understood why her father let her get away with it. But I can't say I've ever understood Ed. He liked her husband, too. And a sorrier S.O.B. I've not run into in years."

"The plot thickens," Chris muttered.

"You don't know the half of it. But we'll get to the good stuff later. For right now, maybe you'd like to tell me how you two turned up here with D.J. in that condition."

"It's a long story."

Dan leaned back against the chair and folded his arms across his chest. "I've got nothing but time."

The phone shrilled a disagreement to his statement, and Franklin expelled a sigh of irritation before unfolding himself from the chair to answer it.

"Doc Franklin here." Chris's mouth twitched at the old-sounding name applied to such a young-looking man. Dan listened to the caller, then his gaze flicked to Chris. The expression in Franklin's eyes made Chris's half smile fade. "Yeah, I hear you. I'll take care of it." Dan hung up. "Does a black van with four men inside mean anything to you?"

Chris came to his feet in an instant. "Where?"

"In town. They've been asking questions. The old-timer who sent you up here thought I should know."

"We've got to get out of here." Chris headed toward the closed door to the office. Dan's hand on his arm stopped him.

"The folks in town sent them off onto the back roads. They'll be driving for hours before they realize they're lost. The townsfolk would never let any harm come to D.J. if they could help it. Her father was born here. So was she. We protect our own."

"Those men—they won't give up. Sooner or later they'll be back. I've got to take her somewhere they can't find us, at least until she's well enough to go even farther." Chris pushed a hand through his hair in agitation. He felt as helpless as D.J. insisted he was. He had no idea where to go, no certain idea where they were. But he did know he had to keep D.J. safe. More so now than ever before. He'd misjudged the danger, and D.J. had paid for his mistake. He wouldn't fail her again.

"I'm sure she meant to go to the cabin," Dan said. "They'll never find you there."

"What cabin?"

Dan's eyes widened in surprise. "She didn't tell you?"

"We didn't have much time. She told me to go to Isadora; then she passed out."

"Her father has a hunting lodge. Very remote. Unless you know where to look, you'd never find it.

"Great. How am I going to get us there?"

"I'll take you."

Chris shook his head. "Thanks, but we can't be left anywhere without a means of escape. It's too dangerous."

"There's a pickup at the cabin. Ed uses it when he's up here. We'll hide your car in my shed. With all the bullet holes and smashed glass, I don't think we'd better let it sit outside too long. Kind of conspicuous."

Chris didn't like involving anyone else in his problems, but he had little choice. With D.J. unconscious, they were adrift in the north woods. "All right. I guess I don't have many choices right now. I'll drive the car around back."

"No, give me the keys. I'll take care of it. Even though those guys left by the other side of town, I'd rather you stayed out of sight until we get you both to the cabin."

Chris dug the keys out of his pocket and handed

245

them to Dan. "I appreciate your help."

Franklin took the keys from Chris's outstretched palm and then stared directly into his eyes. "I'd do anything for D.J. She's had a tough life. I won't stand for her being hurt anymore." Though the words had been said without malice, the warning remained clear.

Chris nodded an acknowledgment. "Neither will I."

The doctor peered at him for a second more; then, obviously deciding Chris meant what he said, Franklin left to take care of the car.

Chris stood alone in a stranger's house. He stared at the door separating him from D.J., and he wondered.

She'd asked for him. *Odd*. Why would his name be the one she spoke upon returning to consciousness? Why not the name of her childhood friend? Or, in her drug-induced disorientation, maybe her ex-husband? Or her father?

She desired him; that she couldn't hide. She didn't attempt to deny those feelings, even though he denied his own. What lay between them was strong. Its force drew him forward, toward the door, enticed him into the room and forced him to stand at her side.

Dan did his job well. The last time Chris had seen D.J. she'd been sticky with blood, and pale as the clean, white sheet that covered her now. Besides digging out the bullet, stitching the hole, and bandaging her shoulder, the good doctor had taken the time to wash the gore from D.J.'s body and clothe her in a flannel shirt—one of the doctor's own, from the size of it. She lay upon the examining table, still pale but not unnaturally so. Her fiery hair needed combing. She'd have a fit if she could see the way the brutally shortened locks curled about her face. She looked too young to have been shot in the line of duty. Too innocent to have lain with him on a hotel bed only the day before and driven him to the point of madness—so close to the denial of everything he'd lived his life believing.

He should leave her now. She'd be safe in Isadora. Safe with her own people. Franklin would take her to the cabin, and no one could find her there. She'd be too ill to get into trouble—at least for the time it would take Chris to draw the danger away from her. They wanted him, after all. He could make them leave her alone—at least until she regained the strength to fight back.

But he found he couldn't leave her. He had no guts, no spine. He couldn't walk away from her while she lay unconscious, and he had no guarantee whoever wanted him dead would stop with him. Though Dr. Franklin looked capable enough, he was no match for the man or woman who pulled the strings in this game. Though Chris didn't know yet who stood behind the threat, he felt in his heart that evil lurked behind a smiling facade. The person who stalked them was someone he knew. The one who had discovered their hiding place at the hotel would find them again—more easily than they could ever dream. Until Chris eliminated such a possibility, D.J. wouldn't leave his sight. Though he'd spent the last eighteen years honing his mind and body into a weapon for his own protection,

Chris found he cared little for himself. He would use his talents to make sure D.J. survived her association with him. She might be a tough cop, but right now she was as vulnerable as a newborn baby—and it was all his fault.

He looked down at D.J. She lay so still; if her chest hadn't risen and fallen in an even cadence beneath the white sheet, he would fear she'd slipped away from him forever. Despite the knowledge such a move could be disastrous, Chris took her pale, cool hand in his.

At his touch, she shifted. Her fingers flexed, enfolding his with her own, and a smile tilted the corners of her lips.

Chris stared in amazement. He'd never seen D.J. smile like that—a smile of true joy. He wished he could see the same joy reflected in her eyes, but he knew too well the depth of sadness within D.J.'s soul. That same sadness resided in his own heart. Like Sleeping Beauty, she awaited a prince to set her heart free. Too bad all she had was Christian McCall. Not much of a prince. But what the hell?

He leaned down and stroked her lips with his own. The contrast of her cool, slim fingers clinging to his and her warm, full lips so still beneath his mouth made him pull back, unnerved.

But D.J. slept on—the curse unbroken.

Ah, well, what had he expected? Eternal devotion? Undying love? From D.J.? He let out what he thought would be a derisive snort. Instead, the sound he emitted wavered into a hopeless sigh.

Once more; just one more kiss while she's sleeping. One more caress when she isn't spitting mad or dazed with passion, when her eyes don't promise eternity, while her mouth mocks everything I hold dear. Once more while I can still believe in miracles.

This time when he kissed her, something moved inside him. Something shifted and ached, then burned hot against the cold, lonely part deep within him.

Chris pulled away with a gasp, and as he stared into her face D.J.'s eyes opened and she stared back—a dazed, soft look, like that of a child who had just awoken in a place where she didn't belong.

Her fingers clenched on his, a needy, frightened grasp, and she glanced around the room in confusion. Then she looked back at Chris and her brow furrowed. He smiled at her and leaned closer. Maybe there were miracles still to be had, after all.

"Danny?" she whispered.

The smile on Chris's lips froze. Another man's name upon D.J.'s lips, whispered in that hoarse, heartbreaking voice, made him want to smash something into bits with his well-trained fists. Why had Franklin told him D.J. had asked for him? The doctor had lied. She no more wanted Chris than she wanted a stranger at her side. Despite the feelings he had for her, that's all they were to each other in truth—strangers.

"I'm here." The doctor's voice came from the doorway, and Chris straightened, pulling his fingers from D.J.'s clutches with difficulty. He avoided Franklin's eyes, wondering how much the man had seen, how much he had heard.

The doctor replaced Chris at D.J.'s side. Chris retreated to the doorway. But he couldn't bring himself to leave—not yet.

"How're you doing?" Franklin asked.

"Fine now. Danny boy, I knew you'd take care of me. I'll always be safe if you're around."

The softness of her voice, the smile he couldn't see but knew lay upon her lips—for Franklin—tore at Chris. He had to remind himself of the truth; he and D.J. were two people thrown together by circumstance. She would never understand him, just as he couldn't understand her. Not the way Franklin understood her. They'd grown up together, shared years of childhood memories—good, happy memories, from the sound of Franklin's name on her lips. Chris could never comprehend such memories. His childhood remembrances fell into two categories—those of extreme happiness destroyed by violence and those of extreme unhappiness with no hope of surcease.

Chris could tell just by her voice how she felt about the good doctor. D.J. cared for Dan Franklin; she respected him. In ways she couldn't or wouldn't care for and respect Chris. Whenever she spoke to Chris the voice of a different woman from the one now speaking quietly to Franklin came from her mouth. When she spoke to Chris more often than not, she called him McCall—in cold anger or heated passion. But she never said his name the way she'd said "Danny boy."

And he knew she never would.

Chapter Twelve

D.J. awoke from a pleasant half dream where McCall kissed her gently and held her hand. That dream was all mixed up with the other dream, if she could call it that, of Josie and the feeling of love the angel had placed in D.J.'s heart.

When she'd opened her eyes and seen McCall hovering above her, his fingers entwined with hers, the strange, suffocating emotion had returned—or maybe it had never left. But even in her foggy, drugged mind, she'd recognized the love for what it was—a counterfeit sentiment forced upon her by a pushy guardian angel. Still, the tender look in McCall's eyes and the warmth of his strong hand in hers almost made all the trouble Josie had caused worthwhile.

Then she'd seen a movement behind McCall, and

the flash of red hair, and joy of a different kind had flooded her. True joy. Honest emotion. Feelings of friendship she'd only had for one person in her life. His name had burst from her lips before she could think, and in less time than it took her to utter Danny's name, McCall withdrew.

She tried to see where he'd gone, but Danny's broad shoulders blocked her view. He spoke to her, and D.J. focused all her woozy attention on his face as she tried to make sense of Danny's words.

"I know you don't feel like moving now, little girl, but we've got to take you to the cabin so you can be safe."

"Safe? I'm safe with you."

"The people who put the bullet in your shoulder are trolling through town looking for you and your friend. He tells me they aren't men to mess with, so I'm gonna drive you guys up to your dad's cabin."

"Ugh." D.J. put her hand to her head as a wave of nausea hit her. Whether the spinning sensation had been caused by the drugs and the loss of blood or the thought of being carried forcibly to her father's cabin, she didn't know. Either way, she was just as sick. "I hope I don't barf all over your pretty pickup, Danny my boy."

"I don't have a pickup anymore; I have a van. But don't worry if you get sick. I'm a doctor. Barf is my middle name."

"I thought barf is a nurse's middle name. The doctor's middle name is golf."

D.J. opened her eyes to see Danny shaking his head. A chuckle came from deep inside his chest. She'd always loved how he laughed, as though he really meant it. "Shot, bleeding, and still a smartass. I should have known better than to hope a little Demerol would hamper your mouth."

"That's right. You of all people should have known." D.J. struggled up onto her elbows. "If we're going to go, let's go."

"Whoa there, little girl. You're not going anywhere under your own power. Not with big, strong me to carry you."

She smiled a little at their easy return to camaraderie. Danny had begun calling her "little girl" when they'd first met—though at the time, a few years before his big growth spurt, she'd been almost as tall as he. She, in turn, had called him "Danny boy." The nicknames had always been their way of showing an affection D.J. wasn't capable of voicing any other way.

"You're not carrying me anywhere, you he-man. I'm not a complete incompetent. Just lend me your shoulder, good man, and we'll be off." She swung her legs over the side of the table and jumped to the floor.

The floor was closer than it looked, and D.J.'s feet hit the tile with a painful thump. The world shimmered and dipped. The room tilted.

"Oh, oh," she muttered, flinching as the floor loomed toward her face.

Strong arms caught, then lifted her, cradling D.J. against a solid chest. She looked up into McCall's face. "Gotcha," he whispered. She opened her mouth to thank him, but he looked away.

D.J. snapped her mouth shut and frowned. He was hiding something. He'd never avoided her gaze before. She put her arms around his neck, for lack of anything better to do with them. He stiffened at her touch.

Yes, something was bugging Mr. McCall. She'd have to interrogate him once they were alone.

"My van's out back," Danny said, leading the way through the house. "It's customized so I can make house calls or transport patients to the hospital if I need to. D.J. can lie on the stretcher I installed. Chris, you sit with her, and stay out of sight."

McCall stepped out onto the back porch. As Danny had promised, a large blue van awaited them. The back doors stood open, revealing an interior that reminded D.J. of a makeshift ambulance. Chris set her down inside the vehicle, then helped her to recline on the padded stretcher bed. He took the bucket seat next to her.

Under normal circumstances D.J. would never have allowed herself to be put to bed like a child. But she couldn't keep her head up without the world starting to spin in a sickening whirl. The way the two men moved, silent but quick, alerted her to the advent of danger. But the leftover lethargy from her ordeal made any sense of urgency fade away on a stream of lassitude. Her shoulder had started to ache, just a whimper here and there, but those whimpers promised screams to follow. D.J. had never been shot before—and she'd already decided she never wanted to be again.

Danny appeared in the open doorway. "We'll be at the cabin before dark. We might have to walk the last mile or so; I don't think Ed's had the road cleared in years. But we'll get there. I promise." He looked at D.J. His eyes narrowed when he spied her tight mouth. "Do you want anything for the pain yet?"

She bit her lip and shook her head. She'd wait until they got to the cabin before she took anything else. There was no telling what could happen before they got there, and she might need a clearer head than pain killers would allow to deal with any trouble.

"Where's my gun?"

"Here." McCall pulled the .9 mm from his jacket. He laid the weapon on the stretcher, within reach of her fingers.

She smiled her thanks. He looked away again, returning his attention to Danny, who still hesitated at the rear of the van.

"You're sure you're all right?"

"Fine, Danny boy. Now get us out of here."

Danny must have heard the apprehension in D.J.'s voice, for he listened to her order without question. The doors slammed, and seconds later the van rolled into motion.

D.J. sighed, though the sound came out more of a moan, and closed her eyes.

"Are you in pain?"

The single light in the back of the van came from the front window, several feet away. Semidarkness shrouded them both, but she could see him if she opened her eyes. She didn't want to. Without the benefit of sight, she heard nuances in McCall's voice that she wouldn't notice otherwise. Right now, despite the concern in the question, he sounded quite angry with her.

"I'm fine," she lied. "Why are you angry with me?"

He didn't answer at first, and D.J. smiled to herself. He'd never figured her for a sensitive soul, able to uncover the hidden agendas in a person's voice. Two days ago she'd have agreed. But Josie and McCall had done wonders for her powers of perception.

"You didn't tell me you'd been shot. You just drove off like a madwoman. Why, D.J.?"

"Why didn't I tell you? Or why did I let myself get shot?"

"Both."

"Good, because I have the same answer to both questions." D.J. opened her eyes and turned on her uninjured side. McCall's eyes shone bright in his still, pale face. "I didn't know. I never felt a thing. And even if I had, what difference would knowing have made? I could still function. We had to get out of there."

"This is all my fault."

"Why? Because you insist on taking the blame for everything? I'm the professional here, McCall. I'm the one who's supposed to be protecting you. I did my job. Getting shot is one of the hazards of being a cop. I'll admit, I don't like it much. But this is my own fault. I wasn't careful enough. Don't take my stupidity onto your conscience, as well as everything else."

If she hadn't been watching him so closely, she never would have seen his withdrawal. He tensed; then his shoulders drew inward just a bit, though not enough to see if she hadn't been waiting for it. Yes, he was angry with her for getting shot, and with himself for letting it happen. But she sensed something more, something he wasn't sharing.

"What do you mean by 'everything else'?"

D.J.'s gaze flicked up to his face, searching for an indication of what he continued to hide. "I'm not sure. But I can see it in your eyes whenever you look at me. I can taste it on your lips when you kiss me. You're punishing yourself for something, McCall. You're one big mountain of angst, and I intend to find out why."

"My problems are none of your business."

"Oh, but they are. You've drawn me into a game without rules. Someone's trying to kill us, and the only way to find out who and why is to take apart your life, Christian McCall. So I'm going to pull every secret from that creative little brain of yours until I understand what's going on here. Because now they want to kill me too, and it pisses me off."

"No one gets into my head, least of all you."

The glacial tone of his voice made D.J. blink. He sounded like . . . like her. When had McCall learned how to be rude?

"My, my, aren't we touchy? Thanks, McCall, you just proved to me there's a mystery in you aching to be discovered."

"Go back to sleep, D.J." His voice sounded as weary as she felt; all the life and joy usually contained in his tone had been drained away.

D.J. lay back on the stretcher and closed her eyes. Poor guy; he'd spent too much time with her, and things would only get worse before they got better. An indeterminate amount of days, perhaps weeks, isolated with McCall at her father's cabin yawned before her. D.J. pushed the disturbing thought from her mind. She was working; she had to keep her mind on the job at hand—not on the strange and new sensations McCall's presence brought to her body and soul.

"I'm starting to despair of both of you." Josie's voice filled her head.

"Shut up and go away," D.J. mumbled.

"I'd be happy to," McCall answered. "But I have a problem leaping out of moving vehicles in the middle of the wilderness."

"Not you." D.J. turned her head away from him and kept her eyes shut.

Josie didn't give up. "I would have thought a brush with death would make you see the light. I showed you what you're missing. What's the matter with you?"

"Counterfeit emotions," D.J. muttered. The soft, fluffy darkness clouded her mind, but she fought against the darkness for a moment longer, anxious to make her point with the irritating angel. "I don't feel the way you do. I don't feel love. I can't. I won't."

Josie didn't answer. D.J. let out a sigh of relief. The angel had finally shut up. Warm, soothing fingers touched her brow, easing away the tension, and D.J. slid away on the sea of sleep.

Chris removed his hand from D.J.'s forehead and sat back in his chair. No fever, so her words weren't delirium-induced. They were a message for him: a message he couldn't ignore.

She'd told him before she didn't believe in love. She couldn't love. Franklin had confirmed a bad relationship with her father and an unhappy marriage. Somewhere in D.J.'s past, as in his own, circumstances had shaped her into the woman he knew. The woman he desired—but could not have. He needed love too badly, he'd waited for love too long, to throw his dreams away on the promise of sexual fulfillment. Maybe he could teach her to love him the way he'd dreamed of being loved—but then again, maybe he couldn't. He'd lived with the Rousseaus for six years and seen how lust could turn into hate. D.J. couldn't be the woman for him. She wanted nothing to do with his dreams, and she possessed none of her own. To delude himself into believing what D.J. felt for him and he for her could ever be the love he'd waited all his life to find was to give in to his loneliness too soon.

The van stopped with a jerk. Chris broke away from his intense contemplation of D.J. Franklin peered around the driver's seat. His gaze touched on the sleeping woman and softened. Chris tensed, his teeth grinding together. He had to fight the urge to tell Franklin to keep his eyes to himself. What was the matter with him? He'd just decided D.J. wasn't for him. Why did the thought of her and Franklin together send a blast of fury through his gut? The doctor's gaze left D.J. and found Chris.

"This is as far as I can go with the van. You carry her, and I'll take the supplies and the luggage." Dan got out of the van, his footsteps crunching as he walked around to the rear doors.

The latch clicked and the doors opened outward. Fresh, cool air wafted in. The sky had begun to darken with the advent of night. "Toss me that pack." Franklin pointed into the van.

Chris hadn't noticed the full knapsack leaning against the driver's seat. Now he nodded and reached for it. Groaning, Chris dragged the bag across the floor and handed the knapsack to the doctor. "What's in here? Rocks?"

Franklin hoisted the bag onto his back. "No. Frozen meat, flour, sugar, coffee. Ed keeps canned goods up here for emergencies. You might have to split some wood for the furnace. The days are still warm, but it'll get cold at night. You'll be all right for a few weeks, if you need to stay that long."

"Is there a phone?"

"No, but I'll leave you a cellular and my pager number. You'll be able to get hold of me any time."

After climbing out of the van Chris turned to pick up D.J. She mumbled something under her breath that sounded like, "Go away, Joe," then subsided against his chest. Chris ignored the stab of curiosity. Who the hell was Joe? For a woman who disparaged emotion she had enough men in her life.

Chris followed the doctor as he walked up the overgrown road. Tangles of grass, small trees, and shrubs hampered their progress. D.J.'s hair tickled him under the chin, and Chris rubbed the tingling skin back and forth against the top of her head to ease the itch.

"What do you know about medicine?" Franklin asked, and Chris's head jerked up. He glanced at the doctor, but the man walked ahead, intent on finding their way to the cabin.

"Enough to know I don't know much."

"She'll need her dressing changed. I'll leave you

an antibiotic. Check her for fever. Watch the bullet area for redness and puss."

"I can watch her for fever and make sure she takes her medicine, but I highly doubt she's going to let me change her dressing or watch her bullet area."

"No?" Franklin sounded surprised. "I got the impression the two of you were—ah—well—close."

"Not as close as you two." Chris heard the jealousy in his voice and winced. He'd never been jealous in his life, and he didn't like the feeling now.

Franklin threw a quick glance over his shoulder before he returned his attention to the trail. Though the darkness hid the man's expression, Chris heard the smile in the doctor's voice. "Me? You've got the wrong idea there. There's nothing between D.J. and me but a very old and dear friendship. We might have made it more once, but she wasn't capable of the kind of relationship I needed."

"And you think she's capable of one now?"

"Maybe. She can't stay inside the shell of ice she's put around herself forever. I figured out a long time ago she needed a different kind of man than I could ever be. I'm not saying I don't love her; I do. But not the way you do."

"Me? I think *you've* got the wrong idea."

"Do I? Well, we'll see. D.J.'s very special. She's had a tough time, and she's become tough because of it. But she's not as emotionless as she'd like everyone to believe."

Chris remained silent, and Franklin didn't pursue the conversation. After another half hour of fighting the weeds and the mud while they turned and twisted on an unknown path, Franklin stopped short. Chris's tennis shoes slid in the mire, and he bumped into the doctor's back. D.J. shifted and moaned. She lifted her head, looked at Chris, then at Franklin, and then at the shadowy structure looming in the darkness several yards ahead.

Her chest hitched, almost like a sob, and Chris held her tighter against him, afraid she'd caught a chill in the damp night air.

"I hate this place." Her voice wavered in a totally un-D.J.like manner.

"I know, little girl, I know."

Chris frowned at Franklin's answer. The two must truly be old and dear friends if D.J. allowed Dan to call her "little girl" all the time. If Chris tried it, she'd probably break his nose. The doctor continued on toward the house, leaving Chris and D.J. at the base of the incline alone.

"Why do you hate this place?" Chris asked.

D.J. turned her head to look at him. Her face was so close to his, Chris could see the bright sheen in her eyes, reminding him of unshed tears. Then her breath hitched again and Chris frowned. Something was wrong. She bit her lip, then looked back at the house.

"Put me down," her voice demanded, and when he hesitated she took matters into her own hands and gave him an elbow under the ribs. His breath left him in a whoosh of pain, and Chris released her legs. She slid toward the ground, a sinuous movement of her body against his that he was unable to enjoy while he gasped for breath.

"Dammit, D.J.," he choked. "What did you do that for?"

But she'd already limped away, following Franklin up the final incline to the house. She tripped over a half-buried rock and went down on her knees.

Chris gritted his teeth, forced air into his lungs, and went to help her up. His tennis shoes slid on the incline again, and he swore under his breath while he scrambled for purchase. He hadn't known they'd be tramping through the north woods when he'd packed for their trip. His hiking boots rested inside the door of his kitchen, back in Lakeview.

He reached D.J. and helped her to her feet. Once she stood on stable ground, she tried to jerk her elbow from his, but this time he was ready for her. Tightening his fingers, he leaned forward. Her knee moved, and he blocked the frontal assault with his own leg. Living with Kirk Rousseau had trained Chris to anticipate the moves of a dirty fighter. "Don't even think about it," he hissed. "I don't know what's gotten into you, but I'm here to help. And you're going to let me."

D.J. glared at him; her mouth tightened into a thin, hard line. She was spitting mad, but not at him. He was just the lucky target for her unhappiness.

Lights inside the house flared to life, bathing them in artificial day. She glanced toward the cabin, unhappiness shrouding her face. All the fight drained out of her and she swayed. Chris scooped her up in his arms and carried her the rest of the way into the house.

She didn't protest when he laid her on the couch. Her eyes stayed closed, her face a mask of indifference. Chris frowned at the sudden change in her—from furious anger to limpid apathy.

Straightening, he stared at her face, which she held perfectly still, except for the twitch of her eyelids that she couldn't control. She knew he watched her. For now he would leave her alone, let her pretend to be asleep. At least until he got rid of Franklin.

The doctor crouched near the fireplace, touching a match to the newspapers he'd stuffed beneath the wood-stacked grate. "You'll have to make due with the fireplace for heat tonight," he said. "Then tomorrow you can put by enough wood to use the furnace." Standing, he turned to Chris. "I'll help you unpack the supplies."

Beep, beep, beep, beep. The sound shrilled through the air, making D.J. start up from her feigned sleep.

"What the hell is that?" she shouted.

Franklin's hand went to the electronic device on his belt. He pushed a button and the noise ceased. A sheepish smile curved his lips. "My beeper." He glanced at the small window on the top of the device, then pulled a flip phone from his jacket and dialed the number. Moments later he broke the connection and handed the phone to Chris.

"One of my patients is having a baby. She has a history of short labor, so I've got to hustle. Keep the phone." He took a card from his back pocket and pressed it into Chris's palm. "This is my phone and beeper number."

As he left, he stopped at the couch to kiss D.J.'s

cheek. "Behave yourself, little girl." Straightening, he glanced at Chris. "I'll be in touch."

Chris nodded at the unspoken message. The doctor would keep a lookout for the black van—as would the rest of the town. Chris doubted they'd get any surprise visits—unless, of course, the thugs learned of Ed Halloran's hideaway. In a town devoted to protecting their own, he and D.J. were as safe as they could hope to be. For the moment.

His gaze returned to D.J. All the danger didn't rest inside a black van. Danger awaited beneath this roof, in this woman he'd come to admire and crave.

She'd given up any pretense of sleep and moved closer to the fire. The dancing flames threw shadows across her face—or perhaps the shadows came from within. Her chin rested on her knees; her hands clasped her ankles; her shoulders hunched forward, as though the cold penetrated her very bones. Chris grabbed a woven throw from the back of the couch and crossed the room to settle it about her shoulders. She jumped at his touch, then mumbled a "thank you" as she pulled the blanket tighter around her.

"I'm going to put away the supplies. Are you hungry?"

"No."

Her voice worried him. She'd always insisted she didn't believe in feelings or emotion, but life had throbbed in her voice whenever she spoke, despite every denial. Now her tone was as cold and devoid of life as she'd always insisted her heart to be.

"Here." He flipped a pillow from the couch onto

the floor next to her. "Lie down. I'll make some tea."

She snorted. "McCall, I hate tea. I'm not an invalid; I got shot. I'll be fine in the morning."

Better, he thought. A tinge of anger shrouded her voice when she spoke his name.

"Can I get you anything?"

She glanced over her shoulder. "Such service. I could grow to like this." Reclining on the floor, she placed her head on the pillow and studied him. "I'm thirsty. Any soda in the kitchen?"

Though the words mocked and sounded more like the old D.J., Chris could tell by her face that she had tried very hard to resemble her usual self. She couldn't quite pull off the act. Something about the cabin upset her too deeply to ignore.

Chris bowed. "Your wish is my command, master." He went into the small utility-sized kitchen and opened the refrigerator. "There's canned tomato juice." A gagging sound told him what she thought of that choice. "Grapefruit juice?" A retch. "And a bottle of wine."

"Bingo. Just what the doctor ordered."

Chris glanced around the wall dividing the kitchen from the living room. "I don't know, D.J. You've had Demerol and antibiotics. You shouldn't drink."

She raised her head from the pillow and grimaced. "Don't be such a goody-goody, McCall. Bodies aren't meant to absorb bullets either, but mine did today. Now bring me the bottle or I'll get it myself."

Chris sighed. He'd give her one glass and wrestle her for the rest if he had to. Moments later, he carried two jelly glasses, the only containers available in the cupboards, filled with amber liquid toward the fire.

D.J. sat up and jerked her head toward the sofa. "Can you move the couch closer to the fire? Then we'll have something to lean against."

Chris nodded and handed the two glasses to D.J. He did as she'd asked, then sat down next to her on the floor, their backs against the couch. The fire cracked and flared. D.J. handed him a glass.

Chris took a sip.

Empty.

He glanced at D.J. She tilted up a full glass of wine, studied innocence on her face. So much for confining her to one helping, Chris thought. He put his empty glass aside.

"Nice place," he ventured.

She made a noncommittal grunt.

"Would you like to share why you hate it?"

"No."

"Did you live here as a child?"

"Yes."

"How long?"

"A few years."

Chris sighed. He was getting nowhere with his game of twenty questions. "Do you plan on acting like a zombie the entire time we're here, or just for tonight?"

She took a sip of wine and stared into the fire. Several moments passed before she let out a long sigh, and her head tipped over onto his shoulder. He captured the glass before the remaining liquid spilled onto his pants and set it aside.

"One glass too many," Chris muttered, thinking she'd passed out.

"No, I'm all right." D.J. turned her body and cuddled against his side. "Just cold. And you're so warm."

Her slurred voice alerted Chris that she wasn't all right, even if her actions hadn't been so out of character. He circled her back with his arm and pulled her closer, attempting to warm her with his own body heat.

"After my mother died my father sent me to live with his mother. He had no idea how to take care of an infant. Gran had moved from Isadora to a larger town when my dad went off to college. She wanted to be busy, so she opened an antique store with one of her friends. Then Gran died too. I was twelve." Her voice held a dreamy quality, as though she was remembering the events for the first time in a very long time.

"Where did your father live when you were with your grandmother?"

"Here. Or, rather, in a cabin he and my mother'd built even farther into the woods. They were kind of weird, I guess. Back-to-nature freaks—live off the land and all that stuff. He was lucky enough to avoid the draft in Vietnam—first because of the lottery, then he got married, then he had me." She tilted her head a bit as she considered a thought. "I wonder if they would have gone to Canada if he'd been drafted, since they were so big on peace and love." She gave a short laugh. "Hard to believe if you'd meet my father now. There isn't a tougher cop than Ed Belmont."

"Your dad's still a cop?"

"No, he's retired now. When Gran died I came back here to live. He'd built this place since he couldn't bear to live in the old one. Ed was the sheriff by then. We stayed here about four years. Then he got the job in Lakeview, and we moved when I was sixteen."

The words came out of her mouth as if by rote. She told Chris the facts, but something was still missing. He waited awhile, and when D.J. had relaxed against him even more, the day's events and the alcohol dulling her senses, he spoke.

"So why do you hate this place, D.J.?"

She sighed, a fluttering breath filled with pain, and Chris hugged her closer. She rubbed her cheek against his chest and placed her hand on his thigh. When he glanced down at her face her eyes had closed, and she looked almost asleep.

"I was so excited to be coming home," she said, her voice low and tight with pain. "My father visited me maybe twice a year at Gran's, and even then I could tell he only came because she insisted. He could barely stand the sight of me. He'd look in my face and then flinch. I remember trying to hug him when I was little, but he pushed me away, and I stopped. But when he came to take me to live with him I had such hopes we could make things better."

Chris sat very still, afraid to interrupt her tale lest she cease the telling.

"We came here and things got worse. He worked as much as possible, to avoid looking at me, I suppose. When he was here he'd read the paper or, if it was deer-hunting season, he'd go out in the woods and sit in a tree stand rather than stay in the house with me. If I hadn't met Danny, I'd have been totally alone. He made the time I lived here worth something. Danny's the only friend I've ever had."

She tilted her head back, opening her eyes to stare into his face. Her pupils loomed large and black, almost obliterating the green of her irises. She looked as tipsy as she sounded. Chris smiled at her gently and pressed her head back onto his shoulder.

"Tell me about your mother," he prompted.

"She died because of me. My dad never forgave me for it. I never had the chance to know her. My father destroyed every picture, so I have no idea what she even looked like. He named me after her, and then refused to allow her name to be spoken. So he called me D.J., and then he didn't have to hear her name ever again. When I turned sixteen I demanded to change my name legally to D.J. Trying to get a rise out of him, I guess." She laughed, a barking sound without humor. "He agreed right away. Said he'd been thinking of changing my name for years but never got around to it. So even her name disappeared from our lives. He loved her so much, and then she died. I think I must have reminded him of her—so much so, he couldn't stand to look at me. I decided very young that if that's what love did to a person, I wanted no part of it. The more I observed of people who believed themselves in love, the more I realized that love is just a word to excuse any type of behavior."

Chris's heart ached at the picture her words painted. No wonder D.J. pretended to be so emotionless; she'd never known anything else. At least he had the example of his parents' relationship to show him how love could be. If he'd had nothing to base his opinion on but the Rousseaus, he'd be in as bad shape in the emotion department as D.J.

"Did you ever ask your grandmother about your mother? She might have told you something."

"Gran never set eyes on her. My mom and dad met at some protest rally in Madison. According to Gran, they saw each other and—bam." D.J. slapped her hand against her thigh. "They were in love. Ed inherited this land from his grandfather. Gran was busy with her antique store and having problems with her hip at the time. She asked them to come and visit, but they never made it. They got married, came to Isadora, built a cabin, and had me. The story goes downhill from there. I think he even became a cop just to get away from me. The hours were long. The job was dangerous. Everyone on the force knew old Ed had a death wish. But no matter how hard he tried, he couldn't get himself killed. He always had to come home to me in the end—the child he couldn't stand the sight of."

Chris winced at the bitterness in her voice. He needed to turn her attention away from her father. She might even start crying in her maudlin state—and he would not know how to handle D.J. in tears.

"So why did you become a cop?"

"To fight for truth, justice, and the American way." She laughed, then hiccoughed and raised her head to put her palm over her mouth. "Why else?"

"Yeah, why else?"

D.J. stared into his eyes, her own shiny and

bright, a combination of mirth and pain. "I wanted him to see me. Just once I wanted him to look in my face and see me, not her. I couldn't expect love, but I thought if I could make him proud of me, if I excelled at the same thing he excelled at, he'd have to look at me—if only once—and truly see me." Her head dropped, and she fell back against his chest—dead weight.

"Did he see you, D.J.?" Chris whispered, smoothing his hand over her tangled head.

Her answer drifted on a sleepy sigh. "Never."

One word, so soft and sad, Chris couldn't be sure he'd heard correctly, but he had.

Chapter Thirteen

"Time is running out, Josie."

"What do you mean? Since when is there a time limit on this assignment?"

Instead of an answer, a whisper of thunder rumbled in the distance.

Josie glanced around, unease filling her. Ever since her death the sound of thunder reminded her of all she'd lost. She hated the sound. She also hated the place D.J. and Christian had run to, almost as much as D.J. did. Josie had recognized Isadora immediately. Though the cabin D.J. resided in now was different from the one where Josie had died, Josie knew the other was not far away, and that knowledge rested like a sharp shard of glass against her breastbone. She did not want to see that other cabin—but she somehow knew she would.

Josie's gaze returned to Raphael. "Is it storming?"

"It's always storming somewhere, dear Josie. Ignore that and tell me, why are you here when your daughter is down there with a bullet hole in her shoulder?"

"Yeah, how did she get that bullet hole in her shoulder? I did everything in my power to keep her safe and she ended up shot. Why?"

"Everything happens for a reason."

"What reason could there possibly be for my daughter to get shot?"

"You told D.J. her getting shot would bring her and Christian closer together."

"I had to tell her something or look the incompetent."

"Well, in this case you were right. They will be thrown together into danger. Nothing makes two people learn the truth of their inner feelings like danger."

"Danger. I don't like the sound of that. What if someone gets killed?"

He didn't answer, just continued to stare at her, his eyes bluer than any summer sky she'd ever seen or imagined.

Josie's fear nearly took away her voice. She swallowed against the hot lump in her throat. "Don't tell me they're supposed to die," she said in a hoarse voice. "Since they can't find their way to each other on earth they get to do it up here? Tell me that's not true. I'm the one who failed. Punish me. Not them."

"Heaven doesn't work that way. We do not punish, and we do not make deals. Everyone has their life lessons, as I've told you before. You have learned yours. If D.J. and Christian don't learn theirs, they

will have to return to earth and learn those lessons in a different life. Once they have, they can be together for eternity once their earthly trials have passed. Just as you can be together in heaven with your husband when the time is right."

"My husband? Is he here? Is that why I haven't seen him yet? Why D.J. hasn't been able to reach him?"

"He's not here yet. He had lessons yet to learn that you were not a part of. Very soon you can be together again."

The thought warmed Josie. She had something to look forward to. Soon she and Ed would be together for all eternity. There was only one other gift she needed to make her existence complete. "When can I tell D.J. who I am?"

"I never said you could tell her, Josie. I said I'd ask."

"And?"

"The answer is no. You were sent to teach her how to love. She hasn't learned the lesson yet. You cannot ruin all you've gained thus far by upsetting her with the truth of your identity. If you do, you'll be yanked back to heaven, and D.J. may very well join you without ever having the chance of finding love. Then she'll know who you are, but I doubt she'll thank you for the knowledge. Is that what you want?"

"No," Josie whispered, her heart breaking. "No. I'll teach her to love. But please, please, ask again. Once she learns to love, can't I tell her I'm her mother? I need her to love me too. If only for a moment in time."

*　　*　　*

"I'm at the cabin, Dad." D.J. didn't bother with greetings or lengthy explanations. She had awoken alone in the cabin, the steady thunk-thunk of an ax telling her that McCall was splitting wood for use in their extended stay. She had taken the opportunity to call her father. Now she wanted to finish speaking with him before McCall came inside or Josie showed up. Talking with Ed always left her an emotional wreck.

"You said you'd never set foot there again."

"I had no choice. Someone's trying to kill me—to kill us."

"Who's us?"

If D.J. had hoped her father would show some concern over her life being in danger, those hopes died at the cool courtesy in his question. She sighed and rubbed her aching head with her fingers. "I'm on an assignment. A guy named McCall—someone's trying to kill him. We went to a hotel in Outgamie. After I called in my location to the station four guys showed up with automatic weapons. I got shot, and McCall brought me to Dan."

"Hmm. You okay?"

D.J. blinked at the question. His voice held an emotion she couldn't remember hearing from him before. Could it be concern? Her heart stuttered with hope for a single second before her well-honed protective instincts reared their ugly little heads.

God, I'm so pathetic. One little sign of interest from dear old dad and I'm ready to go home for Christmas.

"Yes," she snapped, the coldness of her voice dashing the tiny flame of warmth within her. "I'll be fine. But I need your help."

"Shoot."

D.J.'s mouth twitched at his answer, but her father had no sense of humor so she didn't bother to laugh at the pun. No matter how she tried to explain it, he'd never find the humor. "I hate to admit it, but I can't depend on the Lakeview PD. There's a leak there. Like I said, after I called in to Captain Miller, four guys showed up at the hotel we were staying at and tried to kill us."

"What about Lou?"

D.J. flinched. She hated this—she who had always been able to rely on her connections at the police department, especially Lou, could no longer trust anyone. "No. Don't call him. I only want you to know where we are. I don't trust anyone anymore. Can you try to find out what's going on? Run a check on McCall. There's got to be something in his past causing all this hassle. You can call me at this number." She picked up the card Dan had left with them and recited the number over the phone.

"Got it. Anything else?"

"Nope. Just don't tell anyone where I am. No one."

"Rich has been looking for you."

D.J. sighed. She should have known her ex wouldn't let up on his demands for money. She could never understand why one week he had money to burn and the next he was tapped out. All of the cops and all of their friends frequented his store—Ed had seen to that. But Rich always seemed to be on the hunt for more money. When they were married she'd figured it was a mere matter of time until he turned to illegal activities to fund his constant thirst for more, more, more. So far, she didn't think he'd succumbed to that temptation. If he had, he wouldn't need to hassle her about selling their meager supply of stocks.

"D.J.?" Her father's voice came over the wire. "What should I tell him if he calls again?"

"Tell him I've gone off on my honeymoon. That oughta shut him up for a while."

"Your honeymoon? Is there something you're not telling me about this McCall character?"

"No, Dad. I'm just kidding. Ha, Ha." She didn't expect her father to laugh, and he didn't disappoint her. She couldn't remember ever hearing the sound of her father's laughter. "I don't care what you tell Rich, so long as you don't tell him the truth. No one can know where we are, not even Lou. Something's fishy at the station. I plan to find out what it is. And Rich is on the hunt for money again; knowing him, he'd come up here and pester me if he knew where to find me."

"All right. I'll take care of Rich, and I'll get on this check. Shouldn't take more than a day or so."

"I'll be waiting to hear from you."

Not expecting to hear a good-bye, D.J.'s thumb inched toward the OFF button. Her finger froze when her father's voice came over the wire once more.

"D.J.?"

"Yeah. I'm still here."

"Be careful."

Then the line did go dead. D.J. continued to hold the silent phone in her hand, a frown on her face. She had been right: Her father was acting different.

Almost concerned. Fatherly.

She punched the OFF button.

Too weird.

Maybe, just maybe, there was a chance to patch up the dregs of their relationship. If she tried a little harder and he did, too . . . Hope lightened D.J.'s heart.

The steady thunk of an ax against wood continued from outside, and D.J.'s momentary lightheartedness faded. She hoped McCall stayed out there all day. She didn't want to face him—not after her maudlin performance of the evening before.

She rolled her neck, then gave a tentative roll to her shoulder. Flames of agony licked at the wound. She sat down on the couch and closed her eyes against the spin of her stomach. Moving was a bad idea. Maybe she should pop one of those pain pills Danny had left. If she was lucky, she'd pass out; then she wouldn't have to look McCall in the face until tomorrow.

She'd woken on the couch this morning, all tucked in and cozy. But she remembered snuggling against McCall's chest like a kitten. Hell, she might as well have purred and been done with it. Purring would have been a whole lot less embarrassing than spilling her guts about her father.

How could she look McCall in the eye when he knew what a pathetic childhood she'd had? Pity would shine in his eyes, just as it shone in Dan's and Lou's—the only two people in the world, before McCall, who'd known her deepest secrets.

She'd lost her mind. Temporarily to be sure, but the damage was done. She could blame her injury, the Demerol, the antibiotics, and the wine for her lapse in judgment—and she'd be right. But she couldn't explain why telling McCall about her past had felt so damn good.

Something was happening to her she couldn't understand. Ever since she'd met Christian McCall feelings she'd never experienced, feelings she hadn't believed she could experience, had been racing through her without pause.

It had to be the angel's fault.

"Speaking of angels," D.J. muttered, opening her eyes, "what happened to mine?"

"Ask and ye shall receive."

D.J.'s neck snapped toward the sound of Josie's voice from the kitchen. She groaned as the suddenness of her movement caused a resurgence of pain.

"Are you all right, dear?" Josie walked out of the kitchen holding a cup of coffee and a glass of water. She handed the water to D.J., along with some pills. "Take your medicine like a good girl."

D.J. frowned, but a twinge of pain from her shoulder made her obey the angel's soft command. She drained the water and handed the empty glass to Josie, then accepted the steaming coffee with a nod of thanks. "Where've you been?"

"Here and there. Up and down. All around. Angel stuff."

"Did you discover any clues as to who shot me and why?"

Josie shook her head. "But I do know there are just a few days left."

D.J. looked up, then swallowed her mouthful of coffee. The liquid burned a path to her empty stomach and she winced, then put the cup aside. "A few days left until what?"

Josie frowned. "I'm not sure. Until all this," she waved her hands in the air, "comes to a head."

"I've got my father checking out McCall's past. There has to be something he's not telling me. Something that would warrant a hit on him—and on me, too, it seems. I can't believe the black van club would chase us all over Wisconsin for days just because they have nothing better to do."

"You did what?" Josie's voice rose on the last word, and she jumped to her feet.

D.J. blinked in surprise, then swallowed. "What's the matter with you?"

"You had Christian investigated? What on earth for?"

"You won't tell me what he's hiding. And he sure won't—if he even knows what he did or what he knows that set off this mess. I'm sick of floundering around in the dark here."

"Oh, D.J., you shouldn't have looked into his background like he was a common criminal. When Christian wants you to know about his past he'll tell you. If he finds out you went behind his back . . ." She shook her head. "You might have ruined everything."

"Ruined what?" D.J. handed the empty water glass back to Josie.

"Why, your relationship, of course."

D.J. sighed. "How many times do I have to tell you? There is no relationship. There's lust and there could be sex. That's it. I need to find out who's after us, arrest them, and then we can both be on our merry way."

"You believe that?"

"Sure. Why not?"

"Then why did you tell him about your past last night?"

D.J. froze halfway between standing and sitting. Her legs, still weak from the ordeal of the day before, wouldn't support her in such a position, and she fell back onto the couch. Her breath hissed out through her teeth when the jarring movement shot pain throughout her body. When the pain receded she glared at her angel. "How did you know about last night?"

Josie gave a smug smile. "I know everything about you, dear."

D.J. narrowed her eyes and focused on Josie's face. The angel stared back at her with wide blue eyes. "So I suppose you want to pity me too."

"Me?" Josie put her hot pink fingertips against the collar of her flowing dress in an innocent gesture. "I know you too well to pity you. Listen, I don't think you're going to find out anything from Christian's past to explain what's happening to you both now."

"Why not?"

"I can't tell you the details, but I'll tell you the basics: Christian's parents were murdered in front of him on a Lakeview street when he was twelve years old."

D.J. gasped. "Oh, how awful! No wonder he's so screwed up."

"People in glass houses, dear," Josie admonished.

"Are you implying I'm screwed up?"

"If the shoe fits . . ."

"My, aren't we just a barrel of clichés today? Well, let me try one out on you: Spill the beans, Josie. Who killed the McCalls?"

"No one knows. It was a robbery. From Christian's description, three thugs from Chicago, up for the night. The police never caught anyone."

"Hmm." For some reason Josie's description of the crime set off warning bells in D.J.'s head, but she couldn't think why just now. In the back of her brain an idea began to tumble forward. From past experience she knew if she allowed the tidbit to roll around in her brain unfettered, the knowledge would come to the front eventually.

"A random theft," Josie continued. "The murders weren't planned. A trigger-happy kid with a gun he shouldn't have had. You won't find a motive in that crime for what's happening now."

"No. I'm sure we won't. McCall's parents were killed—what—eighteen years ago?" Josie nodded. "A bit too long to hold on to a motive. And if they wanted to kill McCall, for whatever sick reason they might have had to kill a kid, they'd have killed him right then. When he was twelve years old and helpless, not thirty and—"

D.J. broke off. How could she have been so dense? No wonder McCall had trained all those years in karate. No wonder he could fire a gun as well as she. After what had happened to him as a child, McCall never wanted to be helpless again.

The flash of understanding made her smile softly and tilt her head toward the steady thunk-thunk that continued unabated in the front yard. *Protecting yourself.* Now there was a motive she could relate to. Perhaps she and McCall weren't so incompatible after all.

An image came to her of McCall at twelve, alone, orphaned, frightened. She wanted to take that child in her arms and comfort him. Hell, why didn't she admit it? She wanted to take the man into her arms and do the same thing.

D.J.'s throat thickened, and she swallowed against the unaccustomed well of feelings. Early senility had set in for sure. Ever since she'd met Josie her emotions had become increasingly hard to bury. After the angel had put that stupid dream into her head about a family and children D.J. had found herself craving those two things in the dead of night. Ever since McCall had dragged her to his damned day-care center and the sweet little girl had fallen asleep against her chest, D.J.'s arms had ached to hold a sleeping child once more.

D.J. looked away from the window and caught Josie's gaze upon her. The angel had tears in her eyes. Josie smiled gently, then crossed the space separating them and cupped D.J.'s cheek in her hand. D.J. stifled a sudden, inexplicable urge to throw herself into Josie's arms and sob. Instead she whispered, "What's the matter, Josie?"

"Nothing. I was just thinking how much I'll miss you once I'm gone." She took her hand away from D.J.'s cheek and turned away, brushing the back of her hand across her own cheek.

"I'll miss you too." D.J. surprised herself with her answer. She was even more surprised to find she meant what she'd said. She'd been telling Josie to get lost since the first day the angel had arrived, but now she discovered that the thought of Josie's leaving for good pained her. But the angel couldn't stay around forever, could she?

A loud curse from outside made D.J. spin toward the door. She winced when her shoulder protested the sudden movement. When would those damn pain pills kick in? Biting her lip, she grabbed her gun and headed outdoors.

Just as she reached for the doorknob, it turned, and McCall appeared in the opening. He cast an evil glance at D.J. and, wide-eyed, she backed out of his way. Shirtless, sweaty, scowling. He was the most beautiful thing she'd ever seen. She continued to stare at him, but he pushed past her and went into the bathroom.

D.J. glanced at Josie, who shrugged. "Go and help him, dear."

"Help him what?"

"I don't know. All that sweaty, muscled man. You can think of something." Josie disappeared.

"I'm sure I can," D.J. said to the now empty room.

"Who are you talking to?" McCall appeared in the hall connecting the living room to the bath and bedrooms. He held a cold cloth around his hand. His chest still glistened with well-earned sweat.

"Who me? Ah—I was talking to—ah—you. That's right. I asked you what happened." D.J. bit her tongue to keep from cursing. She sounded like a lovesick kid. It wasn't like she'd never seen a half-naked man before. She worked with a building of men, and most of them weren't shy about baring their torsos. She'd even seen this man without his shirt on. But never like this.

The muscles in his chest and arms were sleek and defined, even more so with the sheen of perspiration upon them. Most of the chests D.J. had perused were bulked up, over-pumped, weight-room specials. McCall's lean build appealed to her, as did the springy black hair curling across his chest. His nipples, flat and brown, peaked from the hair and beckoned for her to put her mouth—

"What?" She shook her head and sent the fantasy to the far corners of her mind—with all the others. "I'm sorry. You were saying?"

McCall frowned. "Did you take a pain pill? You seem kind of dopey."

"Me? Dopey? No, I've always been partial to Bashful myself. He's nice and quiet. Kind of shy. Nothing like me at all. But today I'd have to say I'm Grumpy."

"I see." His brow creased into a concerned frown. "Maybe you should lie down, D.J." McCall walked into the room, still holding the cold cloth on his hand. He stopped next to her and reached out to push her onto the sofa. Instead, she grabbed his hand and yanked off the cloth.

Shiny red blisters graced his palm. "Ouch," she said.

"Yeah. Ouch." He tugged on his hand, but D.J. didn't let go. His brow creased in confusion, but he didn't pull away again. "I didn't realize I'd overdone it until I stopped for a minute. I—ah—I had a lot of energy to work off this morning. I woke up early and got started. So, we've got enough wood for quite a while."

D.J. nodded. She still held on to his hand, staring at the angry red skin. The blisters reminded her of the wound he must carry deep within. The wound of his parents' murder. Just as she carried the wound of her mother's death and her father's disgust within herself. Wouldn't it be wonderful if those wounds could be healed? Was it possible they could heal each other?

D.J. leaned forward and pressed her lips to the fevered skin of Christian's palm. She raised her head, then her gaze. "All better?" she whispered.

He stared at her mouth, a hungry look upon his face. D.J. licked her lips. A harsh intake of his breath became her reward. He took a step closer, and she raised her mouth toward his.

The kiss began softly, a tentative meeting of two lonely souls. The caress deepened into much more.

D.J. dropped Christian's hand and attempted to wrap her arms about his neck. The slash of pain from her shoulder made her moan into his mouth, and her hands lowered to rest on his waist.

Christian's lips left hers, trailing a path of kisses across her jaw until he reached her ear. He took the sensitive lobe between his teeth and sucked. D.J.'s fingers clenched into the firm flesh of his stomach.

Christian groaned, the passionate sound arousing D.J. even further. Why did this man's slightest touch make her want him more than she'd ever wanted anything or anyone?

Christian raised his head and pulled her against his chest. She muttered a small sound of protest at his withdrawal, which he soothed by threading his fingers through her hair and making a shushing sound deep in his throat. "D.J., there's a lot about me you don't understand. I'm sure you've wondered why I back away from anything physical between us."

She nodded. An inner voice told her not to speak and break the intimate spell shimmering between them. Perhaps he would confide the story of his parents. Then she wouldn't feel like such a sap after confiding her deepest secrets while under the influence.

"I understand you so much better after last night."

D.J. fought not to cringe at the reminder.

"There's a reason I behave this way, and I need you to understand. I promised my father before—"

He stopped speaking. After a moment of silence D.J. pulled back and looked up into Christian's face. The pain she saw there made her stomach clench with dread. Maybe she didn't want to hear the truth.

Christian glanced down at her, and a small smile curved his lips, though the expression didn't reach his eyes. "I promised him I would wait for the right woman. My one true soul mate. He and my mother had that kind of marriage before—"

His voice broke once more, and D.J., needing to help him through the pain, spoke into the silence without thought. "Before they were murdered."

Christian's gaze snapped up to hers.

Oh, oh, I definitely should have kept my mouth shut.

"How do you know they were murdered?"

"I—ah—I—um—" D.J. bit her lip. How was she going to explain that her guardian angel had told her?

The warmth radiating from Christian's body to hers dissipated as he stepped away. He stalked around the couch, putting the item of furniture between them. The size of the sofa seemed small compared to the mountain she'd just put between them with her ill-timed words.

"You had me investigated." She didn't answer, just continued to stare at him, cursing in silence the lapse of her stupid tongue. "Didn't you?" he insisted.

"No. I mean yes." She took a step toward him, her hand outstretched in a silent plea. "It's not what you think."

"I think it must be nice being a cop. You can invade anyone's life on a whim. Is that how you get your kicks, D.J.? Digging up secret horrors and sharing them with your buddies?"

She shook her head, horrified at his words, but she couldn't seem to speak. She couldn't seem to deny his accusations. Her outstretched hand dropped back to her side unheeded.

He made a sound of disgust deep in his throat. "My private life is private, Officer. What I choose to share is what *I* choose. Not you."

He turned and walked down the hall toward her

father's bedroom. The door closed behind him. In the silence that followed the click of the dead bolt being snapped into place echoed throughout the house and settled into D.J.'s heart.

Chapter Fourteen

The dead bolt on the door beckoned Chris, and he snapped the lock home. Though he doubted D.J. was the type to do so; he was taking no chances she might decide to follow him and explain herself. Right now he didn't want to hear it.

Never mind that he'd been about to unburden his secrets to her; the fact that she already knew them infuriated Chris beyond measure.

How long had she known? Was the softening he'd sensed in her nature a result of pity for the poor orphaned child he'd been? Still was, actually, and always would be. The though of D.J. learning about his childhood terrors in the form of an investigative report compiled by another "just the facts, ma'am" cop, then hiding her knowledge from him for who knew how long, increased Christian's fury. He couldn't stand duplicity or secrecy. D.J. had just proved herself adept at both.

Chris threw himself down on the bed and glanced around the room. Franklin had deposited the computer and Chris's suitcase in the corner of this room. A hint from the good doctor?

Separate rooms—separate beds? No problem there, Dano. You don't realize who you're dealing with.

Chris narrowed his eyes, really seeing the room for the first time. This must be her father's room. In shades of brown and navy blue, the decor emitted a masculine air that would have revealed the owner even without four stuffed deer heads on the walls. The shiny black eyes of the mounted deer stared at Chris, a haunting reminder of the thin thread separating life and death. D.J. could have been just as dead as those deer if the bullet had been any closer to a vital organ. His parents had been alive and happy minutes before they were dead and gone. So what did that all mean? Should he live his life as though every moment was his last? Damn the torpedoes and full speed ahead on the pleasure? Or should he stick to his beliefs and wait, forever if necessary, to have the perfect life he'd dreamed of for so long?

Chris's gaze drifted back to the mounted deer, and he closed his eyes against the sight of death. He closed his mind against the philosophical ravings never far from the surface of his thoughts. Weariness washed over him. Even without a morning spent splitting wood he would be exhausted. After D.J. had fallen asleep the night before he'd lifted her onto the couch and stretched out on the floor below her. He wanted to be close by, just in case she needed him.

Thinking about all she'd told him while they sat together in front of the fire, a long time passed before he fell into an uneasy sleep. Then he'd dreamed—a strange, confusing, beautiful dream.

D.J. was surrounded by a field of wildflowers. The violet, white, and orange blossoms shone in the bright sunlight. Her hair had grown to her shoulders and curled in abandon about her face. She wore a flowing dress—long and old-fashioned, with a lace-trimmed scoop neck. A totally un-D.J.like dress, but for some reason it fit her. The colors of the material reminded Chris of late autumn—muted red, burnt orange, amber. She was the most beautiful woman he'd ever seen.

But the strangest aspect of the dream was the children who followed in her wake—two young boys, perhaps eight and nine, with dark curling hair and bright blue eyes, and a little girl, about four, with long red hair and a dress that matched D.J.'s. The child ran after the boys, who in turn followed D.J. as they made their way across the field, picking flowers. The little girl's laugh still rang in Christian's ears—like sleigh bells echoing in the frosty air.

When he woke on the floor in the morning the dream lingered in his mind. The little boys had looked enough like him and the girl like D.J. for Christian to understand the implications. What confused him was the longing that possessed him to make the dream his reality.

D.J. had slept on while he watched her. He'd had

to fight the urge to kiss her awake and share the dream with her. Instead, he'd searched out his drawing pad and sketched D.J. as she'd been in the dream—the field, the flowers, the children. The beauty was somewhat lost in a pen-and-ink drawing, but he'd preserved the emotion that had burgeoned through him during the experience. The drawing was easily the best work he'd ever done.

When he'd gone outside Chris had seen the field of his dream existed in reality—directly in front of the cabin. Though right now the flowers had faded and the autumn trees blazed all the color, he would know the field anywhere. The question was, how had he dreamed the field just as it lay before him when he'd never seen the place until that morning? When they'd arrived the night before the area had been a mass of dark shapes and treacherous rocks. Since Chris had no explanation for the dream he'd chopped wood until his hands blistered and his mind cleared.

Perhaps he'd been wrong to fight the attraction he felt for D.J. When he'd first met her he'd wanted her. But the example of Kirk Rousseau, who slept with any woman he desired with no feelings for them, then bragged about his conquests until Chris became sickened, had made Chris distrust lust at first sight. He could never be the animal Kirk was.

But as time went on and he got to know D.J., his desire had deepened into something more. She was different from the woman he'd at first believed her to be. Sure, she was tough; she was cold; she was driven. But beneath all those protective devices she was soft and warm and as lost on this earth as he.

Chris sighed and drifted toward sleep. He'd always been too rigid in his beliefs. He'd had an image in his mind of the woman he would spend his life with. Now that he thought about it, the imaginary woman looked and acted a lot like Marianne McCall. Was she the kind of woman he wanted? Or had he thought he wanted someone like her because his mother embodied an ideal he'd clung to throughout his lonely childhood?

When he'd come into the house Chris had meant to tell D.J. about his past. She'd shared her background with him, though he doubted she would have if the circumstances had been different. The understanding of her character that had come with those revelations was so precious, he wanted her to understand him in the same way. Since the night he'd related the facts to the police officers who'd arrived on the scene too late to save his family, Chris hadn't revealed the horror of his parents' murder to a living soul. But he'd planned on revealing the nightmare to D.J., until she'd gone behind his back and torn his secrets loose from the wrong source.

Chris fell asleep with the remembrance of D.J.'s deception on his mind—but he dreamed again of the field and the children and D.J., and the deception shrank in importance when compared with the wealth of love forgiveness could grant him.

D.J. stood outside her father's room and listened for some indication of what McCall was doing on the other side. Ever since he'd slammed the door and locked it she hadn't heard a peep.

"How could I have been so stupid?" She'd asked

herself the question at least ten times since McCall had left her. The entire time she'd cleaned up and changed, washing her hair in the sink to avoid getting the bandage on her shoulder wet, she'd cursed herself for her loose tongue. She was a trained professional who knew better than to spill confidential secrets.

D.J. frowned and put her ear against the bedroom door. She didn't like this lack of sound and movement. A quick trip to her room and a search of her jewelry case produced the key for the deadbolt lock on her father's door. While they'd lived here he'd often disappeared into his bedroom with a bottle—always on the same dates each year, which D.J. had finally understood coincided with important days in her mother's life.

After the first fearful morning when she couldn't rouse Ed from his drunken sleep, no matter how hard she pounded on the door and screamed, she'd called a locksmith to open the bolt. The man had taken her aside and given her a key for the lock when her father wasn't looking. She could still feel the embarrassment stealing over her at the look of pity in the man's eyes. From then on, whenever too much silence came from her father's locked room, D.J. made use of the key.

The dead bolt slid open, and D.J. pushed the door inward a fraction. "McCall?" she whispered. "You all right?"

No one answered. D.J. pushed open the door the rest of the way and stepped inside. The breath she'd held in fear that the room would be empty, the window gaping open to reveal McCall's desertion, rushed out in relief at the sight of him asleep on the bed.

D.J. backed out of the room, closing the door behind her. But just before the latch clicked shut she paused, then opened the door once more. He would get cold lying there, shirtless, without a blanket.

Shaking her head, D.J. chastised herself over her newfound mothering instincts. But she crossed the room anyway, stopping next to the bed. For several seconds she stared at him, memorizing the way the dark locks of hair lay against his forehead, the way the curling hair on his chest lay against his skin. She wanted to touch that hair and discover if the two textures were the same and, if not, how they differed. Instead of giving in to such dangerous desires, she clenched her fists and turned away.

McCall didn't want her. She should be able to understand that by now. If she hadn't been so infatuated with him, she'd have gotten the message the first time he pushed her from his arms. His earlier anger proved the truth. The flash of fury in his eyes had killed the burgeoning sense of intimacy between them. She knew his deepest secret, and he hated her for it. He didn't trust her with that special part of himself, and the knowledge shattered her.

D.J. took an afghan from the bottom of the bed, one of the few homey touches her gran had provided for the cabin, and gave the knitted material a yank to free the fringe from beneath McCall's feet. He didn't move when she covered him and tucked the blanket beneath his chin. His early morning wood-splitting marathon had worn him out. Despite herself, D.J.'s fingers strayed, and she caressed his cheek for just a moment. He hadn't shaved, and her fingertips tingled when they encountered the rough beard.

She'd never touched a man this way—because she couldn't stop herself from giving in to the need to feel his skin against hers. She'd never wanted to touch anyone the way she wanted to touch Christian—the way she needed to touch him. Her brief marriage to Rich had been composed of one disappointment after another. She'd never felt enough for Rich to caress him at all. Her lack of emotion and his biting taunts about her frigidity had turned their mediocre sex life into a nightmare. Any desire she'd convinced herself she possessed for Rich Halloran had gone the way of the rest of the marriage— straight to divorce court. Since then there'd been no one, and she hadn't cared. She'd barely noticed. She had her job and that had always been enough.

But now, suddenly, the job wasn't enough. Christian McCall made her ache for things she'd never thought could be a part of her life. In the space of a few days the all-powerful career she'd wanted didn't look so wonderful. After being on the run, fearing for their lives, getting shot—peace and quiet sounded oh, so very good.

Unfortunately, the threat hadn't disappeared. In fact, according to Josie, the threat was very real and getting closer.

Despite her distaste for this cabin, the place emitted a peace that soothed D.J.'s overtaxed mind. But she couldn't forget what they faced—not for a second. Not if she wanted to save Christian's life. And she wanted to—very badly. Not because keeping him safe was her job, but because she couldn't bear the thought of losing Christian McCall forever.

"Hell's bells," she muttered and straightened, snatching her fingers away from McCall's cheek. Where on earth had such a thought come from?

Fear flooded her. She sounded like her father. What was life without his wife?

Hell. That's what.

She could almost hear her father's smoke-roughened voice shouting about the hell his life had become since the day her mother died. And he'd made D.J.'s life hell too. She wouldn't allow a man to make her suffer ever again. She'd always been in control of her emotions. She could shut them off whenever she wished. Well, she wanted to shut them off now. Right now. And she would.

D.J. turned away and took a step toward the door. McCall's voice stopped her.

"I used to dream about them every night."

The sadness dripping from the words caught at D.J. Though her well-trained, emotion-hating mind screamed for her to run away, a newly awakened heart forced her to turn back. McCall's eyes remained closed, but his face reflected the sadness filling him. D.J. perched at the very foot of the bed and waited for more.

"The dream never changed. Just as the reality never changed. They were dead. They weren't coming back. And I was alive. Alive and alone. More alone than I'd ever dreamed a person could be. I hated myself. Hated myself for living when the two people I loved most were murdered while I stood helplessly by and let it happen."

"You were a child. What could you have done? Do you think they would have been happy if you joined

299

them? If you'd died along with them that day?"

He went on as though she hadn't spoken. "So I lived with the Rousseaus and saw how horrible life could be with hate instead of love to guide you. But I swore that night as I stood over the dead bodies of my parents that I would never feel helpless again." He opened his eyes and looked directly into hers. "I never did. Until I met you."

D.J. couldn't breathe. Every emotion she'd fought to subdue stared back at her from Christian's eyes. The fright that had consumed her moments before returned with a vengeance. She jumped to her feet and backed toward the door.

He watched her go, making no move to stop her. Then he spoke again, and his words stopped her inches from escape.

"Last night I dreamed of you."

"Me?" D.J. cursed the husky rasp of her voice. She bit her lip and forced herself to be quiet.

He nodded his head, slow and sure, then pushed himself up on his elbows to see her better. The muscles in his shoulders bunched, and D.J.'s gaze fastened on them despite her resolve to remain aloof. She forced her gaze back to his face. His dark eyes bored into hers, and she went still, his words washing over her, freezing her in place, trapping her with their power.

"Yes, you. You and our children. Walking in a field of wildflowers. You were all so beautiful, I had to draw the picture when I woke up this morning." He nodded at the sketch pad balanced against the wall just inside the door. "Look at the picture, D.J. Then tell me what you see."

He sat up and leaned back against the headboard of the bed. The afghan slithered downward, pooling at his waist. He folded his arms across his bare chest and waited for her to comply.

D.J. stared at the sketchbook as though the bound papers had come alive and hissed at her. Before she even picked it up and turned the cardboard cover over to reveal the sketch on the first page, D.J. knew what she would see.

A picture of her—some years in the future. She looked different—longer hair, a bit older, but a lot happier, softer. But those changes weren't what caused her stomach to lurch toward the floor, as if she'd just ridden the world's largest roller coaster. No, the part of the drawing that terrified D.J. were the children. Two boys and a little girl, older than the ones in her dream, but undeniably the same children. Hers and McCall's. Dream children put into D.J.'s head by an angel.

My dream, not his. D.J. dropped the sketchbook to the floor and rubbed the pain centered between her eyes. *I don't understand any of this new-age crap. Did he have a dream? Or a premonition? Or are we both being manipulated by a pain-in-the-neck guardian angel?*

McCall spoke again, and D.J.'s questions faded as her attention centered on the man in front of her. "I've spent my life waiting for the one woman I could share my life with." He laughed, the sound disparaging. "I know you must think I'm foolish, but you'd understand if you could have seen my parents."

"They were very much in love?"

He smiled at the memory. "Oh, yeah. Sometimes I felt left out, they were so into each other. But how can you resent a love like that for very long? You just want the same for yourself. Most people would believe I'd gone crazy if I told them this, but since you know the situation, how they died and what happened to me afterward, maybe you can understand."

D.J. opened her mouth to deny such knowledge, but then snapped it shut. She hadn't asked for the truth, but since he wanted to tell her she would listen.

"The day they died, my father made me promise to wait for my soul mate." McCall glanced up, searching D.J.'s face for a reaction. When she stared back without answering he gave a small smile and continued. "I know that sounds hokey—but he believed there is someone for everyone. My parents' marriage showed me he was right—at least in their case. My foster parents' marriage showed me what could happen if you married the wrong person."

Curiosity got the better of D.J., and she asked the question perched on the tip of her tongue, though her rational mind scoffed at her need to know. "Did your father tell you how you're supposed to recognize this person when you find her?"

"He said I'd know. I'd feel it inside."

D.J. remembered Josie telling her the same thing. At the time D.J. had laughed off such an answer as mushy nonsense. But now she wasn't so sure. Maybe McCall's dad had been on to something. Maybe if you believed hard enough, you could make a dream come true.

McCall continued. "So I lived my life with the

memory of that promise. I'm thirty years old, and I've started to despair of ever finding the woman I'm meant to be with. I had an ideal, you see, and no one lived up to my ideal. But my dream last night made everything clear to me."

D.J. looked up, hope lightening her heart. McCall had the answers? Wonderful. "I'm glad someone is clear around here, because I'm totally confused."

He ignored her temporary lapse into sarcasm as if she hadn't even spoken. "The truth didn't become clear to me right away. I've been fighting my feelings because I couldn't believe what my heart kept telling me. My mind insisted I had to remember my promise. I've been telling myself the same thing for so long, you see, it's become second nature. But my subconscious spoke up and sent the dream. And while I lay here, half-asleep, half-awake, you came in." He shrugged and spread his hands wide. "When you covered me up and then touched me." He snapped his fingers. "I knew."

"What?"

"It's you."

"Huh?" D.J. gaped at him. "What's me?"

"You're the one. We're supposed to be together. That's what the dream meant. It showed me the future and how life could be if we were together. We're soul mates, D.J."

The fear returned, stronger than ever. Soul mates? McCall was starting to sound a lot like Josie. The concept of a soul mate terrified D.J. too much to contemplate. What happened if a person lost her soul mate? Did her soul die, too, while she was left to flounder about on the earth for the rest of her days?

303

Such an image reflected her father's life too closely for comfort. The small spark of hope that had sprung to life within her earlier became a tiny pinpoint of pain. D.J. wanted nothing to do with a soul mate. She had to put a stop to this nonsense before things got out of control. "Halt, stop, and whoa, McCall. You're crazy if you think I'm your soul mate. I'm the one who doesn't believe in love. Remember?"

"I'll teach you." He swung his feet over the edge of the bed.

"Freeze." D.J. put all the icy control she could muster into the command. McCall froze. "I don't want to learn. You just stay right there." Her voice wavered on the last word and D.J. winced.

McCall smiled at her, a lazy, sexy smile that started her sluggish heart to beat faster. He ignored her second command and started to walk toward her with all the resolution of the white tiger she'd once admired in the zoo.

D.J. retreated. Her back came up against the doorjamb. The scent of danger reached her nostrils, and she took a deep breath. The oxygen did nothing to calm the blood pumping through her body in an almost painful frenzy. He was going to touch her, to kiss her. He'd murmur in her ear and tell her everything would be all right. He'd hold her and love her and make her need him too much. Then, when he left, part of her would leave with him.

McCall stood two steps away when D.J. spun and ran out the door. He made a grab for her, fingertips brushing the back of her shirt. But she jerked away and, thankfully, he let her go.

She wasn't sure where she was running to. She'd

never run from anything in her life. But she couldn't stand in her father's room and let McCall destroy her—even though a part of her wanted him to.

D.J. didn't stop until she reached a remote section of the woods. She leaned her head against a tree trunk and waited for her breathing to return to normal. She could hear her harsh pants, which seemed unnaturally loud in the stillness of the woods. Even the birds had stopped twittering and flown away when she'd crashed through the brush at a run. She wasn't following the rules of the forest—walk quietly, stay on the trail, don't scare away the birds. Because when the birds flew away, all the other animals followed.

D.J. let out a snort of derision and opened her eyes. She must have absorbed some of her father's north woods philosophy if she remembered those rules. And she'd always pretended to be so aloof, too. Her father had loved these woods—so she, in turn, had hated them. Looking up at the beauty of the autumn trees against the neon blue sky, she couldn't understand why.

She knew this place—her father's place. The place he'd always run when he couldn't stand the sight of her any longer. D.J. tilted her head back, looking up, up, up, the long trunk of the tree until her gaze focused on a wooden platform partially concealed by the tree's leaves.

"Mile high," she said, and put her boot onto the lowest rung of the ladder built into the side of the tree.

Moments later she reached the tree stand and swung her leg over the edge. As she held her sore shoulder still and allowed the pain caused by her climb to recede, she glanced around the small area built into the tree.

She'd never been up here. The stand had been off limits when she'd lived at the cabin with her father. This section of the woods was his place and, as such, she would never have been welcome. But Ed wasn't here; so he'd never know.

D.J. surveyed the area from her bird's-eye view. Interesting how different the world looked from such a height.

She sat down on the small folding chair. Her eyes widened. From this vantage point, she could see the cabin clear as day.

Surprising. She'd always thought her father abandoned her to her fate when he retreated here. But from the location of this chair, he'd been watching the cabin the whole time.

D.J. stood and moved to the end of the platform. From this position the trees obscured the house. No, he'd have to have been sitting to see the cabin—and that's what you did the most while in a tree stand— you sat and waited and remained quiet. She'd never understood his obsession with bow hunting.

"Care to explain your behavior, dear?"

The voice, coming out of the peaceful silence, made D.J. jump, even though she knew who spoke. Her boot slid off the edge of the tree stand. She flailed her arms for purchase, but this close to the edge there was nothing to grab onto. With a strangled little scream she fell forward into the open air.

Chapter Fifteen

Free fall they called it, with a certain degree of awe in their voices. Whoever "they" were, obviously "they" had never fallen from a tree stand thirty feet in the air. Because free falling wasn't cool, it wasn't neat, and it certainly wasn't fun.

Terror ripped through D.J.'s gut so hard she thought she might just throw up on her way toward the earth. Wouldn't that make a pleasant picture when they found her dead on the ground? She'd never cared for heights—now she understood why.

Though the opposite had to be true, it seemed to D.J. she fell slowly, experiencing every sensation of what would most likely be her last seconds alive. Air swooshed past her cheeks as she fell. Her eyes watered. The droplets stuck to her eyelashes, then blew away—tears on the wind. Her heart beat too fast; her arms flailed too slow.

She couldn't fly. Too bad.

McCall's face appeared before her as she'd last seen him—the emotion she'd run from heavy in his eyes—and in a flash of understanding she knew what she'd thrown away.

D.J. landed with a thud on her rear end. "Ouch." She rubbed the bruised area. Even her teeth ached from the impact. But she was alive, unbroken—and sitting on the floor of the tree stand she'd just fallen from.

"Did that hurt?"

D.J. tilted her neck and scowled at Josie, who perched on a tree limb, bare feet swinging.

"Of course it hurt. What do you think?" She continued to rub her injured rear end.

"Good. You needed a little jolt in the right area."

"A kick in the butt, you mean?"

"Exactly." Josie sighed and floated down to sit so close to D.J. their knees bumped. "What are you running from?" the angel asked in a quiet voice just above a whisper. "Why do you continue to fight this gift? A gift that could change your entire life."

D.J. opened her mouth to make a smart retort. Instead her breath came out on a soft sigh of despair. Josie patted her hand. D.J. let her.

"I don't know." D.J.'s voice sounded rusty, as though she hadn't spoken for a very long time. Her chest hurt. Her eyes burned. Delayed reaction from her near death experience, she told herself. But she knew the pain in her chest and the burn in her eyes were unshed tears. She hadn't cried since early childhood—and she didn't plan to start now. D.J.

had a feeling that if she allowed herself such a luxury, she would never be able to stop.

"He loves you. You love him. I know you do." Josie's fingers tightened on D.J.'s. D.J. concentrated on the warmth of the angel's hand. How could an angel's hand be so warm, so real? Had anyone ever held her hand this way? If they had, D.J. would remember. She'd remember because this human contact when she needed the comfort felt too good to forget.

Then the reason she had come to the woods in the first place reasserted itself in her mind. The longing she'd experienced for McCall when she'd thought she would die receded as she recalled the drawing he'd made of her and their children. "You gave him my dream," D.J. choked out past the thickness in her throat. "What he feels isn't real. You made him feel it."

"What dream?" Josie wrinkled her nose in confusion.

"*My* dream. The one about the field and the wildflowers and the children. The beautiful dream you gave me to take away my nightmare. McCall had the same dream last night. Now he thinks he loves me. That we're meant to be together. That I'm his damned soul mate. You tricked him just as you tricked me."

The anger felt good, replacing the tears and making D.J. feel more in control of herself. She removed her hand from Josie's and shifted until they no longer touched. The angel didn't comment on D.J.'s withdrawal, though D.J. saw the hurt flash through Josie's eyes.

Lori Handeland

"I don't know what you're babbling about, D.J. I gave you the dream, but I certainly didn't give the same dream to Christian. I couldn't have. He's not my charge. I can't mess with his head like I can with yours."

The anger left D.J. in a rush, leaving her tired and weak with shock. "You didn't give him the dream?"

"Isn't that what I just said? If he had a dream, then the dream was his. What he feels for you is real. Just as what you feel for him is real. If you'd only let yourself believe."

"B-but I'm *not* his soul mate. There is no such thing as a soul mate. No such thing as love."

Josie shook her head. "You are a stubborn one. At least Christian recognized the truth at last. Now you can get on with your lives, and I can get on with my death."

For once D.J. could think of nothing to say. No snappy comeback, no sarcastic comment. Because now she was really frightened—or, if the truth be told, out-and-out terrified. If what Josie said was true, it was too late for her. The heavy, thick, syrupy feeling lodged deep in her throat wasn't tears; it was love. She loved Christian McCall—and he loved her. And that was very, very bad.

Believing in love meant she could be destroyed by love, just as her father had been. She couldn't face that.

The angel touched her on the shoulder, and D.J. turned to look into Josie's concerned blue eyes. "Why do you fight love, D.J.? You could be so happy. All you have to do is reach out and grab it. It's right there waiting for you."

"I—I can't."

Josie's face fell. "Why not? You said you didn't believe in love, but I can see now that you do. There's nothing stopping you from having a wonderful relationship for the rest of your life. Nothing but your own fears and wrongful beliefs. Tell me what they are and I'll help you. I just want you to be happy. As happy as I was."

D.J. stared at Josie, seeing the true concern on the angel's face. Before last night, she'd never told anyone her innermost fears. But now that she'd told McCall, she couldn't see how it would hurt to tell her angel the truth. "You said you knew everything about me. Then you know about my mother dying and my father—" D.J. broke off with a sigh, then stared off into the woods once more. This was harder than she'd thought.

Josie touched her arm in encouragement. "I know he hurt you. That he wasn't there for you. I'm sorry. I wish I could have done something to heal him before he hurt you so badly."

D.J. shook her head, then swallowed the unaccustomed emotion clogging her throat. "The only thing he wanted was to have her back. Since that wasn't possible . . ."

She shrugged. "After my mother died he was just the body of a man performing everyday tasks without caring about anyone or anything. I can't live the way he did, waiting to die so I can be with the one I love." D.J. looked up, then away from Josie's tear-filled gaze. "I just can't."

Silence hung between them for several moments.

D.J. stared out at the brilliantly colored trees once more, her mind a blank.

Josie spoke, her voice no longer soft but shaded with an anger D.J. had never heard her express before. "You'd rather live your life the way you have been? Working, existing, never feeling joy or love or hope? You're more pathetic than your father. At least he took a chance. Just once in his life he took a chance. Did you ever ask him if that chance was worth the pain? Did he ever say he regretted the time he had with your mother?" D.J. didn't answer. Josie reached out and shook her. "Look at me." D.J. looked. "Did he? Did he ever say he regretted loving your mother?"

"No," D.J. whispered.

"Of course not. Because even a short time on the earth with someone you love is better than a lifetime alone. I'm sorry your father set such a bad example for you. He didn't deserve to have the gift of a child. He should have realized some of his wife lived on in you and been grateful. But I'm not here for him. I'll deal with him later. I'm here for you. You can experience something wonderful if you'd just have the courage to take a chance."

D.J. saw her perched once again on a tree limb high above the earth.

"Take a chance, D.J. You won't regret it. I never have."

D.J. climbed down and started off through the woods. A few feet away, she turned to thank Josie. But the angel had disappeared into thin air.

* * *

Chris had watched D.J. from the window until she disappeared into the woods; then he took a shower. As the heated water relaxed the tense muscles of his shoulders and back, his troubled soul calmed as well.

He'd waited all his life for D.J., and now that he'd found her she ran from him. But since he'd waited this long, he had faith that if he waited just a little longer, she would understand the gift they'd been given and come to him. Once she did, they would have the rest of their lives to be together.

Chris got out of the shower and dressed. Thinking he'd try and work, pass the time until D.J. returned in industrious pursuit, he pulled the packet of pictures from the pocket of his computer case and dumped them out on the bed. But he couldn't bring himself to go any further. His mind wasn't on the task at hand. His mind was filled with D.J.

Chris went to the window once more and looked out, hoping to see her materialize from the woods and return to him. At a movement from the edge of the trees Chris smiled and headed for the front door. His fingers touched the doorknob, and he glanced outside once again through the window set into the door.

The smile froze on his lips, and he jerked his body to the side, pressing his back to the wall to avoid being seen through the window. How could he have forgotten the danger stalking them both?

A man approached the cabin. He walked as though he knew the area—and he must, to have reached the isolated hunting lodge without guidance. Though he seemed at home in the woods, he

313

glanced at the cabin as though he felt a need for stealth.

Chris peeked out the window once more. The man stared at the cabin with a frown on his face. While he looked around the area once again, Chris studied the stranger. Dark hair, young, handsome—though the scowl on his face marred his looks a bit. He wasn't one of the three men who had accosted Chris in Outgamie. Chris had never seen the fourth, the one who'd driven the van and shot D.J. Still, Chris knew this man. The face was familiar, as was the set of the man's shoulders, and the way he walked on the balls of his feet, as if he needed to be ready for anything. Chris had met him before. But where and why? Though Chris couldn't remember who the man was, he did know one thing instinctively: This man hadn't been sent by the person who wanted Chris dead. This man was the faceless, nameless stalker who had haunted his and D.J.'s every move for the past few days.

Panic flared to life within Chris.

D.J.

She could come out of the woods at any moment, unaware that their hideaway had been discovered. He needed to find her.

Chris dashed for the kitchen, where another door led outside. He exited in silence, just as the front door opened. Chris didn't look back. He didn't pause to see what the man did next. He sprinted for the trees, on the hunt for D.J.

D.J. took her time returning to the cabin. Her entire life had been upended like a wastepaper basket—all her beliefs tumbling to the ground like discarded letters. Now she had to pick up the letters that held the truth and burn those that told lies.

Back at the cabin Christian awaited her. The man who believed himself to be her soul mate. The man she could spend the rest of her life with if she could only change her entire belief structure and thought processes.

Halfway back to the cabin, as the sun began to set and the shadows of night spread long fingers through the trees, D.J. called out to Josie. She waited, straining her ears for the trill of Christmas-bell laughter, straining her eyes against the darkness, searching the treetops for a glimpse of bare feet. But the angel didn't answer or appear. Had Josie returned to her heavenly reward, her mission complete?

D.J. hoped so. Josie deserved eternal happiness. D.J. just wished she'd been given the chance to say good-bye.

Good-bye and thank you.

Reaching the edge of the trees, she stopped short and frowned in the direction of the cabin. Though night approached, no lights blazed within. Perhaps McCall had fallen asleep once she'd left and now slept on undisturbed. Perhaps, but she didn't think so. Something wasn't right here. D.J. could smell it.

She reached for her gun, then swore when her hand encountered the small of her back and nothing more. Her service weapon lay on the coffee table in the living room, useless to her and available to anyone inside.

Captain Miller would have her hide if he ever

found out that she'd left her side arm lying around loaded. Of course, if the captain were involved in this mess, he'd be happy she had. D.J. shook her head against the thought. She couldn't believe her by-the-book captain had turned into a criminal, nor Lou, her closest friend in Lakeview. It made her sick that she'd felt even a moment's distrust for people she'd once trusted with her life. But she wasn't talking about just her life now; she had another life to worry about—a life that meant more to her than her own ever had.

D.J. continued to stare at the cabin, looking for a sign of movement to indicate whether anyone lurked within the building. Nothing moved. Finally, when she could stand the suspense no longer, D.J. made her way around the cabin, staying in the shadows of the trees until she reached the back door.

The door stood open, revealing a deserted kitchen. D.J. ran up to the house, breathing a sigh of relief when no gunfire answered her actions. She crept through the open doorway and peered around the wall between the kitchen and the living room. The fading light from the windows revealed an empty room—empty now, but not empty for long. Whoever had invaded her father's house had come looking for something.

The furniture lay upended, stuffing spilling from the slashed pillows on the couch. The bookcases rested on their sides, the books spread across the floor. The place looked like McCall's house after it had been ransacked.

McCall.

Panic flared through D.J.'s mind. Where could he be?

The deathlike stillness of the house told D.J. she was alone. At least the intruder had gone—but so had McCall. Unless, of course, someone had killed him.

A sound erupted from D.J.'s throat that was too much like a sob of pain for her comfort. Biting back on the panic threatening to take over her cool head, she stood and crossed the room to the coffee table, where she'd last seen her service weapon. The table lay on its side. D.J. picked it up and looked on the floor for the gun. The weapon wasn't there. A quick but thorough search of the area revealed the truth.

Whoever had been inside the cabin had taken her gun.

"Hell's bells," D.J. muttered. She took a deep breath and glanced down the hall toward the bedroom. Fear of what she might find there lay heavy on her mind—but she had to go on. Right now she'd give anything for Josie's reassuring presence. When the angel didn't appear, despite her wishes, D.J. had no choice but to walk down the long hallway toward the bedrooms alone. She, who had walked alone for most of her life and liked it, now realized how lonely being one against the world could really be.

Both rooms stood as empty as the rest of the house—and in as neat an order as they had been when she'd left. Whoever had ransacked the front room hadn't reached the bedrooms.

Why? Had they found what they were looking for and left? Where the hell had McCall gotten to?

D.J. couldn't believe he'd been taken away without a fight. But the intruder had her gun—and probably one of his own. If McCall had been kidnapped, where had he been taken?

There was a frightening truth she didn't want to contemplate but she knew she had to consider: Someone wanted McCall dead. They didn't want to kidnap him. If they'd found him, they wouldn't have taken him anywhere alive, or if they had, they wouldn't have let him live for long.

She bit her lip until the pain made the panic recede enough so she could think. The lack of blood in the house soothed her a bit. McCall hadn't been killed inside this cabin. But that didn't mean he hadn't been killed in the woods. Still, she'd heard no shot—and she knew very well how loud a gunshot could be in the stillness of the forest.

How had the men who had stalked them found her father's cabin? The only people who knew she'd come here were her father and Danny. She hadn't spoken with Captain Miller or Lou since the fiasco in Outgamie and still someone seemed to know their every step before they took it. Lou knew about her father's cabin. She'd trust Danny with her life—and her father, too, she supposed. But it wasn't just her life she was talking about now. It was McCall's, too, and she wasn't sure she was willing to trust anyone with his life.

D.J. made a disgusted sound deep in her throat. She hated this feeling. Suddenly she trusted no one—not her boss, not her partner, not her childhood friend, not even her sole surviving parent. If trusting them meant risking McCall, she couldn't do it.

D.J. sat down on her father's bed, trying to think around the fear and suspicion clouding the edges of her mind. Something crunched beneath her, and she pulled out several photos. A quick glance revealed them to be pictures of the Lakeview police station. The pictures McCall had taken for his book, a lifetime ago, when they'd had nothing more serious to worry about than his deadline and her suspension—and putting up with each other until they could complete their jobs. Had only a mere week passed since she'd shot a teenager? She'd put a bullet in that kid and then pushed the reaction away into the sad, cold part of her where she kept all her emotions. Then she'd met Christian McCall and Josie—two people who had shown her what she lacked in her life. Could she ever go back to the way things had been before she'd known them? Did she want to?

While her thoughts tumbled over each other in her mind, D.J. rifled through the photos. The last picture made her stop and stare, her questions fleeing in a sudden flash of understanding.

A picture of the holding cell at the station—and inside it a member of a prominent Chicago gang who had been picked up dealing in Lakeview the same night she'd shot the kid. She'd forgotten about him in all the excitement. She and Lou had thought this gang member might be a link to the money man in Lakeview—the man who'd been putting kids in touch with the criminal elements that could explode gang activity throughout the streets of their town. Someone with money, opportunity, and the connections to start such activity. Someone who seemed to know the police department's moves before they made them.

Why? Because that someone had a lot of friends who were cops. That someone had been married to a cop.

That someone had been married to her.

"You son of a bitch," D.J. muttered, staring at a picture of Rich Halloran in earnest conversation with the gang member residing in the Lakeview holding cell—an area off limits to the general public. How had both Rich and McCall gotten back there where they didn't belong? Heads were going to roll over this.

D.J. shook her head as questions, then answers, pounded through her brain. Had Rich been behind all the problems in Lakeview recently? She wouldn't put it past him. He had no scruples. He cared only about himself and money. He could easily learn about the activities of the Lakeview PD because he was a friend of many of the officers. Hell, someone had let him into the off-limits holding cells. Whoever that someone was would lose his job for sure once D.J. got her hands on him.

She continued to unravel the pattern while she stared at the picture in her hands. Rich had access to guns through his shop—though she wasn't sure how he worked that part of the operation, since all guns had to be registered and serialized. And all the gang connections? Had he made those during the years he'd lived in Chicago with his aunt? If so, then how had he kept them quiet for so long?

More important to D.J. right now was the question: Did Rich stand behind the attempts on McCall's life? All because he'd seen McCall take his picture speaking to a person Rich wanted no one to know he'd spoken to? Murder seemed a long way to go for something so minor. Whatever Rich had involved himself in must be more far reaching and dangerous than D.J. could fathom right now. To try and kill McCall, and D.J. as well, a police officer and his ex-wife, seemed more stupid than she'd given Rich credit for being.

But someone wanted them both dead, and the picture held the first clue she'd been able to discover that pointed to anyone. Rich had been looking for her—she'd thought to get money, but maybe for another reason. Rich knew about this cabin. Her father had brought him here to hunt whenever Rich came home from Chicago as a teen, continuing to do so after Rich and D.J. married. Rich surely remembered the lodge and easily could have come hunting for her, and McCall, this time.

D.J. stuffed the picture down her shirt and crept toward the front of the house. She'd seen the phone on the floor next to the couch. She had to get help. She had to find McCall, and they both had to get the hell out of there before Rich came back from wherever he'd disappeared to. She wouldn't make the mistake of thinking Rich Halloran had returned to Lakeview without finding what he'd come looking for. She of all people knew how tenacious Rich could be when his own neck rested on the line.

She found the phone and dialed her father's number. Her breath came in harsh gasps. The pain in her shoulder had intensified with all her extra exertion. If she hadn't needed her mind clear to think, she'd be popping those pain pills like peanuts right now.

The line was picked up at her father's house, and D.J. almost groaned with relief. Then the recorded message started playing and she swore.

"Please leave your message at the tone." *Beeeep.*

"Dad, I'm at the cabin and I've got trouble. If you're there, pick up. I need you."

She waited. No one answered. "Dad. Pick up!" she shouted.

Nothing.

D.J. disconnected the line with a furious jab of her thumb. "There's never a cop around when you need one," she muttered.

Now what? She needed help. She no longer trusted the Lakeview PD. Whoever had allowed Rich near the holding cell had undoubtedly leaked her whereabouts in Outgamie to Rich or his thugs. Even if she did trust anyone in the department, they were over four hours away. She could call the sheriff in Isadora, but what would she say?

I think my ex-husband is a gang lord, and he's kidnapped the man I was supposed to have in protective custody.

The sheriff in Isadora was sixty-seven years old. Nothing happened in this town except drunk-and-disorderly on Saturday nights. He still carried the gun he'd bought when he was elected to the position over forty years before. He might have a shotgun somewhere, but neither weapon would be a match for the kind of firepower she knew their pursuers possessed. If she called him, he'd be duty bound to race up to the cabin and save her. She would have to do this herself—find McCall, if she could, and then get the hell out of the woods. Once they were safely away she could call in the big guns from a larger town.

The phone she still clutched in her hand started to ring, and D.J. jumped, her pumping heart nearly choking off her breath. She jabbed the "on" button, hope filling her as she put the phone to her ear. "McCall?"

"D.J., it's Dan. I've been calling there for over an hour. Where the hell were you? Where's Chris?"

D.J. hesitated. She had to trust someone. Her father was unavailable; Danny was right here, right now. She wouldn't be so alone anymore if she enlisted Danny's help. "I'm in the cabin now. I was walking in the woods, and when I got back McCall was gone. Someone trashed this place. They took my gun." Her voice wavered on the last sentence, and she exhaled a harsh breath of irritation. She couldn't fall apart now; McCall needed her.

"Rich." He said the name with all the distaste he'd always held for her ex-husband. Danny had always fancied himself in love with her, but she hadn't been able to return the feeling. He'd understood and been her friend. A friend she desperately needed right now.

"D.J.?" Danny's voice broke off her thought. "Are you still there?"

"Yeah, I'm here. You just proved my theory. I figured Rich was around somewhere. The mess in the cabin has his name stamped all over it."

"He came here this afternoon looking for you. I told him I hadn't seen you, but if you came to town you'd certainly come to me first. As you can imagine, he didn't take kindly to my remark."

D.J. made a sound of understanding. Rich had always been jealous of her relationship with Danny. While she'd been married, she'd avoided her friend just to avoid the inevitable scene with Rich when he found out she'd talked to her "lover boy," as he'd called Danny. Rich, in his typically macho way, hadn't been able to comprehend that a man and a woman could be "just friends."

Danny's voice continued. "He left when he realized I wasn't going to change my story, and the sheriff followed him until he got on the highway toward Outgamie, but he must have doubled around and come to the cabin the back way." He sighed, and D.J. could almost see the chagrin on his face. "I'm sorry, D.J., I should have come up there, but I had a patient who was bleeding all over the room and—"

"Never mind, Danny boy. I wasn't here when he came, and he's gone now. At least for a while. I'm just worried about McCall."

"I'll be right there."

"No. Stay where you are. Rich is around here somewhere; I can feel it. I'm going to find McCall if I can." She dearly hoped he was somewhere close by, in the woods, alone. If she couldn't find him, she'd have to walk out tonight and start a manhunt for both McCall and Rich as soon as possible.

Right now she needed to get out of the cabin and back to town. These woods were becoming too crowded for her taste. "When I find Chris we'll start down toward Isadora. I think Rich is involved with some nasty stuff. He'll be back, and I don't plan to be here when he shows up. Call the sheriff and tell him what's up. Have him get some help from the next town—younger guys with bigger guns. With any luck we can bag Rich and his buddies before they cause anymore trouble."

A soft rustle at the back door reached D.J.'s ears and she froze.

"D.J.? What's happening there?"

D.J. turned toward the sound, hope and fear at war within her. The door inched open in the wind. No shadow appeared in the doorway. Nothing else moved but the breeze.

"I've got to go," she whispered. "I'll see you as soon as I can. Just don't come up here, Danny. It's too dangerous." She disconnected the line, cutting off Danny's protest in midsentence.

D.J. went to the window. Night had fallen in earnest while she was speaking on the phone. Heavy clouds shrouded the stars and moon, turning the woods into a black cavern. The wind had picked up, and she could smell electricity on the breeze. A storm was headed their way—a big one, from the looks of things. She'd always hated thunderstorms. When she'd lived with Gran she would crawl into bed with the older woman until the storm passed. Once she'd lived with her father he'd put a sleeping bag on the floor next to his bed, and she'd crawled in there and pulled the blanket over her head whenever the storm became too much for her to bear alone. Though her father had never mentioned it, she'd sensed he somehow understood and empathized with her irrational fear. Maybe he had loved her just a little, though he couldn't show it. She'd eventually grown past the need to hide during a storm—though the desire to do so had never left her.

D.J. clamped down on the unreasonable fear—a weakness she'd always detested. She would just have to hope she found McCall before the rain began. As time had passed and he hadn't appeared, her fear for him had increased. But the urgency to get out of the cabin pulsed at the forefront of her mind. Rich could get her here, and she would have nowhere to run. In the woods she had a better than average chance to get away.

D.J. paused long enough to grab a jacket and stuff the phone into her pocket. Then she slipped out the back door and entered the woods.

Thunder rumbled in the distance and lightning flashed. The frigid air around her promised snow. It had been a long time since she'd seen a lightning snowstorm, a rarity that frightened her just as much as an old-fashioned summer thunder boomer. She hoped she wouldn't have to walk through the woods alone in the middle of it. Or maybe she should hope she could make herself do so if the need arose. She'd never been outdoors during a thunderstorm in her life.

An animal crashed through the brush to her left and she jumped, then relaxed when she recognized the waddling gait of a raccoon. She walked on. If McCall was hiding in the woods as she was, he couldn't have gone far. And if he wasn't in the woods, then he was with Rich—and she didn't want to think about what had happened to him then. If she did, the panic pulsing at the edge of her consciousness would invade her thoughts full force and she would be unable to function. She would make a circle of the area, and if she didn't find Chris, she would walk out and get to the sheriff's office.

The longer McCall remained missing, the more worried D.J. became. What she wouldn't give to have him whisper in her ear, to have him kiss her and touch her and tell her she was his soul mate. They'd found each other at last. All the words she'd disparaged earlier would sound like wondrous promises when contrasted to the intense fear growing inside her—the very real fear that Rich had found Christian before she had, and that she'd lost the love of her life before she'd ever had him.

"Christian, where are you?" she whispered on a sigh.

A hand clamped onto her shoulder. She winced as pain shot through her injured limb. D.J. opened her mouth to scream. Another hand clamped over her lips, stifling the sound of terror before it could be born.

"Don't scream. Don't fight. Just stay still and shut up, D.J."

The voice in her ear was as familiar as her own. D.J. shut up, but she didn't keep still. She turned her head and met the eyes of the man who held her captive.

Chapter Sixteen

One minute Josie had been talking to D.J., joy and pride flooding her as her daughter started back to the cabin to meet Christian and her destiny. She couldn't wait to see Christian's face when D.J. admitted her love for him. She wanted to follow D.J., but the next thing she knew she was facing Raphael once more.

"You've done your job well, Josie. I must admit, I wasn't certain you'd be able to pull this one off. But according to the word from upstairs, you have. Congratulations."

"Thank you. I think. Now that she's learned what she needed to know, can I go back and tell her who I am? Since I won't be distracting her, I can't see how it will hurt." Josie held her breath, the hope in her heart almost bursting from her lips.

Raphael shook his head, and Josie's heart stuttered

in pain. *"You've got to let her go now, Josie. Your work there is finished. She'll find out who you are in due time in her own way."*

"But I want to tell her. I want to touch her just once and have her know her mother is holding her. Why can't I?"

"I told you everything happens for a reason. D.J. was meant to go through life without a mother on earth. I can't change that."

Josie searched her mind in desperation. She couldn't believe she'd been taken away from D.J. without a chance to even say good-bye. She had to get back to earth somehow. *"But what about the threat to Christian's life?"* she blurted. *"If he gets killed, D.J. won't be able to handle his death. She'll need me."*

"The events of the next few days are not your concern. It is your turn to have faith, Josie. D.J. has absorbed all you had to teach her. When there is nothing between her and disaster she must rely on faith and love. She must make a conscious decision to believe. Only then will she have learned the ultimate lesson."

The ultimate lesson?

Josie didn't like the sound of that. She searched her heart for news of her daughter. She didn't like what she learned. Five men approached the cabin—D.J.'s ex-husband, a man she couldn't remember seeing before but who must have been driving the black van, and the three who had accosted Christian on the highway. They were up to no good.

Josie turned to meet Raphael's gaze.

"No," he said.

"But—"

"No," he repeated, his voice booming like thunder. *"Your mission is complete. You aren't allowed back to the earth for any reason. Things are meant to happen as they happen. Any further interference from you could have disastrous results. I thought you wanted her to be happy."*

"I do." Josie sighed. How could Raphael expect her to leave D.J. and Christian now, when they needed her the most?

Her shoulders itched, and she reached to scratch one of them. Her fingers encountered a substance with the consistency of feathers. With a gasp, Josie twisted her neck to the side. She stared in awe. She had wings—big, beautiful blue and white wings. They shimmered and sparkled as though they'd been sprinkled with angel dust—and no doubt they had. She couldn't stop staring at them.

"You've earned them, Josie," Raphael said. *"Now leave the rest of D.J.'s problems to God. You have a date to keep."*

Josie tore her gaze away from the new wings. *"A date?"*

Raphael smiled, obviously thinking her new wings had removed her attention from her daughter's problems. He couldn't be further from the truth. *"Yes. You need to go to orientation. Then there will be a new arrival for you to greet. Someone I think you'll be very happy to see."*

"Who?"

Raphael shook his head. *"Patience is a virtue, dear Josie. We like to have new arrivals attend orientation with a loved one."* He turned his head. *"And here's your guide."*

Josie followed his gaze, and her heart skipped a beat. Her eyes filled with tears to match those of the woman approaching her. Josie's heart warmed with love.

"Mama?" she whispered.

Chris kept his hand over D.J.'s mouth until the tension in her eyes ebbed, then flowed away. The readiness of her body, the fight-or-flight reflex, had passed the second he'd whispered in her ear. But the wariness took longer to leave her. Though she wasn't terrified of him, his presence didn't soothe away her fears as her presence soothed away his. For some reason unease still hovered at the back of her eyes as she stared at him. What had happened to her while she walked in the woods?

Confident she wouldn't scream now that she knew who kept her company in the dark, Chris took his fingers away from her mouth and his hand away from her shoulder. She kicked him in the shin.

His breath came out on a hiss of pain and anger. "What the hell did you do that for?"

"You—you—you—creep."

Chris raised his eyebrows at the uncharacteristic mildness of her name-calling. "Creep? That's a new one, D.J. Can't you come up with anything better?"

"Lowlife. Vermin. Stinking, sneaking terrorist."

"Much better, and without a swear word in the bunch. I'm impressed. Now tell me what's gotten you so upset."

"What do you think? You scared me to death. I thought they'd gotten you. Taken you somewhere and killed you—or worse. And all the while you were following me. Why did you grab me, you fool? I could have shot you."

Chris focused on her last sentence and forgot, sort of, the stinging pain in his leg. "You've got your gun?"

Even in the darkness he could see her frown. "No. I suppose it's too much to hope that you've got it."

"Yeah, that's too much to hope. And I left the other one in the cabin too. In my suitcase."

"Damn. I should have looked for it. I guess I got preoccupied."

"You were inside?" Chris looked down at D.J. She glanced back at the cabin, a shadowy shape in the distance, while a thoughtful expression came over her face.

"Uh-huh."

He spun her around to face him, anger at her lack of caution getting the better of him. "Dammit, D.J., he could have hurt you. What did you go in there for?"

She tilted her head back to look into his eyes. "Relax, McCall. No one was there when I went in looking for you. I didn't know Rich had been here, though once I got inside it was obvious someone had been, since the living room resembles a barn after a tornado's been through its middle. I didn't know about Rich until I found the—"

Chris shook her, once, and she stopped talking. "Rich? You know the guy? Dark hair, perfect clothes, mean face."

D.J. nodded. "That's him. Rich Halloran." She shook her head in disgust. "I still can't believe I married the guy."

Chris released her and ran his hand through his hair. "Your ex-husband is the guy who's been trying to kill us?"

"Looks that way." She paused. "How do you know about him? You saw him? Talked to him?"

"I saw him." Chris shrugged. "I didn't wait around to talk. I could tell by his face he meant trouble. The way he crept around told me he hadn't come on a social call, and since we *are* on the run from someone who wants us dead—I put two and two together."

She nodded. "I hear you. For some reason he's got it into his head we're dangerous to him. Although he could just be looking for me, I doubt it. I think he's looking for this." She paused and dug inside her shirt, producing a photograph, which she held out toward him. Chris squinted but could see nothing in the dark.

"I can't see a thing."

She folded the picture and put it into the breast pocket of her shirt. "It's a picture you took at the station. The holding cell. How did you get in there? It's off limits to the public."

"The mayor told Captain Miller I was to have full run of the station."

"The mayor: I forgot about him. All right, that explains you, but not Rich."

Chris shook his head. He'd never known D.J. to babble except when she was very nervous. "Calm down. You're not making any sense. What's so great about this picture?"

"A Chicago gang member is in it, inside the holding cell, having a cozy conversation with my ex-husband."

"So? I didn't notice."

"Rich must have thought you did. For quite a while now Lou and I have been trying to find out who's trying to start up gang activity in Lakeview. It looks like Rich is the guy we're looking for, though how he's managed everything is beyond me."

Chris shook his head slowly. "Seems kind of far-fetched for him to try and kill us over a photo, which in the end proves nothing. Are you sure he's not just jealous? Jealousy is a more believable motivation for murder in my book."

"What would you know about jealousy, McCall?"

"Plenty," he muttered, remembering the sound of D.J.'s voice when she'd said "Danny boy" after waking up from her enforced rest. Chris grit his teeth to avoid saying anymore.

"Jealousy?" She said the word as though she had never heard it before. "What could Rich have to be jealous of?"

He breathed a sigh of relief that she hadn't probed any further about his own feelings. They had no time for that now. "He might be jealous of you and me."

D.J. laughed—the first true sound of mirth Chris could recall her uttering. "I don't think so, McCall. First of all, when we were married he was possessive, not jealous. He liked to tell me I was his and all that macho garbage. But he had no reason to be jealous. He knew better than anyone how I was—" She broke off and her gaze flicked to his, and then away. She continued without finishing her sentence. "Now that we're divorced Rich hates my guts—almost as much as I hate his. One thing we've always had in common is the ability to feel anger—and not much else." She paused for a moment, as though contemplating the similarity. Then she glanced up and saw Chris watching her. D.J. cleared her throat and held up her hand. Two fingers stood up in a peace sign. "Second—there wasn't any 'you and me' for him to be jealous of, even if he'd been around to see something that might have made him jealous, which he wasn't." She allowed her hand to fall back at her side, then turned to stare at the darkened cabin once again. "No, something else has set him off. And I'll bet this picture holds the key. This must be what they were looking for at your house and in the cabin. But now they want to kill us too. Probably because they think we've seen it and recognized Rich."

Something D.J. had said, and the way she'd said it, caught Chris's attention. He took a step closer, and his body brushed hers. She started, like a frightened doe, turning back toward him, her wide-eyed gaze meeting his. Her lips parted on a sigh, and he reached for her slowly so as not to frighten her further, then curled his fingers around the nape of her neck.

"What?" she whispered.

"You said there *wasn't* any us. Is there now, D.J.? Is there an 'us' now?"

She stared at him without blinking. He pulled her forward, bending to touch her parted lips with his. She moaned and leaned into him. He ran his tongue over her lower lip, then turned his head to delve deeper into her mouth.

"Over here," a voice shouted from the woods to their left.

They both tensed, frozen in a kiss, as though the lava from Pompeii had stilled them forever in the middle of the embrace.

Chris inched his mouth away from hers. "Shh," he whispered at the same time she did, warm breath mingling against damp lips.

Five bobbing lights approached the cabin from the far side of the forest. The lights solidified into flashlight beams and five men. They came around to the front of the house and stopped. D.J. took Chris's hand, and they crept closer to the cabin until they could see and hear everything clearly.

"They didn't come back," one of them said.

Though the night was dark and he couldn't see their faces clearly, Chris recognized the men—the three who had attacked him in Outgamie, a fourth who must have driven the van, and the man he now knew to be Rich Halloran.

"They will," Rich stated. "And if they don't, I'll find them tomorrow. We'll wait here overnight. Come on." He flicked his flashlight beam toward the house. "I didn't get to finish searching the place before you morons called me to come and show you the way. Let's finish it now."

"If we find the picture, we can get out of here tonight," the first man said as he walked toward the cabin. "I fuckin' hate the woods."

Rich's hand shot out with a speed that belied his well-dressed, laid-back exterior. The back of his hand connected with the speaker's nose. Chris heard the crunch of the bone breaking all the way into the woods. D.J. flinched, and he put his hand on her shoulder to calm her. She shifted and linked her fingers with his.

"Shit!" the man shrieked. "What did you do that for?"

Rich stepped toward the man and the three others fell back. The injured man went very still, then glanced up at Rich. Though Halloran spoke softly, the menace in his words punctuated them enough so Chris, and D.J., could hear him quite well.

"We aren't going anywhere until they're both dead. Can you get that through your thick skull? I paid you guys well to do the job, but you screwed up. Now I have to do it myself. There is no statute of limitations on murder. And though I won't fry in this state, I don't plan to spend the rest of my life behind bars. McCall and my sweet little bitch of a wife are going to die. Tonight or tomorrow, I don't care which. But they're going to be dead."

"All right, all right." The man sidled away from Halloran and walked into the cabin, holding his hands to his bleeding nose. The other three followed, and seconds later the lights inside the house flared to life. Rich stood outside a moment longer. He turned and swept his flashlight around the perimeter of the woods. D.J. shrank back from the searching light. Chris squeezed her fingers, warning her not to move. For a long minute, Rich stared into the darkness, and Chris could almost feel the man's evil gaze creep over them before moving on. Seconds later, Halloran looked their way again, and his eyes narrowed. He took a step forward just as a crash of thunder shook the earth. Halloran looked up. The sky poured icy rain into his face. He hesitated another second, then shook the water from his slick, black hair and turned toward the house. Chris and D.J. both sagged in relief.

What was it about Rich Halloran that made Chris think of another long ago night when another, younger man had sought his death on a city street?

Chris stared at Halloran's retreating back. D.J.'s hand tightened on his in the darkness, and he returned the pressure with a squeeze of his own fingers. She gave a soft sigh of comfort. Halloran froze with his hand on the doorknob. He spun around, the beam of his flashlight honing in on them as they huddled in the woods.

D.J. jumped and gasped in shock. Halloran smiled, a smug, evil smile that tugged another cord of recognition in Chris. But he had no time to analyze the pull.

"They're here," Halloran shouted to his cronies. He yanked a gun from his shoulder holster as he ran toward them.

"Run," D.J. hissed and yanked Chris along with her as she did just that.

The last thing Chris saw before he turned and followed her was Halloran sliding in the icy mud, then falling to his hands and knees. His men came out of the door and promptly fell on top of him. The sound of curses followed them into the night.

D.J. ran with unerring instinct through the dark woods—almost as though she had a destination in mind. The trees shaded the ground from the worst of the icy rain and helped them to keep their footing. Whenever lightning flashed or thunder crashed D.J. flinched, but she kept on running. If Chris hadn't known better, he would have thought she feared the storm. But that couldn't be—D.J. feared nothing.

They had a head start on Halloran's hoods, but Chris could hear them crashing through the brush somewhere behind. A gunshot echoed and a bullet sliced through the trees above them, far enough away to show that their pursuers shot in vain.

"Where are we going?" he asked.

"Shut up and run, McCall. Rich knows these woods almost as well as I do. If we didn't have this storm to help, he'd be on us, and from the sound of things we'd be dead."

They continued to run for another fifteen minutes. The sounds behind them faded and stopped. D.J. had begun to tire, favoring her shoulder as she ran.

"Stop, D.J. Just for a minute. You've got to rest."

"No. We're almost there. If I can just find the right path, we'll be safe." She continued to jog, her head moving back and forth as she searched in the dense brush for the path she'd mentioned.

"If Rich knows the woods as well as you, won't he find us?"

She stopped and bent down, focusing her gaze on the overgrown ground. "I said he knows them *almost* as well. *Almost.* There's a back way to town. A path—little more than a deer trail, really. It'll take a while and it won't be easy, but we'll come out right behind Danny's house. He and I used the trail

339

all the time when we were kids."

"And Rich doesn't know about the trail?"

"No. It's pretty treacherous. I wouldn't try it if we had any other choice." She used her forearm to push aside some long grass and revealed an overgrown path. "Bingo."

A shout from behind them made her tense and cast a wary glance back at the woods. Then her eyes met his, and Chris read the fear there. He had never seen fear in her eyes before. He didn't like it. Since when had D.J. cared enough about anything to be afraid?

"Let's go," she said, and crouched to enter the tunnellike path. Chris followed her. She brushed the grasses back into place, curtaining off the entrance. "If we're lucky, the rain will wash away our tracks and they'll go right past this."

"If we're lucky," Chris muttered.

They were both soaked. The rain continued to fall in increasing torrents, the freezing temperature making Chris's body tingle with cold. D.J. took one step forward—and slipped. Chris grabbed for her, but his grasping fingers met thin air. He looked down, but she had disappeared. Under his feet the rain had made the small gulley of a trail into a creek. As he watched, another flood of water came from behind him and his feet slid too. Seconds later he slid downhill amid icy mud and water to land in a large, chest-deep puddle next to D.J.

"What the hell happened?" he asked.

"The northern Wisconsin version of *Romancing the Stone*. Mud slide à la ice storm."

Voices from above made them both go still and quiet.

"I don't see them."

"They couldn't have disappeared. They're hiding somewhere."

"Come on, Halloran. Let's get back inside. They'll still be here to kill in the morning. In this storm no one could get back to town without a car."

"Shit. This is a waste of time." Halloran must have stopped right at the top of the trail; his voice drifted down to them quite clearly. Chris had a sudden vision of the ground beneath Halloran's feet giving way as it had moments before beneath Chris's own. Then the man who stalked them would land in their laps, and their lives would be measured in seconds. A quick glance at D.J.'s white face told Chris she'd had the same thought. He reached for her hand, taking her icy, stiff fingers into his equally cold palm.

"Let's go."

The voices receded in the direction from which they'd come, and Chris breathed easier. He looked at D.J., who'd closed her eyes in relief. When she opened them he smiled at her. She smiled back—a bit shaky, but a smile nonetheless.

"Now what?" he asked.

"The trail's washed out."

"Really? I didn't notice."

She rolled her eyes at his sarcasm. "There's one other way out of here, and that's the trail in front of the cabin."

"I don't think so. I've had enough of Rich Halloran for the night."

"I've had enough of him for a lifetime. If we wait until morning, this excess water should wash down to the river and we ought to be able to get out on this back trail."

"Sounds good, but what about tonight?"

D.J. remained silent for a long minute, her gaze focused on a point in the distance. Then, as though she'd made a tough decision, her shoulders raised and lowered and she turned back to him.

"There's a place. A cabin in the swamp where we can stay."

"Your ex-husband won't come knocking on the door in the middle of the night, I hope."

She held out her hand to him, palm up. "Trust me, McCall. I'll keep you alive until the morning."

He laid his hand in hers. "Promise?"

"I'll promise you anything if you'll follow me anywhere." She didn't smile, but Chris heard one in her voice.

"You've got a deal. Just tell me where we're going."

"My mother and father had a cabin much farther back in these woods. No one's been there since my father built the new house closer to the road."

Chris remembered the trip they'd taken to reach the cabin. "The new house is closer to the road?"

"Just wait until you see this place, McCall. You'll think you were in a four-star, luxury hotel last night. No electric, no heat, no plumbing. My parents were nuts."

"Speaking of nuts, you're sure Rich doesn't know about the place?"

"I'm ninety-nine percent sure he doesn't know

this cabin exists. The only reason I know is because my gran told me, and I searched the place out when my father wasn't around to stop me. I can't believe he'd tell Rich about the old cabin. He'd have no reason to."

"All right," Chris agreed, and gave her fingers a squeeze of encouragement. "We've got to go somewhere for the night. Right now any roof is better than no roof at all."

"My sentiments exactly." She pulled her fingers from his grasp and stuck her hands into the pockets of her jacket. She went still, then pulled the cellular phone from one pocket.

"I didn't know you had that. We can call for help."

She shook her head. "Not anymore. It's soaked." She flicked the button, listened for a moment, then tossed the phone into the water. "I owe Danny boy a phone."

Thunder rumbled, farther away now, but D.J. flinched anyway.

"You don't like the thunder, do you?" Chris asked.

She glanced away, staring into the trees.

"Do you?"

"No. I hate it. I always have. I know it's stupid. Danny used to try to talk me out of the fear, but even his psychoanalytical bull didn't help. Let's get out of the rain." She strode off into the swamp.

Chris smiled to himself. At least D.J. had one irrational fear. He liked that in a woman. He had a feeling she wouldn't flinch at snakes, mice, or spiders—but thunderstorms were another story.

They slogged out of the waist-deep water and made their way to slightly drier ground. D.J. zigged and zagged through the trees as though her way was marked in tiny lights, like the small county airport runways he'd observed throughout the state—most often located in the middle of a field. Chris had all he could manage to hold on to her hand and avoid knocking himself unconscious on a low-hanging tree branch. Bushes and trees with sharp prickers snapped at their clothes and tore at exposed flesh. His hands stung with minor scratches. His cheeks and nose stung with cold as needlelike sleet slapped against his face. The night became ever darker as the trees above thickened in rhythm with the thickening of the cloud cover. By the time D.J. slowed her steps Chris could barely make out the outline of her body in front of him. He took a step closer, trying to see what she stared at with so much interest. His shoe squelched ankle deep into icy mud.

"The heart of the swamp," she said. "If it was spring, this place would be waist high in green water."

"Sounds terrific. Let's come back for a visit then."

"I'll never understand why my father built the original cabin right off the edge of the swamp. The deer hide here. I guess he thought they might as well too. So can we."

She started off, and Chris hurried to catch up with her. Out of the black misty darkness appeared a cabin.

Mist? Chris looked up at the pitch-dark night. When had the mist descended?

The creeping, smoky tendrils looked pretty spooky. The building looked like an escapee from the back lot of the "Beverly Hillbillies." The porch tilted at an impossible angle. The roof had caved in on one side. The windows gaped black and empty.

D.J. stepped onto the porch, and one boot broke through the rotted wood. Chris caught her arm as she teetered backward. Yanking her foot clear with a curse, D.J. continued to mutter under her breath as she picked her way to the door. Chris followed with equal care.

The entire area held a surrealistic air—if Chris hadn't known better, he would have thought he'd stepped into a Stephen King film. Maybe *Pet Semetery*, when the poor, beleaguered hero finds the cursed pet burial ground. Any minute now Chris expected to see a cat zombie appear in the window.

The door swung open without a creak. Chris frowned. So did D.J.

"He's been up here."

"Who?" Chris said, hoping she didn't mean her ex-husband.

"Ed. My father." She shook her head. "I didn't think he'd ever come back here. The place reminds him too much of her. But someone oiled this door." She stepped inside and fumbled around. After several curses a match flared, and a soft, wavering light crept out the doorway, silhouetting D.J. just inside, holding a lantern. She held it up higher and looked around the one-room cabin. Chris stepped up behind her and peered over her shoulder. "And someone cleaned this place up."

"I'll say." The inside looked as neat as the outside didn't: the fireplace stocked with wood, the bed made up with quilts, everything dusted and washed. The lantern light showed the gaping windows didn't truly gape since they had been covered in plastic. A rough cabin, but not as rough as it had looked at first glance.

Chris gave D.J. a little push. She looked at him with a frown marring the bridge of her nose, her mind still focused on the mystery of the cleaned cabin. "Inside, D.J." He indicated the direction with his head. "I'm cold. And my rear end is getting mighty wet out on this porch."

"Oh, yeah. Sorry." She stepped further into the cabin and set the lantern on the kitchen table. The wooden structure had been made by hand, heavy and sturdy, crafted roughly but well. Furniture wrought by the same hand peopled the cabin. The quilts and pillows on the bed and couch were also handmade, by another hand. The cabin spoke of the two people who had lived there long ago.

Chris closed the door. His fingers searched for but didn't find a lock. But why would there be a lock out here, where the most dangerous predators feared man more than man feared them? Or at least such had been the case until Rich Halloran had invaded the forest. Chris turned away from the door with a shrug. If Halloran and his thugs found them here, they'd need more than a locked wooden door to keep the five men out.

He glanced up to find D.J. staring at the room as if in a trance. She turned in a slow circle as she spoke. "The other times I came here the place stood abandoned. Dirty. Animals living inside. I couldn't understand how anyone could be happy here. As happy as they must have been for my father to fall apart when he lost her. But now, with the place like this, I can see how they lived. What life must have been like for them. I've been thinking about her so much lately. I don't know why. Maybe it's being in these woods again." She looked at him, and Chris saw the tears threatening in her eyes. "I can almost feel her, Chris," she whispered. "Can't you?"

D.J. with tears on her eyelashes did funny things to Chris's insides. He swallowed against the thickness in his own throat and crossed the room toward her. With no encouragement on his part, she came into his arms, wrapping her uninjured limb around his neck, and leaned her head on his shoulder. He held her close. When he heard the water drip from their bodies onto the floor Chris pulled back.

"We've got to get out of this wet stuff before we freeze."

She nodded and stepped away. "Start the wood stove. I'll get some towels."

"Do you think we should have a fire? What about the smoke?"

"We'll warm up the house and then put the fire out. Rich and his buddies are warm and toasty in the cabin. They won't come out again until first light."

Chris nodded and did as she'd asked. By the time she returned, her hair toweled dry and her body wrapped in a blanket, he had an admirable fire glowing in the wood stove.

D.J. handed him a blanket and a towel, then sat on the couch in front of the stove, her back to him, and stared into the flames.

"I was born here, you know."

347

Chris had just taken off his shirt. He paused in the act of unzipping his jeans and glanced at her. She continued to stare at the fire. "No, I didn't know."

"In the middle of a thunderstorm, just like this one. I was born. My mother died."

That explains her thunderstorm problem. Chris kept the thought to himself as she continued to speak.

"I never knew her, but I missed her. Gran did her best. Ed did his worst. I survived. But it would have been nice to have a mother."

"It is nice. Take my word for it." Chris positioned his wet clothes on the kitchen chairs as D.J. had done, then wrapped a blanket around his body and joined her on the couch. "Wasn't there anyone else in your life you looked up to—a teacher, a coach, a Girl Scout leader? There must have been one woman somewhere in your life who mothered you."

She glanced at him. Her gaze focused on his bare chest, then slid away. "After Gran, no one. At least no one until—" She stiffened and broke off.

"Until . . . ?" Chris put his arm around D.J. and drew her against his side. She cuddled up to him, her head resting in the crook of his neck. He pushed away the thought of D.J., as naked beneath her blanket as he was beneath his. She wanted to talk now—and he would listen.

D.J. shook her head, the movement of her hair tickling his chin. "I don't want to talk about her right now. Maybe someday."

Chris liked the way she said "someday," as if

there was a future for them. He hadn't brought up the topic that had made her run from him earlier. Since they had all night, perhaps now presented a good time. The words Dan Franklin had spoken to him—was it only a day ago?—ran through his mind.

She never told me her real name either. I always imagined if D.J. ever let her guard down enough with someone to reveal such a secret, her cold heart might thaw a bit.

"What's your real name, D.J.?"

"Huh? What on earth does my name have to do with anything, McCall?" The ice had returned to her voice. D.J. sat up, pulling herself from his embrace. When she made a move to stand, Chris grabbed her hands and pulled her back down onto the couch.

"Don't run away again." When her lips tightened, as though she would refuse, Chris leaned forward and placed a soft kiss on those tense lips. "Please," he whispered. "Trust me, D.J. I only want to love you."

She pulled back and stared into his face, searching his eyes as if looking for a deeper truth. "Love? I don't know what love is. I don't know if I can give you what you need."

"All I need is you, D.J. I've waited for you all my life. Now that I've found you I'm not going to let you go. You just have to trust me. Can you trust me? Can you give us just one chance?"

"I don't know if I love you. I can't promise I'll be able to love you. I don't think I could stand it if you grew to hate me because I couldn't be what you needed. And tonight, when I thought you might be injured or dead—I hurt, Chris. I couldn't think. I couldn't breathe. I can't live like that."

"So you won't take a chance? You'll give up something wonderful so you can be safe but never happy?"

"God, you sound just like . . ." She sighed and shrugged. "Maybe I don't have the guts. You don't understand all the fears and the insecurities in my screwed-up little mind. You don't know what you're getting into, McCall."

He let go of her hands to clasp her upper arms tightly. He'd had enough of her I-don't-believe-in-love nonsense. They both could have been killed today. The time for prevaricating was past; the time for truth at hand. He gave her a little shake, hoping to joggle some sense into her. "Don't call me 'McCall.' I know you're trying to push me away when you do that, and it won't work. I'm here to stay. I know more about screwed-up minds than you think. Yours isn't so bad—when compared to my own."

He could see the hope flickering in her eyes, the desire hovering on her lips. They could have so much if she'd only just believe.

She smiled, and his heart turned over with love. When she smiled just so she looked like an angel. Chris released her arms. One hand reached out and cupped her cheek in his palm.

She closed her eyes and turned her mouth toward his hand. Her lips touched the softer skin at the center; then her tongue flicked out and tasted him. The caress made him catch his breath against the desire surging through him.

She turned her head, rubbing her cheek along his palm once more, and her eyes met his. He read the same desire in those eyes that tingled throughout his body.

"Now, Christian. Make love to me now." She leaned toward him, her eyes shining bright green in the reflection from the lamplight. "Show me the difference between having sex and making love. Make me believe. I think you're the only one who can."

He didn't answer her with words. He let his lips prove to her the truth of that statement.

Gently he kissed her face—her cheeks, her chin, her closed eyelids. Then he moved to her mouth. He wanted to be gentle, to show her his love in such a way that she would always know he cherished her. But when their lips met and hers parted her soft sigh of trust mingling with his haggard breathing, the raging desire he'd banked within him since the first time they'd kissed sparked to life.

Needing to be closer, he pulled her into his lap, then froze when she uttered a small whimper of pain. He raised his head, but she pulled him back, her fingers strong on his neck.

"No, don't stop. I'm all right," she said before her lips met his once more.

Her firm buttocks pressed against his arousal and he shifted to relieve some of the pressure. She moaned and pressed herself against him harder. Sweat broke out on his brow. He'd waited so long for this—could he wait any longer?

As though they had a mind of their own, his

hands had strayed to the top of the blanket. One yank and the covering pooled at her waist. She gave a startled gasp as the cooler air met her warmed skin, then clutched his fingers and drew them to her flesh.

As he'd expected, she wore nothing under the blanket but the bandage protecting her wound. He had no interest in her wound just now. Instead, he cupped her full breasts in his palms. They filled his hands to perfection, as though she'd been made just for him, which he knew she had. Her lips left his as she arched into his palms. His thumbs rubbed over the hardened nubs, and he watched in fascination as they hardened further. He bent his head and took one into his mouth.

The effect on them both was electric. D.J's fingers clenched in his hair, bringing him closer. Her bottom shifted against him, and he clenched his teeth against the urge to throw the blanket aside and bury himself inside her without any more preliminaries. He took a deep breath and focused his mind on the love brimming over in his heart. He wouldn't act like an animal; he would show her love or he wouldn't do this.

Concentrating on D.J. with all his might, he pushed the rush of lust back for a moment. He drew her nipple into his mouth, using his tongue against the nub to push it against the top of his mouth as he suckled.

She cried out his name and turned in his lap, her thighs on either side of his so she straddled him. She pushed against him again, and he grasped her hips to still her.

"Easy, D.J. Not so fast, honey. We've got all night."

She took a deep breath and nodded.

"Let's move this to the bed, shall we?" Chris found talking helped to calm the blood pounding in his ears. They stood, and he took her hand. She clutched the blanket around her waist as though the covering were all that remained between her and disaster. He led her the short distance to the bed. Still holding her fingers in his, he drew back the quilt, then turned toward her.

He placed his hand over hers and tugged her fingers away from their stranglehold on the blanket. The covering fell to the floor at her feet. D.J. avoided his gaze as he perused her full breasts and long, toned legs. Chris put his palms against her waist and rubbed his thumbs over the prominent bones at her hips. He bent to kiss her neck.

"You're beautiful, D.J. So damn beautiful you make me ache."

"I'm not, Chris. I've never been beautiful. My hair's too red and too short. I'm too big in some places and too small in others. You don't have to tell me I'm beautiful. I want you anyway."

He lifted his head and looked into her face. She still avoided his eyes. Chris put his fingertip under her chin and drew her head up until he could look into her eyes. "I don't know who told you those things, though I have a pretty good idea. Don't tell me you're not beautiful. I can see the truth."

The corners of her lips tilted upward in a small smile of pleasure. In answer, she tugged his blanket free and it joined hers on the floor under their bare

353

feet. Now he stood as naked as she, and D.J. did the perusing.

"I know beautiful when I see it." She drew her finger down the middle of his chest, twirling a curl of black hair around the tip. "And you're it. I've always loved your body."

"The feeling's mutual." Chris sat on the bed and pulled D.J. closer until she stood between his legs. The time they'd spent undressing and talking had done wonders for his self-control. Though he still had a near painful erection, his head had cleared to the point where he could concentrate on D.J. once again.

Her breasts were even with his mouth. *Perfect.* He nuzzled his lips against the underside of one, tracing a path with his tongue until he found a nipple once more. Round and round his tongue rolled, then his lips closed on her and he sucked. One long pull was all it took for her knees to buckle. Her body leaned heavily against him, and they fell backward onto the bed, her length pressed to his own.

Chris turned, and D.J. tumbled onto the soft sheets at his side. He came up onto his elbow, his head resting in his hand so he could look at her. Her eyes were half-closed as she watched him watch her. She smiled when their gazes met, and she reached for him, her fingertips grazing his nipples. They hardened at her touch, the drawing sensation shooting straight to his groin. He leaned forward and kissed her, their tongues stroking and melding in an erotic dance that parodied the final act of love.

Her earlier shyness receded and her fingertips

danced down his chest, splaying along the tense muscles in his stomach. She didn't stop her exploration until her fingers grazed his shaft. Chris started at the sensation of her callused hands on his hardened flesh. Her fingers closed around him, warm and sure, drawing upward from the base to the tip, then returning for another stroke. The pleasure became almost painful, and he put his hand on hers.

"Stop. I'll—" He sighed and bit his lip.

"You'll what, Chris?" She made a sound deep in her throat—halfway between a chuckle and a sigh. Ignoring his hand, she continued to stroke him.

When he perched so close to the edge he could barely keep from tumbling into the abyss she drew him over her, guiding him to her moist entrance. He clenched his teeth and held back.

"What?" she gasped, her voice a sob. "You can't do this to me again, Christian. I'll kill you."

"I don't have anything."

She shook her head, moving it back and forth on the pillow. Her eyes met his and she smiled, her breath puffed out in harsh little pants. "The only thing I'll catch, Christian, is a part of you. That's all right." She touched him again, and he moaned. "It's all right," she whispered.

She raised her legs to his hips and placed her palms against his buttocks, pulling him toward her once more. He went with a deep forward thrust that had them both groaning. His arms began to shake with tension as he held his upper body still above her while his lower body moved in slowly, sinuously.

The waves started deep within her where he lodged, and his body answered them with waves of its own. She arched her back, pulling him more deeply inside. Her body tightened and released around him, and he understood what he'd been searching for during all the long, lonely years until he'd found her.

D.J. opened her eyes and caught his gaze. Their souls met and mated as their bodies did the same, and as the storm receded, she pulled him to her and held him close to her heart.

A long time later, when the night reached its darkest point, the thunder and lightning ceased and the forest around them slept. Inside they drowsed, warm in each other's arms. D.J. shifted. "My name," she whispered into his ear, her warm breath stirring Chris to life once more. "My name is Daphne Josephine."

Chris smiled into the darkness. He was halfway home. He gathered her close and held her next to his heart throughout the rest of the long, but no longer lonely, night.

Chapter Seventeen

D.J. slept in Christian's arms. Sometime in the hours between midnight and dawn they awoke and made love once more. This time the pace was as slow and leisurely as the first had been fast and frenzied. Both ways had their assets. She planned to spend the rest of her life learning all the ways she could make love to Christian and he to her.

He'd told her he loved her, over and over as he moved within her, and she believed him. But she still couldn't bring herself to return those words in kind. She could tell the omission hurt him, though he said nothing. She didn't want to hurt him, but she still couldn't form those three words on her lips even though they were imprinted upon her heart. They'd have plenty of time for words later, she assured herself. Someday she'd tell him.

Someday.

The fear that had stalked her throughout their rush through the woods to the cabin had receded at the first touch of his lips on hers. The cabin seemed an enchanted place where nothing and no one could hurt them. Throughout the night, D.J. slept safe in Christian's arms, their bodies curved around each other, hands entwined.

The sun didn't awaken them. The crash of the front door splintering inward did.

"What the—?" Chris sat up.

D.J. did the same. She clutched the quilt to her chin while the blood drained from her face.

Rich Halloran stood at the foot of the bed. He stared at her with dislike as he pointed the missing .9 mm at her head.

Rich's cold gaze switched to Chris and his eyes narrowed. "You're in bed with my wife, McCall. Get out." He motioned with the gun.

Chris tensed. D.J. put her hand on his thigh beneath the covers, a signal to keep still and quiet. He got the message.

"I'm not your wife, Rich. Not anymore. What do you want?"

Rich ignored her. "I told you to get away from my wife, McCall. Do it now or I'll shoot her where she lies." The gun swung back toward D.J. and Chris got up.

"I thought you said he wasn't jealous." Chris reached for a towel and twisted the material around his waist.

D.J. didn't take her eyes off Rich. He kept his gaze on Chris. "He's not. Like most guys who aren't secure in their masculinity, he likes to play macho man."

Rich ignored her taunt, swinging the gun back and forth as he motioned for her to get out of the bed. He kept a wary eye on Chris while he stared at her with a cold, purposeful gaze. "Now you, D.J. Get up."

The thought of getting out of the bed and standing stark naked before Rich made D.J. swallow hard to keep from gagging. But the way he stared at her convinced her he meant what he said. Would she rather be dead or embarrassed? D.J. moved to the edge of the bed.

"No. Don't move, D.J."

She turned and looked at Chris with a frown. He didn't look her way but remained focused on Rich. The two men stared at each other like two wolves standing over a single kill in the dead of winter.

"Get up," Rich ordered. "I've seen it all before, McCall. I'm not interested anymore."

"I don't care. She's not getting out of the bed until she has her clothes on."

"I came here to kill you both. It would suit me fine to do the job now and get out of here." He cocked the gun.

"No!" D.J. jumped from the bed and ran across the room. With her back to the two men, she stuffed her body into her still damp shirt and jeans. She grabbed Chris's jeans and tossed them to him.

"I didn't say he could get dressed," Rich snapped.

"Be a sport and let the guy die with his pants on. It won't kill you."

Rich narrowed his eyes at her tone, then

shrugged his acquiescence. Chris dropped the towel and replaced it with his jeans. He motioned for D.J. to come to him and she did. Chris put his arm around her shoulder and drew her close. Despite the relaxed pose, she could feel the coiled tension of his body. He waited for an opening. When he found one he would strike. She remembered how he had taken out the three men in Outgamie. Even though they'd had a knife and Rich had a gun, some of D.J.'s fear left her at the memory. If she had to face a nutcase like Rich, Chris would be the one she'd chose to have beside her.

Rich stared at the two of them, jealousy shining from his eyes. Rich had never been jealous—but then, he'd never had cause. Until Chris came along she'd had no interest in men, sex, or anything but work.

"I could have told you she isn't worth the trouble," Rich sneered. "I've never had a woman more frigid than D.J."

"Frigid? D.J.?" Chris laughed. "I don't think so. Not with the right man, anyway."

Rich's lips tightened.

D.J.'s lips were numbed by fear. She dug her fingers into Chris's side, warning him to shut up. Rich had always been unpredictable. She had never known what he would do when he got angry. She still had a hard time believing he meant to kill them both. She had to keep him talking—find out why he'd do such a thing. Then maybe she could figure out a way to talk him out of whatever he had planned. Or at least keep him occupied in the hope her father or Danny made their way up here before

Rich lost patience. And if not earthly help, perhaps heavenly . . . D.J. looked up, hoping with all her heart to see bare feet swinging above her. No luck. How could Josie, her guardian angel, have deserted her in her greatest time of need? Unless D.J. and Chris were meant to be together in heaven as they hadn't been on earth. Coldness seeped into her bones at the thought.

No way. She would fight such a fate with every resource she could dredge up. D.J. bit her lip until she tasted blood and feeling flooded back into her body. "Rich." Her voice wavered, and he glanced at her with a smirk. Like an animal, he could smell her fear—and he loved it. She cleared her throat and tried again. "You could care less about me, about Chris and I. You just want to control me as usual. You know being possessive doesn't work— and hitting me didn't either."

"He hit you?" Chris's voice, usually so calm, always the voice of reason, now contained an undercurrent of fury she'd never heard in it before. She looked at him and saw the same fury clouding his face.

"Once. He never tried it again."

Chris glanced at her and she shook her head, one small shake. *Let it go,* she thought. *Don't lose your temper and get us killed because of something that's over and done with.*

He nodded, as though he'd heard her, then returned his gaze to Rich. The fury faded from his face, but she could still see the anger in the way he clenched his hands.

"Tell us what you want, Rich. Then get out."

Rich's gaze flicked away from Chris and settled on her. He stared at her for a long time, measuring her words. Finally he laughed. She didn't like the sound of that laugh. "I'm holding a gun, threatening to kill you, and still you're giving me orders. You always were a gutsy broad, D.J. I hated that about you. I still do. But in this case you're right. I could care less who you screw. I know what a cold little fish you are. If McCall here thinks you were good, who am I to argue? You'll both be dead soon enough, and no one will be the wiser."

She ignored the insults and the threats in an effort to keep him talking. "How did you find us?"

"I made it my business a long time ago to know everything about you and your dad. Information is power. Once, when we were up here hunting, your dad got drunk and told me all about his dead wife and the cabin. I checked the place out in case I ever needed to hide somewhere. When you disappeared last night I knew where I'd find you in the morning."

"What happened to your thug friends?"

"I left them at the cabin. I've found murder is best accomplished on your own. The fewer witnesses, the better."

D.J.'s heart gave a stutter at his cold-blooded statement. She'd been married to this man. Admittedly, the marriage had been a mistake, but she'd once hoped to make a future with him. Had he changed so much over the past year? Or had she been too preoccupied with her career and her problems to see the truth? There was so much going on here she didn't understand. "Murder, Rich? You talk like you've done a lot of killing. I know that's not true."

"You don't know a damn thing. I used to laugh myself sick over the stupidity of my cop wife. Both you and your dad. And Colleen, too. She was always mothering me. But she comes in handy on occasion."

A flash of understanding came to D.J. If she hadn't been so preoccupied with guardian angels and gangs and love, she would have figured out Rich's contact a long time ago. She gave herself a mental kick. "The holding cell. Colleen has the keys. And the phone. When I called Captain Miller the phone kept clicking. Colleen was on the switchboard. She listened in and told you where we were."

"Yeah. As I said, she comes in handy on occasion. I told her we were trying to get back together and had had a little disagreement. So she took pity on me and told me where you were." He laughed at the older woman's gullibility. "And I told her I wanted to talk to that gang kid—to set him straight. She thought Ed had done the same for me, so she bought it. The three of you always thought you were saving the poor, misguided Irish kid, when all along I used you and your connections to keep my true business from being discovered."

"Trying to start up gang activity in Lakeview."

"Yeah. I guess I should have known you'd figure everything out eventually. Especially with lover boy here to help you out. All those years I spent in Chicago with my aunt gave me the knowledge and the connections. Back then, the gangs weren't what they are now. But I was in at the beginning on a lot of them, and I learned how to get things rolling. When I returned to Lakeview, married you, and opened my shop, I had the perfect legitimate front for what I really wanted to do—start up a network of gangs, first in Lakeview and then throughout Wisconsin. I tell the kids where to get their drugs and their guns, then take a cut from both parties— sort of a finder's fee. Making money is almost too easy."

"If you were making so much money, how come you kept hitting me up for more?"

"The more money I've got, the more connections I can buy, the more money I make." He shrugged. "It's not really about money anyway. It's about power. Control. My parents and your father sent me away when I had no say in the matter. I swore then that I'd find a way to be the one in control someday. Now I am. As for the money, every time I came around the station asking for more I had an excuse to hang around and check the place out. Until lover boy took my picture."

"You're going to kill us over a picture?" D.J. still had a hard time believing all their troubles were because of one stupid picture. "Don't you think the results will be more trouble than they're worth? Killing a cop is big time, Rich. You won't get away with it."

He shook his head at her, a smirk twisting his mouth. "But I will. I've got the perfect plan, as always. Once I kill you two, you're going for a swim in the swamp. Up here, it'll be months, maybe years, before they find you."

"No, it won't ," D.J. snapped. "Danny knows we're

here. So does half the town. And you've been seen in Isadora, Rich. They'll be looking for you."

He shrugged away her warning. "You'll have been shot with your own gun, so for all anyone knows, you were the victims of a murder-suicide. Everyone at the station always thought you were nuts anyway, D.J. Officer Ice who threw away a great man for her job—this will just prove them right. I'll take care of Franklin on my way out of town. That one will be my pleasure. By tonight I'll be out of the country. I've set up the network; now all I have to do is keep the connections flowing. I can do that from anywhere. Once I know things have calmed down and I'm off the hook I'll come back and do the same deal in another town."

The callous threat to Danny made D.J. grind her teeth, but she let it pass, not wanting to bring up her friend's name again and incite Rich's anger. "Why are you going to so much trouble? The picture Chris took won't prove anything against you. So you were talking to a guy in the holding cell? Big deal. Why chase us all over the state to kill us for something like that?"

Rich started to laugh. He couldn't seem to stop. D.J. shifted to glance at Chris. He watched Rich like a tiger who'd just come upon a deer. His arm dropped away from her waist. He took a step forward. Rich stopped laughing and brought the gun back up.

"Stay right there, karate boy. I heard what you did to my men. I should have known better than to send them, since I heard all about you years ago from your dear brother."

Chris frowned. "Kirk? You know him?"

"Of course. I make it a point to know everything I can about all my victims. Kirk and I have been pals for a long time. He's one of the main delivery people for my business—both legit and illegal. Traveling salesmen are the handiest of assets. I searched him out first to keep tabs on you—but when I discovered we thought a lot alike I took him into the business with me."

"Figures. You two are made for each other."

"Thank you. Kirk has quite a few traits I admire. Namely, he hates your guts, which was something I could work on for my own needs. A little unreasonable on his part, but I'm not going to argue family business. I should have let him get rid of you years ago; God knows he wanted to badly enough. But I took pains to make sure we never crossed paths. Surprisingly, it wasn't hard to stay out of your way—we don't exactly travel in the same circles."

"Thank God," Chris muttered.

Rich's lips tightened at the insult. His voice, which had been deceptively calm, now took on an edge. "At least we didn't until you decided to invade the police station and hit on my wife. Maybe there is such a thing as fate, or predestination. We certainly seem to keep crossing paths, and always with such terrible results. It's a shame. Though I don't mind killing, I prefer to avoid it if I can. Too messy—and there're always questions, questions, questions."

D.J. had remained silent, trying to follow Rich's meandering speech. She couldn't. Finally her curiosity got the better of her, and she blurted out her questions. "Rich, you've lost me. You didn't see

Chris until last week at the station. How can you say you've been watching him for a long time? None of this makes any sense."

Rich shook his head. "D.J., D.J., D.J." He made a *tsking* sound with his tongue. She wanted to smack him in the mouth. "Sometimes I wonder how you have the brains to come in out of the rain. There's more to this than you know." He looked at Chris. "Isn't there, McCall? A lot more."

Though they no longer touched, D.J. stood close enough to Chris to feel his start of surprise. "I don't know what you're talking about."

"You don't? Well, I'm sure you'll remember real soon. I recognized you the second you walked into the station, and I knew you'd place me eventually. Especially once you'd seen my picture and had a chance to study it. I wanted to get it away from you before that happened, but the boys couldn't seem to find the thing when they searched your house." He glanced at D.J. "Then you started hanging around and we didn't get another chance to look. I figured McCall had seen it by then and maybe shown it to you—you two were so tight. So I knew I'd have to kill you both. I don't look that much different now than I did as a teenager. And after the night we shared, McCall, I must have been a prime figure in a lot of your nightmares." Rich grinned, relishing the idea that he'd starred in someone's bad dreams. "Heard any tigers roar lately, karate boy?"

D.J. let out a sigh of exasperation. Rich had always talked too much, but this was getting ridiculous. He was ranting. "What are you talking about, Rich?"

Before he could answer Chris took a staggering

step sideways and bumped into her. She turned toward him with a gasp of fright. He stared at Rich as though he'd seen a ghost. The sudden paleness of his skin scared her. His hand came out and clasped her shoulder as he steadied himself. She grasped his other hand. Ice cold. She held his fingers between her palms. "Chris? Christian? What is it?"

"Leave him alone," Rich snapped. "He's remembering now. Aren't you, McCall?" He took a step forward, his gaze focused on Chris's white face, as though he was enjoying the pain he saw there. "I knew you hadn't figured out the truth yet because no one came looking for me. After Colleen listened in on D.J.'s call to the captain I sent the boys to Outgamie to steal the picture and get rid of you both. As you both know, the incompetents didn't do the job. When they called and said they'd lost you near Isadora I knew where you'd gone and came up here myself. I couldn't take any chances with you two loose ends. There's no statute of limitations on murder, after all."

"You said the same thing last night," D.J. muttered. "What does the statute of limitations on murder have to do with starting gangs?"

Rich turned his gaze back to her, and D.J. flinched away from the hatred in his eyes. "I'm sick of your mouth, D.J. I've always been sick of it. It'll be a pleasure to get rid of you once and for all." He raised the gun and pointed the weapon at her head. "Close your eyes, little girl. Listen to the tiger's roar and dream of better things."

D.J. stared at the barrel of the gun in horror. Rich had definitely lost his mind. If he hadn't been ranting before, he certainly was now. What was all this nonsense about a tiger?

"He says the same thing to all his victims," Chris blurted, his voice hoarse and choked. "He said those words to me once. Eighteen years ago on a dark street." D.J. turned her rapt gaze away from the gun pointed at her head and stared at Chris in amazement. This entire mess had gotten way too complicated. She needed a map to understand all the implications.

"Chris?" she whispered.

He didn't look at her. Instead he stared at Rich, undiluted rage on his face. "He said the same words right after he shot my parents in cold blood and then turned his gun on me."

Josie could barely hear what was being said between D.J., Christian, and Rich, but what she could hear she didn't like. Ever since she'd been yanked back to heaven, her knowledge of D.J.'s world had been steadily fading.

Someone placed a hand on her shoulder.

"Mama, I've got to go down there and—" Josie broke off at the sight of Raphael. Her mother, and the others who had been attending the orientation class, had all disappeared.

"And what, Josie?"

Josie straightened and looked the archangel straight in the eye. "And help her, that's what. There's a maniac with a gun down there. He's going to kill them both. I don't plan to let my daughter get murdered because that's part of her life lesson. I won't!"

Thunder rumbled and Josie winced. "You are not to go back there, Josie." Raphael shouted so loud her ears hurt. "Disobeying my orders could result in forfeiting your eternal reward. Is that what you want?" He sighed and lowered his voice. "Please, Josie. I know this is hard for you. But you have to meet a new arrival very soon. That is what you should be concentrating on. You've done everything you can for your daughter."

Josie's heart gave a painful thump. They had sent her mother to greet her. Did that mean she was being sent to greet . . . "Not D.J." Josie reached out a hand in supplication toward Raphael. "Please tell me she isn't going to die today."

"I can't tell you the future."

"Why not? You know it."

"And you will, too. Very soon. Let D.J. meet her own destiny. I guarantee it will be the right one for her. Have faith, dear Josie. We know what we're doing."

Josie closed her eyes and tried to find her faith. But it was all twisted up with fear for her daughter, and she just couldn't do it. Then a new and just as frightening thought came to her.

What if the new arrival turned out to be Christian? D.J. would be devastated. Just as Ed had been. Becoming like her father was D.J.'s greatest fear—the fear she'd love someone so much, then lose him and lose herself. There was no way in heaven or earth Josie would allow D.J. to suffer that way. Josie only cared about her daughter. Her eternal reward meant nothing if D.J. had to pay the price.

Now she just had to figure a way to get rid of . . .

Josie turned. She was completely alone. A smile curved her lips as she returned to earth.

Chris could barely think past the orange haze of fury clouding his brain. The second Halloran recited his pre-murder ritual, everything clicked into place in Christian's mind.

Dickey.

The name of the thug who'd killed his parents. Dickey—short for Richard, just as Rich was short for Richard. Richard Halloran. The man who stood before him with a gun pointed at the head of the woman Christian loved. History did repeat itself. But this time there would be a different ending to the story.

"Y-y-you killed Christian's parents?" D.J. asked, her words muffled as she pressed the back of her hand to her mouth. Her fingers shook. She stared at her ex-husband as though she meant to be sick all over his silk suit. Chris kind of hoped D.J. did just that. She'd give him a second's distraction, which would be all he'd need.

"Bingo, D.J. Give the girl a cigar." Rich kept his gaze on Chris, despite addressing his comments to D.J. The two men stared into each other's eyes. They understood each other. One of them would die before this ended. But Rich didn't know one thing—Chris had too much to live for now to let anything or anyone stand in his way.

A deep calm settled over Chris and his head cleared. He would bide his time and make his move at the first opportunity.

"Th-this is too weird." D.J.'s teeth chattered with

shock, making her words come out in staccato bursts. Chris hoped she remained in shock for a while and didn't do anything stupid. He'd seen how reckless she could be. But maybe now, with something to live for as well, she might exhibit a newfound caution. "H-how could you have done such a horrible thing? I never knew—never suspected you could be so, so, so—"

"Of course you didn't, little wife. If you'd suspected, you'd have put me away."

"Don't call me your wife. You make me sick. I can't believe any of this. What you're saying is that you killed Chris's parents when you were fourteen? Fifteen? How could you be so brutal at that age? I can't believe you've gotten away with the crime this long."

"I'll get away with it forever, don't you worry. I didn't live this long outside the law without knowing what I was doing at all times." His gaze had flicked over D.J. for a moment, as though assessing her willingness to cooperate. Rich must know D.J. and her propensity for heroics well. When he saw she had no intention of fighting him, for the moment, he returned his gaze to Chris. "No one ever suspected me. I lived with my aunt for so many years, I wasn't considered a resident of Lakeview. And the trouble I got caught at in both places was so minor, I wasn't even questioned. Me and the boys came up from Chicago just for the night."

Chris nodded. "That's what the police figured. A Chicago gang up for some petty theft that turned bad."

"And they were right. I have to tell you, McCall, I never planned to kill anyone. The gun just went off when your dad ran at me. But once I killed him I saw how easy killing could be. Your mom—" He snapped his fingers. "Even easier. You would have been the easiest of all."

"Pig," D.J. muttered. Chris put a hand on her arm, afraid she meant to do something foolish. Rich saw the movement and his eyes narrowed. Chris took his hand away. He didn't want to draw attention to what existed between the two of them. As long as Halloran believed Chris had been after D.J.'s body and not her soul, the man wouldn't think to use her as a weapon against Chris.

Rich continued to explain, and Chris breathed a sigh of relief. The longer the man talked, the more chance Chris had to make his move. And Rich Halloran loved to talk. "I have Ed to thank for my time in Chicago. He convinced my parents to send me to my aunt's and get me away from the bad boys I'd started to hang with in Lakeview. At the time I was angry that my parents dumped me so easily. But I found ways to make up for their desertion. There were even worse kids in Chicago to play with. After I killed the McCalls my status went up. I became a silent leader—the money man, the brains behind the muscle. I liked being in charge. I still do. I'm a businessman now. I get respect from the community. But I pull a lot of secret strings in Lakeview."

"How could you have hidden this from me? From everyone?" D.J. asked.

"It wasn't so hard. You were always wrapped up in your career—you didn't want to be married to me any more than I wanted to be married to you. But being married to one cop, and having another as a self-appointed mentor, I knew what the police did in Lakeview at all times. You didn't actually think I married you for your charming personality? Or perhaps your great looks? No, no, I remember now. It must have been your spectacular performance in bed."

D.J. tensed at his taunts but remained silent. Chris's fury returned and pulsed hotter than before. D.J. had come so far, and Halloran was ripping out all of her newfound confidence in her womanhood and trampling it under his snakeskin boots.

Rich watched D.J. draw in upon herself and his lips turned up in a thin smile. He was enjoying himself too much, and he was far too calm for Christian's plan. For the plan to succeed he had to get Halloran to lose his cool and drop his guard.

"Leave her out of this, Halloran." Chris stepped forward, putting himself between D.J. and the gun. Though Halloran had never stopped watching Chris, he'd kept the weapon trained on D.J., leaving no question of who he'd shoot first if crossed. That had to end right now.

"Won't work, McCall. She'll still die, same as you. I think I'll enjoy killing her the most. She's been nothing but a pain in the ass since the first day I met her."

"You're a sick son of a bitch," Chris said.

Rich's eyes narrowed. "Watch your mouth. I'll shoot you here if I have to, though I'd rather shoot you out by the swamp and save myself some work."

"I wouldn't want to make you work, Rich. Lord knows you never were much good at it." D.J. had stopped stuttering, and her voice sounded so much like the old D.J, Chris winced.

Not now. Not when he'd been getting to Halloran and had the man's attention focused off D.J. and onto him. Chris grabbed for her wrist and squeezed it to warn her, but she ignored him, coming out of her shock with her mouth in full gear. "I can't wait to see you in jail. I'm gonna sit outside the bars for hours just watching you, Rich. It'll make my millennium." She yanked her wrist from Chris's grasp and moved around him. He tried to shove her back, but her anger outweighed the warning and she sidestepped his arm. Chris took a step after her, but Halloran waved him away with the gun.

D.J. marched up to her ex-husband, fury in every step. "You're a pathetic excuse for a man, Richard Halloran. You always were. I only wish I'd had the guts to stand up to my father back then. The fact I shared your house, your bed, and your name sickens me."

"Doesn't do much for me either, baby." He grabbed her by the arm and pointed her toward the door. "Time to shut your smart mouth for good, D.J. Let's go."

Chris tensed. He would have to make his move now or risk losing D.J. forever. Almost as if she'd heard his thoughts, D.J. wrenched her arm from Rich's grasp. He swore and backhanded her across the mouth. Her head snapped back with the force of the blow.

Chris gave a roar of fury and launched himself at Halloran. The man shoved D.J. so hard she flew sideways and landed in a crumpled heap on the floor. Rich brought the gun up at the same time. He smiled as his finger tightened on the trigger.

"Listen for the tiger, McCall," he shouted.

And then everything happened at once.

Chapter Eighteen

D.J. hit the floor, pain shooting up her injured shoulder and clouding her brain for a second. Blood trickled down her chin from the cut her teeth had made in her lip when Rich struck her.

She shook her head and the fog cleared from in front of her eyes. "No!" she screamed and lurched to her knees. She stopped there, frozen, as Chris launched himself toward Rich, and Rich pointed the gun at Chris's head. Small details imprinted themselves on D.J.'s mind: Rich's thin smile; Christian's face, calm as death, as he rushed toward danger.

Her ex-husband's fingers tightened on the gun's grip, and D.J. glanced up. She'd do anything, say anything, believe anything, if Christian could live. They needed a miracle.

The first prayer she'd ever uttered ran through her mind.

I never told him I loved him. Dear God, he's going to die and he'll never know. Three little words I was too frightened to say. I'm not frightened now. Please, give me another chance. Save him, and I'll spend the rest of my life telling him I love him. I'll spend the rest of my life showing him how much.

A flash of blue from the ceiling made D.J. gasp. Josie swooped down and knocked the gun from Rich's hand. The bullet sliced into the dilapidated ceiling. Chris plowed into Rich, and both men fell to the floor in a tangle of legs and arms.

Josie landed next to D.J. and helped her scramble to her feet and retrieve the gun. Impulsively, D.J. turned to the angel and hugged her. Then she and Josie watched Chris take Rich apart.

The fight progressed, brutal and dirty. Rich outweighed Chris, but Chris was the taller and stronger of the two. Though Rich fought as though his life depended upon the outcome—and he probably thought it did—Chris fought with the memory of his murdered parents fresh on his mind.

They came to their feet and circled each other. When Rich lunged toward Chris, Chris stepped into the lunge. He used none of the karate D.J. had seen him apply in Outgamie, though his grace reminded her of that morning. While Rich threw himself into the fight, arms flailing, fists punching in a random pattern, Chris approached the matter with a calm thoughtfulness. His very lack of anger in the face of Rich's fury seemed to make Halloran all the more furious. As a result, Rich's technique went out of control.

Chris used his fists and forearms to meet and match any punches thrown by his opponent. His face was set, his concentration on one final goal obvious. D.J. held the gun ready; Rich wouldn't get away no matter what the outcome. But she wouldn't need to use the weapon. By the time this was over her ex-husband would be the loser—something she'd always known he was anyway.

Rich landed a shot to Chris's face. D.J. flinched and tightened her grip on the .9 mm. But Josie, embracing D.J. with one arm, placed her other hand on the gun and frowned. D.J. relaxed. The angel was right. Chris didn't need her help. He never had. He could take care of himself and anyone else, including D.J., all by himself.

Rich's ring had sliced a thin cut under Christian's eye, and blood trickled down his cheek in a glistening red path. D.J. bit her lip against the cry in her throat. She would take care of his cut when this was over, she promised herself. Once Rich was behind locked doors she and Chris would be safe. They could get on with their lives—together. She'd made a promise to God just moments before, and she wouldn't break her promise. She didn't want to.

God had sent Josie to save Chris, and D.J. would never forget His gift.

D.J. returned her attention to the two men just as Christian glanced a blow off Rich's temple. He followed that punch with a shot to the stomach and then one to the nose. Only when Rich staggered and shook his head to clear away the haze did Chris step back and make use of his training. Just as Rich looked up, his eyes searching for Chris, Chris's foot shot out, clipping Rich under the chin with bone-crunching impact.

Rich Halloran hit the floor, unconscious. D.J. leapt over him and threw herself into Christian's arms.

"I love you, Christian. I love you, I love you, I love you."

He staggered back as her full weight hit him in the chest, but he recovered quickly. "All right, all right." He wrapped his arms around her. "If I'd known all I had to do was beat your ex-husband unconscious to make you love me, I would have done it days ago."

The grin he sent her way lost some of its allure because of the blood on his lips. D.J. wiped the redness away before she pulled his head down so she could kiss him.

"I have to be going, dear. But I can see you've got everything under control."

D.J. yanked her mouth from Christian's. "No, wait. I want to thank you."

"You're doing just fine," Chris said, and pulled her back into his arms. "We don't need words."

"No, not you. Her."

Chris looked up, his gaze touring the room. "Who?"

"D.J.!" Dan Franklin's voice calling from outside interrupted any explanation. "McCall!"

Chris released her. "We'll get back to this later." He walked toward the door, shaking his head. "I don't understand how the gun flew out of his hand.

I wasn't even near the guy." He disappeared onto the porch, and D.J. heard him greeting the cavalry.

D.J. walked toward Josie, her hands held out to the angel who had saved her life in more ways than one. Just as she reached for her, Josie's eyes widened and her face went sheet white. D.J. snatched her hands back as the fear she had so recently banished returned full force.

"Josie? What's the matter?"

Josie stared at the doorway to the cabin, then her gaze returned to D.J.'s. Her mouth opened and closed helplessly. Then she just pointed.

D.J. turned, half expecting to see Rich with another gun trained on her back. But neither Rich, nor Chris, nor Danny stood in the doorway. The man staring at her was . . .

"Dad!" D.J. exclaimed. "What are you doing up here?"

"I—had—I had to—"

D.J. frowned. Her father looked as bad as Josie. She glanced at the angel. Josie began to fade.

"Wait!" D.J. cried, reaching out for her angel. Her hands passed through Josie's body.

Josie turned her gaze on D.J., her eyes a well of sadness where before there had been only joy. She tried to speak, but no sound came out of her mouth. She reached for D.J., but her hands became wisps of smoke. D.J. blinked, and the angel disappeared.

"Good-bye," she whispered to the empty air. "I'll never forget you."

"D.J. Help me."

Her father's hoarse cry startled D.J. She turned just in time to see him clutch his chest and slide toward the floor. She caught him before he fell. "What's the matter with you?"

"My chest. Hurts like hell. Shouldn't have run all the way up here. But I had to make sure—" He broke off on a groan of pain, and his eyes fluttered shut.

"Danny!" she screamed.

Chris and Danny came through the door at a run. They saw the situation at once. Chris pulled D.J. away from her father while Dan knelt next to the fallen man.

D.J. fought against Christian's hold. "No. He can't die now. Not when I understand at last what he suffered all these years. I have to talk to him."

"I know, honey. I know. Just let Dan look at him."

Having Chris's arms around her helped, more than she'd ever dreamed a human touch could soothe. She watched as Dan worked over her father. The sheriff and two deputies entered the room and removed Rich, but D.J. barely noticed. She would have to fulfill her threat to Rich another time. Once her father was better they'd both go and stare at Rich through the bars of his prison cell. She held on to that dream.

Dan looked up. His eyes met Christian's, and he gave a little shake of his head. D.J. knew what that shake meant, and a sob escaped her throat.

"Help me get him onto the bed, Chris. All I can do is make him comfortable."

Chris hugged D.J., a quick pull and release that she leaned into and savored. When he moved away to help Danny the loss of his warmth returned the frightening chill. D.J. wrapped her arms around

D.J.'s Angel

herself in an effort to stop the cold from seeping into her bones. It did no good. By the time Chris and Danny had moved her father to the bed and made him comfortable, her teeth chattered so loud their clicking hurt her ears.

A blanket flopped around her shoulders. Danny's warm, steady hands tucked the covering closer as he led her toward the bed. They both stared down at the man whose harsh breathing filled the silence of the room. Her father looked old. Amazement filled D.J. at the revelation. He'd always been a robust man who kept himself in shape for his job. Since he'd retired he'd let his stomach go a bit, but nothing to speak of. Years of drinking had tinted his face a ruddy red. His strawberry blond hair had thinned and the tense lines about his mouth and eyes had deepened. But until this moment D.J. had never seen her father look old and sick and pale. The sudden change made her stare without speaking.

"Talk to him, D.J." Danny's palm on her back prodded D.J. forward. "Tell him what you want him to know."

D.J. turned her face up to her childhood friend. "Can't you do something? You're a doctor, Danny. Make him better."

The doctor sighed and glanced at Chris, a helpless expression on his face. Chris looked just as helpless. Danny closed his eyes and took a deep breath; then he put his arm around her shoulders and pulled D.J. close to his side. His warmth didn't soothe her as Christian's had, but he still felt good. D.J. had learned a lot about the value of human

383

contact over the past few days. She leaned against Danny, and after he recovered from his surprise at her easy acquiescence to his comfort he spoke again, softly, quietly, his words a knell in D.J.'s mind. "He's had heart trouble for a long time now, D.J. Bad trouble."

"He never told me."

"No. He didn't want you to know. I told him to tell you, but he said he'd given you enough grief and he didn't want to give you any more. Since I had to agree with him, and he is my patient, I couldn't tell you either."

D.J. nodded her understanding. "Why did he come up here if he's not well?"

"For you."

D.J. rolled her eyes. "Right, Danny boy. He wouldn't walk across the street for me."

"You're wrong. He came up here to save you today. I told him to wait in town. The climb was too dangerous after the storm, but he wouldn't hear me. He's as stubborn as you when he makes up his mind about something. Whatever you might have believed, however he's acted in the past, he loves you, D.J. He just wasn't capable of showing it."

D.J. nodded. She recalled small things her father had done, things that her bitterness had blinded her from noticing before now: the chair in the tree stand positioned so he could watch out for her, even though he couldn't be with her; the sleeping bag on the floor of his room, always available without a word of reproach for her irrational fear; and the greatest sacrifice of all: today he had come to her rescue, though the trip would cost him his life.

She understood his pain now. If she'd lost Christian today, she might have ended up living the same bitter existence her father had led. Sure, he'd withdrawn from life in a cowardly and selfish fashion. But right now D.J. couldn't swear she would be able to behave any better if Christian were to be taken from her.

Dan led her a few short steps and helped her onto a chair next to the bed. "McCall, the sheriff wants to talk to you outside." With a last awkward pat on her shoulder, Danny left the cabin.

Chris took his place. He put his hands on her shoulders. She stared at her father's still, gray face and tried not to cry. "I love you, D.J." Chris whispered in her ear. "We have a lifetime ahead of us, right outside that door. I'll be waiting, as soon as you're ready to join me."

She nodded, unable to speak. Chris would be there for her; she knew that in her heart, where it mattered. Right now she had to close another door of her life.

Chris left. She could hear the three men speaking in low-voiced murmurs on the porch. Scooting her chair closer to the bed, D.J. took her father's hand into hers and leaned forward.

"Dad?" Not even a flicker of his eyelids showed he might have heard her. His chest continued to rise and fall, though his skin had cooled to a temperature even lower than D.J.'s own. She'd read hearing was the last sense to leave a dying soul. If that was the case, then he could still hear her, despite his lack of response.

"I understand now, Dad. Why you were so miserable. Why you made me so miserable. I can't say I enjoyed it. But I understand."

His fingers moved a bit in hers, and D.J. sat up straighter. Perhaps he did hear her. She continued, her voice becoming stronger as she went on. "I'm in love, Dad. He's wonderful. I didn't want to love him. I didn't believe love existed, or if it did, I thought it made a person as miserable as you were all your life. I didn't want to be so miserable."

His fingers grasped hers with surprising strength, and Ed's eyes snapped open. Green eyes met green eyes as he stared into her face." Grab love while you can, Daphne." D.J. blinked when he used her true name for the first time she could remember. "I was wrong to behave the way I did. I ruined my life and nearly ruined yours. I should have cherished the one gift she was able to give me—you. But I didn't have the strength to live the life we'd planned together without her to share it with me. And I didn't have the strength to give up and go to her either. You're stronger than I ever was. You're just like her, a fighter from the beginning. You might look like me, but you always reminded me of her."

"I thought I looked like her. I thought that was why you couldn't stand to look at me."

He shook his head. "You act like her. You talk like her. You hold your head just like her. She was strong. So are you. You'll be okay."

"Yeah, I will." She squeezed his hand and leaned closer. They had so little time, and she had so many questions. "Tell me more about her, Dad. If you don't now, I won't have a part of her to keep when you're gone." His eyes slid closed, and D.J.'s heart gave a painful thump. "Dad?"

"I'm here. I was just picturing her as she looked and acted when I first met her—the complete opposite of everything I'd ever known. Happy, free, so beautiful she made my eyes hurt just to look at her. All she ever wanted was to be my wife and your mother. She counted the days until you were born. And then she never even got to hold you in her arms. I don't know if she died thinking you—" He broke off with a grimace of pain and his eyes opened. He clutched D.J.'s hand so hard, she thought her fingers might break. "I see her." He stared at a point just behind and above D.J.'s head.

D.J. remembered the angel's sudden appearance and odd fading out afterward. Had she returned? Had the barrier between the earth and heaven thinned just enough so her father could see Josie? D.J. snapped her head around and looked up.

A breeze from the doorway, carrying the scent of damp earth and burning leaves, wafted through the empty air above her.

D.J. turned back to her father with a frown. He nodded and smiled at the same place above D.J.'s head. Whatever he'd seen before he still saw it.

"Daphne Josephine." His voice rasped with such love, D.J.'s eyes widened, then filled with tears. He'd never said her name like that before, as though all the joy in his world were contained in two little words.

"I'm here, Dad."

"No, not you. Her. She always hated her name. Wouldn't answer to anything but—" He coughed, long and hard, and D.J. had to stifle the urge to smack him on the back. She didn't think Danny or the American Medical Association would approve.

The coughing fit at last subsided, and her father calmed enough to resume speaking. "She's here." He lifted a shaking hand toward the ceiling, pointing at the same spot he continued to stare at with a joyous smile lighting his too pale face. "Right there waiting for me. I'm coming." He tore his gaze away from the ceiling and smiled into D.J.'s face. "Good-bye. I did love you. I just couldn't say it."

"I know. I had the same problem. Once upon a time. Who's waiting for you, Dad. Is it my mother?"

He nodded. "She's wearing her wedding dress." He laughed. D.J. stared. She had never heard her father laugh before. Never. Her amazement turned to shock as he lurched up onto his elbows, still staring at the ceiling.

"Dad!" She jumped to her feet and tried to push him back onto the bed. "Stop this. You'll hurt yourself."

He ignored her, his struggles surprisingly strong considering his condition. "Her feet are bare. Never could get her to wear shoes unless she had to. That's Josie. My sweet Josie." His breath came out on a sigh of pleasure. D.J. tensed, waiting for him to draw in another breath. She shook him. He remained as still as—

Death.

D.J. released her hold on her father's shoulders. He fell backward onto the pillow, his gaze fixed on the ceiling.

"Josie?" she whispered and looked upward, her heart pounding a combination of hope and loss.

Laughter like the trill of Christmas bells filled the air, and Josie appeared in the hole in the roof. She held a piece of paper in her hand, and as D.J. watched in confusion, Josie opened her fingers and sailed the paper free.

D.J. reached out shaking fingers and caught what she could now see was a photo. Swallowing against the thickness in her throat, she blinked back the tears flooding her eyes and focused on the scene she held in her hands.

A wedding picture, the couple standing together amid brilliant wildflowers, the trees circling the field an array of summer greens. The bride in a dress of flowing blue, feet bare beneath the long hem. The man smiling into the woman's eyes, his love clear for all to see.

Looking up once more, D.J. met the gaze of the woman above her. They smiled into each other's eyes as the truth flowed between them. D.J.'s fingers tightened on the picture in her hand.

A picture of her father and Josie—D.J.'s angel.

Epilogue

"Josephine Marianne McCall! Spit out that worm this instant!"

The red-haired toddler glanced up at her mother, a look of amazement filling her bright blue eyes. Then she opened her mouth and allowed the still wriggling earthworm to fall from her dirt-encrusted lips.

D.J. rubbed at the ache in the middle of her forehead and counted to ten. Then she opened her eyes and glared at the two boys who rolled around on the ground at her feet in a burst of giggles.

"Brian. Eddie. On your feet, boys." They continued to giggle as they got to their knees. "Now," she shouted in her best drill sergeant voice. They complied—still laughing.

The volume of D.J.'s voice brought her husband

to the door of their house. Shielding his eyes against the late afternoon sun, he stepped outside and started toward them.

D.J. allowed the boys to giggle a while longer while she watched Christian approach. Six years of marriage and she still got all choked up every time she looked at him.

"What's going on out here? he asked, taking one look at D.J.'s face and putting his arm around her shoulders to pull her close.

"*Your* sons convinced their sister to eat an earthworm."

"Liked it, Mama," Josie announced, picking up another worm and dangling it in the air.

The boys fell, giggling, to the ground. Chris choked on a laugh, and D.J. elbowed him in the ribs.

"What?" he asked with an innocent smile.

D.J. threw her hands up in the air and started back toward the house. "I have to go to work. You can handle this one."

Christ caught her before she'd walked three steps. He could still move as quick as a tiger—though she usually let him catch her without much of a fight.

"I just love a woman in uniform," he whispered as he nuzzled her neck. "And those handcuffs are sooo sexy."

"Stop it." She laughed, batting his fingers away from the cuffs dangling at her belt. "I've got to get to the station. I am the sheriff in these here parts, you know."

"Oh, I know. I won't give you any trouble,

ma'am." He let her go **with a qui**ck kiss on the lips, then turned to deal with **their** children.

D.J. walked toward the squad car sitting in front of the house. Reaching it, she opened the door, put her foot inside, then turned and stared back at her family.

A lot had happened since the morning over six years earlier when she'd lost her father and gained a mother. Rich had been sentenced to two consecutive life sentences in Columbia Prison for the murders of Marianne and Brian McCall; with extra sentences added on for his other crimes, he wouldn't know freedom for a very long time. With Rich out of the way, the tentative gang structure had collapsed, and Lakeview had regained its reputation as a midsized town with a small-town flavor.

Chris never brought up the subject of the flying gun, or D.J.'s desire to thank an empty room, and she never explained. She often reflected upon the time with her mother—remembering each moment, each word, each lesson as a special gift. But she kept the truth to herself—the secret of Josie Belmont—her mother and guardian angel.

When the sheriff in Isadora retired D.J. took the job. Though leaving the old Victorian house in Lakeview had pained her, she'd come to understand that she'd craved the house for what it represented, not the house itself. She'd wanted a home. Now she understood that wherever Christian and their children resided her heart and therefore her home would lie. All in all, their lives were so close to perfect, sometimes D.J. got scared.

Funny thing was, whenever she became frightened she might lose everything she'd once disparaged but now needed with a desperation that terrified her, she'd hear her mother's laughter, and her father's, too. D.J.'s parents lived together now, up there, and they watched over her, and Christian and the children. D.J. was sure of it.

With a sigh, D.J. slid behind the wheel. She honked her horn. Four hands waved from the field. Four voices shouted, "Love you. Bye-bye."

Her heart warmed as it did every day when they said the very same thing. And as she did every day, D.J. looked up at the setting sun and whispered, "I love you. Bye-bye."

Ed and Josie reclined in the thin air above D.J.'s car, bare feet swaying back and forth, back and forth. The two lovers smiled at each other, then at their daughter.

"I miss her," Josie said.

"Me, too. It's nice of Raphael to allow us these visits."

"Yes, it is. Especially after I disobeyed him and came back to earth to help D.J. and Christian."

"Raphael said Christian would have been wounded, not killed. Your interference wasn't necessary."

"I didn't know that."

"You did know you weren't supposed to tell her you were her mother."

Josie looked down her nose at him. "I told her

nothing. I showed her. Raphael never said I couldn't show her."

"You're splitting hairs."

Josie just smiled.

Ed sighed. They'd been over this ground before. They'd also been over his treatment of their daughter. She'd read him the riot act on that one, but in the end she'd forgiven him. She'd understood he'd been lost without her. He was lost no longer. "It's all over now. Everyone's fine. D.J.'s happy. We're together, and you have all those children to mother in heaven."

"Marianne McCall is a wonderful help. You know she and Brian have been paying visits down here, too?" Ed nodded. "They were happy to be together, but Christian's pain didn't allow them to enjoy heaven to its fullest. You're right—now everyone's happy. I love my job. Though it's hard when one of the little souls leaves me to come to earth and live their life."

"They always come back."

"I know. I enjoyed having some time with our grandchildren before they were born."

"Me, too." Ed looked down at their daughter once more. Josie took his hand.

As D.J. drove down the long gravel driveway toward the main road, the Belmonts flew low over Christian and the children.

Little Josie looked up and smiled when she saw them. She raised her arms, a beautiful beggar asking for a lift. Her grandparents smiled indulgently, swooped down to kiss her on the head, then waved good-bye.

The toddler squealed with laughter. She put her

*palms into the dirt, hoisted her diaper-clad behind
into the air, and stood. Clumps of earth showered
around her as she waved her dirty hands at the sky
and shouted, "Love you. Bye-bye."*

LORI HANDELAND

On the run from his past, Charlie Coltrain never plans on rescuing a young nun in the desert. Charlie tells himself he wants only the money she offers him to take her to the convent. But hiding away such shimmering beauty is a sin he couldn't abide, and he yearns to send her to heaven with his forbidden touch.

Hoping to find happiness, Angelina Reyes is ready to follow her calling and dedicate her life to the Church. But the first soul she finds that needs saving belongs to a gunslinger wanted by the law, not the Lord. Determined to help Charlie at any cost, Angelina discovers that he is far more than a mere man—he is her mission, her temptation, her greatest love.

_3776-9 $4.99 US/$5.99 CAN

SHADOW LOVER

Lori Handeland

"A powerhouse of a story...one you don't want to miss!"
—*Rendezvous*

Devastated by the loss of her brother, Rachel Taylor vows to avenge his death. And after three long years, only one unforeseen problem will make her well-laid plans go awry: She is falling under the seductive spell of the man she blames for her pain and suffering.

The victim of a horrible accident, Michael Gabriel hides away from all save his most trusted friends. Yet the talented singer can't deny his growing attraction for Rachel—or his fear that secrets from his past may destroy her life.

Night after night, Michael and Rachel draw closer, unleashing long-suppressed passion. But someone will stop at nothing—not even murder—to come between them and keep Rachel from the love that can heal her heart.

_52010-9 $4.99 US/$5.99 CAN

An Angel's Touch *Where angels go, love is sure to follow.*

Don't miss these unforgettable romances that combine the magic of angels and the joy of love.

Daemon's Angel by Sherrilyn Kenyon. Cast to the mortal realm by an evil sorceress, Arina has more than her share of problems. She is trapped in a temptress's body and doomed to lose any man she desires. Yet even as Arina yearns for the safety of the pearly gates, she finds paradise in the arms of a Norman mercenary. But to savor the joys of life with Daemon, she will have to battle demons and risk her very soul for love.

_52026-5 $4.99 US/$5.99 CAN

Forever Angels by Trana Mae Simmons. Thoroughly modern Tess Foster has everything, but when her boyfriend demands she sign a prenuptial agreement Tess thinks she's lost her happiness forever. Then her guardian angel sneezes and sends the woman of the nineties back to the 1890s—and into the arms of an unbelievably handsome cowboy. But before she will surrender to a marriage made in heaven, Tess has to make sure that her guardian angel won't sneeze again—and ruin her second chance at love.

_52021-4 $4.99 US/$5.99 CAN

Dorchester Publishing Co., Inc.
65 Commerce Road
Stamford, CT 06902

Please add $1.75 for shipping and handling for the first book and $.50 for each book thereafter. NY, NYC, PA and CT residents, please add appropriate sales tax. No cash, stamps, or C.O.D.s. All orders shipped within 6 weeks via postal service book rate. Canadian orders require $2.00 extra postage and must be paid in U.S. dollars through a U.S. banking facility.

Name _____

Address _____

City _____ State _____ Zip _____

I have enclosed $_____ in payment for the checked book(s).

Payment **must** accompany all orders.☐ Please send a free catalog.

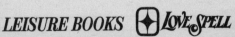